PLAYING WITH FIRE

*L*et the world say what it would. She was sure—absolutely sure—that what she was doing was not wrong.

Barnes took her face in his two work-hardened hands and kissed her hard. Feeling his cool hands on her cheeks as his warm tongue found her own, it was as though a switch flipped in her. She stopped being the clever, self-possessed daughter of an earl and started being simply a vessel for her own desire.

She reached her hands behind him and ran them down his ass. She was surprised by its muscular compactness. Although he was large and she was small, she could almost cover each cheek with one of her hands. She squeezed and pulled him closer.

She felt herself widen to accommodate him, and relished the slowness with which he eased himself into her. He stopped halfway, and she instinctively tried to push herself down so he would be completely inside. But he held her feet, and she couldn't move.

Her body, almost of its own accord, wanted to move. She wanted to feel him deeper, deeper. She squirmed, and he held her fast. She knew he was in control, and she gave herself over to it. She was surprised, though, when he reached down and picked something up. She propped herself up on her elbows and looked at him quizzically. Was he getting dressed?

"This may seem strange to you, but I think it will add a whole new layer of pleasure," he said, smiling. . . .

MY LADY'S PLEASURE

OLIVIA QUINCY

A SIGNET ECLIPSE BOOK

SIGNET ECLIPSE
Published by New American Library, a division of
Penguin Group (USA) Inc., 375 Hudson Street,
New York, New York 10014, USA
Penguin Group (Canada), 90 Eglinton Avenue East, Suite 700, Toronto,
Ontario M4P 2Y3, Canada (a division of Pearson Penguin Canada Inc.)
Penguin Books Ltd., 80 Strand, London WC2R 0RL, England
Penguin Ireland, 25 St. Stephen's Green, Dublin 2,
Ireland (a division of Penguin Books Ltd.)
Penguin Group (Australia), 250 Camberwell Road, Camberwell, Victoria 3124,
Australia (a division of Pearson Australia Group Pty. Ltd.)
Penguin Books India Pvt. Ltd., 11 Community Centre, Panchsheel Park,
New Delhi - 110 017, India
Penguin Group (NZ), 67 Apollo Drive, Rosedale, North Shore 0632,
New Zealand (a division of Pearson New Zealand Ltd.)
Penguin Books (South Africa) (Pty.) Ltd., 24 Sturdee Avenue,
Rosebank, Johannesburg 2196, South Africa
Penguin Books Ltd., Registered Offices:
80 Strand, London WC2R 0RL, England

First published by Signet Eclipse, an imprint of New American Library,
a division of Penguin Group (USA) Inc.

First Printing, July 2010
10 9 8 7 6 5 4 3 2 1

SIGNET ECLIPSE and logo are trademarks of Penguin Group (USA) Inc.

LIBRARY OF CONGRESS CATALOGING-IN-PUBLICATION DATA

Quincy, Olivia.
    My lady's pleasure/Olivia Quincy.
        p. cm.
    ISBN 978-0-451-23007-2
    1. Aristocracy (Social class)—England—Fiction. I. Title.
    PR6117.U356M9   2010
    823'.92—dc22   2010009815

Set in Adobe Garamond
Designed by Ginger Legato

Printed in the United States of America

MY LADY'S
PLEASURE

ONE

"You did that deliberately," said Jeremy when the other guests had gone, leaving him alone in the drawing room with Lady Georgiana Vernon.

"I beg your pardon, but I haven't the slightest idea what you could mean," said Lady Georgiana archly, but with a knowing half smile that revealed that she did, in truth, know exactly what the tall, sandy-haired young man meant.

"Ah," said Jeremy, whose manners were impeccable, as became a viscount's son. "In that case, I made the statement in haste, and I withdraw it with a sincere apology." But his half smile mirrored hers exactly. The game he'd been playing with the eldest daughter of the seventh Earl of Eastley had been going on much too long for either of them to confuse dialogue with action. "I had thought, when your dress caught on that low table and revealed a length of ankle—a slender, shapely length of ankle, if I may say so—that you might, out of your kind heart and generous nature, have so managed it for my particular benefit," Jeremy continued, with an exaggerated half bow.

"You, sir, should know that my good breeding matches your own," replied Lady Georgiana with mock stiffness, "and that I take great pains to remain decently covered in decent company." As she said this she slowly began lifting the skirt of her brocaded frock, revealing the lace-trimmed petticoat beneath. Then this, too, began to rise, showing stockings and then, just below the knee, where the crocheted cuffs of her drawers should have been, bare skin.

"I take it this means I don't qualify as 'decent,'" said Jeremy, crossing the room to sit beside her on the sofa.

"You most certainly do not."

"Am I irredeemably indecent?"

"Absolutely irredeemably."

"Do I understand by this that I am unfettered by the societal conventions that prevent me from, for example, running my hand under your dress and up the length of your thigh?" Jeremy asked, matching the gesture to the words.

"Completely unfettered," said Lady Georgiana, lying back on the couch to savor the warm, dry roughness of his hand on her skin.

Although she had been Jeremy Staunton's lover for more than a year, Georgiana still thrilled at the first touch of each encounter. Perhaps it was the necessary secrecy that kept their physical meetings so vital. They'd known each other all their lives, and they met frequently in society, their friendship on display in the drawing rooms and country houses of the best families in England. Each was generally thought to be an excellent match for the other, and their eventual marriage was sometimes quietly spoken of.

The two principals had different ideas. Lady Georgiana, particularly, thought of marriage as something she would undertake later in life, if at all. She didn't despise the institution, but she considered it a pastime for someone older and duller, rather like cultivating roses, or knitting. She had no interest in entertaining the idea just now, when she was so busy exploring the much more compelling idea that chastity shouldn't be a young woman's lot in life. Jeremy, for his part, found flouting chastity far more interesting than affirming marriage, and so the two had embarked on an exciting, adventurous, and mutually satisfying affair.

Somehow, over the course of that year, the affair had retained almost all its heat and air of illicit pleasure and, as Georgiana lay back on the sofa in the drawing room at her father's home at Eastley, she felt the same electric response she had the first time Jeremy had touched her.

He ran his hand from the outside of her leg to the inside, and her muscles tightened as she gave a quick, anticipatory quiver. He flipped her dress and petticoats up. She was naked from waist to knees.

"It was thoughtful of you to dispense with your drawers," he murmured, as he kissed the inside of her left thigh, just above the knee.

"It took some doing," Georgiana replied. "After she dressed me, I had to send Hortense on a sham errand so I could take them off and squirrel them away back in the bureau." Hortense was her lady's maid, and Georgiana didn't get dressed without her.

"I think perhaps I can make the squirreling worth your while," said Jeremy.

"You generally do," she said as she sat forward and pulled him up so she could look him in the eye. "You generally do," she repeated softly, and kissed him. She knew well the feel of his lips on hers. The first time he'd kissed her, she'd been surprised by their firmness. Until then, the only lips she'd known well were her own, which were full and soft. His, though, were strong, almost muscular. When they kissed, her lips always yielded to his, as they did now.

His taste was deeply familiar, but Georgiana couldn't say exactly what he tasted of. He simply tasted of Jeremy, she thought. His smell, though, was easier to place, and Georgiana breathed in the odor of tobacco, and stables, and the laundry soap his housekeeper made with oil of rosemary.

She found the scent of him wonderfully arousing, and she ran her hands down his chest. She pulled his shirt out of his trousers and ran her hands back up, under the fabric. She spread her fingers and put her palms flush against him so she could feel the fine, soft hair on his chest slip through her hands as she traced the line of each side of his rib cage, up to where his ribs came together just below his nipples.

Georgiana loved both his compact, dusky nipples and the full, firm pectoral muscles beneath them. She traced the outline of those muscles, and then circled in, tighter and tighter, to the nipples. She knew they'd be hard and sensitive, and she covered each with a palm and pressed, at first gently and then a little harder. Jeremy's eyes closed as he took in a quick breath. Georgiana reached around his waist to where his trousers buckled in the back, but he stopped her. He inhaled deeply to get his own sensations under control, and then he gently took her forearms and returned them to her sides. "Not yet," he said. "Lie back down."

She did as she was bidden, not quite knowing what to expect. Jeremy had been her only lover, but she assumed he had had others, given his way of surprising her.

He stood over her as she lay on the sofa, and put his hands between her slightly open thighs. He eased her legs apart, and she had to put her right foot on the floor. He sat on the edge of the sofa between her legs and ran his fingertips up and down the insides of her thighs. He pressed hard enough not to tickle, but not hard enough to satisfy her craving for his touch. Feeling his fingers on the soft skin that no one but Jeremy ever even saw, let alone touched, always opened her to him. She felt the beginning of wetness deep inside her, and half sat up so she could reach out for him again.

Again, he didn't let her. Instead, he put one of the cushions from the sofa behind her. "Lie down," he told her. "Be comfortable."

She did, and was, and he sat back down between her legs. He leaned in close and kissed the inside of first one thigh, and then the other. His firm lips had never felt so soft. And then those lips opened, and she felt his warm, wet tongue on her skin. It worked its way up, up one leg and then the other, closer and closer.

She knew where he was headed, and she had the fleeting urge to stop him. They had gotten to this point before, and she *had* stopped him, but had later been ashamed of what she thought of as cowardice. As a young woman, she had gone out into the world determined not to be bound by the constrictions society placed on her sex, and of all those constrictions, chastity bothered her the most. That ladies were required to sit in their drawing rooms painting or reading, playing whist or piano, while men prowled the streets, the clubs, and the theaters in search of thrills and adventure, had enraged her from her adolescence, when the wonder of her body first began to be revealed to her.

Jeremy had helped her understand that wonder—what her body could give, what it could receive, what it could feel, and the pleasure it could bring others. Why, then, did she balk? Where did it come from, that visceral reaction that prevented her from accepting the ministrations of his tongue? Why did it feel *dirty*?

Intellectually, she didn't believe it was dirty or wrong, and she was determined that her head would triumph over her viscera in this battle. It felt odd for Georgiana to lie practically naked on a sofa, with her lover's head between her thighs, and will her intellect to assert itself, but that was what she did.

She found, though, that circumstances had compromised her intellect, and she couldn't stop herself from sitting up once more, taking Jeremy by the shoulders, and pushing him away. When he looked up at her, she didn't say a word, but her conflicting emotions were written clearly on her face.

"It won't do, you know," he said to her with a small, sympathetic smile. "You're going to have to learn to let me do this."

"I want to," she said, hesitating. "I do. But it's as though my body tightens automatically, all on its own, against my express wishes."

"Then we shall have to find a way to make your body submit," he said simply. He pressed her to lie down once more, and again ran his hands over her legs. This time, though, he headed toward her feet. He unlaced her delicate little boots and took them off. He held her feet in his hands for a moment, pressing his thumbs into their fine, high arches. Georgiana closed her eyes and savored the sensation that was part sensual, part sexual.

Then Jeremy put her left leg down on the couch and held her right in one of his hands as he ran the other up the length of her ankle and calf, which were covered by a sky blue stocking of the sheerest silk. He released the stocking from its elastic garter, and expertly rolled it down her leg, leaving Georgiana wondering just how a viscount's son learned to remove a lady's stocking. The thought had barely entered her mind when it was displaced by curiosity. What was he up to?

Jeremy had taken both her slender wrists in one of his hands, and lifted them above her head. He put one of her hands under the arm of the sofa, and one over. He brought her wrists together again, and wrapped the stocking around them so that Georgiana was tethered to the sofa's arm.

"What are you doing?" she asked with a curiosity just tinged with alarm.

"I'm making sure your body will obey your express wishes," said Jeremy. "We are ensuring that *it* does what *you* want, and not the other way around." He paused. "Does it hurt at all?"

Lady Georgiana considered. "No," she said. She was about to add that she wasn't sure she was quite comfortable, but Jeremy didn't let her.

"Good," he said as he stood up and took his position between her legs again. "If it begins to hurt, tell me."

It took a moment for Georgiana to reconcile herself to the situation. Yes, she was helpless to stop him, but wasn't this what she wanted?

It was, and she trusted him. He had earned her trust over the course of a year of generous and considerate lovemaking. As she gave herself permission to let this happen, she was awakened to a very new sensation— the confluence of extreme arousal and enforced passivity. The idea that she was powerless to participate, powerless to manipulate, powerless to do anything but focus on her own sensations was a new one for Lady Georgiana, and it didn't at first sit comfortably with her. She was determined, in all things, to control her own destiny; the very act of taking a lover had been an exercise of control. And yet here she lay, all her control, all her power, wrested from her.

But then she realized that it hadn't been wrested from her. She had given it. With that realization, she began to truly relax. She began to see that her mind, freed from worry about what she should do next, could focus completely on what was happening to her.

And *oh*! What was happening to her!

She didn't feel just his lips as they danced up her inner thighs; she felt the smallest movement, the subtlest change in texture, in temperature. She was more aware of her own response than she ever had been. In all their lovemaking, there had never been even a moment when some part of Georgiana's mind wasn't occupied with Jeremy—what he was feeling, what she'd like him to feel, and how she could make him feel it. Now, though, there was only her own self. Her skin, and how he felt against it. Her desire, and the way it turned her insides to honey. Her need, and how it was growing.

When Jeremy reached the velvet junction where her legs met and her sex flowed, the first touch of his tongue was revelatory. She had imagined it many times, and she had imagined that it felt good, but this was beyond good. The warmth and the wetness were just the beginning. The way his tongue moved over her, following her contours, now skimming, now diving, sent impulses of pure pleasure the length of her body. He pressed the very tip to the button of her clitoris, and moved it almost imperceptibly back and forth. Just as a tremendous, insistent orgasm started to build deep inside her, Jeremy pulled back. She gasped, and fought to contain the sensations his mouth had unleashed.

When those sensations had subsided, she felt his tongue return, going around and around her pussy in ever-tightening circles. By the time he came back to that magical button, she knew, as he did, that there would be no more containment. He slowly, deliberately, moved his tongue back and forth, and she felt as though he were touching her very essence. Her orgasm consumed her. It rose up and took up all the space not just in her body, but in her mind and her spirit. She had never, never felt its like, and as it ebbed she marveled at its power.

She didn't realize her eyes were closed until she opened them and saw Jeremy standing over her, smiling and wiping his mouth with the back of his hand. She'd also forgotten that her hands were tied until Jeremy bent down to release them.

"Are you all right?" he asked as he handed the silk stocking back to her, quite a bit worse for the wear.

"I am," she said, and looked at the torn, misshapen stocking a little ruefully. "But had I known what was in store for my stockings, I think I would have chosen the cotton ones."

Jeremy laughed. "I'm terribly sorry about your stocking," he said. "If you let me have it, I will try to find a replacement of the same color next time I go up to town."

"That's very kind," said Georgiana, "but I think I shall keep it as a memento."

"My memento will be your scent," said Jeremy, holding his hand to his nose and inhaling deeply. "I'm not going to wash until you get back from Penfield," he said. She was planning to leave the next morning, and this would be the last time she and Jeremy would meet until she returned.

"But I can't leave you like this," Georgiana said, tracing the clear outline of his erect penis through his trousers.

"Ah, but you can," he said. "I want what you just felt to be the feeling you take with you. That is," he added, "if you really must go."

"It's not a question of must," she said. "I want to go. Paulette is a dear friend, and the party is one of the best in the country." Paulette was Lady Loughlin, and the party was the annual masquerade ball that the Loughlins hosted at Penfield, their country estate in Hampshire.

"Why don't you come?" she continued. "I know your father frowns on masquerade balls, but really—we're only five years shy of the twentieth century. Can't you convince him that what simply wasn't done when he was a young man is now done by just about everyone?"

"It's not just masquerades in general, as you very well know," said Jeremy. "It's the Penfield masquerade. It has something of a reputation, and not the kind that my father looks kindly on."

They both smiled, he ruefully and she expectantly. He needed to stay in his father's good graces in order to keep both his allowance and his expectation of financial independence once his father went to his maker. As the younger of two sons, he was at his father's mercy. The estate was entailed on his elder brother, John, but the crumbs—substantial enough to support a family in something like high style—were his father's to distribute as he would. If Jeremy started socializing with the likes of the Loughlins, the Viscount Newbury most certainly wouldn't distribute them to his younger son.

Lady Georgiana understood all this, and didn't press her lover.

"I'm sorry you won't be there," she said, "but I'll be back in a fortnight, at the most."

He kissed her hand with a gallant intimacy. "Enjoy yourself, but come home to me," he said, and took his leave.

TWO

As she rode to Penfield, Lady Georgiana thought about what Jeremy had said. When they first became lovers, they had agreed that theirs was an intimacy without conditions and without expectations, but Georgiana was beginning to think that Jeremy was repenting of his bargain. Lately, she sensed in him a seriousness, a determination that their relationship be something more than ephemeral pleasure. She had the idea that he wanted to *keep* her. It was an idea that flattered, but also chafed.

She prided herself on being forward thinking. She was of the twentieth century, although she wouldn't be in it for five years yet. As fond as she was of Jeremy—and she was very fond indeed—marriage to him would be capitulation to a convention that the nineteenth century, and all centuries previous, had foisted on women: Get married, young, to a gentleman of your class, and bear him an heir as soon as ever you can. She didn't object to marriage, or gentlemen of her class, or heirs; she objected to their being her only choice.

Strength and independence were, for her, cardinal virtues, inextricably linked. She strove for them herself and looked for them in others, men and women alike. Where men were concerned, the world's views were aligned with hers. When it came to women, the situation was more complicated. Females were expected to be, if not weak and clinging, at least delicate and submissive. To defy those expectations required not just a degree of boldness, but also societal latitude—latitude much more readily granted to a scion of nobility than a scullery maid.

Lady Georgiana wasn't a fool, and she understood that her freedom was a function both of her personality and her position. She was, perhaps, inclined to overvalue the first and undervalue the second, but that's to be expected in a girl of spirit.

Spirited she certainly was. Her wit was sharp and her mind was keen. While her education had been only middling for a girl of her class, she had read widely, and was conversant with matters of politics, and agriculture, and even natural philosophy. What she couldn't do was draw. Neither could she sing. She couldn't arrange flowers or embroider handkerchiefs. Her piano playing was so rudimentary as to be embarrassing.

She had steadfastly refused to acquire those accomplishments, partly from a natural disinclination borne of her understanding that she lacked the gifts of ear and eye, and partly from sheer obstinacy. She sought the traditional occupations of men as assiduously as she shunned those of women. She smoked cigars. She read newspapers. She would have opinions, and freedom, and lovers.

It was lovers she was thinking of as she rode the last few miles to Penfield.

An observer would have seen a lithe, pale-skinned girl, deep in thought. He might have taken her for a man, as she dressed and rode like one. When she was seventeen, after she had taken a tumble jumping a hedge, she decided that serious horsemanship required riding astride, and she pilfered a pair of riding breeches from her fourteen-year-old brother, the nascent eighth earl. She told the groom to saddle Senator, the most independent-minded horse in the stable. "And not with the side-saddle," she added with a self-conscious imperiousness. "I will be riding astride."

The groom, well trained, blinked once and did as he was bidden. She mounted and rode out of the stable yard with all the dignity she could muster. Although she'd had a couple of stealthy practice sessions, she wasn't used to swinging her right leg over the horse's back, and she managed it gracelessly. But she sat up straight, with her heels down and Senator's torso firm between her knees, and headed out to Eastley's grounds.

She never rode sidesaddle again, and now, five years later, she was a skilled and confident rider. On this occasion, though, neither skill nor confidence was required. The path underfoot was well-worn and, even though the sun had been down an hour and more, there was enough moonlight to render the path faintly visible. Lady Georgiana knew that her horse's excellent vision and sure-footedness would keep them both on track, and her reverie began to take on a more physical quality.

For her, there was always something about being on a horse. She'd discovered this unexpected pleasure of having a moving saddle between her legs the very first time she took Senator around the grounds at East-ley. She'd been too uncertain of herself then to relax and let it overcome her, but it didn't take many outings before she understood how to stay on the horse while letting the smooth leather of the saddle pitch up and down against her, raising her temperature, quickening her heartbeat, and moistening her core.

Now all she could think about was the rhythm of the ride and the gradually increasing waves of pleasure working their way through her body, almost of their own accord. Alone on the trail, shrouded by darkness, Georgiana abandoned herself to the steady climb toward the explosion she knew would come. She focused on letting it happen, and not making it happen. She kept her sensations under control by tilting her hips a tiny bit backward to minimize contact, and then forward again to bring her right to the brink. She'd been in the saddle for two hours already, and had the luxury—which she never had, or perhaps just never exercised, with Jeremy—of building up and then pulling back, and then doing it again, at whatever pace pleased her, for as long as she wanted.

And she wanted. The freedom to move as she liked, to have to focus on no one else, to abandon herself to the rhythm, meant that some of her most intense pleasure, her most body-enveloping orgasms, had come on horseback.

The horse continued his steady walk, the saddle moving up and down, with each lift having a slight forward motion that pulsed against her. The pulsing went on and on, out of her control because the animal she was riding made it happen, but within her control because the slightest motion determined the intensity of her feeling.

As she neared the point at which control ceased, she tried to relax every muscle that wasn't needed to keep her in the saddle. She resisted the deep-seated impulse to grasp, to clench, to hold. When she was with Jeremy, she loved that sensation—of taking him in, of keeping him in, of trying to bury him deeper and deeper inside her. His hardness and his urgency were part of her pleasure. Without that, her pleasure was different. It was soft and slow, almost slack. Even as she knew she was approaching her climax, she was relaxed and passive.

Then came the tingling she recognized as the first note of fulfillment. It started in the backs of her calves, the sensation of being overcome by a gentle warmth; it traveled up her legs and into her chest before it trans-formed itself from a lapping wave to a perfect storm, involving every muscle and every nerve. Her deliberate relaxation succumbed to the force of her ecstasy. Now she contracted everything to lengthen, to intensify. She felt as if her very body were transformed to some other material. She didn't just feel pleasure; she *was* pleasure, a pleasure that was both suf-fusing and acute. She made no noise, but exhaled sharply.

Her orgasm left as it had come, subsiding back to the lapping wave and then ebbing altogether, leaving her profoundly satisfied. It took several minutes for her breathing to return to normal, and another few for Georgiana to be fully aware of her surroundings. As she became attuned again to the darkness, and the breeze, and her horse's steady footfall, she saw a line of lights, dim in the distance. It was Penfield.

Penfield was undoubtedly the finest house in Hampshire. Not the biggest, not the oldest, but the most pleasing and complete. It wasn't just a box on a hill, like so many of the country houses she'd visited. It had long, lean lines, and nestled comfortably in the rolling terrain of its grounds. The house had been built a hundred years ago as the country home of the Earl of Tewksbury, and had seen that family through three generations. The fourth, though, did them in. With family finances brought low by the gambling debts of a dissolute brother, the great-grandson of the original owner was forced to sell. Lord and Lady Loughlin bought. The Loughlins had lived there twenty years already, but decades mean little when real residence is measured in centuries.

As Georgiana rode up the broad drive that looped in front of Penfield, she noticed again how fine it looked, illuminated by the torches set out to welcome late-arriving guests.

Lady Loughlin came running downstairs when she heard a horse's hooves on the gravel drive and the ring at the front door. She'd expected Georgiana hours earlier and, even though that young lady never came anywhere on time, the lady of the house was relieved to hear her friend's voice greeting Dodson, the Loughlins' longtime butler.

"Georgiana!" she cried, racing into the entrance foyer. "We've been expecting you all evening."

"Paulette," said Georgiana, embracing her hostess. "I'm sorry to be so beastly late. I hope you haven't worried."

"If I worried every time you were late," said Lady Loughlin, chuckling, "I'd be able to think of little else."

The women embraced again, and Lady Loughlin said, "I'll show you to your chamber, even though I know you can find it perfectly well by yourself." Then the older woman looked around. "But where are your trunks?"

"They'll be along tomorrow, with Hortense. I wanted to ride alone. I brought enough to get me through the night," Georgiana said, pointing to a small valise.

Lady Loughlin shook her head in some wonder. She was used to her friend's eccentricities, but surely no young woman, no matter how spirited or self-sufficient, should be riding alone at night. She knew from experience, however, that no good would come of suggesting a more prudent course, so she simply took her friend's elbow and led her to her room.

As they went up the great stairway that led to the guest wing, Georgiana asked who else was in the house.

"Oh, we're full up," said Lady Loughlin. "We have the Graftons, and the Carlisles, and the Sheffields. And of course Robert's cousins the O'Maras."

"That *is* a houseful," said Georgiana.

"At least the boys aren't here." Paulette was referring to her two grown sons. "Robbie's in Scotland and Freddy's gone up to Oxford. But we are expecting the Earl of Grantsbury," she continued, as though as an afterthought.

"An earl!" exclaimed Georgiana, who could take liberties with her friend, "And not just any earl—it's Peter!" Georgiana had known Lord Peter Halsey, Earl of Grantsbury, for some years. "I'm delighted to hear that you've managed such an earl as that."

Paulette had managed such an earl as that. But earls hadn't always been within her grasp.

Lady Loughlin was the former Paulette Carston, heiress to the fortune made by her grandfather, who had formulated Carston's Complexion Cream. The lotion had become a staple on ladies' dressing tables, and made the family very rich indeed. But the cream's admission to dressing rooms didn't guarantee the heiress's admission to drawing rooms, and Lady Loughlin's path through English society had been uncertain.

Her marriage to Robert Loughlin had helped. He was a baron, but an Irish baron, and so the status his family connection conferred gave his wife entrée into a larger circle than she'd known before, but doors to some of the very best houses were still closed to her, at least early in her marriage. Lady Loughlin, though, wasn't one to dwell on her failures. Overall, she thought her living a fine thing, and took some pride in her ability to take whatever came.

She had been a merry and mischievous girl, and had grown into a charming and gregarious woman. She was forty-one or forty-two, or possibly forty-five—no one could pin her down—and she'd borne two sons, but neither the years nor the children showed in her figure. Her waist looked as narrow as it had been at nineteen, her breasts as buoyant. Only her husband and her maid could say how much tighter stays and stiffer corsets contributed to the effect.

Lady Loughlin and Georgiana Vernon were as great friends as two women separated by two decades could be. The older woman admired the younger, and saw something of herself in her friend. Had Lady Loughlin, as a girl, gone out into the world with noble, rather than commercial, antecedents, Miss Carston might have been much like Miss Vernon. As it was, though, Paulette had understood from a very young age that it was incumbent upon her to play by the rules. Coming from a manufacturing family, she knew how precarious her social standing was. The slightest lapse from the proper would brand her boorish and crass. "What do you expect?" the bona fide ladies would ask. "She was born into complexion cream."

When she met Robert Loughlin, she knew nothing of the private side of men. She knew their public side well; since her first season in London, when she was just sixteen, she'd spent as much time as she could in society. A good match would be crucial to her prospects, and she meant to put herself in the way of making one. Before Lord Loughlin, there had been several other suitors, but none had met her rather exacting standards. Not relishing the idea of having to turn down a request for her hand, she had found ways to make it clear to them before the offer had ever been made that an offer would not be accepted.

Lord Loughlin, though, she would not discourage. Besides being tall, broad, and handsome, he was thoughtful and well-informed. His manners were pleasing, his conversation entertaining, and his style winning. His hair was undeniably a shade too red, but the Miss Carston she had been had graciously decided to overlook that flaw. She hadn't known him more than two or three weeks before she noticed a constriction in her chest, a tightening around her quickening heartbeat, when he entered a room.

He was also noble and, while he certainly didn't have income to spare, he wasn't downright destitute. Although she didn't need a husband to bring money to their union, she didn't want to give the impression she had been married for hers. She also wasn't willing to connect herself simply for status. Her family ties would always be considered a liability, she knew, but she appraised her personal charms and her financial wherewithal at their true value, and calculated—rightly—that their combination would merit a husband of substance, one she could love.

She did love Robert Loughlin, and had thrilled at his asking to marry her. The day they were wed, she shut the door on Miss Carston and wholly embraced the newness, the excitement, the stature, and the responsibilities of Lady Loughlin.

One of those responsibilities, though, gave her some trepidation. She had never so much as kissed a man until she agreed to be Lord Loughlin's wife, and knew little about what went on between a man and a woman behind their closed bedchamber door. Her mother, she knew, would be of no use; that good lady was so prim that she had trouble discussing even the complexion cream that made the family's fortune; she believed anything that couldn't happen in a drawing room, for all to see, shouldn't be part of a lady's conversation. In the weeks before her wedding, Lady Loughlin–to-be spoke with several of her married friends, but her necessarily oblique approach to the subject occasioned equally oblique responses.

And so, when she stepped out of her dressing room at the inn at Dover in which they were to spend the night before crossing the channel to begin their Italian honeymoon, she wasn't sure what to expect. Her husband was dressed in a simple cambric nightshirt, lying in the canopied four-poster bed with his head propped against the pillows, reading a book. When she stepped into the room, he looked up, smiled at her, and put the book down on the nightstand.

She sat down on the opposite side of the bed and smiled in return. Robert piled pillows in front of the headboard, and motioned her to sit beside him. He didn't say a word, then or later.

She'd heard tales—ribald jokes, risqué stories—of men's wolfish nature, and knew, in the indistinct way affianced girls knew such things, that her husband had been adventurous in those private matters, so she was a little surprised when he simply took her hand. He turned it over and gently ran his fingertips over her palm. He traced its lines softly. He ran his index finger down the inside of her thumb, over the smooth muscle where it met her hand, and down to the underside of her wrist.

Her nightgown was of fine, supple muslin, with Belgian lace at the collar, placket, and cuffs. There was a drawstring where the lace cuffs met the muslin sleeves, and Robert untied it by pulling gently on the pink grosgrain ribbon that her maid had tied so carefully. He pushed her sleeve up her arm and ran his hand over her forearm—always gently, gently.

Paulette was astonished at how intensely her body reacted to such a simple motion. What she'd felt seeing him in public had given her only the merest inkling of what it would be like feeling him in private. Every nerve in her body was focused on the point of contact between her and this man; every thought was for what was happening between them. Never had she known such single-minded concentration, or such inner turmoil. It was as though the tightness were melting her, and the intensity focusing itself between her legs.

Each time Robert's hand touched a part of her he hadn't touched before, a wave broke inside her. And, as though he knew it—could he? did he?—he let his hand stay in one place while her urgency subsided. Only then would he move on, reawakening the tightness, the turmoil, the melting.

His expert touch brought her own inexperience home to her, but she despised the idea of the naive little virgin meekly letting her husband take her on their wedding night. She was a full-blooded woman, and she wanted both the giving and the taking to flow both ways. She took both his hands in hers and looked at him for a long moment. She leaned in and let her lips just skim over his, and then worked her way around to his cheek, and then his earlobe. Almost instinctively, she moved to his neck and kissed him, hard. He groaned as he felt her lips, her teeth, her tongue.

Her aggressiveness surprised him, and he looked at her with a fresh curiosity. He reached out and untied the pink ribbon at her neck, not quite so carefully and slowly as he had untied her sleeves. He unbuttoned the six buttons that went from the collar to the end of the lace placket, just above her waist. He traced a line from the hollow between her collarbones down to where her breasts met. He turned his hand over so his palm was up, and cupped her left breast, still under the fabric of her nightgown. She watched as he moved his head to her chest and gently kissed the inch-wide strip of bare skin exposed between the two bands of lace. He widened the gap, moving his lips back and forth, first to one side and then the other, each time pushing her nightgown a little farther open.

And then, almost before she realized it, her nipple, erect and sensitive, was in his mouth. She gasped, the first sound that had passed between them since she sat down on the bed. Her body, moving of its own accord, arched toward him. She knew, as he did, that she was ready for him. He sat up and pulled his nightshirt over his head, and she saw what a man looked like. The outline of the male body, its basic composition, was familiar to her from statues and paintings, but art hadn't prepared her for his cock, so hard it was almost vertical. He took her hand in his and put her index finger in his mouth. The sensation of his tongue on her finger brought her right to the edge. He took that finger, wet, and guided her to run it up the underside of his penis, and the groan he gave let her know that his urgency was as acute as hers.

The feel of his erection surprised her. It had a core like steel, but it was surrounded by smooth, soft skin. The vein running its length had pulsed under her finger, and she found that his heart was beating as quickly and insistently as her own. She reached her hand around its girth at the base, and found it was as big around as her wrist. She started to move her hand up the shaft, her exploration motivated by both desire and curiosity. As hard as it had been, it became harder still. She continued to move one hand slowly up and down his cock, and took his balls in the other. She felt their slippery looseness as she rolled them over her fingers.

And then she let them hang as she used both hands to hold his cock. She wanted to know how to touch it to please him most, and she used her hands in different configurations, with varying pressure, and paid attention to his response. Touching the tip, she found, elicited the most intense reaction, and she slowly ran her finger up and down the small slit that ran up the bottom of the glans. Then she wet her finger and did it some more.

Robert was at the point where he could no longer trust himself in her hands. He pulled himself away from her and then reached under her nightgown, one hand on the outside of each leg. He ran his hands straight up the sides of her body, lifting the nightgown as he went. She moved to free the fabric, and raised her arms so he could lift it off her. Then his hands ran back down her naked body, retracing their path. They stopped when they got to her hips, and he eased his thumbs around to her inner thighs, and then up, straight up, to the source of her pleasure. He separated the lips of her cunt and slowly inserted his thumb. She was so wet that it slid in effortlessly, and she felt its presence as a preview of what was to come.

Robert was kneeling between her legs, and as he pulled his thumb out, he slid his penis in—just the tip, at first. The sensation was breathtaking. She felt him move the tip in and out, and all she wanted was more. She tilted her hips toward him and, in one motion, he sank his full, hard length into her wet, warm center. She cried out at the sudden pain of her lost virginity, but it was over almost instantly, replaced by the most acute arousal she had ever experienced. Robert moved slowly in and out of her, and she had a sense that he was containing himself only by a supreme effort.

Then she knew there would be no more containment for her. Everything in her contracted toward his presence in her, and she came in great, convulsing waves. The first wave unleashed Robert, and together they consummated their marriage.

Now, twenty-two years later, Lady Loughlin thought back on that night with both pleasure and sadness: pleasure for the purity of the experience, sadness for what she and her husband had lost since that night. In the time they'd been married, their lovemaking had become more skilled, more imaginative, more sophisticated, but a distance had also developed between them. They still made love, but less frequently and less wholeheartedly. They had found that creating a home, navigating society, and raising two sons had divided them into their respective roles. They both felt as though they lived two individual lives, rather than life as one.

This week, though, Lady Loughlin had little time for such thoughts. Georgiana's arrival marked the beginning of the busiest and most exciting week of the Loughlins' social calendar. The life she led the rest of the year went into a kind of suspended animation as her house began to fill with guests who looked forward for months to visiting Penfield and to attending her masquerade. And she couldn't say but that she didn't anticipate it more than any of them.

"And we're off," she said to herself as she went up to bed.

THREE

~❧~

The morning after Lady Georgiana arrived at Penfield, she was late coming down to breakfast. Hortense had arrived with the luggage early enough to see that Georgiana had tea and toast in her room, and so had deprived her mistress of any incentive to get out of bed, get dressed, and join the rest of the Penfield guests in the breakfast room.

It was almost ten o'clock when she finally made her way downstairs, and the only people who joined her over the kippers, for which she had a particular fondness, were Mr. and Mrs. Henry Sheffield, who were still chatting about the day's plans over plates with discarded toast crusts and cups with cold tea leaves.

"Ah!" said Georgiana. "Mr. and Mrs. Sheffield! How glad I am to see you." She knew the Sheffields slightly, and had enjoyed the company of the husband sufficiently to be willing to overlook a certain shrewishness in the wife.

"And how glad *we* are to see *you*," said Hermione Sheffield, with a chilliness that gave the lie to the words. Mrs. Sheffield valued respectability above all else, and she had much too great a veneration for propriety to approve of Lady Georgiana's conduct at the party the year before, when the earl's daughter had spoken familiarly with all the servants—made friends with them, almost—and then appeared at the ball in a scandalously abbreviated costume. She had been Diana, goddess of the hunt, if Mrs. Sheffield's memory served her, and that good lady was certain that no self-respecting goddess would ever have made an appearance in a robe that parted almost to the knee with every step she took.

Mr. Sheffield, for his part, didn't share his wife's disapprobation of revealing robes, and liked Georgiana very much.

"What are you planning for the day?" Georgiana asked them, between bites of kipper.

"We were just deciding that very thing," said Henry Sheffield. "Several couples decided to take advantage of the fine weather to have a picnic at Linwood"—a large house with a lovely park about ten miles distant—"but Hermione and I thought we'd like to see the new pleasure grounds here before we wander farther afield."

"I am entirely of your mind," said Lady Georgiana. "Lady Loughlin kept me abreast of the construction, and I simply cannot wait to see them." The Loughlins had spent the previous year transforming their park, and the results were the talk of horticultural England.

Mr. Sheffield was just about to invite her to join them to walk the grounds, and Mrs. Sheffield, seeing her husband's intention, was trying to think of a way to head off the invitation, when a deep, gravelly voice came from the door. "I'd be happy to show them to you," it said.

All eyes moved to the doorway of the breakfast room, which was almost filled by a very large man with dark eyes and a wide smile. He was dressed like a gentleman, but his sleeves were rolled up, his hair was shaggy, and his boots were splattered with mud, so the impression he gave was that of a laborer.

"Forgive me for interrupting your breakfast," he said to the company as he helped himself to a piece of bread and slathered it with marmalade. "I heard you talking about the grounds and thought I should introduce myself. I'm Bruce Barnes." He shook hands with Henry Sheffield and bowed to the ladies as the three of them introduced themselves in return.

They all knew his name, and even some of his history. He'd been born the son of the gardener of an extremely wealthy country squire, and had risen to become one of the foremost designers of estate grounds in all England. He'd shaken up his profession by breaking from the graveled walks and formal gardens of the past, and installing artificial ponds and intricate topiary in the parks of his clients. Although some of England's oldest, most venerable clans would never countenance such modern innovations, Barnes had caught on with a smart set of rich families, and his services were in great demand.

"There are a few areas that aren't quite finished," Barnes told them. "We'd hoped to have everything completed for the masquerade, but the weather wasn't cooperative. But if you're willing to overlook a few bare spots, I think I can show you almost everything," he said.

Lady Georgiana and Mr. Sheffield agreed readily, and Mrs. Sheffield couldn't decline without seeming ungracious. The two women went upstairs for wraps, as there was a hint of a fall chill in the air, and they met Barnes and Mr. Sheffield in the foyer. The foursome set out for the grounds.

Penfield's lands were extensive, and two hours later the group still hadn't seen all of what Barnes had done. They'd seen how a field had been transformed into a lake, complete with an island and a flotilla of punts. They'd taken a few steps into a boxwood maze. They'd seen exotic plants from halfway around the world, and the modern greenhouses that made their cultivation possible. They'd seen hedges trained and trimmed into elephants, camels, and lions. And they'd seen peacocks. Hundreds of peacocks.

"Wherever did you get them all?" asked Mrs. Sheffield in frank amazement.

"I know a man in Dorset who breeds them for the purpose," said Barnes. "There's quite a bit of demand."

"Aren't they tropical birds?" asked Georgiana.

"They are. Over the winter, we'll keep them indoors. We've built a pavilion for them over the hill south of the house."

"A pavilion?" Georgiana couldn't suppress a smile. "For peacocks?"

"A pavilion for peacocks," Barnes said definitively, his smile matching her own. "Should you like to see it?"

"I most certainly should. I've never seen a peacock pavilion before."

Barnes turned to the Sheffields. "Will you join us?" he asked.

Neither Mrs. Sheffield's boots nor Mr. Sheffield's constitution could manage the walk around the house and over the hill—it was over a mile—and they excused themselves and headed back to Penfield in search of a cup of tea.

For her part, Mrs. Sheffield was glad to have a reason to excuse herself. She prided herself on having an uncanny sense of the improper, and she had seen the glances that passed between Lady Georgiana and the man Mrs. Sheffield considered a glorified gardener.

"Did you see the way they were looking at each other?" she asked her husband as they made their way back to the house.

"No, my dear," said Mr. Sheffield, suppressing a sigh, "I didn't notice."

Before she had been Mrs. Sheffield, his wife had been Miss Hermione Preston, a moderately pretty girl from a moderately prosperous but eminently respectable family. She had been unremarkable but for two things: a rectitude unusual in a girl so young, and the most astonishing breasts Mr. Sheffield had ever seen. He still remembered the way that even the best-tailored, most modest dress could barely contain them. Always there had been the luscious twin hillocks, with the tantalizing crevice in between, escaping from the confines of her bodice.

The rectitude, had it been fed by confidence and generosity, might have turned, in time, into the flexible backbone of a fine, upstanding woman. Starved by insecurity and petty jealousies, though, it had become a pinched and poor smallness of mind. Mr. Sheffield had often pondered the folly of marrying breasts without duly considering the woman to whom they were attached. Still, he was a cheerful and optimistic man, and was determined to make the best of it.

"I'm sure you'd like a cup of tea," he said to his wife by way of distracting her from the iniquity that had gone on right under her nose.

"I would at that," she said, and couldn't help but think of those crumbly little scones with the raisins that Stevens, the Loughlins' cook, invariably served with tea.

"Then let us go find some, shall we?" said Mr. Sheffield with a smile.

As the Sheffields went in search of their tea, Lady Georgiana and Bruce Barnes headed to the peacock pavilion. The two walked in silence, each noting the change in the atmosphere now that they were alone. When the Sheffields had been with them, Georgiana had assessed Barnes coolly, from the distance that the company of others always interposed between a man and a woman. The company had gone, and with it the distance, and she felt his presence in a new way.

She saw the pavilion as they crested the hill that hid it from the house. It was a big, square, low-ceilinged building nestled in a little dale. "We have to keep it warm in the winter," Barnes explained, "so we sheltered it from the wind."

Her mind hadn't been on the peacocks for quite some time, and she just nodded rather stupidly. "I see," she said.

Barnes looked at her a little sharply. The woman who'd sparkled all morning was now answering him in monosyllables. She seemed distracted.

She was distracted. She found this man profoundly alluring, and her mind was attempting to penetrate the fog of her physical attraction to him to try to decide what she wanted to do about it.

Barnes turned toward her and looked her straight in the eye for a long moment. "Would you like to see the inside?" he asked in a low voice.

She nodded again, not sure that she ought to go in, but also not sure that she ought not to. Although Barnes seemed a rough man beneath his gentlemanly veneer, Georgiana didn't think there was any danger in him. She started down the hill, with Barnes close behind her.

The building had a double door in the center of the wall, and Barnes opened one side of it. Although the doorway itself was wide, when only one of the doors was opened, the space leading into the building was quite narrow. The gardener held the door open for Lady Georgiana to pass, but to walk in she would have to all but brush against him. She paused a moment but, having committed herself this far, she refused to be deterred. She walked past him, leaving as much space between them as she could without obviously avoiding the contact.

She felt her skirts brush his boots. She smelled his raw, earthen smell. She saw the large, calloused hand that held the door, and couldn't help but imagine how it would feel on her skin, caressing her thigh, cupping her breast.

She walked into the building. She heard the door close behind her and stood for a moment recovering herself, letting her heartbeat slow and her eyes adjust to the relative dimness. As they did, she realized that she must be looking at the least remarkable building in all England. It was a large, empty space with four walls. It had a wooden floor, and a stove in the center. There were bales of straw piled up against one wall. And that was all there was.

The anticlimax brought her back to the here and now. "So this is a peacock pavilion," she said dubiously as she looked around. "I always thought pavilions were luxurious and well-appointed."

Barnes laughed. "This is luxurious and well-appointed, if you're a peacock," he said. "It's got warmth, food, protection from predators, and the companionship of other peacocks. Do you think they'd ask for up-holstered furniture and electric lights?"

Lady Georgiana laughed in turn, and looked up at him, almost re-lieved that the tension between them seemed to be dissipating. But with one step, Barnes brought it once more to bear. That step took him so close to her that only inches separated them. He seemed to be forcing his presence on her, but he didn't touch her. He looked at her, and she heard his breath and smelled his smell again. He stood so very close that she felt his heat, yet he didn't touch her. It was as though he were waiting for her.

Her eyes were level with his chest, and she saw the red-tinged hair that showed where the first two buttons of his shirt lay open. It was dense, curly hair, with none of the silky smoothness of Jeremy's. It covered a chest that was tanned and hard. His outline was clear through his thin cotton shirt, and Lady Georgiana could see that it wasn't quite symmetrical. His right side—shoulder, chest, arm—was perceptibly more developed than his left, the result, she assumed, of the work that he did.

And those hands! Even as they hung relaxed at his sides, she could sense their power. Here was a man whose body was built not by lawn tennis and riding to hounds, but by good, honest work. His was strength that came straight from the land, strength he built establishing his mastery over it. No man had ever seemed more virile, more genuine to her. He made the men she was accustomed to meeting in society look effete and ineffectual, hothouse plants beside the oak that was Bruce Barnes.

He stood so close to her, and she ached to close the gap, to cleave her small body to his large one. She felt as though her desire could be quenched by his merest touch.

But something stopped her, and she didn't quite know what. Perhaps it was simply the suddenness of it all that prevented her. Two hours ago, she hadn't known this man. Two days ago, she'd been in the arms of a very different man. She'd come to Penfield resolved on asserting her freedom, but freedom thought of in the comfort of her bedchamber at Eastley seemed different from freedom standing in front of her in firm flesh and hot blood.

When she'd walked down the hill to the pavilion, she'd told herself that there was no danger in this man. And there wasn't, not in the sense that she'd thought of it then. Now, though, she saw that there was danger, but the danger was in her, not in him. It was the danger of passion, the danger of unbridled animal attraction. The thought of it kept her from closing the gap between them at the same time that it intensified her desire to close it. She looked up at him, willing her gaze to stay steady and her pulse to stay calm.

Almost before she realized she had decided what to do, she took a step back. Barnes didn't move. His gaze held her eyes, and she knew that she was still in his thrall. To break the spell, she would have to break the silence.

"We should get back before luncheon," she said a little haltingly. "I don't want to be missed." Still, she couldn't look away from him, and he didn't answer. What was it about this man? Finally, she looked down at the floor and the spell was broken at last.

"You're right," said Barnes, "we should." He said it cheerfully, as though nothing had passed between them, and for a moment Georgiana thought she might have imagined their connection. But then he held the door open for her, and she had to pass in front of him to go out just as she had passed in front of him to come in. Once again, her skirts brushed his boots. And again, his scent of the soil and all that grew from it suffused her senses. As she walked past him the feel of his eyes on her back was as real, as tactile, as the feel of his hands would have been. It had been real, she knew. It *was* real.

They walked up to the house together in silence. Lady Georgiana didn't even attempt conversation; she was entirely focused on being able, once they reached Penfield, to appear as though this had been an ordinary garden tour.

This she was able to do, and, when they got there, she thanked him prettily for his time.

"It was my pleasure," he said, and watched her go up the stairs.

As she went up to her room to gather her wits and change her clothes, both of which had been more than a little disordered by her morning's activities, he went back outside and around to the kitchen garden in the back of the house. He slipped through the back door that led into the scullery. There, a buxom, strapping, red-cheeked girl of about nineteen was ironing and folding freshly laundered sheets.

"Ah, Maureen," said Barnes. "I thought I might find you here."

"Ah, Bruce," said Maureen, echoing his tone with a subtle but discernible Irish brogue, "you can find me here most times, as you well know."

"I do," he said, as he walked up behind her. "But I never know if I'll find you alone." As he said it, he swept her auburn hair away from the back of her neck and kissed her just under her left ear.

Maureen put her iron down and leaned into his kiss. She was a smart, resourceful girl, and until she met Bruce Barnes she'd managed to keep clear of the men of Penfield and their guests, some of whom thought it was their God-given right to have their way with any scullery maid who struck their fancy. Barnes, though, struck *her* fancy, and when he had first appeared at Penfield the previous year, she had decided that he would be the one she'd let have her. She'd never regretted it.

Maureen closed and bolted both the door to the garden and the inner door to the kitchen, and then walked behind Barnes just as he had walked behind her. She put her hands on his shoulders, and then traced the contours of his back down to the waist of his pants. She slipped her hands under the waistband, and then circled them around to the front so her arms were around him and she gripped his already erect penis.

He had both hands on the table she'd been using to iron the sheets, and he bent over at the waist. He stretched his left leg behind him and she straddled it, rubbing herself against the back of his thigh as she stroked his cock and felt it grow harder in her hand. The suddenness of his appearance, the lack of any preamble to their sex, and the insistent throbbing of his penis in her hand set her on fire. She moved her hands back to his waist and turned him around to face her. They didn't kiss; they seldom did. Instead, she unbuttoned his shirt and pressed her mouth against his bare chest, hard.

Her mouth moved to his nipple, and she took it in. Her teeth played along the edges of the areola, hard enough almost to bruise. Barnes was breathing deeply, holding her hips hard against his. As she bit, she circled her tongue around his nipple, feeling it firm, yet strangely yielding in her mouth. And then her teeth closed and clamped on, and she worked his nipple slowly back and forth, all the while keeping her tongue on its tip. He let out a cry that was part pain, part pleasure.

She stopped abruptly. "Hush!" she said. "Cook will hear you."

He could only grunt in reply.

He took her by the waist, lifted her off the floor, and turned to put her on the table. He made short work of her apron, dress, and drawers, and pulled her to the very edge of the table. He took his cock out of his pants, stepped between her legs, and with one motion was inside her—deep inside her. She gasped. It almost hurt.

She moved even closer to the edge of the table until her thighs were completely off it and she could straighten her body at the hips. Only then did she feel the full, explosive power of his contact with her. She wanted him ever deeper, to feel him reaching to her core, and to feel the lips of her pussy pulling him in.

He took her firm young ass in both his hands so he could push deeper, and he squeezed the two muscles of her buttocks, hard enough to leave marks—he'd left them before. The harder he gripped her, the more the pressure intensified her pleasure. She was tight to him, and she felt her clitoris graze the base of him every time he moved into her. Every thrust seemed just a little deeper than the one before, and every thrust brought her closer to climax.

Together they rose to that climax, and together they reached it. Just as she turned liquid, she felt him shudder and pull her to him. The liquid turned to fire as she succumbed to her orgasm, and she held him close as he tightened, tightened, and then slowly relaxed.

She released him, and they smiled at each other conspiratorially as they rearranged their clothes. She watched as he tucked the instrument of her satisfaction back into his trousers, and gloried in the afterglow of her animal excitement.

For his part, Barnes gloried in the idea that an earl's daughter might be within his grasp.

FOUR

The Loughlins' dining room, small for the house, sat twenty comfortably. When more than that number were to dine, Lady Loughlin preferred laying the food out in a buffet to converting another, larger room to accommodate the crowd at table. She had always preferred the ad hoc to the formal, and enjoyed letting her guests spread out through the various drawing rooms and parlors, with groups forming as they would.

There was still the best part of a week to go before the masquerade, and the party at the house was still small. It was nevertheless too big to sit in the dining room, and the evening after Georgiana's excursion to the peacock pavilion, Lady Loughlin watched with interest to see how the guests would divvy themselves up.

Lady Loughlin's taste in people was more varied than that of most others of her class. She took pleasure in populating her house with men and women who interested her, regardless of rank or background. When she was younger, she tempered this inclination in the interest of her own social mobility, but now that she was secure in her position she felt free to indulge it.

The eclectic, almost haphazard mix of people didn't always put her guests completely at their ease, but the mistress of the house found that a bit of social friction made for a much more interesting assembly. Her husband had, on more than one occasion, expressed concern about the jumble of humanity his wife liked to bring together under their roof.

"Oh, rot," said Lady Loughlin. "Are our friends so fragile that we risk their well-being simply by putting them in a room with people who don't see the world quite as they do?"

"It's not their well-being I fear for," said Lord Loughlin with equanimity. "Only their comfort." Although he was loath to admit it to his wife, he also enjoyed the sparks that flew when like met unlike, and he lodged his mild protest more for form's sake than out of any genuine anxiety.

When her guests didn't seem able to arrange themselves in a satisfactory way, Lady Loughlin intervened, and on this occasion that was exactly what she did. It started with the Sheffields, who were always a problem. Although Mrs. Sheffield was exactly the kind of woman Lady Loughlin disliked most, her husband was genial and sociable—as well as being one of her father's oldest business associates. The combination of Mr. Sheffield's trade associations and Mrs. Sheffield's manners tended to keep other guests at bay.

But Paulette Loughlin wouldn't have it so, and she scooped up three other guests as they were leaving the buffet with full plates and deposited them on chairs next to the sofa the Sheffields were already occupying.

"I don't believe you are acquainted with the Carlisles," she said to Mr. and Mrs. Sheffield. "They're our neighbors in London, and this is the first time they've been down to Hampshire with us." The two couples nodded to one another as Lady Loughlin went on.

"And this," she said, holding the arm of the third guest she'd commandeered, a round-faced, cheery-looking man who appeared to have already had several glasses of Lord Loughlin's excellent burgundy, "is Alphonse Gerard, but everyone calls him Gerry."

"Hullo!" said Gerard with more enthusiasm than the situation seemed to warrant. "I'm pleased to know all of you." He sat down and immediately went to work on a very large veal chop.

The Sheffields and the Carlisles began exchanging the usual pleasantries, inquiring about the nature of the others' connection to their hosts, and their lives when they weren't visiting Penfield. This led to a discussion of Penfield itself, which the Carlisles were seeing for the first time that day, having arrived only a few hours before dinner.

As they were talking of the house's beautiful exterior, its modern improvements, its convenient layout, Mrs. Sheffield saw Bruce Barnes heading toward the buffet. Lady Loughlin made a point of having him eat with the family and the family guests, and not with the servants, but the sight of him doing so surprised Mrs. Sheffield enough to make her break off almost in midsentence.

"That's Bruce Barnes," she said generally to the company. And added, after a pause, "I wonder that he eats with the guests."

"I shouldn't wonder in the slightest," said Alphonse Gerard through a mouthful of veal, put out by Mrs. Sheffield's obvious disapproval. "The man's a genius."

"But he's a gardener," protested Mrs. Sheffield.

"Certainly he knows how to tend plants," responded Gerry. "And I know how to saddle my horse. Does that make me a groom?"

"Of course it doesn't. But if you earned your bread by saddling other people's horses, you would indeed be a groom." Mrs. Sheffield was rather pleased with her own quickness on the subject.

"Fiddlesticks," expostulated Gerry. "Barnes doesn't earn his bread tending plants any more than I earn mine by saddling horses. He earns his bread designing the most astonishing gardens in England, and I'm more honored than otherwise to share a meal with him."

At that moment, Barnes's entrance into the room stopped their conversation. He took a seat in the corner farthest from them, on a chair grouped with several others around a low table. He didn't betray the slightest discomfort at being alone, but then, he wasn't alone for long. As if to confirm Alphonse Gerard's view of the man, three other guests entered the room and made straight for the empty chairs around Bruce Barnes. Two of the three were Robert Loughlin's cousins the O'Maras, and the third was one of the most beautiful girls in England.

She was tall. She would have been too tall had her perfect proportions not turned her height into an asset. She had dark, rich hair pulled up and back, but with gently curling tendrils escaping at her nape and temples. Her shoulders were perfectly straight across, strong and broad enough to support the perfect body that hung from them. Her brimming bustline tapered to a waist so neat and narrow that it led every man she met to wonder whether his two hands could span it. Her eyes were wide-set and so dark a brown as to be almost black, and their color was set off by that of her lips, which were an arresting sepia-tinted red with a soft matte shine. If she had a flaw, it was that her face and figure were too perfect, without the interest of any blemish or asymmetry.

"Who's the girl?" Gerry asked his dining companions, staring at her openmouthed, his disagreement with Mrs. Sheffield instantly forgotten.

"That's Alexandra Niven," said Mr. Sheffield, whose appreciation of the girl's radiance matched Gerry's own, although his expression of it was necessarily more muted. "She's the ward of Lord Bellingford, who was due to come with her but was laid up with gout, so she's here with her companion, Miss Mumford."

"A beautiful young girl with a gouty guardian and a companion named Mumford?" said Gerry with a laugh. "It sounds like something out of Dickens. No doubt this Mumford is a dried-up old crone."

"On the contrary," said Henry Sheffield, who knew the details of the story from Lord Loughlin. "She's not yet thirty and attractive in her own right. But she's had to make her way in the world and worked as

Miss Niven's governess since the girl was eleven or twelve. But when the girl got too old for a governess she couldn't bear to see Miss Mumford go and asked her to stay on as companion."

"And where is she now, this companion?"

"She has an acute sense of her own position and generally remains in the background. She prefers that Miss Niven go out in society unfettered."

"By Jove, this is shaping up to be an interesting visit!" said Gerard, with a sideways glance at Mr. Sheffield. It was the kind of glance that ordinarily wouldn't elude the watchful propriety of Mrs. Sheffield, but she missed it entirely, absorbed as she was in the drama of Alexandra Niven talking with Bruce Barnes.

"Henry," she said, elbowing him in the ribs. "Will you look at how that gardener is talking to that girl?"

Mr. Sheffield knew from long experience that the nuances of how people talked to one another and how people looked at one another, so clear to his wife, were opaque to him. Where he saw only a man and a woman conversing, his wife saw impropriety and even scandal.

"They seem just to be talking, my dear," he said to his wife.

"Talking!" exclaimed that lady. "He's looking at her exactly the way he was looking at the Vernon girl this morning."

On hearing this, Alphonse Gerard turned toward Mrs. Sheffield. "Lady Georgiana Vernon?" he asked. "Here?"

She answered in the affirmative, and told Gerard of their tour of the grounds. "He spoke to Georgiana the same way he's speaking to Miss Niven over there," she said indignantly. "He leans in too close, and he speaks very softly. And then he touches her arm—see! Just like that!"

Gerard did see, but was more inclined to admire the man's technique than to share Mrs. Sheffield's disgust. "And what is wrong with an unmarried man talking softy and touching the arm of an unmarried girl?" he asked. "Are young people to court by shouting at one another from across the room?"

Mrs. Sheffield's already sour expression turned sourer still. "You know perfectly well that there are ways of doing things that are proper, and ways that are not. And making love to two girls in the space of a few hours is most certainly not."

"It's a rum kind of lovemaking if it includes the O'Maras," said Gerry, drawing her attention to the fact that the conversation clearly included them.

Mrs. Sheffield was saved from having to answer by the entrance of Georgiana herself, who had appeared in the doorway and was clearly trying to decide which group to join. She had been there long enough to see what Mrs. Sheffield had seen and Mr. Sheffield hadn't—that Bruce Barnes was indeed, after his fashion, making love to Alexandra Niven. The sight had given rise to a very unpleasant constriction in her gut. She had spent the better part of the afternoon thinking about Barnes, and had by no means decided what she wanted to do about him. But the idea of him with another woman hadn't entered her thoughts. Being confronted with that idea, in the flesh, made her realize the depth of the impression the man had made on her.

But it also gave her pause. When she'd stood with him in the peacock pavilion, she'd felt as though he had singled her out, that he thought the two of them had a special connection. Seeing what looked like an attempt to single out another young woman—and in the same day!— made Georgiana think this was simply how he treated young women, and it made her think less of him.

Her first instinct was to take refuge at the Sheffields' table, but she quelled it and walked resolutely to the other side of the room.

She put on a confident smile and made her voice sprightly. "May I join you?" she asked the foursome.

"Oh, please do," said Alexandra Niven, with a touching ingenuousness. "You are Lady Georgiana Vernon, are you not?"

"I am," said Georgiana, slightly taken aback by the enthusiasm of a girl she had already started to think of as a rival.

"Lady Loughlin told me I should meet you here, and I have so looked forward to it," said the girl. "My name is Alexandra Niven."

Lady Georgiana recovered herself. "Lady Loughlin has also talked to me of you," she said, "and I, too, am glad that we should know each other."

Georgiana nodded her greeting to the O'Maras and, as casually as she could, to Barnes, and sat down next to Miss Niven. No one at the table was aware that their little drama was being minutely observed by the people across the room, who had ceased their own conversation to better hear what the two girls would say to each other, and to Barnes.

They were at first disappointed.

"Do you play tennis, Lady Georgiana?" asked the dark-haired beauty.

"I do, and I imagine you do as well, since Lady Loughlin always takes pains to make sure I have a worthy opponent."

"I do play, but I'm not sure how worthy an opponent I'll be. I have heard, though, that there is a wonderful new court on the grounds." Miss Niven turned to the gardener. "Mr. Barnes has agreed to show it to me, and give me a tour of what he has done, have you not, Mr. Barnes?"

Across the room, Mrs. Sheffield's eyebrows shot up, and she gave her husband a knowing look. Gerry laughed softly. "By Jove, it's as good as a play!"

Barnes looked steadily at Miss Niven, and then at Lady Georgiana. He neither blushed nor blinked. "I have, and if the weather is fine we can go directly after breakfast," he said.

"Make sure you see the peacock pavilion," Lady Georgiana said pointedly. "It's certainly one of the highlights."

From there, the conversation at both tables turned general, and Barnes and the young ladies spoke of the house, the grounds, and the masquerade. Before they went up to bed, the two girls made an appointment to play tennis the following afternoon.

Only Henry Sheffield and Alphonse Gerard were left downstairs when Robert Loughlin, who'd been dining in the adjoining parlor, came in and sat down with them.

"Hello, gentlemen," he said, "I see you've divested yourself of all the ladies."

"That we have," said Gerard, "but I wouldn't be quick to divest myself of either Lady Georgiana or Miss Niven, were I ever so fortunate as to invest myself of them in the first place."

Mr. Sheffield was willing to overlook the omission of his wife from the list of women not to be divested of. "They are fine girls, certainly."

"That gardener of yours seems to have a magical hold on pretty young girls," said Gerry, never one to beat about the bush. "What's his secret?"

Lord Loughlin laughed. He'd noticed the way the women in his household responded to Barnes. "Damned if I know," he told his friend. "It must be some primal attraction to men who work the land. You know, a kind of salt-of-the-earth mystique."

He turned and pulled the cord that rang for the servants. It was barely a minute before the parlor maid, a slightly coarse-looking girl some years past thirty, came in and curtsied.

"Will you ask Dodson to bring us some port, please, Rose," said Loughlin. "There's a 'seventy-seven in the cellar that I opened just the other night."

"Yes, sir," said Rose, and left to find the butler.

"Salt of the earth, fiddlesticks," said Gerry with disgust, picking up the conversation where they had left it. "It's raw animal magnetism. He's big and he's strong and he's handsome, and they can't get enough of it. They're like bitches in heat. I was hoping to have a go at one of those girls myself, but I'll be lucky if either one of them gives me the time of day."

"Well, you may not be big or strong or handsome," said Lord Loughlin, laughing, "nor are you young. But you are awfully rich."

"That won't take me very far with girls who are rich themselves," scoffed Gerard.

"Georgiana is, certainly, but Miss Niven, I'm told, is sorely in want of a fortune."

"But I thought Bellingford was as rich as Croesus. Surely he'll provide for her."

Lord Loughlin lowered his voice. "I'm told he suffered very heavy losses speculating in American railroads."

"He did, at that," said Mr. Sheffield, joining the conversation now that it had left the mysterious subject of women and moved to the firmer footing of finance. "I almost bought some of the same shares myself, but there was something about the offering that didn't seem quite right."

"Has he gone to smash then?" asked Gerry.

"Not entirely, I understand," said Sheffield. "He had a great deal to begin with, and I believe he has enough left to try to make a go of it without selling the estate. But he won't have much to settle on his ward. It's lucky his daughters are grown and married already."

As Gerry pondered this new opportunity, the butler came in with the port. After he left, Gerry looked at his host with a more serious expression.

"Do you think I have a chance, then?" he asked.

Lord Loughlin looked at his friend. Gerard's appearance wasn't prepossessing. His face was a little too round, his hair was a little too sparse, and he was undeniably awkward. But his smile was winning, his good nature was genuine, and he moved with a certain grace. And, of course, he was certainly rich.

"I think you do," he finally said.

"Hmmph," grunted Gerry. "Damn fine port, this."

The three men drank in silence for a few minutes, and then said their good nights.

On his way up to his room, Alphonse Gerard met Rose, the parlor maid, coming down from upstairs, carrying a tray with the remains of a meal. She nodded to him and moved to pass him, her head down.

"Rose, is it?" Gerard said to the girl.

"It is, sir."

The evening's conversation had left him feeling a bit randy, and he thought he might have a go at her. Experience, moreover, had taught him that the most effective method of having a go at a servant was picking one who wasn't especially pretty and telling her she was. But first he had to break down her reserve a bit.

"Whoever ate that dinner, give him a wide berth," he said, in a tone of dire warning, pointing at the tray.

Rose looked uncomprehendingly at him, and at the tray.

"You can't trust anyone who doesn't finish a dish of strawberries and cream," said Gerry, breaking into a broad grin.

The girl laughed. It had crossed her mind that something must be wrong with a person who wouldn't eat such a delicacy. Strawberries and cream were a rare thing in her world.

"It wasn't a him, sir; it was a her. Miss Mumford, sir."

"Well, I see her loss has been your gain," said Gerry, pointing to a small dollop of cream on Rose's left cheek.

Rose colored. "I couldn't bear to see all of them go to waste like that."

"I'm sure, had they made it all the way to the kitchen, that they wouldn't exactly have gone to waste," he said, smiling.

Seeing that he wasn't going to take her to task emboldened the girl. "Well, then, why not me as well as them? After all, I was the one as had to fetch them down from Miss Mumford's room."

"Why not, indeed?" Gerry laughed. "The only flaw I can see in your line of reasoning is that you didn't eat them all." He picked one of the strawberries out of the cream and held it up to her mouth. "You missed this one, for example."

The girl looked at him curiously, and backed away. After a moment,

Gerry put the strawberry in his own mouth, and licked his fingers deliberately.

"By the by, my name's Gerard," he said. "Alphonse Gerard. You're new here, aren't you?"

"Yes, sir, I've been here three months, sir."

"Tell me, Rose, do you have a young man?"

"A young man, sir?" The girl almost snorted with derision. "No, sir."

"What! A fine girl like you with no young man? What's the world coming to?" Subtlety was not in Gerard's nature, and he had learned that, anyhow, it generally didn't answer in situations like this. He took the tray from her, set it on a small side table, and moved in close to the girl.

Rose kept her distance, but didn't absolutely make a run for it. Gerard read curiosity and excitement in her face, but they were tempered by something else. Not fear, he thought. Skepticism, maybe. He took one step closer, reached up, and ran the back of his fingers down her cheek. Her skin still had the softness and suppleness of youth. He used a fingertip to skim the dab of cream off her cheek, and then licked his finger clean.

For the first time, she looked him full in the face. Her eyes were brown tinged with green, and Gerard saw the living, breathing being inside the parlor maid's uniform. And then she said something that surprised him.

"I noticed you in the drawing room."

"You did?" Gerry asked with genuine curiosity.

"I did. I was glad to see that Mrs. Sheffield taken down a peg. She was poking her nose in where it don't belong."

Gerard laughed heartily. "She most certainly was."

"If Mr. Barnes and Lady Georgiana want to hide out in the peacock pavilion, it ain't no business of hers. They're grown people, and can do as they like."

"And were they hiding out in the peacock pavilion?" Gerard asked cautiously. He wanted badly to know what had happened, but he didn't want to be seen sticking his nose in where it didn't belong and categorized with Mrs. Sheffield.

"Well, I can't say as they were hiding out, but they went there together, alone, and stayed for some time. Everyone in the servants' quarters knows about it, thanks to Little Eddie."

"And who, may I ask, is Little Eddie?"

"Oh, he's the groom's son. He does odd jobs around the grounds, and he seems to know everything about everyone. If you want to have a secret around here, you'd better stay out of the way of Little Eddie."

"I'll keep that in mind," said Gerard. "Would Little Eddie be anywhere in the vicinity right now?"

"Oh, no, sir! He works outside, and almost never comes in the house."

"Well, that's good news," said Gerard. "Because I think, perhaps, we're about to have a secret."

The conversation had thawed Rose considerably, and when Gerry reached for her hand she gave it, if a little tentatively.

"Tell me, Rose," Gerard said with a lowered voice, gesturing down the corridor, "do you know if any of these rooms are unoccupied?"

"Yes, sir," she said, lowering her own tone to match his, "that one there on the right is for Lord Peter Halsey, and he won't be coming for three days yet."

"Excellent," said Gerard. "Come with me."

Gerard glanced both ways down the hallway, and led Rose by the hand to the empty room. They went in, and he was about to close the door when something occurred to him. "Wait just one second," he said, and dashed out. He was back before she had time to wonder where he had gone, with the bowl of strawberries in his hand. "We can't let them go to waste now, can we?" he asked conspiratorially.

"No, sir." She grinned at him.

"You'll have to stop calling me 'sir,' you know."

She grinned again. "Yes, sir. I mean, yes, uh . . ."

"Gerry," said Gerry.

"Oh, no, sir, I can't call you that!"

"And why ever not?"

"It's too . . ." She thought a moment. "It's too personal."

"Too personal?" asked Gerry, with mock incredulity. "And is this too personal as well?" he asked as he cupped one of her ample breasts with his hand. He hefted it, as though judging its weight, and began to fondle it in a way that was almost kneading.

The feel of her breast in his hand fueled his increasing arousal, and it took him some moments to realize she seemed somewhat bemused. He took a breath and a half step back.

"You're a damn fine girl, you know," he said. He didn't really believe she was a damn fine girl, but because she seemed to have something to say for herself, he genuinely liked her. If she wasn't a damn fine girl, she was certainly above middling.

But Rose was clear-eyed, and she knew the difference between damn fine and above middling.

"I'm not a damn fine girl. If I was, I'd already be married with a bunch of little ones, and that would probably be a mixed blessing, so I'm not sorry," she said, the words tumbling out of her. "I'm a grown woman, and a red-faced, thickset fireplug of one at that. But I'm an honest one, and I work hard, and I'm not stupid."

Gerard was thoroughly taken aback by this. But Rose wasn't finished yet.

"If I'm going to duck into Lord Halsey's room with you, it won't be because you feed me strawberries and call me a damn fine girl. It'll be because I want to, pure and simple."

At this, Gerard was completely thrown. Although he didn't make an absolute habit of it, he had seduced servant girls before, and never had any of them talked to him like this.

He looked at her with a mixture of astonishment and admiration. "And do you want to, pure and simple?" he finally asked.

She didn't answer. Gerard wasn't sure if she hadn't decided yet, or if she had but wasn't ready to let him in on the secret.

"I hope you do," he said in a whisper, and kissed her.

He didn't kiss her the way he kissed servants. He kissed her the way he kissed lovers, with his lips soft and barely parted. But he didn't linger; he didn't feel he had permission quite yet.

"I do," said Rose, "on one condition."

"And what's that?"

"That you never call me a damn fine girl again."

"Only if you promise not to call me 'sir,' at least in private," he said, grinning.

"Done," she said. "Gerry." She giggled a little at the idea of calling one of the Loughlins' guests by his given name.

They were standing just inside the closed door of the room, in a little hall that led to the bedchamber. Gerry put his hands on Rose's hips and pushed her backward against the wall. He reached his hands around to cup her ass and pull it toward him. By this time he had a full hard-on and he groaned as her hips met his.

The circumstances were such that Gerry had to be careful not to let his arousal get the best of him. That this girl had been unknown to him that morning, that he had gone from introducing himself to grinding his pelvis into hers in the space of ten minutes, that her surprising self-assurance attracted him, all created a confluence of novelty that made him feel as if he were nineteen again. And at nineteen, he remembered with some embarrassment that helped check his passion, he hadn't been completely master of himself.

He put his hands back on her hips and pushed himself away. He turned her around so she faced the wall and traced the lines of her back. It was a strong, muscular back, and her firmness and solidity appealed to him. Somehow it seemed right that her strength of body matched her strength of mind.

As he pressed himself against her again, he reached around and took one breast in each of his hands. He started with his hands at their base and caressed them, circling first inward, and then outward, with the thumb and forefinger of each hand coming closer to her nipple each time. When he reached the nipples, and touched them lightly, Rose responded by groaning and moving her hips backward to meet him. Her hands were on the wall and she bent at the waist, moving her ass side to side against him. He let her breasts go and reached for the buttons on the back of her uniform. He hadn't undone more than half of them before the girl turned around and shimmied out of the bodice of the dress.

Her bodily firmness extended to her lovely round breasts. "No fireplug ever sported a pair like that," he said.

Rose looked taken aback, and Gerry was afraid he'd blundered. But it took her only a moment to remember that she had described herself that way not more than a few minutes ago. To his relief, she laughed heartily.

Gerry leaned down and kissed each in turn, just on the top where they rose enticingly from her chest.

He had put the strawberries and cream on a small bookshelf that was next to them, and he reached over to dip his finger in the bowl. He held his cream-covered finger out to Rose, and she took it in her mouth. He watched as she closed her eyes, and relished the feeling of her tongue on his skin as she licked it clean.

She in turn fed him some of the cream, and he kept her forefinger in his mouth and sucked it. She felt his tongue on her skin, warm and wet, and the warmth and the wetness spread through her. She arched toward him; she ached for him. She felt the hollowness at her center that she knew she needed him to fill.

He took the hand that still had a finger in his mouth, and guided it to the bowl. He held her forefinger in his hand and used it like a spoon to get a dollop of the cream. Then he led that hand to her breast and ran her own finger around her nipple, spreading the cream at its base. He licked the remaining cream from her finger, slowly. He started at the base and flicked his tongue over the webbing between her forefinger and middle finger. In her entire life, she'd never been touched there by another human being, and she was surprised at the sensitivity, the eroticism of it.

Gerry ran the very tip of his tongue up the underside of her finger, and then took the tip in his mouth. Rose was consumed by the sensuality of the tiny point of contact between her hand and his mouth. It was as though her finger was the proxy for her body, and he was licking all of her.

And then he leaned over and took the nipple, cream and all, into his mouth, and Rose felt enveloped. And she felt the need to envelop in return. She pushed him back until he was against the opposite wall of the narrow hallway. She deftly unbuttoned his waistcoat and shirt and ran her hands up and down his chest.

He wasn't a beauty; that she had to admit to herself. He was growing a bit stout, and the rough hair on his chest was already graying. But his eyes were kind and his smile was quick, and it was, perhaps, because he didn't have such a fine figure that she could feel an attraction to him that was honest, free of worry about her own looks or the social chasm between them.

Whatever the reason, she couldn't deny the attraction. She took a deep breath to cool herself down, and then she took another fingerful of cream. She ran her finger down the center of his chest, slowly, and then let her tongue follow her finger. She lapped up the cream with little darting motions, starting at the top and working her way down, down. When she reached the waist of his pants, she fell to her knees and worked the buttons deftly.

His cock was as hard as a billy club, and he didn't think it could get any harder. But when Rose ran her fingers lightly up its sides and made that darting motion with her tongue on the underside of its shaft, it got harder still. She reached again for the cream and put one small dab on the very tip of his penis. Then she encircled the tip with her wet, soft lips and sucked gently.

This drove him mad. He had an almost uncontrollable urge to take her by the shoulders and shove the full length of his cock in her mouth, but it was as though she knew this, and she was testing to find out whether he was a lover or merely a brute.

Brute he would not be. He did take her by the shoulders, to ease her away.

"I can't take much of that," he told her as he raised her off her knees.

Rose knew she could have finished him off in a moment, and she liked him for stopping her—it made her want him all the more. She had, in her years, experienced sex without any liking at all, and she thought it rather a luxury to have them both together.

He backed her from the hall into the bedchamber, and onto the edge of the bed, her feet still on the floor. With adeptness born of practice, he flipped her skirts up and pulled her drawers off. He stood between her knees, cock almost vertical. He put one hand on each of her thighs and leaned over so that much of his weight was on them, and then he moved them up toward her hips. The pressure of his weight, and the roughness of his hands on her skin, sent a tingling excitement toward her center, and she again felt the insistent ache of longing. Her pussy, she could feel, was hot and soaked and ready.

Neither of them wanted to wait another instant. Gerry moved his hands around under her and pulled her toward him, to the very edge of the bed. She felt his entrance into her as a completion, a satisfaction that made her perfect pleasure possible.

His thrusts started gentle and long, each time withdrawing the entire length of his cock and then slowly and deliberately pressing back into her. She felt the bulge of its tip against her clitoris each time he brought it out or put it in, and her body responded with a rhythm of its own.

She knew his urgency was heightening as his strokes grew shorter and more insistent. She wrapped her legs around him to keep him tight to her, and his thrusting became a rocking of his hips that ground against her.

Until that point, they had been almost silent—the possibility of discovery had been at the back of both their minds. But now the silence was broken by his long, low moan and her answering gasp. The orgasm she felt was acute, intense, almost sharp. It wasn't just a fulfillment; it was a release of desires that had been pent up for far too long. For several seconds she was aware of nothing but her body, consumed completely by her pleasure.

When she came back to the present and opened her eyes, she saw Gerry, eyes still closed, in the last throes of his own climax. When his eyes opened, they met hers and the two smiled at each other. She unhooked her legs and released him, and he withdrew and began reassembling his clothing.

She did the same, and they faced each other a trifle awkwardly.

"It's been a surprising evening, Rose," he said.

"That it has, that it has."

They walked toward the door, and Gerry picked up the bowl of strawberries and ate one of the last two remaining. The last he fed to Rose.

"I'd say they didn't go to waste," he said as she ate it.

"I'll thank Miss Mumford in the morning," Rose said with a half smile.

FIVE

The next morning held the promise of a fine, fair day, at least as far as Georgiana could tell from looking out the window of her room. She had lingered long in bed and asked Hortense to bring breakfast to her there; she wanted to avoid the appearance of interest in Barnes's promised tour of the grounds for Miss Niven.

When she finally came downstairs it was nearing noon, and the very first person she saw was Barnes, coming in the main door as she was going out of it.

"Good morning, Lady Georgiana," he said. "It's a fine day for a walk."

"It certainly seems to be," she said with some hauteur. "I see you've already been out."

"I have," the man said with something like amusement. "I had promised Miss Niven a tour, and I was as good as my word."

"And was she quite in raptures over your work?" asked Georgiana archly.

"Perhaps not raptures, but she certainly was admiring." After a beat, he added, "Of course, I didn't take her to the peacock pavilion."

"Why ever not?"

"We took the long way 'round, and she seemed a little piqued. I told her the pavilion was a bit far, and perhaps she should go in for a cup of tea."

"I see," said Georgiana.

"Do you?" Barnes leaned almost imperceptibly closer. "Do you really?"

Georgiana looked at him. She couldn't quite make this man out. Whenever she saw him, she felt the certainty of the connection between them. But there was something about his manner, and the way he behaved with Miss Niven, that warned her to keep her distance.

"I'm off for my walk." She turned away from him. "Good day to you, Mr. Barnes," she called over her shoulder.

"Lady Georgiana," he said in a voice low enough to make her turn around. "What time is your tennis match?"

She scowled. "Three o'clock." And off she went.

As she walked down the front steps to the drive, a carriage pulled up. The driver climbed down from the box to open the door, but his passenger beat him to the punch. The door opened from the inside, and a rangy young man with a floppy blond forelock and a wide grin stepped out. Georgiana was the only person there to greet him, but she was too surprised to muster words of welcome.

The young man had no such trouble. "What ho, Lady G!" he said.

"Freddy!" she said. "What are you doing here? Your mother said you'd gone up to school."

"You know my mother never lies. I had indeed gone up to school. But I've been sent down again."

Georgiana gasped. Sent down from Oxford! And within weeks of having gone up.

"Whatever did you do?" she asked.

"Oh, it was just a prank gone wrong," said Freddy breezily. "I suspect a few letters from the right places will have me back up again."

Georgiana didn't know much of Oxford, but she did know that, once a student was sent down, it was almost unheard-of for him to be taken back into the fold. And she knew Freddy must know it too. She marveled at his insouciance. Here he was, grinning ear to ear about being sent down, knowing full well that his father would be furious.

But she had to know. "What was the prank?" she asked, lowering her voice to a confidential tone. "And how did it go wrong?"

"Well," said Freddy, equally confidentially, "it was all Stiffy's fault."

"Stiffy?"

"John Stiffson. He's in my college. His father made an absolute fortune in some kind of shipping—I'm rather hazy on the details—and he's simply loaded. But he can't stand that his money isn't aeons old, so he puts on the most horrible airs. You wouldn't believe it, Lady G. The man's as pompous an ass as ever brayed."

"Do asses bray?" Georgiana asked. "I thought only donkeys bray."

"You have led a sheltered life, dear Lady G, and you have not been subjected to many asses. I assure you that asses in general, and Stiffy in particular, are masters of the art of braying." said Freddy, and went on.

"So Stiffy's old man used some of his wads to bring one of those new motorcars over from Germany, and Stiffy brought it up. I'm sure you've seen pictures—it's the Benz Patent Motorwagen—and it seems to be all the rage on the continent. And so Stiffy, who had been just barely tolerable—his free-flowing liquor counterbalanced his beastly manners—crossed the line to unbearable, what with his acting the swell because he has a motorcar and you don't."

"And naturally, you couldn't just leave him be . . ." said Lady Georgiana, wryly.

"And live with myself?" asked Freddy incredulously. "Certainly not."

"So?" Georgiana knew she ought to be more severe, but she couldn't help being drawn into sympathy with Freddy.

"Well, for Stiffy, the internal combustion engine was food and drink. Better than food and drink! It was better than booze, better even than women! Well, if it was that good, he ought to be going to bed with it, oughtn't he?"

Georgiana looked at the ground and put her hand over her mouth to hide her smile.

"So I rounded up a bunch of rather large chaps, and we broke into the barn where he kept the precious thing. It was a matter of minutes to unbolt the engine from the frame. We popped it in a wheelbarrow and rolled it around to his rooms. Good thing he was on the ground floor!"

"Good thing, indeed!" Georgiana didn't bother to hide her smile now. The prank seemed harmless enough.

"So we heaved the thing into his rooms and put it in his bed. We even drew the covers up and added a frilly nightcap."

Georgiana waited for the "went wrong" part of the story.

"And the sad part is, Stiffy never even saw it. The stupid thing had some oil or some petrol or something in it, and it leaked into the bed-clothes and onto the floor. When the porter came in to make up the fire, a spark caught it and it went up like a bonfire."

"Oh, dear," said Georgiana. It had indeed gone wrong. "What happened?"

"Well, the fire was put out right quick, and didn't do much damage. But the porter was terribly burned." Freddy either felt very bad about this, or had the good sense to look as though he did.

"Oh, dear," Georgiana said again.

"As soon as I heard," Freddy continued in a sober tone, "I told them I'd done it, and I was sent down before you could say, 'Jack Robinson.'"

"You told your parents?"

"There was no point in writing when I'd be here before the letter arrived. No, Lady G"—he grinned again—"you have the honor of being the first to know."

"Not much of an honor, I'd say." Georgiana, thinking of what a blow this would be to the Loughlins, was having less trouble being severe. "And your parents won't think so, either."

"Oh, Mama will take it all right, but the pater will have kittens." Freddy rolled his eyes.

Georgiana thought Freddy's assessment accurate. Paulette thought of Oxford as just another hoop you jumped through to be welcomed in the highest social circles. Her husband, though, thought it a badge of all that was right and proper, a validation of worth. He would indeed have kittens.

Freddy was looking at his shoes and shuffling a bit, but he evidently decided he had been abashed for long enough, and he looked up and brightened.

"Where are you off to?" he asked.

"Just for a walk."

"Topping! It's a grand day. Shall I come with you?"

"You shall not," she said firmly. "You shall walk directly into that house and tell your parents what has happened."

"I can do that anytime. But right now the sun's out and you look ripping, if I may say so, and who knows when we'll have another moment like this. Carpe diem and all that, you know."

His manner would have been ridiculous in an older man, but Freddy was only eighteen, and his blatant disregard of what was clearly his duty came off as youthful ebullience and high spirits. It was difficult to speak to him sternly, but Georgiana made the effort.

"You will indeed carpe diem," she said, "and you will do it by marching into that house, finding your parents, and telling them what has happened."

Freddy cocked his head and looked at her fixedly, with an expression resembling seriousness. "You must still think of me as a little boy, to talk to me in that way," he said. "I left the nursery years ago, you know."

Georgiana was a bit abashed. In her head, she replayed what she had said to him, and the tone in which she had said it, and found that it sounded terribly matronly and stiff. She *did* still think of him as a little boy. She had known him as one and, as he had grown up, her image of him hadn't adjusted commensurately. She knew herself to be in the right to tell him to see his parents, but she realized she should have moderated her tone. Freddy was a grown man.

"You are entirely right, Mr. Loughlin," Georgiana said, and curtsied. "I apologize unreservedly."

Freddy's high spirits were back in an instant. "Oh, I think you can still call me Freddy." He gestured down the walk. "And you can still take that walk with me."

"Thank you for that offer," said Georgiana, with exaggerated politeness, "but I'm afraid I must decline. And I will add that it is my considered opinion that you should go and greet your parents."

Freddy guffawed. "I'm dashed if I know whether that's better or worse! But I suppose I should get it over with." He bowed as formally as she had curtsied, and went inside. Georgiana headed down the walk alone.

Once Freddy had made up his mind to break the news to his parents, he wasted no time. He found them in one of the drawing rooms, his mother finishing her tea and his father smoking a cigar. They looked up as he entered the room, and it took a moment for them to understand that his presence at Penfield boded ill.

"Freddy!" his mother said. "Whatever brings you here?"

The young man went straight to the point. "Mama, I've been sent down."

"Sent down!" his father positively roared. *"Sent down?"*

"Yes, Father. Sent down." Freddy tried to look neutral. He knew he must take this seriously, but he didn't think what he had done was so very bad, and refused to look ashamed. A stoic dignity was what he aimed for.

He told his parents what had happened, and they reacted essentially as he had predicted to Georgiana. His father absolutely raged. His mother was irritated, but neither furious nor surprised.

She had never breathed a word of her preference, but she had always felt closer to Freddy than to his elder brother, Robert. Robbie was like his father, but Freddy had inherited her own spirited cheerfulness. That, coupled with a rambunctiousness she always attributed to his gender, got him into all kinds of scrapes. When he had gone up to Oxford, she would have been willing to wager that he would be sent down again—although not quite this soon.

And now, when her blue-eyed son stood before her, making an obvious effort at stoic dignity, she could not find it in herself to be angry. Scrapes were Freddy's lot in life, and if this was the worst one he ever found himself in, he led a charmed life indeed.

Her husband had enough anger for both of them. After spluttering almost incoherent expostulations of his son's thoughtlessness and stupidity, he realized he needed to calm down before he discussed this any further.

"We'll talk about this later," he growled to his son. "Right now, I need you to get out of my sight."

Freddy was happy to oblige. He ran up to his room, changed his traveling suit for riding clothes, and headed for the stables—via the kitchen garden, where he pulled up two fat carrots. He was in no mood to explain his presence to any of the servants, and he went through the back door to the stall where his favorite of the Penfield horses was contentedly eating oats.

"Prancer, old girl," he said to the horse, and she came over, nuzzling him to find the food she knew he inevitably brought. He gave her the carrots and stroked her nose. "I'm glad to see you," he said softly, and he meant it. Freddy's heart was soft and permeable, and a lively horse or a loyal dog could find its way in with very little trouble.

He saddled Prancer and rode off to the north, to the far end of the Penfield lands. There was a small dairy farm that abutted the estate, and the farmer was a German named Glück with a remarkable knack for cows. He owned only twenty acres, though, and such limited grazing could support only a small herd. Fifteen years before, he had approached the Loughlins and asked about leasing grazing rights for a thirty-acre portion that bordered his land.

The Loughlins liked Glück, who was enterprising and hardworking, and they were glad to grant him the lease. When Glück asked the price, they told him that he could have it for a thrice-weekly delivery of milk and butter to Penfield.

Glück protested that he couldn't do business on such terms, that he felt as though he were stealing the valuable grazing rights for such paltry payment, but the Loughlins wouldn't have it any other way, and the deal was sealed with a handshake. Twice since, the parcel Glück used had been expanded, and Penfield had been plentifully supplied not just with milk and butter, but with cream and Hirtenkäse, the dense, creamy cheese Frau Glück grew up making in her native country.

The leasing arrangement paved the way for friendly relations between the two families, and Freddy, as he grew up, often took a cart to the Glücks' dairy to fetch what the farmer would otherwise have to deliver. In that way, he got to know the Glücks' daughter, Gretchen.

Gretchen, Freddy thought, must have been the model for the milkmaid archetype. Fair skinned, peach cheeked, buxom, and firm, with a perpetual smell of new milk, Gretchen had been irresistible to Freddy from the day he knew what it was to want a girl.

The two were almost exactly the same age, and they couldn't have been more than thirteen when they first began, haltingly and clumsily, to explore each other's bodies in the fragrant hay of the cowshed. It wasn't long before they were less halting and less clumsy, and Freddy owed his not inconsiderable experience to the fortuitous combination, embodied in Gretchen, of fondness for him and sexual curiosity.

Freddy had found women a bit hard to come by at Oxford, and as he rode to the Glücks' his desire mounted. Unless their patterns had changed, he knew he'd find Gretchen in the barn at this hour, cleaning up from the morning milking. Thinking it might be inconvenient to be spotted by the farmer or his wife, he skirted the house and went straight out to the barn. He tethered his horse and went in.

And there she was, washing out the buckets they used for milking, her sleeves rolled up past her elbows, her heavy blond hair escaping its braid in curling damp tendrils. She was glistening from the exertion and her apron and clothes were stained with dirt, but that in no way diminished the appeal she had for Freddy.

She hadn't heard him approach, and he watched her for a few moments before he said, "Gretchen, my girl, you look good enough to eat."

Startled, she turned around and said, "Freddy! I thought you'd gone off to school."

"And so I had, but I missed you dreadfully and so I've come back again."

She laughed as he put his arms around her waist and leaned over so he could bury his face in her neck. "You are a liar," she said, "but you are a charming liar."

"I never lie about anything of substance," Freddy said, "and so when I tell you that you taste marvelous, you can believe it as though it were one of the gospels." He kissed her neck and ran his tongue up to her earlobe. He added, whispering in her ear, "And I did miss you, you know."

Freddy slipped the string off the end of her braid and worked his hands through her hair to release it. He loved the feeling of her cool, fine hair running through his fingers, and pulled her to him as he ran his hands from her hairline to the back of her head, and then out to either side, over and over.

Gretchen buried her face in his chest—she was a full foot shorter than he was—and closed her eyes to better focus on the feel of his fingertips on her scalp. He pressed harder, and then harder still, and she groaned softly.

The responsiveness of her body had always been a wonder to Gretchen. When Freddy touched her breasts, or her pubis, or her inner thighs, the cascading warmth of her response made sense to her. But she realized years ago that he could touch her anywhere—the backs of her knees, the soles of her feet, the top of her head—and she would have that same response. A man's touch made her feel as though she were made of nerves extending from a center somewhere between her hip bones, and radiating out to every square inch of her surface.

Freddy took the full heft of her hair in his left hand and pulled it, forcing Gretchen to look up. She did, and he kissed her fully and deeply. His tongue, flirting with her own, made her feel as though she were glowing, lit from within.

She ran her hands up the insides of his thighs until she found his balls. She took them in her two hands and manipulated them, one against the other, in opposing circles. Now it was Freddy's turn to groan. She moved her hands up to his cock, which, while not long, was as thick as a sapling and hard as a cable pulled taut. She reached one hand down his trousers and held him, at first loosely and then tighter and tighter. As she squeezed, she started working up and down, up and down, and felt as the cable pulled tighter still.

Freddy was clearly nearing his limit. He put his palms on her shoulders and bodily separated himself from her. He took a deep breath and, leaving one hand on her shoulder, used the other to trace the outline of her breasts with his index finger, cupping each in turn as his finger went around the bottom.

After he'd made several circuits, he found the little hollow in her chest where her ribs met, and ran his hand straight down over her firm, slightly rounded belly, to the mound between her legs.

Neither of them could tolerate the layers of clothing between them, and Gretchen held up her skirts obligingly while Freddy took off first her boots, and then her drawers. He took the entire mound of her pubis in his hand and worked his middle finger inside her. She felt the pressure of the heel of his palm against her clitoris as he circled the finger inside, and she let out a sound that was part gasp, part moan.

Freddy released the pressure and stopped the movement, and he felt Gretchen's muscles contract as though willing him to start again. Her eyes opened in time to see him smile, and he waited just a beat before he renewed his efforts. The next time he stopped, he knew she was too close for him to start again, and he removed his hand. He put his finger, wet from her juices, into his mouth and licked it clean.

There was a narrow, steep wooden stairway that led to the hayloft, consisting of two long pieces of wood with boards nailed across them, and Freddy backed her against it. They knew from long practice that, if she stood on the first step, she was at just the right height for him. He lifted her up, pulled up her skirts, and pushed them behind her, between two steps of the ladder, to keep them out of the way.

Freddy took two steps back. As he admired the sight of Gretchen, naked from the waist down, standing on the step and leaning back against the stairs, he unbuttoned his trousers and took his cock in his hand.

"I think that belongs to me," Gretchen said, motioning him over to her. He came over to the ladder, and she took his penis in her hand once more. This time, though, she guided it inside her.

Gretchen loved the feeling of Freddy's fully erect cock inside her. It was so broad that it seemed to plug her as snugly as a cork, and her insides felt almost pressurized. As he started slowly pulsing in and out, she lifted her right leg and wrapped it around his waist so she could work him in deeper. He held her leg up with his left hand and leaned fully against her, pulsing faster. With his other hand, he reached around behind her and gathered her hair up through a gap in the stairs. He gently pulled, forcing her head up and exposing her neck.

Gretchen was pinned to the stairs, and the vulnerability heightened the excitement for her. She gave herself over utterly to the sensation, letting the crescendo happen.

And it did. She hadn't seen Freddy in weeks, and her body was more than ready to receive him. Every nerve, every muscle was doing its part to bring her to climax. And then she was there. The epicenter was the warm wetness between her legs, with Freddy's cock driving in and pulling out, but there were tremors in every extremity.

Freddy was there a second behind her, and they reveled in their joint orgasm, almost as though they could feel each other's pleasure. As it subsided, she leaned back against the stairs and he leaned forward against her, both attuned to the lingering softness of their intermingling.

They were spent, and they disentangled and put themselves back together. When they were presentable, Gretchen said, "Well, now that we've gotten that out of the way, tell me what happened."

"Let's go for a walk, and I'll tell you the whole story." They spent the next two hours wandering the fields, each telling the other everything that had happened since they had last met. Freddy basked equally in the warm sun and the warm affection, and told himself that he couldn't regret Oxford when home held such pleasures.

SIX

It was midafternoon by the time Freddy finally returned to Penfield. As he rode up, he saw a crowd headed for the tennis lawn. He had no idea so many people were staying with his parents, and he wondered what was bringing them all out. Then he saw the two young ladies—one of them Lady Georgiana, the other unknown to him—dressed for the game, and it all became clear.

He was about to join his parents' guests, but thought better of it when he reasoned that his parents themselves would probably arrive any moment. He wasn't yet ready to face his father again, but he wanted to watch the game. He took refuge in the boughs of a beautiful copper beech tree that he'd climbed at least a thousand times. At eighteen, he was still almost as nimble as he'd been at eleven, and he had settled himself on a comfortable limb with an excellent view before anyone had noticed his presence.

The two women approached the lawn, walking companionably together. Miss Niven was wearing a tennis frock with a white bodice and a full light blue skirt. Lady Georgiana maintained that attempting to run around a lawn chasing a ball was a silly enough pastime, but to do it in a dress was ridiculous. She wore white trousers and a white blouse that buttoned down the front.

The contrast between the two women didn't stop there. Georgiana was lithe to Miss Niven's robust, fair to her dark, slim to her voluptuous. Most observers would have pronounced Miss Niven the more beautiful of the two, but Lady Georgiana's sylphlike figure and knowing smile would always win over a small, unconventional minority.

Bruce Barnes was in that minority. He'd been at the tennis lawn an hour and more, overseeing the efforts that ensured it was in perfect condition for the contest. As he watched the two girls come over the rise, accompanied by several other guests interested in watching the match, he thought that any man who preferred Miss Niven must not understand the essence of female beauty. The sight of the small, athletic, agile girl in the white trousers compelled him in a way he had seldom experienced.

Freddy, from his beech, was also drawn to Georgiana. He'd known her for years, but had never before seen her through any but a boy's eyes. *She's smashing,* he said to himself. And then, as an afterthought, *But that other one isn't half-bad either.* He settled in to enjoy the match.

The lawn itself was probably one of the finest in England. It was perfectly flat, with close-cropped grass growing uniformly on firm soil. It was built in a natural hollow surrounded on three sides by hills, to minimize the wind, and the slopes had been carved into risers for spectators. The fourth side faced the path to the house, and was guarded by two topiary lions whose fierceness was undermined by their stubby little tails. Mature hedges had been carted in, at great expense, to form the bodies and heads of the lions, but there were still visible wires where Barnes was training the plants to grow to form full, brushy tails.

Barnes had seen to it that the lines were freshly chalked, and the net was new and taut.

As the girls put down their gear on the benches placed behind each of the lions for the purpose, Miss Niven surveyed the court. "Oh, Mr. Barnes," she said, "it is indeed a wonderful lawn. I have been looking forward to playing on it ever since Paulette told me you were building it."

"I hope it lives up to your expectations," said Barnes, with a small bow. "And yours as well," he added, nodding to Lady Georgiana.

"Oh, for my part, I have no expectations whatsoever," said Georgiana with studied breeziness. "I always enjoy a pleasant afternoon's tennis."

This was nonsense. Lady Georgiana, like her opponent, had heard about the tennis lawn from Lady Loughlin, and she was eager to try it out. Furthermore, she took her tennis quite seriously, and was determined to trounce the lovely young woman who was just then taking her place across the net.

As they started to limber up by lobbing a ball back and forth, more of the Loughlins' guests appeared on the path from the house. Word of the match had gotten out, and the consensus was that it was not to be missed. The Loughlins themselves were the last to arrive, and their guests shifted around to make room for them courtside.

"You two girls have completely emptied the house," Lady Loughlin said to the contestants. "I'd have thought only a fire could do that."

"I think fire is precisely what we're hoping for," said Gerard under his breath.

The game began, and it became clear that the women, whose styles were quite different, were nevertheless evenly matched. Lady Georgiana's quickness and strategy had her placing balls all over the court, but Miss Niven's raw athleticism and long reach enabled her to return almost every one.

The game commenced with genuine nonchalance on Miss Niven's part, and the appearance of it on Lady Georgiana's, but each young lady thought she would win. Miss Niven simply expected to, and Lady Georgiana was determined to. Each was surprised by the skill of the other.

After the first two games—one went to each—there was no more nonchalance. The women were focused, getting the most from their respective games. Georgiana was certainly running her opponent around the court, but Miss Niven was handling all she was dealt, and it was her unexpected returns that scored points. The rallies were long, the action was fierce, and the spectators were delighted.

After the first two sets, which they split, the two took a moment to catch their breath and get a drink of water. They were both in high color, and sweat soaked their underarms and backs. The stains were particularly apparent on Miss Niven's dress, with its relatively snug bodice. Georgiana's blouse was loose, and the circulating air had kept her cooler. Miss Niven looked enviously at her opponent's clothing, and wished that she herself had the nerve to wear pants and a shirt.

She wasn't the only person on the court with that wish. Some of the men there had never even seen their wives in so formfitting an outfit, and Lady Georgiana's trim waist and gently rounded backside distracted many of them from the action of the game. When she ran and stretched and reached, she revealed a female form in all its details. It was a revelation that captivated the men, but some of the women present didn't approve.

Mr. Sheffield knew his wife would think Georgiana's dress scandalous, and he steeled himself for her comment. It came, but it wasn't nearly as damning as he had expected.

"She's not wearing much of anything, is she?" Mrs. Sheffield said. Even that lady was fascinated by the match.

Going into the third set, the two players began to flag. They had been running back and forth for over an hour, and neither was accustomed to that level of exertion. Lady Georgiana, though, was used to outdoor activity, and took exercise every day that weather permitted. Those habits now stood her in good stead. Each player made more mistakes than she had at the beginning of the match, but the drop-off in Miss Niven's skills was the steeper.

Georgiana realized her advantage and pressed it. She concentrated on trying to minimize her own exertion and maximizing that of her opponent, and her strategy was successful. Miss Niven won two of the first five games, but Georgiana swept the last three to win the set and the match.

As the girls walked off the court, Lady Loughlin approached with two glasses of cold lemonade.

"Well played, my dears, well played," she said as she handed a glass to each.

Some of the guests started back toward the house, but several remained to congratulate the two players. Miss Niven, however, didn't want to linger.

"I must get back to the house to change," she said, gesturing ruefully at her grass- and sweat-stained dress.

"You should be proud of it," said Bruce Barnes. "It's the evidence of skillful play and honest exercise."

She didn't look convinced.

"Well, I'd certainly be proud to walk you back to the house," he said, and offered her his arm.

She laughed and took it. "If *you* don't mind my sorry state, I don't see how *I* should," she said.

Lady Georgiana thought this a prime bit of sycophancy on Barnes's part, and looked down at the ground so no one would see her roll her eyes. Exhausted from the match, watching him with Miss Niven, she thought the strength of her attraction to him was on the ebb, and she was glad.

The entire party made their way back to the house, and Georgiana went to her room to wash and change.

Not two minutes after she'd closed the door behind her, she heard a knock.

She opened the door, and there was Barnes.

"Are you here to tell me about my skillful play and honest exercise?" she asked with a sneer.

"No, I'm not," he said calmly. "I'm here to tell you that if you took a little bit of topspin off your forehand you'd send fewer of them into the net."

She looked at him blankly for a moment. She knew that she put too much topspin on her forehand, and had been trying to correct the problem. But that was about the last thing she expected him to say to her.

"You're the better player," he went on.

"Maybe," she said. "Although if Alexandra worked at it, she'd be better than I am. She has a remarkable natural ability."

"I'm not sure about that." Barnes had one hand on either side of the doorway, and he leaned into the room. "You're faster, and you're smarter."

"Maybe," she said again.

He didn't answer. He just looked at her. And his gaze held her almost against her will. It was only a half hour ago that she'd thought herself well on her way to being through with him, and now here he was, flooding her all over again.

She looked back at him, but she wasn't seeing him. She was feeling him. His presence had a palpability for her. She felt as though he were touching her even though he was on one side of the threshold and she was on the other. It didn't matter. He was somehow projecting his essence into the room, and she felt an incipient tightness in her chest.

Georgiana's body was sending her many different messages, and the confusion froze her. She felt his attraction, even more powerful than before, but she couldn't say for certain whether she liked this man. Her body practically ached for him, but her consciousness held her back.

She was on the verge of simply excusing herself on whatever flimsy pretext came to mind—a letter to write, a previous engagement—when Barnes, apparently sensing her conflict, somehow managed to scale back the intensity of his presence. Although he kept his hands on the doorframe, he straightened so he was no longer leaning into the room. He softened his expression and smiled. And he started talking about tennis again.

"You *are* faster," he said, picking up the thread of their conversation, "and you *are* smarter. She plays by instinct, but with you, it's skill."

Georgiana was by no means immune to this kind of compliment, and hearing it settled her a little. It also gave her time to gather her wits and try to decide how she wanted to navigate the situation.

"I sense I'm being flattered," she said, with an attempt at flippant lightness.

"I never flatter a woman," Barnes said, looking more serious.

"Nonsense," said Georgiana, "sometimes I think that's all you do."

"So you think that when I pay you a compliment it's because I'm a flatterer and not because you're extraordinary?"

Extraordinary. Although she didn't have the hubris to apply the word to herself, even in thought, she did think herself, with some justification, a cut above other girls. By using the word, Barnes insinuated himself into the club of people with the discrimination to see her value. It was as though he had admired an obscure poet she loved, or praised an opaque work of philosophy in which she herself had found wisdom. With one word, he had widened her attraction to him so it was no longer limited to his physical being. She felt it almost like a puzzle piece snapping into place, a connection made.

Barnes stepped over the threshold, but didn't come any farther into the room. "I've never met a girl like you," he said, his tone low and husky, personal.

A snide remark about Alexandra Niven rose to Georgiana's lips, but she swallowed it. She need not fear Miss Niven as a rival. That woman's attractions were confined to a pretty face and figure, and fine, studied manners. A man like Barnes could wade in Miss Niven, but he could dive into Georgiana, and Georgiana knew it.

He reached out a hand and put it on her hip. He didn't pull her to him, and she again had the sense that he was waiting for her to come to him. And she did. She stepped toward him and put her arms around his neck.

He backed her into the room, closed the door behind them, and they stood just inside. He could feel the points of her hip bones in the palms of his hands. He stroked her taut belly with his thumbs, just above the waistband of her pants, and found her navel through the fabric of her shirt. He pressed gently, and she felt as though he had tapped a nerve that ran from the back of her neck straight to the lips of her vulva. He encircled her waist with his hands, and when they didn't quite meet, he squeezed her to fit. She gasped at the constriction.

And then he picked her up from the waist, as though she were a child. He raised her so high that her hair brushed the ceiling. The suddenness of the movement made her a little dizzy, and before she had regained her bearings he was lowering her, slowly. When her feet were still almost a foot off the floor, he widened his grip and she slipped down through his hands. She felt their pressure moving up the sides of her rib cage and then coming to rest on the outsides of her breasts as her feet touched the floor.

She felt his hands move to her back and finally, finally pull her to him. He tilted her head up with the touch of a finger under her chin, and leaned down to kiss her. She felt an overwhelming sensation of warmth. His body, his lips, his hands, all possessed a penetrating heat, as though he were made of pure animal energy. His tongue just barely met hers, and then retreated. He tasted of sweat, and she remembered his smell—earthen and green.

She remembered also the reddish hair showing where his shirt had been unbuttoned—was it only yesterday?—when they had stood together in the peacock pavilion. She reached up and unbuttoned one button, and there it was. She pressed her cheek against it, and felt his heartbeat, strong and insistent.

When she looked up at him, he surprised her by saying, "Come to the window. I want to see you in the light."

Together they stood in the early evening sun that shone through the leaded panes of the bay window, and he undressed her. There was no haste, and no sense of abandon. He deliberately unbuttoned her blouse and pulled the muslin camisole she wore underneath over her head. Her pants fastened on the side, and he undid them and slid them down over her slender hips. She hadn't had underthings appropriate to the pants, and so there was nothing else to take off.

She stood before him naked, and it felt right. He looked at her fully and frankly, and traced the lines on her body where the windowpane frames cast their shadow. She felt a combination of urgent arousal and absolute calm. She had, somehow, consigned herself to him, and was content to see what he would make of her.

"You're lovely," he said, but then checked himself. "No," he corrected, "you're flawless."

He put his hands on her shoulders and pressed her gently down to the window seat, and then he took off his own clothes with a heedlessness that contrasted with the care he had taken with hers. He stood before her with neither modesty nor pride. This was who he was, and this was what he had to offer.

The only penis she had ever seen was Jeremy's, but she somehow wasn't surprised that Barnes's was different. It was larger, but he was the larger man. She reached out and took it in her two hands, feeling the veins running up its sides. This cock was somehow definitive, purposeful. She stroked its underside with one hand and, with the other, reached for his balls, which were taut and tight to his body.

The hair at the base of his penis was redder than the hair on his chest, and covered the point of the V shape his sharply defined stomach muscles made as they tapered down at his hips. She traced those lines up with her hands, and her eyes followed until she looked him in the face. His eyes, bright with desire, held hers. His large hands covered her small ones, and then moved up her arms to her shoulders, and then down to her small, firm breasts. She felt a tingling in her nerves and a sensitivity in her skin as goose bumps rose.

Barnes kissed her between her breasts, and at that moment their urgency broke through the calm, and they let their passions loose. They kissed deeply, greedily, each seeking to close the distance between them. She felt his hands, rough and hard, on her back and buttocks and thighs as she stood up, and she felt completely surrounded. She was hot, she was drenched, she was salty with the residue from the tennis, and she wanted him inside her as badly as she had ever wanted anything.

He put his hands in the crease where her ass met the backs of her thighs and lifted, his natural strength amplified by his desire. She briefly felt the air cool on her pussy as he opened her thighs, and then she wrapped her legs around his waist and he was inside her. For a long, tantalizing moment he held her still and they both felt the fit, tight and strong.

"It's as though you were made for me," he said a bit hoarsely.

"Perhaps I was," she said, and smiled at him.

Entwined in front of the window, by the light of the reddening sunset, they made love. She cleaved to him, her arms on his shoulders, her thighs on his hips, and he slowly rocked her back and forth, starting small and slow. She arched her back and tightened her ass to feel him better, and feeling him brought her almost instantly to the brink. She relaxed again to recover herself, and he started moving her faster and harder against him.

She was so wet that he moved effortlessly in and out of her, and each time he thrust in, she felt a pressure deep inside her, where the tip of his cock was touching a part of her that had never been touched. The sensation was new, and powerful, and intimate, and she stopped him with her legs while he was deep inside. With him fully buried, and her clitoris hard against the base of his penis, she rocked her hips from side to side, the movement reverberating from the lips of her cunt up through his shaft, and dispersing through her entire body.

And then she lost control, and no force on earth could have stopped the pulses of all-encompassing pleasure from tearing through her. She moaned, low and long, and it was that moan, combined with the feel of her orgasm, that made him come. He held her like a vise against him as he erupted inside her, his orgasm peaking just as hers was subsiding.

He remained standing, and as her thoughts returned to her, she wondered that he could stand holding her, apparently effortlessly, seemingly forever. He put one forearm under her and held her to him with the other. Their sweat and their heartbeats mingled for a few moments, and then he set her down on the window seat. His softening penis glistened with her juices, and a small bead of semen hung on its tip. She took the drop on a fingertip, and ran the finger down his chest, tracing a line in the already damp hair.

He smiled at her and turned to collect both his clothes and hers. He handed her trousers and blouse to her, but she shook her head.

"I think I'm going to want a bath before dinner," she said, and walked to her wardrobe for her dressing gown. As she wrapped herself in it, she actively wondered what she should say to him. She was still coming down from her high, and somehow, with Barnes, words didn't seem quite the thing anyway.

"I won't be at dinner," said Barnes, "and I'll be gone most of the morning tomorrow. I'm going to look at an estate in Romsey. Lord Chiltenham is thinking of buying it, and wants my opinion as to what might be made of it."

"Oh," said Georgiana, eyebrows raised. "It must be a fine thing to have one's opinion solicited by such a man as Lord Chiltenham."

Barnes looked as though he were about to demur, but then a grin broke out on his face. "It is at that," he admitted, "it is at that."

"Well, I hope it is all an estate should be, and that you have fine weather for your journey," Georgiana said rather stupidly.

"May I come to see you when I return?" he asked, with a straightforward frankness that appealed to her.

"Yes" was the only answer she was able to give, and she gave it. They walked to the door, and he opened it. He kissed her softly and left.

After he was gone, Georgiana rang for Hortense and asked her to draw the much-needed bath. When she stepped into it, she thought a bath had never felt so good. She luxuriated in the big claw-footed tub and let the water's warmth penetrate her tired body. The exertion first of the tennis, and then of her interlude with Barnes, had exhausted every muscle she had.

"Hortense!" she called, and her maid came into the bathroom. "Could you let Lady Loughlin know I won't be coming down for dinner? I can't bring myself to get dressed and face the company." Knowing that Barnes wouldn't be at dinner made the prospect of that meal much less compelling.

"Certainly, my lady," said Hortense. "Shall I prepare a tray for you?"

"Just some tea and toast. I find I'm not hungry."

When Hortense returned with the tray, she found her mistress already asleep. She left the tray on the night table and tiptoed out.

SEVEN

G eorgiana slept soundly and long, and woke up refreshed, just in time for breakfast.

As she dressed and ran through the previous day's events in her mind, she found she was not without misgivings. Her liaison with Barnes was quite different from her relationship with Jeremy Staunton. She and Jeremy were social equals; she and Barnes most certainly weren't. And there were things about the man himself that gave her pause. She felt as though she were seeing only what he wanted her to see, that she didn't know the whole man.

She was glad to meet Lady Loughlin on the stairwell as the two were going down to breakfast. She had resolved to tell her friend all, and seek her advice.

"Good morning, Paulette," Georgiana said. "You're looking well."

Lady Loughlin was indeed looking well, happy and robust.

"Oh, I thrive on company, and we have it in abundance," said the mistress of the house, laughing. "The only fly in my ointment is poor Freddy. For my part, I must admit I'm happy to have him home again, but his father is not of my opinion." A momentary frown flashed over her face. "I daresay he's coming 'round, though," she continued, smiling again. "He was a shade less angry this morning than he was yesterday evening."

"I haven't seen him this morning," said Georgiana. "Actually, I haven't seen anyone. Where are they all? The house seems empty."

"After yesterday's match, everyone seems to have decided that tennis is quite the thing. Gerry challenged Alexandra to a match, so the poor girl is at it again. Most everyone else is in the gallery, watching age battle beauty."

"The smart money's on beauty," said Georgiana. "Miss Niven is an excellent player."

"Don't count Gerry out. He's a wily old creature, and if she's got an Achilles' heel, he'll find it."

"I certainly couldn't find it, but I wish him luck."

The two women walked companionably into breakfast, and took tea and what was left of the kippers and toast.

"Are you horrendously busy this morning?" Georgiana asked.

"I don't have a thing, my dear," answered Lady Loughlin. "I did all the planning ahead of time, and the house should run like clockwork, even if I were to drop dead on the spot. Do you have something in mind?"

"There's something I'd like to talk to you about."

"Well, fetch your bonnet when you've finished your kippers, and let's go for a walk. We can try the labyrinth. It's perfectly private."

This suited Georgiana admirably, and the two women set out directly after breakfast.

As they walked across the grounds, Lady Loughlin asked Georgiana if she had been through the labyrinth already.

"Mr. Barnes showed it to me, but we didn't go in," she said. "He said he was afraid we'd never get out again."

"Oh, rot," said Paulette. "It's not that difficult, and he knows it like the back of his hand. He was just trying to be mysterious."

"Mrs. Sheffield was with us, and I suspect he didn't want to prolong the tour," said Georgiana rather ungraciously. But it was not the kind of slight to ruffle her hostess, who agreed with her friend's assessment of her guest.

"I imagine you're right. She has a way of making people want to limit the time they spend in her company." And then Lady Loughlin's expression changed, and she said slyly, "You, on the other hand, have a way of making people want to spend every spare moment with you."

Georgiana reddened, and looked at her friend in surprise, not sure of the implications of this remark.

They had by this time reached the labyrinth, and Lady Loughlin stopped just outside its entrance. "That is what you want to speak to me about, isn't it, dear?" she asked more gently. "Mr. Barnes's spare moments?"

In the novels Georgiana was fond of reading, people's jaws were always dropping when they were astonished. She hadn't thought it really happened until she felt her own chin drop almost to her chest. "You mean you know?" she asked after a moment.

"Oh, dear, the whole house knows. It's very difficult to keep a secret at Penfield."

"But . . . how?" Georgiana spluttered.

"I don't know the details," said Lady Loughlin. "I never do. But I take it Barnes was spotted going into your room last night. And since Little Eddie saw the two of you in the peacock pavilion the previous day, the servants' hall put two and two together. I'm afraid the cat's out of the bag."

Georgiana was speechless, and her friend led her into the labyrinth, giving her some minutes to absorb this information as they progressed into the maze.

The absorption didn't go well. Georgiana had been prepared to empty her heart, to tell her deepest secrets to this woman who was her friend. She loved Paulette, and thought much of her judgment. But now this conference, far from being a heart-to-heart, was an exercise in damage containment. Everyone in the house knew of her intimate affairs! Georgiana was mortified.

Her distress was written plainly on her face, and Lady Loughlin felt for her young companion.

"Oh, my dear," she said with compassion, "it isn't as bad as all that."

"Isn't it?" asked Georgiana, almost in tears. "Isn't it as bad as ever it could be?"

Lady Loughlin stopped, put a hand on her friend's arm, and turned to face her. "I have a question for you. It's an impertinent question, no doubt, and you are under no obligation to give me an answer. But it's a question you need to answer to yourself, if not to me."

Georgiana was all attention.

"Are you ashamed of what you have done?" Paulette asked her.

Georgiana was silent as she thought about this. She was uncertain of her feelings for Barnes. But she was certain that women should have the same kind of sexual freedom that men enjoyed, and she would not—no, she would not—be ashamed of exercising it.

"No," she said, quietly but firmly, "I am not ashamed."

Paulette nodded, having been almost certain that this would be Georgiana's answer. As they resumed their walk through the maze, she said, "If you are not ashamed, then you should not be distressed."

"But there are things that, while not shameful, one would not want the whole world talking of," said Georgiana.

"Certainly there are, and when the whole world *does* talk of them, one is likely to be discomposed. But not distressed, my dear. Reserve your distress for situations that merit it. I understand that you are upset—with good reason. And I hereby give you license to be annoyed, but not distressed."

Georgiana had to laugh, and she thought there was a great deal of sense in this. While she would have preferred to keep her affair with

Barnes private, that was no longer possible. Since it was public, she would hold her head high. She would not be cowed by criticism she knew to be unwarranted. She would hold firm to her principles.

She felt the flush that had come over her when Paulette told her the news begin to ebb, and as they wound their way through the labyrinth she found she was able to tell her hostess all about her feelings for Barnes with relative equanimity. By the time they exited the maze—Lady Loughlin was as good as her word, and they had no navigational trouble—the women were talking of other things as though nothing had happened.

Had they turned around as they were walking away, they would have seen Bruce Barnes emerging from the maze after them. He had seen them enter just as he was riding back to the estate from his visit to Romsey, and he couldn't stop himself from following them in. He knew the maze well enough to keep a path parallel to theirs, and he'd heard every word that passed between them.

Barnes turned toward the stables to see to his horse, which he'd left saddled and unfed while he followed the women. Paulette and Georgiana headed toward the house, which they reached just as the large party was returning from the tennis courts.

"And who is the victor?" asked Lady Loughlin.

"That honor belongs emphatically to Miss Niven," said Alphonse Gerard. His face had turned bright scarlet, and his clothes were sweaty and disheveled. His wide smile, though, was intact.

"But Gerry put up a good fight," said Miss Niven, who looked as though she had barely exerted herself.

"Fiddlesticks!" said Gerry. "Whatever points I scored were results of your extraordinary generosity, not my superior play."

Miss Niven demurred, but not very convincingly. "You play with heart," she added.

"Heart? I play with heart, do I?" Gerry laughed. "Well, perhaps there's something in that. I have so much heart that I will gladly lose to you again tomorrow."

Miss Niven, who had enjoyed herself, agreed readily. The appointment was made, and the entire party went in to lunch.

When lunch had been eaten, the houseguests dispersed to their afternoon activities. Lady Georgiana had correspondence to attend to, and she was steeling herself to the task with one last cup of tea. She was sitting on a window seat overlooking the expanse of lawn, lost in her own thoughts, when Freddy sat down opposite.

"Hullo, Lady G."

"Hello, Freddy." She smiled at him. She was going to make a remark about the fine weather or the tasty lunch, but she decided she didn't have to stand on such social niceties with this young man. "Have you made it up with your father yet?"

Freddy grinned. "I think he's coming 'round. He glared at me this morning, but he seems to have left the horsewhip in the stable. He didn't even shout, which I regard as a good sign."

"A good sign, indeed," Georgiana said solemnly.

"Are you engaged for the afternoon?" Freddy asked. It was a perfectly commonplace question, and if it had been asked by Paulette, or Mr. Sheffield, or Miss Niven, it would not have caught her attention. There was something in Freddy's tone, though, that made her take particular notice.

"I am engaged in my correspondence, I'm afraid," she said, slightly warily. "I've neglected it far too long."

"But surely you can't just shut yourself up in a musty old room when the sun is shining and the grounds are calling," said Freddy, in a tone Georgiana could only describe as suggestive. Could this young man possibly be making a lover's overture?

"My room is hardly musty," she answered, with not a little hauteur. "And there are some responsibilities that supersede even sunshine." She hated the way the words sounded as they left her mouth. She could have been some dried-up old harridan! Why did she feel the need to take this tone with the boy, even if he was trying to bill and coo?

She deliberately softened. "I do feel the call of a beautiful day," she said. "That is, in fact, why I've fallen behind in my letters—we have had day after day of sunshine and warmth. We're all quite spoiled."

"So split the difference," said Freddy in a husky voice, flashing hooded eyes. "Come for a walk with me and then attend to your letters." He stood up and held his hand out to her.

Now there was no mistaking the tone. "Freddy," she said, smiling but serious. "Are you making love to me?"

Freddy blushed to the roots of his white-blond hair. "If you insist on putting it that way, I suppose I am, but a chap's not used to being called out on it."

Georgiana laughed softly. "I wouldn't say I'm calling you out, Freddy. I was only asking because it seemed so unlikely. After all, I'm several years older than you are, and I've known you since you wore short pants."

Freddy considered this a blow to his manhood, and didn't like it at all. "Every man wore short pants once, and not one of them likes to be reminded of it by the girl he's got his eye on." His husky tone was gone, replaced by one of indignation. "If you've been paying one whit of attention, you will have noticed that I no longer wear short pants, and I daresay I'm as much of a full-blooded man as any you know."

In all her acquaintance with him, Georgiana had never seen Freddy even annoyed, let alone angry, and she was astonished. She started to say something, but he wasn't finished yet.

"If you don't care for a chap, you're perfectly entitled to say him nay, but to say he's not man enough to speak to you in the first place isn't cricket." He gave her a look that was almost a glare, and Georgiana saw his point. But then Freddy made a mistake. "I'm every inch the man Barnes is," he said.

It took her a second or two to realize his meaning, and then she was on her feet in an instant. "You impudent pup," she said, and slapped him, hard, across the face. "You know nothing of manhood. Or manners." She turned on her heel and left the room.

She knew it would be hopeless to sit at a writing table and attend to correspondence, so she headed, hatless, out to the grounds, thinking through what had just happened. Freddy, like everyone else in the house, knew of her private affairs. Could he really think that, because she was intimate with Barnes, she wanted to be intimate with every man who crossed her path? That would make her a wanton harlot.

But what, after all, was the difference between what she was doing and wanton harlotry?

The difference was Barnes himself, and the connection between them. There was nothing random or casual in what they were doing. They were driven to each other in a way that transcended social mores. It was very clear to her, but the only other person who seemed to understand it was Barnes himself.

After she'd walked long enough to calm down, Lady Georgiana headed for her room to catch up on her letters. As she reached her door, she saw Barnes coming down the corridor in the other direction, and she found herself a bit flustered.

"Mr. Barnes," she said. "Good afternoon."

"If anyone should call me by my Christian name, I think it's you."

"Perhaps you're right. Bruce." She tested the name on her tongue.

She found, somewhat to her surprise, that her fight with Freddy, coming on the heels of her conversation with Paulette, had made her easier in this man's presence, and more inclined to indulge her visceral attraction to him. Let the world say what it would. She was sure—absolutely sure—that what she was doing was not wrong, and letting the world's opinion override her own would be unconscionable weakness.

"Bruce," she repeated as she opened the door to her room.

The two went in, and as she closed the door behind them, Barnes took her face in his two work-hardened hands. She turned to face him and he kissed her hard. She felt his cool hands on her cheeks as his warm tongue found her own, and it was as though a switch flipped in her. She stopped being the clever, self-possessed daughter of an earl and started being simply a vessel for her own desire.

She reached her hands behind him and ran them down his ass. She was surprised by its muscular compactness. Although he was large and she was small, she could almost cover each cheek with her hand. She squeezed and pulled him closer to her.

She felt his erection at her waistline, and she leaned back just enough to leave room to work her hand between their two bodies so she could feel its length and strength. It was still pointing downward, imprisoned by the fabric of his trousers, and she reached under his waistband to release it. She put her hand around it, just under the glans, and felt the skin of his penis slip over the iron-hard core beneath as she stroked him up and down.

Only then did Barnes's hold on her face loosen, as he closed his eyes and groaned.

"I thought about you all the way to Romsey and all the way back," he told her. "I had a hard-on the entire trip."

She smiled, thinking of her own experience with the confluence of arousal and horse riding.

"It was all I could do not to stop and take care of it myself," he went on. "But I was hoping to see you this afternoon."

"I'm glad you saved it for me," Georgiana said, her hand still caressing his cock.

She unbuttoned his pants and reached both hands down between his legs. She cradled his balls and ran her thumbs in the crevice where the top of his thighs met the base of his genitals. She felt the roughness of his hair and the firm contours of his body. Still holding his balls, she turned her head, placed her cheek against his chest, and was still for a moment. She heard, and felt, his heart beat.

Barnes took her by the waist and lifted her, and her hands came out of his trousers as she rose. She wound her legs around his waist, and he turned and walked to the big four-poster bed. At its edge, he bent over and she fell to its soft surface.

He slipped his shoes off, stepped out of his pants, and almost ripped his shirt from his body. As she had before, she marveled that he could stand before her naked without a trace of self-consciousness.

He lifted her foot, unlaced her boot, and took it and her stocking off. He held her foot in his hand, and she felt his thumb press her instep. The sensation ricocheted up her leg, and she wondered how such a small touch could elicit such acute pleasure.

Barnes took off her other boot and stocking, and then her drawers. She lay on the bed, skirts flipped up, naked from the waist down. Barnes stood between her knees, with one foot in each hand. He pressed so that her knees came up to her chest, and she felt momentarily vulnerable, with her pussy and her ass exposed like that.

But it was only a moment. She felt the tip of Barnes's cock circling and then entering her, and any sense of discomfort was forgotten.

She felt herself widen to accommodate him, and relished the slowness with which he eased himself into her. He stopped halfway, and she instinctively tried to push herself down so he would be completely inside. But he held her feet, and she couldn't move.

"Stay right there," he whispered hoarsely.

She felt the tantalizing denial of his grip. Her body, almost of its own accord, wanted to move. She wanted to feel him deeper, deeper. There was a chasm where his cock ought to be, and she needed to fill it. She squirmed, and he held her fast.

He eased himself out of her as slowly as he had eased himself in, and Georgiana felt the coolness of the air on her wet pussy. She wanted desperately to have him back inside her, but she knew he was in control, and she gave herself over to it.

She was surprised, though, when he bent down and picked up his own shirt. She propped herself up on her elbows and looked at him quizzically. Was he getting dressed?

He wasn't. He picked up her left foot and tied one of the sleeves around her ankle.

"This may seem strange to you, but I think it will add a whole new layer of pleasure," he said, smiling.

And then he reached up and tied the other sleeve to the top of the bedpost, well above his head.

"You're tying me to the bed?" she asked with wonder at the novelty of it, and curiosity about this whole new layer of pleasure he was promising.

"I am," he said, and picked up his pants.

He tied her other leg to the top of the other bedpost, and Georgiana lay with her legs suspended in a V. She couldn't help thinking of the only other time she'd been intimately restrained, with Jeremy. With him, her powerlessness seemed playful, and she knew he would have untied her instantly had she asked. With Barnes, she felt truly powerless, and she wasn't sure at all he would release her if that were what she wanted.

But release was most certainly not what she wanted. She wanted to know what he was going to do. Her body ached with wanting to feel what was coming next.

Barnes put his hand under her backside and spread his fingers. From the tip of his thumb to the tip of his pinkie, he could almost span her entire width. She felt his finger in the cleft between the cheeks of her buttocks, and she tightened her muscles automatically.

"Relax," said Barnes. "Just let it all happen."

She was vaguely uncomfortable, but her desire for him, and her desire to explore all that her body had to offer, overrode her discomfort. She made a conscious effort to relax, and she felt his finger work around the rim of her anus. She had to consciously stop herself from pressing her buttocks together again, to keep him out, but she made the effort and concentrated on the sensation.

And then she knew what he was talking about. It was a feeling she'd never experienced, a deep, dull, spreading pleasure. Barnes put his fingertip inside, and circled slowly to press the rim all the way around, and Georgiana felt it as though it were electric.

Then he turned his hand and reached his thumb into her pussy, and it was like a waterfall let loose inside her. He held all her desire between his two fingers, one in her cunt and the other up her ass. He pulsed his hand, and her pleasure rose and fell with the pressure. Her breathing quickened, she closed her eyes, and she unconsciously gripped the bedclothes. The restraints on her ankles were forgotten. The time and the place were forgotten. There was only his hand, and the astonishing sensation emanating from it.

She was on the verge of orgasm when he took that hand away. She breathed in sharply and opened her eyes. He had stepped back from her and was watching her reaction with a half-smile.

"You can't stop," she said before she had a chance to think about what was coming out of her mouth.

"I can't?" he asked.

She squirmed against her restraints. "Don't stop; please don't stop."

He stepped back between her legs, and brushed her pussy very lightly with the back of his hand. She tried to push against him, put he simply moved his hand to keep the pressure as light as possible.

She moaned in a mixture of pleasure and frustration, and, after making her wait another beat or two, he reinserted his fingers back where they'd been.

"Oh my god," she said, almost involuntarily.

It didn't take long for him to coax her back to the verge of orgasm. When she was there, he stopped again.

"No!" she almost shouted. But this time, when she raised her head, she saw him step again between her legs and guide his cock into her. He slid in effortlessly, his entry eased by the juices she had in such abundance. They groaned simultaneously, and he fell back into the same rhythm he'd had with his hand.

She kept herself flush against him by holding the bedclothes, and all the muscles in her legs and her ass held fast to him. She was so ready for him, so hot, that as soon as she felt his cock harden that last little bit and she knew he was going to come, she was over the edge. She cried out at the searing ecstasy that swallowed her whole. She was subsumed for several seconds, and she let the waves overcome her. When the pleasure began to fade to contentment, she opened her eyes and saw him in the last throes of an ecstasy of his own.

Only then did Georgiana became conscious once more of the fact that her legs were tied to the tops of the bedposts with his clothes.

She gestured at her restraints. "I think you'll be needing those," she said with a smile.

"It would be quite a scandal if I left without them," he said, as he untied her.

It seems to be quite a scandal even when you leave with them, she thought, but didn't say.

As he dressed, she shook out her legs and rearranged her clothes.

"You look a bit the worse for wear," she said with a laugh, gesturing to his hopelessly wrinkled clothes.

"Do I?" he asked, looking down at himself.

"Look in the glass." She gestured to the mirror over the dressing table.

They both looked at his reflection and, for the first time, she noticed the beautiful bouquet of autumn flowers someone had left for her.

"What lovely flowers!" she said. "I wonder who could have left them." She reached out to pick up the vase to get a better look when he stopped her.

"Don't touch these," he said, looking strangely at the bouquet.

"Why ever not?"

"See those bright red leaves all around the base?" he asked.

"Of course," she said, puzzled.

"That's poison ivy."

She looked more closely and could see that he was right. The beautiful, bright leaves were indeed poison ivy.

She laughed. "I'm afraid that whoever put this together is going to pay an exorbitant price."

He didn't laugh. "I don't think so."

"Why not?"

"Because whoever put this together might have known exactly what those leaves were, and included them deliberately—using gloves, of course."

"You think this was deliberate?" she asked, astonished.

"I do. I think anyone who would take the trouble to assemble such a bouquet as this would have to care about plants. And anyone who cares about plants can identify poison ivy."

She laughed again. "I hardly think—"

But he cut her off. "You'll know soon enough. There's a card." He pointed to a small white envelope nestled in the flowers.

Lady Georgiana was itching with curiosity to know what the card said, but she didn't want to open it in front of Barnes.

"You must let me get dressed for dinner," she said, looking pointedly at the clock on the mantelpiece. "I have less than an hour."

It was a transparent ruse, but Barnes recognized that Georgiana wanted to open the card in private. "You're an astonishing woman, you know," he said, and then kissed her forehead and took his leave.

Georgiana closed the door behind him and extracted the envelope from the bouquet, being careful not to touch the red leaves. Inside was a card with one word written on it.

Harlot.

EIGHT

◦━◦

Georgiana was shaken, and all the misgivings she'd felt on first hearing that the entire company knew of her affair with Barnes came flooding back. Her knees weakened and she felt herself go faint. She sat down on the bed, still with the card in her hand.

"Who could have done such a thing?" she asked aloud. She ran through the visitors at Penfield, but could venture no guess. And then she thought of Freddy. Could this be his revenge for that slap? She dismissed the thought. He might be rash and occasionally ill-mannered, but he wasn't venal.

She thought she must tell Lady Loughlin, and reached her hand out to ring the bell for Hortense, but then she thought better of it. Hadn't Lady Loughlin, just that morning, lectured her about having the courage of her convictions? Hadn't she herself decided, just that morning, that she wouldn't allow the opinion of the world to influence her decisions about right and wrong? And now, mere hours later, she was reduced to a quivering jelly by a silly insult from an ignorant prig?

Lady Georgiana Vernon was made of sterner stuff than this, she told herself, and matched her actions to the thought. She tore up the card and threw it and the flowers into the fireplace, where they would serve the only purpose she would permit them: kindling the fire her maid would light for her after dinner. She would *not* allow them to disturb her.

Georgiana bathed and took some time with her toilette. She assumed she would be facing her anonymous enemy at dinner, and she wanted to do it looking her best.

Her best was very good indeed, and heads turned as she came down to dinner in a sapphire-blue silk gown with a very snug waist and a very low neckline. More guests had arrived that day, and there was some nudging and whispering among the people who were seeing her for the first time as they identified her to one another and remarked on her appearance, which was indeed remarkable.

Georgiana looked around for Freddy. She wanted to make things right with him, but he wasn't in the room. She certainly wasn't in the mood for strangers, so she took the last of four chairs grouped around a low table in the corner. The other three chairs were occupied by Gerry, Miss Niven, and a woman Georgiana didn't recognize but assumed to be Miss Niven's companion.

And so she turned out to be.

"Lady Georgiana," said Miss Niven with enthusiasm. "I'm glad you could join us."

Georgiana smiled her greeting.

"I don't believe you've met Miss Mumford," Alexandra continued, and introduced the two women properly.

Miss Mumford nodded coldly, with barely enough civility to avoid being flagrantly rude. Georgiana felt her hackles rise, but she chose to ignore the slight, and smiled warmly at Alexandra's companion.

"I'm so very glad to meet you," she said with exaggerated sweetness. "Miss Niven speaks very highly of you."

Miss Mumford nodded again, and mustered up a wan smile.

Georgiana, having done her social duty, turned to Gerry and Alexandra. "Tell me about your tennis game," she said.

"I'm glad you weren't there to witness the carnage," said Gerry, laughing. "I didn't even give Miss Niven a reasonable challenge. She simply trounced me from start to finish."

"That's not quite true," said Alexandra. "But you're a good sport, at any rate."

"Good sport! I'd dashed well better be a good sport. If you're no good at a thing, being a good sport is all you have left."

Georgiana, when she met Gerry, had thought she might like him, and now she was sure she did.

"I must say, I think qualities you develop in yourself, like spirit and perseverance, are to be valued much more dearly than qualities that are God-given, like athletic talent," she said.

"Spoken like a woman with athletic talent!" Gerry said.

"Oh, you can't be serious for even a moment," said Alexandra to Gerard. "Lady Georgiana is right, of course. I certainly take pleasure in playing tennis, but I try to take pride only in the effort, and not the result."

At this point, a pause in the conversation gave Miss Mumford an opportunity to address her charge.

"Alexandra, dear," she said, pointing to the girl's empty plate, "as you have finished your dinner, perhaps we should pay our respects to Mr. and Mrs. Churchill. They just arrived today. You met them last year in London, do you remember?"

"Of course I remember," said Miss Niven wonderingly. "And I will make it a point to speak with them after dinner."

"You wouldn't want them to think you aren't being attentive," Miss Mumford went on.

"I really don't see how they could think that," Alexandra said, finally understanding what her companion was driving at. "I will most certainly speak with them later," she said definitively, and turned back to Gerry and Georgiana.

Georgiana had understood this exchange fully as well as Alexandra had. Miss Mumford clearly thought that she—Lady Georgiana—was an inappropriate companion for a young lady of virtue, and had made a clumsy attempt at separating the two young women. Georgiana's heart warmed to Alexandra for rebuffing that attempt.

Determined to turn the conversation, Georgiana addressed Gerry: "Perhaps we can find an activity where spirit and perseverance carry the day, and talent plays little part."

"Are there any ditches to be dug?" asked Gerard. "Or perhaps some coal to be shoveled?"

The two girls laughed. "I was thinking perhaps we could take a punt out on the pond," said Georgiana. "We will let you do all the work, and we will sit on pillows and admire your technique."

Alexandra seconded the idea.

"By Jove, that's a fine plan," said Gerard with gusto. "If the weather holds, I consider you engaged to punt on the pond with me after breakfast."

The three continued to discuss the many opportunities the estate offered for entertainment, with Miss Mumford saying not a word.

When dinner was over and the last guests were straggling upstairs to their rooms, Lady Loughlin sought out Georgiana and took her arm. "Come upstairs with me," she said to her young friend.

They went to Paulette's room, where her maid, Jean, was just finishing laying out her mistress's nightclothes.

"Thank you, Jean. That will be all."

"Yes, my lady." Jean nodded and left the room.

"Sit down, Georgiana. After this morning's conversation, I just want to make sure all is well."

"All is certainly well," said Lady Georgiana, her sense of well-being perhaps heightened by the several glasses of wine she'd had with dinner. "Although what I've done has not been without repercussions."

"Repercussions?" her hostess asked with surprise.

Georgiana told her the story of the flowers, and took some perverse satisfaction in Paulette's evident surprise. It was her turn to be blasé to Paulette's perturbed; their respective roles of the morning had been reversed.

"I'm very unhappy about having such a thing going on under my roof."

"Oh, I shouldn't take it so seriously," said Georgiana. "I don't think there's any harm in it."

"But I wonder who could have done it," Paulette mused.

"I couldn't begin to guess, and so I'm not going to," Georgiana said, keeping the thought of Freddy to herself. "And I don't think you should either. It's only important if we make it so."

"I suppose you're right, but I still can't say I like it. It's very unsettling." She shook her head. "I think I'm going to need a sleeping draft." She reached for the bell to ring for Jean.

The women exchanged other news of the day as Paulette waited for her maid, who didn't come.

"Where can she be?" Paulette asked with some annoyance.

"You did tell her there would be nothing further."

"There are sometimes further things that one cannot anticipate." She rang the bell again, but to no avail.

"Bah!" said Paulette. "I am so tired of waiting that I suspect I will be able to sleep without the draft after all, so I will say good night."

The two kissed affectionately and Georgiana went to her room.

Jean, meanwhile, was as otherwise occupied as it is possible for a lady's maid to be. When her mistress dismissed her for the evening, she didn't go straight to her room in the servants' quarters. She went first through the drawing room where Lord Loughlin, with a few of his guests, was taking advantage of the dying warmth of the fire to smoke a last cigar before retiring. Jean curtsied to the group.

"Good night, my lord," she said as she passed them on her way through the room.

But when she shut the far door behind her, she still didn't go upstairs. Instead, she went through the kitchen—empty, clean, and quiet at this hour—and took a key from her pocket. She checked that no one was watching, and fitted the key to the lock in the door that led to the wine cellar. She slipped through and closed the door quietly.

She turned on the electric light that had been installed only the year before, and made her way carefully down the steep stone stairs, breathing in the familiar smells of must and dust and age. She walked slowly in the narrow aisles between the racks and racks of Lord Loughlin's wines until she heard the creak of the door at the top of the stairs and the muffled click of footsteps on stone.

And then he stood in front of her, Robert Loughlin himself.

"Hello, Jean."

"My lord."

"You've been dismissed for the night?"

"Yes, sir."

"Good," he said, and took a bunch of keys from his pocket. He walked toward the back of the wine cellar, with Jean following. When he reached the end of the aisle, he turned right. In the far corner of the cellar was a narrow, iron-barred door. Lord Loughlin unlocked it and held it open for Jean. He followed her in, and closed it behind him.

They were in a small, dark space, a kind of a cage not more than eight feet by ten. It was lined with wine racks, which were filled with the very best wines the cellar contained, wines Lord Loughlin wouldn't entrust even to Dodson, his butler of many years. On the floor, incongruously, was a thick, lush Persian carpet. In the middle of the rug, on a small stand, was a cask of Chateau Laballe Armagnac, which Lord Loughlin shared only with his most favored friends.

Without a word, Lord Loughlin bent Jean over the cask and flipped up her skirts. He stood between her legs and kneaded her buttocks through the thin cotton of her drawers, hard. She took a deep, quick inhale to steel herself against what was almost, but not quite, pain. She always found a strange satisfaction in this, the inevitable prelude to their sessions in the wine cellar. It made her feel flushed and excited, and ready for whatever her master had his mind set on that day.

For Lord Loughlin, the sight of his wife's maid's firm young ass, and its succulence in his hands, did more than arouse him. It took him to the point where he could get past his discomfort with having an affair behind his wife's back, and primed him to indulge proclivities that he almost thought shameful. The sight, the feel of that ass in his hands, and all was put behind him.

His cock was standing at attention when he stepped away and half sat, half leaned on a tall stool in the corner.

"Get undressed," he said to Jean, almost gruffly.

Jean got up from the cask, and then leaned against it to unlace her boots. Lord Loughlin, she knew, liked her to take her time.

He leaned on the stool, one hand caressing his cock through his trousers, as he watched Jean carefully and deliberately roll down her stockings. The sight of her hands against her legs mesmerized him.

She felt the cool air of the cellar as a balance to the heat she was generating from within. She had learned to love this part of their ritual, to feel the pleasure of her own touch. She folded her stockings inside her boots and began to undo the buttons on her dress.

She stepped out of the dress and stood before him in bodice and drawers. She stepped closer to him, her breasts at his eye level, and reached her hands around to her back to untie the laces that kept her white muslin bodice bound. The motion of moving her shoulders back thrust her breasts forward, and they were only inches from his face. He looked, he closed his eyes for a moment, and the motion of his hand on his penis quickened.

None of this was lost on Jean, and his arousal contributed to hers.

As she untied the laces on her own bodice, her eyes were on his hand, and his cock, and she was attuned to his pleasure.

When she loosened her bodice and pulled it off over her head, Lord Loughlin stopped touching himself so he could touch her. He took one breast in each hand and buried his head between them, breathing in the combination of Jean's spice and the must of the cellar. He held her breasts tight to his cheeks and filled his lungs.

Abruptly, he stood up and stripped without ceremony. Naked, he turned away from Jean and walked to the end of one of the racks, where there was a large wooden cabinet. He opened it and surveyed its contents. From the array of toys, tricks, and leather he took out one of his favorites, an ancient Chinese cock ring carved in ivory. It was in the form of a dragon, curled around so its tail met the base of its neck.

He knew he couldn't get it on when he was in a state of full tumescence, so he used the trick he always used to calm his erection: He thought about fishing. One mental picture of the trout he stocked his pond with, and he felt his attention straying and his penis softening.

When it had lost enough strength that he could fit the ring on, he didn't put it on himself, but handed it to Jean. She knew to act quickly, and she slid his balls through it—first one, then the other—and then maneuvered his cock in. She adjusted it, holding his entire apparatus in one hand, and moving the ring into just the right spot with the other.

Once it was in position, she gently stroked the underside of his cock, using only her fingertips. He got steely hard under her touch, and gave her a meaningful look. He went back to the cabinet, and returned with a tangle of leather straps, horsehair, and brass fittings, along with a whip.

He handed it all to Jean.

She took it, and the expression on her face underwent a startling transformation. Her mouth hardened, her eyes narrowed, and she seemed to grow an inch or two taller. She took the whip and cracked it on the cellar floor. In a heartbeat, *she* became *his* master.

"Turn around!" she demanded in a harsh voice.

Lord Loughlin did as he was told, and felt the intense mix of excitement and trepidation that came of relinquishing control.

Jean separated some of the straps until she was holding a harness in her hand, ready for him to slip into it, which he did.

The harness had originally been made for a mastiff Lord Loughlin had gotten when his two sons were young. The dog had been big enough for the small boys to ride, and the riding apparatus was all of a size to fit Lord Loughlin, if not perfectly, then well enough.

Jean buckled the straps across his chest, and attached the reins to the back of the harness. She was left holding the whip, a riding crop, and what looked like a horse's tail—which it had been, at one point. Now strands from that tail were attached to a small cylinder of black rubber.

Jean cracked the whip again. "Down!" she barked, and Lord Loughlin got down on his hands and knees. Jean went over to the cabinet and took out a jar of Carston's Complexion Cream. She opened it, rubbed a large dab of the cream on the rubber cylinder, and went back to Lord Loughlin. "Lean down!" she ordered.

Lord Loughlin put his head to the floor and presented his ass to Jean. She inserted the rubber plug far into his anus, and the horsehair made it look for all the world like a tail.

Jean yanked on the straps. "Up!"

He came back up to all fours, and groaned as his ass closed around the butt plug. Jean cracked the whip again. "Quiet!"

Then she put the whip down and straddled his back, holding the riding crop. She slapped the crop on his ass. "Forward!" she ordered.

At this, Lord Loughlin started forth on all fours, with Jean riding him.

Although Jean still found her master's proclivities peculiar, she loved the sensation that he needed her. She understood that he showed her a side of himself that no one else knew, and that it was the deepest secret of his soul. It made her feel singled out, special, and that sense contributed to the pleasure she got from their games in the wine cellar.

The power also contributed. She spent most of her life doing the bidding of others, but down here, once she held that whip in her hand, she was in control. Exercising that control heightened all her other sensations, including the feel of her clitoris on her lord's back, pulsing against it with his motion across the cold stone floor.

"Faster," she said, and hit his ass again with the riding crop. She could feel him strain with the exertion and the excitement. She reached around and took the horsehair tail in her hand and twisted it until it was taut enough so that her twisting motion turned the plug itself.

He groaned again, and she stopped twisting immediately. "Be quiet!"

He fell silent and continued his cycle around the cask of Armagnac, and she started twisting again. Whenever he slowed down or made a noise she stopped twisting and made him speed up or stay quiet. As long as he continued at a pace she deemed acceptable, and made not a murmur, she twisted.

All this time, Lord Loughlin felt his persistent erection pulsing against the cock ring. Jean felt the same rhythm radiating from her pussy—now so wet that she was slipping on his back—up her spine and down the backs of her legs.

They reached the point where they both knew the climax was coming.

"Stop!" Jean said, and hit him again with the crop. He stopped. She put her feet on the floor and made him lie down on the carpet between her legs, and then turn over on his back. He lay on the floor looking up her body to her glistening cunt and then farther up to her full breasts and erect nipples.

Jean dropped to her knees and impaled herself on him. The dragon's head on the cock ring hit her in just the right spot, and the sensation of the shaft of him inside her, and the hard surface of the cock ring outside, took her right to the brink.

But she didn't want to be at the brink—not quite yet—and she stopped her motion midstroke. He kept moving under her, and she reached behind her with the riding crop, still in her hand, and gave him a sharp rap on the thigh. "When I stop, you stop!" she demanded.

He stopped, with a visible effort. If he hadn't had the cock ring to help him control his hard-on, it would have been all over right then.

She waited a few beats, and began again. This time, he was attuned to her motion, and when she stopped again he stopped with her.

"Very good." She rewarded him with a sly smile.

She started again, for what she knew would be the last time. She was too close to the edge to keep this up. She started to come and, at that moment, he knew he was released and came right in time with her. Their game had been going on long enough that each had built up tremendous excitement, and the release was volcanic. Together, but separate, they rode the wave of it—toys and games forgotten.

As it waned, they both came back to the here and now, and they disentangled themselves and their accoutrements as the last flush faded.

Lord Loughlin hastily dressed and put everything back in the cabinet in a heap—he would come back the next day to clean and rearrange it—as Jean put her dress on over her naked body. She quickly laced her boots and stood with her drawers, bodice, and stockings in her hand, knowing that her master didn't like to linger after their interludes.

He opened the door to the cage and gave her a genuine, warm smile. She knew he was grateful to have an outlet for his desires, and felt a real affection for her. She, in turn, had been introduced to pleasures she hadn't known existed, and the arrangement worked for both of them.

She smiled back.

They left the cage, and he locked the door behind them. Then, as was their habit, he left the wine cellar first, alone. A few minutes later she followed, and went up to bed and to sleep.

NINE

The next day broke clear, warm, and fine. Looking out over the morning light on the manicured grounds, Georgiana made an effort to shake off the residual bad feelings from the poison ivy bouquet, dressed, and went down to breakfast.

The house was buzzing with guests and their servants. The masquerade was just three days away, and the festive spirit was beginning to infect the company. As Lady Georgiana walked down to breakfast she heard laughter and good cheer coming from every corner where guests sat with their plates on their knees and their teacups on the tables. All this helped her put the events of the previous day behind her and face this new day with bright optimism.

She hadn't forgotten her engagement to go punting with Miss Niven and Alphonse Gerard, and she looked for those familiar faces as she walked through the rooms. She didn't see Gerry at all, and Miss Niven was sitting with the severe Miss Mumford and a couple Georgiana didn't recognize. Since she didn't want a reenactment of yesterday's uncomfortable scene with Alexandra's companion, Georgiana chose to join the Sheffields and O'Maras instead.

It was an inauspicious choice. Mrs. Sheffield, whose manner to Georgiana had seemed to thaw a degree or two after her tennis match with Miss Niven, had now turned icy cold. When Georgiana sat down between Mr. Sheffield and Mrs. O'Mara, the nod she got from Mrs. Sheffield was curt, the face unsmiling. She had gotten her reenactment after all, she mused, but she thought too little of Mrs. Sheffield to let the incident dampen her mood. She ate her breakfast and made her escape as quickly as she could.

As she stood up, she saw Miss Niven making her way across the room toward her.

"Lady Georgiana," Miss Niven said, slightly flushed, "I hope you haven't forgotten our plan to go punting on the lake with Mr. Gerard."

"No indeed," she replied. "On the contrary, I have been looking forward to it. But I don't see Mr. Gerard," she continued, glancing around the room.

"He was here earlier, but he left to see to the boat."

"Well, then, we should be on our way, should we not?"

"We should," said Alexandra. "I just need to pop upstairs and get my bonnet."

A few minutes later, the two girls met at the front door and set out across the lawn.

"I am so glad to talk to you alone," said Alexandra. "I really must apologize for Miss Mumford's behavior last night. She is a good creature, but she has some old-fashioned ideas of what's proper for a young lady." Alexandra blushed at the mere thought of what those old-fashioned ideas were in reference to.

"There is no need for you to apologize for the behavior of another person," Georgiana said with emphasis. "You are not Miss Mumford, and not only did you do nothing objectionable, you rebuffed her efforts to separate you from a young lady as improper as I am." Both girls smiled.

"For that," Georgiana went on, "you have earned my affection." She took Miss Niven's arm.

Alexandra glowed at this expression of friendship. Although she had grown up accustomed to wealth and rank, she was aware that her guardian had suffered serious financial setbacks and knew that her position in society was not what it had been. Even if Georgiana hadn't been an earl's daughter, she would have responded with warmth to this overture—she was a good-natured, openhearted girl—but knowing that she had such a friend as this suffused her with good feeling.

And it gave her courage.

"There's something . . ." Alexandra faltered, and the question she wanted to ask trailed off into silence.

"Yes?" Georgiana urged her to continue. She wondered what the girl could want to ask her, but a moment's reflection gave her a good idea of what to expect.

"It's about . . ." This second foray of Miss Niven's wasn't any more successful than the first. She blushed deeply, and thought she must give up this line of inquiry.

"Is it about the impropriety that so injured the sensibilities of our good Miss Mumford?" Georgiana asked gently.

"It is." Miss Niven blushed deeper still. "But I don't even know what I want to ask." And then the floodgates opened. "It's just that I'm nineteen years old and I don't have the first idea of what relations between men and women really are. I've been shielded, protected from ideas and facts that are supposed to do me harm, but I don't see how ideas and facts can do me anything but good. How can ignorance possibly improve me?"

Georgiana laughed, and then hurried to assure her companion that she was laughing at how completely she agreed, and how she had had those same thoughts herself. She laughed because, beneath the naive ingenuousness of her new friend, she had found a kindred spirit.

"Ignorance cannot improve you. And it has always rankled me that it is only women who are thought to be better by knowing less. Men are expected to know even what might be thought distasteful, but knowledge of the venal, or the carnal, is supposed to taint women." Georgiana's blood rose as she tapped into this old resentment. "It's positively infuriating."

Alexandra was a little taken aback at the vehemence of this response. Her own thoughts on this issue were limited to her own discomfort, her own experience, but Georgiana's thoughts ran to their whole society. She was more comfortable with the particular than the general.

"I certainly think Miss Mumford believes that knowledge will taint me," Alexandra said. "And I have never been sure whether my curiosity about what I have been protected from is sensible, or merely prurient."

"How can curiosity about things that affect you intimately possibly be prurient?" asked Georgiana.

"Well, because it's curiosity about . . ." Alexandra trailed off once more.

"Sex?" Georgiana asked bluntly.

There. The word was out.

Alexandra blushed crimson. She was determined, though, to take advantage of the situation to find out from her new friend what no one else would tell her.

"Yes," she said, willing her voice not to quaver. "Sex."

What followed was a candid explanation of what had been to Alexandra, until that day, a mystery shrouded in euphemism and obfuscation.

She heard Lady Georgiana through without comment, taking it all in. When her friend had laid it all out for her, she took a moment to absorb her new knowledge.

"Well," she finally said, "that doesn't seem so very horrible."

Georgiana laughed. "No," she said. "It isn't horrible at all. In fact, it is quite wonderful." But then she paused, and realized that her words might be interpreted as advice, or even a recommendation.

It was Georgiana's turn to feel awkward and embarrassed. "But it can also have devastating repercussions," she said. "Its being wonderful would be cold comfort if all the world turned its back on you."

For all her ingenuousness, Alexandra Niven was not a stupid girl.

"You mean that the world would be quicker to turn its back on one such as me than one such as you."

"It would," said Georgiana. "But that is not to my credit. It is rather to the world's discredit."

She looked Miss Niven full in the face. "I recognize my good fortune. Because I was born into a particular family, I have more leeway than most girls. I have pushed that leeway to its very limits, and the Miss Mumfords of the world have indeed turned their backs on me. But I have the luxury of not giving a fig what the Miss Mumfords of the world think or do."

"I do not have that luxury." Miss Niven looked at the ground. "And perhaps it is because I want courage, or because I have been so thoroughly schooled in what is thought right and what is thought wrong, but I do not regret my constraints. It is much easier to navigate the world knowing exactly what is expected of one. Knowing that the world would turn its back on me if I"—here Miss Niven paused, searching for the words—"experimented as you do makes my course of action very clear."

Georgiana heard this with some relief. If she had been the catalyst for this girl's downfall, she could not have forgiven herself for her carelessness.

"My guess," she said, lightening her tone, "is that a girl such as you will not suffer from want of offers of marriage, and you will soon enough be able to experiment from the safety of the marital chamber."

Miss Niven was saved having to respond to this by the appearance of Alphonse Gerard.

"Good morning," he said cheerily. "I was preparing the punt and saw you coming down the path. Allow me to escort you the rest of the way." He stepped between them with exaggerated gallantry and offered an arm to each young woman. They took it, and the threesome walked down to the pond.

The punt was onshore, ready to go. The bow was filled with pillows, and the two girls climbed in and made themselves comfortable. Gerry positioned an umbrella over them, took his place in the stern, and shoved off.

The three made their way leisurely around the small pond, and their laughter rang out over the water. The girls enjoyed themselves immensely, and Gerry was positively in clover. He couldn't remember the last time he'd spent a morning so pleasantly.

After an hour or so, his arms gave out and he could punt no more, and they took the boat in.

"Can we help you put things away?" Miss Niven asked.

"No, no," said Gerry. "It won't take more than a few minutes. You girls go back to the house. I'm sure you'll want to freshen up before luncheon."

The girls took their leave, and Gerry put the pillows, pole, and umbrella back in the boathouse. He turned the boat over so the next rain wouldn't fill it and, finding himself quite tired, sat down on a bench overlooking the little pond.

Miss Niven was much on his mind. He'd never married, mostly because he valued his freedom, but partly because he was aware of his rough edges and worried that he didn't have enough to offer any girl that he'd like to have for a wife. As he got older, though, his freedom didn't seem quite so worth protecting, and his rough edges didn't prevent him from developing the confidence of a man who knows he's sound at bottom.

He had no doubt that Miss Niven was a girl worth having. She was innocent, but she was not insipid. She seemed to have something to say for herself. And she was so very beautiful. The fact that she had beaten him at tennis tended to make him like her even more.

He pulled his watch from his pocket and realized he had just a half hour before he, too, was due at luncheon, and he took a last look at the clear, flat water and turned to go back to the house.

Guests who'd been engaging in the various activities that the estate had to offer were straggling back to the house, and Gerry greeted several of them on the way to his room, which was in a far corner of the guest wing. As he approached his door, he was surprised to see Rose coming out.

"Hullo, Rose," he said warmly.

Rose looked a little taken aback. "I didn't expect you back so soon," she said. "I was making up your room."

That wasn't the whole truth. She had wanted to run into him, but she hadn't wanted to look as though she did, and she calculated the timing so that it was likely that she'd see him, but also likely that her protestations that she didn't expect him would be believed.

Gerry didn't bother to think whether he believed her or he didn't. He was glad to see her, and he still had a few minutes before he had to be downstairs.

"Do you have other rooms to make up just this minute?" he asked with a conspiratorial grin.

"Not this very minute," she said, smiling back at him.

Gerry took her hand and pulled her into his room.

The combination of the unexpectedness of the encounter—Gerry wasn't expecting it at all, and Rose wasn't at all sure it would materialize—and the press of time immediately rekindled the heat they had felt in their last encounter. Gerry closed the door with one hand as he reached his other around Rose's waist and bent his head to her neck.

Rose felt the warmth and the wetness of his tongue on her skin, and she leaned her head back, elongating her neck. Gerry worked his way up, running his lips and his tongue over its length, relishing the sweet-salty taste of her skin. He followed the soft ridge of a tendon that led up to her ear, and took her earlobe between his teeth. He bit down just enough for Rose to feel a prick of pain through her growing arousal, and she was surprised to find that the contrast of the two feelings focused her even more on the cascade of hot dew building within her.

She took Gerry's head in both her hands, her fingers running through his hair, and kissed him, hard. Her tongue found his, and they held each other as if they were becoming one. She felt as though she couldn't cleave close enough to him, that the urgency of her need to have him inside her couldn't be denied.

Through his trousers and her skirt she felt the hard shaft of his cock, and she knew his need was as urgent as hers. As their bodies, still fully clothed, moved against each other, the friction fueled both of them. She felt the constriction of her breasts pressed up against his chest, her erect nipples straining at the fabric. She traced the outline of his erection with her mound, and the feeling of his hardness against her clitoris drove her wild.

The clothes came flying off. He unbuttoned her with fumbling fingers, as she released him from his trousers. She stepped out of her dress and shift, he pulled his shirt, still buttoned, over his head, and they were on the bed, limbs and tongues entwined.

Gerry took her breasts in his hands.

"Your tits are magnificent," he said as he pressed them together and buried his face between them. He put first one nipple, and then the other in his mouth, and Rose felt the tip of his tongue circling. She ran her hands down his back, feeling his muscles and shoulder blades, holding him against her. She was supremely aware of every sensation—of the softness of his seemingly prehensile tongue, of the warmth of his hands on her breasts, of the slight roughness of his cheeks against her chest. And of the steely-hard feeling of his cock, lying in the crease between her thigh and torso.

With an effort she shifted him to her side and rolled him over on his back. She straddled him and ran her hands through the hair on his chest, starting at his belly and moving up to his nipples—as erect as her own. She pinched his nipples and he gasped, and she felt the reverberation as his penis strained under her.

She moved back a little, so she was straddling his thighs, and took his cock in both hands. It was slick with her wetness, and she held it firmly in her palms, rolling it between them and slowly working her way up toward its tip.

Gerry moaned, and Rose felt him gripping her thighs so hard that there were little white circles of flesh where his fingertips dug in.

She worked her way up and down the shaft of his cock twice more, and then positioned herself over him.

She slipped the tip of him in between the lips of her pussy. "Is this what you want?" she asked. "Do you want my cunt?"

He opened his eyes and looked at her. "I do want it," he said urgently. "I need it."

"It's ready for you," she said, but she didn't move. "It's warm and it's wet and it's ready."

He let out a groan that was almost a grunt, and tried to pull her down on him, but she resisted.

"Just imagine your cock sliding in, into that hot, wet hole," she whispered, all the while moving just a fraction of an inch so the very tip of his penis was moving in and out of her.

He moved back and forth under her with the frustration of imagining that very thing. And just when she thought he might pull her down by brute force, she sat down, engulfing the whole of him.

The sound he made was indescribable, loud and low at the same time.

"You'd better fuck me now," he said, and put his hands on her ass to keep her down on him. "I can't stand any more of that."

Fuck him, she did. She felt his length and breadth filling her, satisfying her. And with each stroke up and down she felt him anew. She lifted herself up and down, up and down, her hands on his chest.

His hands were still on her thighs, and she felt him lifting her, accelerating her pace. Her strokes got faster, and her cunt gripped him harder. She could feel every ridge of him as she moved, and as she reached her climax she felt him get even harder and knew he was reaching his own. He held her down on him, and the throes of his orgasm lengthened and heightened her own. She rocked back and forth, just a hairbreadth, to keep the waves coming, and then sat still as they subsided.

She opened her eyes to see that his were still closed. She smiled at what looked like his perfect happiness, and his eyelids fluttered open to her smile.

"Ah, Rose," he said, "you're a marvel."

She laughed. If she hadn't already been so flushed, she would have blushed at the compliment. She'd been called many things in her life, but never a marvel.

As reality set back in, she knew she had to get on with her work before she was missed, and she climbed off him and got dressed with easy efficiency.

Gerry looked ruefully from the clock to his clothes, lying in a heap on the floor. He pulled his dressing gown around him, and took Rose by her upper arms.

"Thank you," he said simply, looking her straight in the eyes.

She did blush now.

"I don't know why it's you who should do the thanking and not the other way around," she said.

"Well, I certainly feel as though you've given me something, and good manners dictate that I should thank you," said Gerard. "If you feel that *I* have given *you* something in return, then it's all the better."

"It's all the better, then," answered Rose. "But I've got to get back to my work."

She grinned at him, and was gone.

TEN

~

Gerry looked at the clock again. He should have already been downstairs. He opened the doors to the wardrobe, and was surveying its contents when he heard a bloodcurdling scream.

He ran out his door and looked both ways down the corridor. There, three doors to his right, he saw Lady Georgiana backing out of her own room, her face drained of its color.

He ran to her. "Lady Georgiana! Whatever is the matter?" As he asked the question, he followed her gaze into the room and saw for himself what the matter was. There was a dead peacock, a noose around its neck, hanging from the top of one of the bedposts.

"My dear," said Gerry, after he took a moment to absorb the scene. "Please come in and sit down. The bird is dead, and it will do you no harm now."

Georgiana did as she was bidden. By this time, several other people were gathered outside the door to her room, brought there by her scream. Among them was Lord Loughlin, who rushed in and knelt at Lady Georgiana's feet. "Are you hurt?" he asked anxiously.

"No," she said. "I am not hurt in the least." She was beginning to recover her wits, and was a little abashed at having attracted so much attention. "I am sorry to have frightened everyone. It's only a dead bird."

"It's a dead bird hanging from your bed," said Lord Loughlin hotly, "and you needn't apologize for your alarm." He was extremely perturbed at having such a situation in his house, and felt acutely for the girl. But he didn't want to make it any worse than it was, and he rose and urged the spectators in the hall to go down to luncheon.

Gerry remained behind, in part because he felt a responsibility because he was first on the scene, and in part because he couldn't very well go down to luncheon in his dressing gown.

"Tell us what happened," he said.

"There isn't much to tell," the girl said. "When we parted, Alexandra and I came back to the house to change, but I was waylaid by the O'Maras, who asked me about the grouse at Eastley. And once you start talking about grouse . . ." She shrugged, her humor returning with her equanimity.

"In any case," she went on, "I realized I had barely enough time to wash my face, and I came rushing upstairs. I opened my door, and that's what I saw."

"Did you see anyone in the corridor, anyone who didn't belong?" asked Lord Loughlin anxiously.

"I didn't see a soul. Everyone had already gone downstairs."

"A servant, perhaps?"

Georgiana paused, and thought. Yes, she had seen someone in the corridor! She was so used to having servants come and go that the sight hadn't even registered.

"I did see a servant. It was your parlor maid. Is Rose her name?"

"Rose?" Lord Loughlin asked, surprised. "It's hard to imagine that Rose would do such a thing."

Gerry, who knew exactly why Rose had been in the corridor at such an inopportune time, hastened to second Lord Loughlin. "I've spoken with her once or twice," he said, his face coloring, "and she seems like quite a nice girl. Besides, why on earth would she hang a dead peacock on your bedpost?"

"Why, indeed." Georgiana pondered the question. "It's certainly possible that she was simply making up the rooms, and had nothing to do with it."

"I will have a word with her," said Lord Loughlin, "but it could have been anyone with access to your room while you were gone. What time did you leave your room this morning?"

"It was about nine o'clock. I met Alexandra downstairs, and we went punting with Gerry. And I haven't been back to the room from that time until this."

"Then there were several hours in which the bird could have been put there," mused Robert Loughlin. "I suppose, theoretically, it could have been anyone, not just Rose."

"I daresay it could have been." Here Lady Georgiana hesitated. But she thought she owed these two men, who clearly cared for her, a complete explanation. "I am afraid I have made some enemies since my arrival here."

Both gentlemen knew what she referred to, but neither of them wanted to discuss it explicitly. "I am aware . . ." Lord Loughlin trailed off.

"And this is not the first incident," she went on.

The two men looked at her in surprise, and she told them the story of the poison ivy.

As she finished her narrative, they were interrupted by the arrival of Bruce Barnes. "Lady Loughlin told me what happened, and asked me to send someone to dispose of the peacock," he said. "But I thought you might not want the servants seeing this, so I came myself."

He looked at the bird. "It's Eustace," he said.

"Eustace?" Georgiana asked in surprise. "Do you name all the peacocks?"

"Not all of them. But Eustace was a kind of paterfamilias. He was one of the first birds we had, and was cock of the walk until recently, when he started to get feeble. He was a good bird, but I thought he might be nearing his end."

"So no one killed him just to do this?" asked Loughlin.

"I don't think so, no." Barnes released the peacock from its noose and took it down with real gentleness. Georgiana liked him for caring, and smiled sadly as she watched him.

As he put the bird under his arm to take it out, a note fluttered out of its mouth and landed on the floor. Georgiana bent over to pick it up, but she didn't have to unfold it to know what it said. She didn't want to display it with Barnes in the room, and she crumpled it in her fist.

None of the men asked her what it said.

There was an uncomfortable moment, broken by Lord Loughlin saying to Barnes, "Let's dispose of that, shall we?"

The two men took the carcass and left Gerry alone with Georgiana.

"Steady on, my dear," Gerry said with a smile. "It's a stupid prank, and you mustn't let it bother you."

Georgiana smiled wanly. She couldn't quite agree that it was a stupid prank. She felt the menace beneath its surface, and that made it hard for her to laugh off the incident. Still, she thought she must be a poor creature if she couldn't stand up to this.

She forced her smile to brighten. "I'll admit that it shook me, but I'm fine now. Let us both get down to luncheon before all the best bits are gone."

Gerry wasn't quite convinced that she was fine, and he took a long look back at his young friend before he went out and shut the door to her room behind him. He went to his own room, traded his dressing gown for the first clothes that came to hand, and went downstairs.

It took Lady Georgiana a bit longer before she felt she could go down and join the company. It hadn't been difficult to laugh off the bouquet of poison ivy, but a dead peacock in a noose hanging from her bedstead felt much more threatening. But if it was threatening, what, exactly, was she being threatened with?

She told herself that it was highly unlikely anyone in the house would take the fanatical step of doing her harm. It was much more probable that this was a prank, or the venting of hatred, or an extreme sign of disapproval. She had nothing to fear, she told herself, only something to bear.

She sighed, put on a favorite white sprigged muslin dress that never failed to improve her mood, and went downstairs. Once she was able to put the peacock incident in the back of her mind, her desire to make things right with Freddy gravitated once more to the front. Although she still believed that what he had said to her had been unconscionably rude, she realized that she'd been treating him like a child, and thought he had the right to resent it. Besides, it was more important to her to be on good terms with him than it was to see every slight avenged.

She spotted him as she came down the staircase, lunching with Miss Niven. Although she would have preferred to have spoken to him alone, there was nothing she had to say to him that her friend couldn't hear.

"Freddy!" she said, as she approached them. "I've been searching for you high and low."

"When it's me you're looking for," he said, grinning, "you should always try low first." He didn't seem in the least put out at seeing her.

"That must have been my mistake," said Georgiana, falling into the same bantering tone. "I've only just finished high. But here you are, and I want to apologize." Her expression turned serious.

Miss Niven's eyebrows went up. There didn't seem to be any constraint between Lady Georgiana and young Freddy Loughlin, whose acquaintance she had just made, and she wondered what the offense could have been.

"Nonsense," said Freddy. "Old friends are entitled to take liberties, you know." He smiled at Georgiana and turned back to Alexandra. "I have heard you're a smashing tennis player," he said, with his most winning smile.

But Lady Georgiana couldn't have the incident of the slap glossed over so quickly.

"Freddy," she said. "There are liberties that even old friends are not entitled to take, and yesterday's was one of them." She took a breath and was going to continue, but Freddy cut in before she could go on.

"Oh, rot," he said. "But even if there are, least said, soonest mended and all that." He smiled again at Lady Georgiana, and turned to Alexandra. This time, though, he turned his body ever so slightly to face the woman he so clearly wanted to talk to without interruption.

"And is it true?" he asked, as though Georgiana had never interrupted.

Alexandra, profoundly uncomfortable, looked at Freddy, and then at Georgiana, and then back to Freddy. She didn't have any comment immediately to hand that could pour oil on these waters, so she simply answered the question. "'Smashing' would most certainly overstate the case."

Georgiana saw her friend's discomfort, and came to her rescue. "'Smashing' most certainly would not overstate the case," she said, taking Alexandra's arm and giving it a squeeze. "And neither would 'modest.'" She told Freddy he ought to challenge Miss Niven to a game only if he was prepared to be taken down a notch or two, and then excused herself to get lunch.

It was only as she walked to the buffet table that the confusion cleared and she understood why Freddy hadn't wanted to talk about what happened between them. He'd moved on to Alexandra, and in the space of just one day! The thought didn't anger Georgiana. She rather marveled at the very plastic affections of young men as she sat down to cold beef and biscuits.

The peacock incident had made her late for lunch, and she was still eating after everyone else had moved on to naps, walks, correspondence, or whatever else they had planned for the afternoon. Rose, the parlor maid, had just finishing clearing away the dishes and was hovering in the background, waiting as unobtrusively as possible for Lady Georgiana to finish her meal.

"I'm so sorry," Georgiana said to the maid. "Here you're trying to get things cleaned up and I'm daydreaming and lollygagging." She took a last sip of tea and started to get up, trying to imagine this woman hanging a peacock on her bedpost.

"Oh, no," said Rose. "Please don't rouse yourself on my account. I can come back for your dishes later." Rose, like everyone else in the house, had heard the stories of their noble guest's dalliance with Barnes, but she was inclined to like Georgiana for it. Had they been born in the same sphere, the two women might well have been friends. She had no idea about either of the notes Georgiana had received, or that her very own name had been spoken in connection with them, and she went about her work in perfect innocence.

Georgiana appreciated Rose's willingness to accommodate her, and couldn't imagine that the maid was the culprit. She protested that she wouldn't prolong the clearing of lunch any longer than she already had, and went up to her room.

Rose took the dishes down to the scullery and handed them over to Maureen, who was standing in the middle of her spotless domain, wiping down a perfectly clean table.

"Here's the last of it," Rose told her.

"I thought that last batch was the last of it," said Maureen, looking at the dishes with distaste. "I've already washed everything up."

"Sorry," said Rose. "Lady Georgiana was late to lunch."

Maureen made a face. "That one's quite the princess, isn't she?" She took the dishes and had them cleaned, dried, and stored away in a matter of ten minutes. Then she wiped her hands on a dish towel, took off her apron, and left the scullery, knowing she had at least an hour before she had to be back. She headed out across the grounds to Bruce Barnes's cottage.

Barnes lived in the old gamekeeper's cottage, a small, ancient stone house about a quarter mile from the main house. When the Loughlins had engaged his services, they offered him a suite of rooms in the house itself, but Barnes preferred the more austere, but private accommodations of the cottage.

He and Maureen had met there many an afternoon, and he often made it a point to be at home, dealing with paperwork or letters, when he knew she would be free. Today was no exception.

When he began his intrigue with Lady Georgiana, his first impulse was to keep Maureen at arm's length. Although he couldn't have known that the intrigue would be public knowledge, he did know that information like that had a way of seeping into servants' quarters, and he didn't think it likely he could keep the secret. His life would be simpler, he knew, if he limited his intimacy to one woman at a time.

Two things got the better of him. The first was that Maureen didn't seem to mind. The only remarks she made about it were amused. The second was that he thought he would have a better chance of controlling himself with Georgiana if he had a safety valve in Maureen. He'd always been a man of animal appetites, and when those appetites were whetted, he sometimes had less control over himself than he would have liked. And so he was glad to hear Maureen's familiar knock at his door.

He opened the door and smiled at her. He stepped aside and, without a word, she walked in. He closed the door and shot the bolt.

"You look happy to see me," she said, a sly look on her face.

"When have I not been happy to see you?"

"But when have you had an earl's daughter at your beck and call?"

"I'm a gardener, Maureen," he said. "Maybe a glorified gardener but, even so, I hardly have an earl's daughter at my beck and call."

"So you're not proposing to marry her, then?" Her voice dripped sarcasm. She wanted him to know just how likely she thought it that Barnes would marry Georgiana.

This hit him hard, because it went straight to the heart of the conflict in his own breast. On the one hand, he genuinely believed that glorified gardeners didn't have a fighting chance with earls' daughters. On the other, though, he harbored a hope that maybe, just maybe, Lady Georgiana was unconventional enough and their magnetism was strong enough . . . He didn't articulate the thought, even to himself, but he knew it was there. What a triumph that would be.

Aloud, he simply scoffed. "Don't be daft." He stepped toward her, took her hand, and pulled her toward him.

"You can't blame me for pursuing the novelty," he said. "I'm a man, after all." He slipped his arm around her waist. "But it's nothing like what we have."

It was her turn to scoff. "What we have?" She gave a harsh laugh. "What we have is a jolly good time, nothing more." But she harbored a conflict similar to Barnes's. He wasn't as far above her in social standing as Georgiana was above him, but the difference in their status was large enough to render it unlikely that he would ever marry her. But not impossible, she told herself, not impossible. What a triumph that would be.

She knew, though, that if he even suspected that she had such thoughts he would be lost to her, and she wasn't ready to give him up. She ran her hands up his chest and began to unbutton his shirt.

Barnes was relieved that the conversational part of their meeting appeared to be over, and they were moving on to the physical. He let her finish unbuttoning his shirt, and turned her around so he could unbutton her in return. Her blouse had a nearly endless series of tiny buttons running from her neck to below where it tucked into her skirt, and his big fingers fumbled with them.

She smiled to herself as she sensed his frustration, and reached her hands behind her to run her hands up the inside of his thighs. She found his cock, which was not yet hard. Through the stiff fabric of his trousers, she fondled it gently. He groaned softly, and stopped fussing with her buttons.

She pressed the fabric on either side of his penis hard against his hips, imprisoning his cock beneath the taut cotton. Then she lightened one hand's pressure while pressing harder with the other, and then switched. As she did that, the fabric pressed against his cock, pushing it to one side and then the other, all the while keeping it trapped, still pointed toward the floor.

As his erection mounted, it was almost painful to be kept in that position, but the combination of the pressure and the emerging pain was exquisite. He put his hands on Maureen's shoulders and wasn't even aware that he was gripping her hard enough to turn his knuckles white.

She knew where his threshold was, and when his cock got so stiff that it pushed hard against the fabric, she released it. She slipped her hand under his waistband and took it in her hand, letting it, at last, point skyward. Then she took her hand away and backed against him. She stood on tiptoe so she could let his cock nestle between the cheeks of her ass, and she swayed back and forth.

Barnes grabbed her by the hips and ground so hard against her that they almost lost their balance.

"I need to finish your buttons," he said, and went back to that task.

The unbuttoning finally complete, he eased her out of her blouse. Underneath, she wore an old-fashioned whalebone corset, laced loosely.

"Ah," he said. "The corset."

"I haven't worn it in a while," she said. "I thought it was time."

She made short work of taking off her boots, stockings, drawers, and skirt, and stood in front of him naked but for the off-white muslin corset. She was firm and succulent in thigh and breast, narrow and delicate in wrist and ankle. Her skin was milky white, set off by her reddish brown hair. She had freckles on her arms and back, but none on her belly or thighs.

"This is a view I could never tire of," he said as he reached out and ran the back of his hands down the front of her thighs and then up again, finishing where they came together in a small triangle of hair two shades darker than that on her head.

He traced the twin crevices where her thighs met her pubis with his index fingers, and she involuntarily stepped her feet apart, responding to the stimulus of his touch. From the tops of her thighs, he moved up to the points of her hip bones jutting out on either side of her smooth, firm, slightly rounded belly.

He turned his hands so the palms faced him, and edged his fingers under the bottom of the corset. It was loose, and his hands fit under it easily. He followed the curve of her waist around to her sides, and then took his hands out from under the corset and let them sit on her hips.

And then he kissed her. His tongue was as soft as his hands were rough, and Maureen thought he tasted faintly sweet. Every time she kissed him she was surprised anew that such a tender, sweet kiss could come from such a large, hard man.

She could still taste him as he turned her around and walked her into his bedchamber.

His bed was a large, elegant four-poster, incongruous in the modest stone cottage. When he'd first arrived, the house had been equipped with nothing more than a straw-filled mattress on a makeshift platform, and the Loughlins had been quick to send down a proper bed from the main house.

Maureen, her back still to Barnes, took hold of one of the posts at the foot of the bed and braced herself. He took the grosgrain ribbon laces in his hands and began to tighten the corset. He started at the top and pulled it so tight that she gasped. Then he put a finger over where the laces crossed between the top eyelets, to hold it tight, and went on to the next set of eyelets. In this fashion, he worked his way down.

He used his considerable strength to tie her in so tightly that she could take only the shallowest of breaths. She could take in enough air to stay conscious, but the quick little breaths made her feel light-headed almost immediately.

Barnes finished lacing her in, tied the ribbons securely, and turned her around. Her waist, narrowed by the corset, accentuated her round, firm breasts and full, strong thighs. He put his hands around that waist— they almost went all the way around—and buried his head between her breasts, which were held high by the top of the corset.

He ran his hand up her back, and then up to her hair. He pulled her head back and kissed the side of her exposed neck.

Maureen felt his lips, and then his tongue, and then his teeth, and her own arousal began to mount. The more pleasure she felt, the more air she needed, and the harder it was to get enough. The giddiness that resulted heightened the experience for her in a way she didn't quite understand.

Barnes, still wearing trousers and his unbuttoned shirt, pushed her backward onto the bed and removed the rest of his clothes. He knelt, straddling her legs, and her perspective was such that his fully erect cock looked even larger than it was. She reached up to take it in her hand, but he brushed her hand away.

"You're not allowed to move," Barnes said, roughly but quietly. She spread her arms wide and gripped either side of the mattress to keep herself from touching him.

He moved up the bed until he was straddling her midsection, and then came down on all fours. He worked his penis between her breasts and pulsed gently forward and back.

All she could do was watch. She yearned to be in contact with him, to hold him in her hand, to feel his pressure against the mound between her legs, but she knew that if she moved he would withdraw altogether.

The waiting drove her mad, and she felt herself growing faint as she panted for breath.

Barnes sat up again, and finally—finally!—touched her breasts. He started making gentle circles around her nipples, but soon held the twin orbs fully in his hands, moving his fingers over them as though he were testing their texture.

Then he reached across her to open a drawer in his nightstand and pulled out a length of bright red silk. He balled it up in his hand and put it in her mouth.

The gag was the last restriction on her airflow. Now, with her breathing restricted two ways and her excitement on the increase, she felt herself slipping to the edge of fainting. Half her attention was on her breath, and the other half was on the fact that Barnes was easing his cock into her.

His slow, shallow thrusts brought Maureen almost to the brink. The room was spinning; she couldn't keep her lover in focus. Her lungs and her cunt were competing for her attention, and she was engulfed in a whirlwind of sensation.

And then he was in her all the way. Deep, hard, insistent. Through her fog, she heard his climactic moans, and her own orgasm took on a life of its own. Her light-headedness made her experience it almost as though it came from without rather than within. It engulfed her completely and there was a moment—there always was—when she did think she would lose consciousness.

She didn't, though, and Barnes took the gag out so her heartbeat and her breathing could slow. When the last vestiges of sensation had ebbed, she turned over and Barnes loosened her laces. She filled her lungs over and over, experiencing the simple pleasure of breathing again.

Barnes watched her recover herself as he pulled on his trousers and shirt.

"I love it that you like that," he said. "Not every girl would."

She took one last deep breath and sat up. "I'm not every girl," she said and stood up to collect her clothes.

"I've got to get back. Dinner service starts soon."

He smiled at her with uncharacteristic tenderness. "Thank you for visiting," he said, with only the barest touch of irony.

She smiled back, got dressed, and was gone.

ELEVEN

Lady Georgiana little knew what was going on in other parts of the estate that afternoon, as she sat in her room after lunch, an unread book lying closed in her lap. She sat in the window seat and was just feeling the heavy-lidded sense that she was about to fall asleep when there was a knock on the door.

She shook her head briskly to rouse herself. As yet, the only unexpected visitor she'd had at Penfield had been Barnes, and she expected that this was him. She took a moment to arrange herself to appear to best advantage. "Come in," she called.

Georgiana experienced a frisson of disappointment when it wasn't Barnes, but Alexandra who walked into her room.

"I'm so sorry to bother you," the girl said. "I hope I'm not interrupting."

"Not in the slightest," said Georgiana, recovering herself. She held up the book, John Stuart Mill's *The Subjection of Women*. "I know books are supposed to improve one's mind," she said with a laugh, "but I suppose one must actually read them for that improvement to take place. You have interrupted me staring out my window while not reading my book."

Alexandra, who had felt some trepidation about coming to her friend's room, was put at her ease. Still, she hesitated a moment.

"I have come to ask a favor," she said.

"I will certainly grant it if it is in my power to do so."

"I'm engaged to play tennis with Freddy this afternoon, and I wonder if I might borrow the trousers you wore to play with me the other day."

Georgiana laughed aloud.

Miss Niven blushed and went on. "I'm not sure that they'll fit. I'm larger than you are. But they seemed to have some extra room when you wore them, and you looked so much more comfortable than I felt, and I'd hoped . . ." She felt herself to be babbling, and stopped talking.

"Of course you must have them!" Georgiana said with enthusiasm. "And I'm sure they'll fit you." She realized that it took some courage both for Alexandra to wear trousers and for her to ask Georgiana to borrow them, and she wanted to encourage her friend.

She went to the armoire and took the trousers down from a shelf where Hortense had put them after they'd been washed and ironed.

Alexandra took them, unfolded them, and held the waistband up to her own waist a little skeptically.

"Don't worry," Georgiana told her. "Once you take off your skirt and drawers, they'll fit perfectly."

Alexandra looked worried. "Drawers?"

"Oh, you can't wear drawers underneath. They just bunch up and chafe, and then you can't run."

"Then what do you wear underneath?"

"Nothing whatsoever." Georgiana saw Alexandra's look of consternation. "And you'll feel free and liberated, I promise. Besides," she added, picking up the book, "John Stuart Mill would certainly approve. Tennis skirts certainly qualify as subjection of women."

Miss Niven didn't look quite convinced, but being around Georgiana made her feel daring, and she took the trousers, determined to wear them.

"Will you come and watch us play?" she asked.

Georgiana considered. It would certainly be a game worth watching. But, remembering Freddy's reception of her at lunch, she thought it prudent to decline. She was sure he would prefer to be alone with Miss Niven.

"I'm sure it will be an excellent game," she said, "but I have a prior engagement with Mr. Mill." Here she waved the book. "And I am determined to find out how women are subjected and what we should do about it, all before dinner."

"Well, thank you for the trousers. I hope they improve my play."

"I'm sure they must. Good luck, and tell me all about the game at dinner."

Alexandra went back to her room to change. She took off her skirt and drawers and pulled on the trousers. Her waist was as narrow as Georgiana's, and the waistband buttoned easily. The difference in their figures was in the hips, and Alexandra's rounded bottom and curved thighs filled the pants more fully than Georgiana's boyish shape did.

She took a few steps and marveled at the feel of it. Since she was a little girl, she'd never been out-of-doors in anything other than a skirt with drawers and stockings underneath. To feel only one thin layer of fabric between her skin and the air was a revelation.

She ran across the room to see what it felt like. She was unimpeded! Nothing got in the way when she put one foot in front of the other. Nothing swished or swirled or tangled!

The doubts she'd had about appearing in trousers evaporated in her enjoyment of the sensation of wearing them. Her interaction with Georgiana, combined with an unexpected swell of confidence borne of something as simple as freedom of movement, led her to leave her room with something almost like a swagger.

She met Freddy at the front door.

"You've got Lady G's trousers!" Freddy said in astonishment before his better judgment had a chance to tell him that Miss Niven would perhaps prefer not to have attention drawn to her attire.

She reddened. "She seemed so comfortable playing in trousers, and, as I have none of my own, I thought to borrow hers."

"You look smashing!" Freddy did nothing to hide his admiration, and looked unabashedly at the shape, so clearly visible, of her buttocks and thighs. Had Alexandra been aware just how clearly visible her shape was, she might have reconsidered her decision.

She reddened further. "Shall we go?" she asked, not being able to think of a better way to change the subject.

"We shall." Freddy opened the front door for her with exaggerated gallantry, and they headed out to the tennis court.

All the necessary equipment was waiting for them, and they each picked up a racket.

Freddy had grown up with the game, and thought himself to be, if not an expert, at least a skilled player. His assessment of his play, though, had more to do with his conception of himself as an all-around accomplished young man than with his actual level of expertise. To his mind, witty, rakish, charming young men all played tennis well, and Freddy was certainly witty, rakish, and charming. Ergo, reason dictated that not only did he play tennis well, but he rode to hounds, held his liquor, and could engage any eligible young lady on any subject.

Reason, though, wasn't winning the day. Freddy found that the distraction of Alexandra's movement put him off his game. He missed shots he should have reached, and sent too many balls out of bounds or into the net. Alexandra, by contrast, was at her very best. She leaped and ran and stretched and smashed, and was exhilarated by her own prowess.

After a stretch when Alexandra won five points in a row, Freddy made a concerted effort to gather his wits and focus his energy. He blocked out the image of the beautiful girl in the alluring trousers across the court and pictured instead Stiffy, his Oxford nemesis. By this means he was able to muster what skill he possessed, and the score began to even out.

Alexandra, though, still had the lead, and she was determined to hold on to it. She exerted herself in a way Freddy had never seen a girl do, until she was wet with sweat and panting like a racehorse. There was nothing delicate or ladylike in her demeanor or appearance, and Freddy found the novelty and physicality to be a very compelling combination.

Still, compelling or no, he didn't want to lose to her. He conjured Stiffy once more and, in answer to a brisk forehand from Miss Niven, he placed a precise little drop shot just over the net. He'd thought it unreachable, but she ran for the net with all her strength. As she lunged for the ball, her left foot slid on the grass, and she buckled with a cry of pain.

Freddy was over the net in an instant, kneeling at her side. It was clear from her grimace that she'd hurt herself. "Miss Niven, you mustn't move until we can find out if anything's broken."

"I don't think it is," she said through clenched teeth as she shifted her weight to take the pressure off the ankle that had slid under her. There was relief in her voice when she found she could move her foot. "It does hurt awfully, but I don't believe it's broken."

The ankle had already begun to swell. "It's a nasty sprain, then," Freddy said.

Once his fear that his companion had been seriously hurt was allayed, Freddy saw that the situation was ripe with possibilities.

"It doesn't look like you can walk," he said, with something very like hope in his voice.

"I can try," Miss Niven said dubiously, trying once more to move her foot, and wincing with the effort.

"No," said Freddy definitively. "You mustn't try. I can carry you back to the house."

"You most certainly cannot," she told him, alarmed at the prospect.

"I can and I will. You're just a slip of a thing."

She blushed, and almost smiled. "When I said 'cannot,' I did not mean that you weren't capable. I only meant that I could not submit to it."

"Submit, rot! Why ever not?"

What could she say? The real answer was, *Because you would touch me in places where there would be only a thin layer of cloth between your hands and my skin*, but she couldn't very well say that. The best she could do was, "I'm not sure either your dignity or mine could withstand the assault."

Freddy laughed. "For my part, I cannot see how carrying a beautiful, injured girl to safety could do anything but bolster my dignity. And I promise to do it in such a way as to protect *your* dignity in the process." He knelt down and started to slip a hand behind her knees to pick her up, but she pushed him away. "Can we not get a cart?" she asked feebly.

"No, we cannot get a cart. It is imperative that we get you back to the house so we can sit you on cushions, put ice on your ankle, and feed you restorative beef broth." He tried again to pick her up, and this time she made no protest.

He lifted her, one hand under her knees and the other behind her back, from the lawn. "There, now, put your arms around my neck." She did as she was bidden, and he started back toward the house.

The effort required to carry a girl—even a slim girl—a quarter mile is not insignificant, but Freddy felt it not a whit. His left hand was on her thigh and his right on her rib cage, and her breasts were pressed against him as she hung on his neck, and those were the only things he could think about. He felt the muscles in her legs ripple as she changed position, and her breasts bounced gently with his gait. And her smell! She smelled of soap and sweat and sweetness, and he breathed her in.

His erection had begun as soon he'd picked her up, and as they walked to the house it got harder and harder. Eventually, it pointed straight up so as to be grazed by Alexandra's buttocks with every step he took. The feel of her against him aroused him more than he thought possible, and he subtly adjusted her position against him to maximize the contact between her ass and his cock.

Had she not been caught up in her own thoughts, Alexandra might have realized what he was doing, and been mortified. But in her consciousness the idea that his touch, through so few clothes, was improper was doing battle with the sense that his touch, through so few clothes, was wonderful, and she had no thoughts to spare for *his* consciousness.

He looked at her face, and saw with relief that she wasn't looking at his. Her eyes were cast down, trying not to engage with him any more than she had to. And so he let it happen.

He slowed his walk just a bit and focused on the feel of the weight of the girl against the stony hardness of his penis, first on one side, then on the other, as he took each step. He wondered that she could have no awareness of it, but she seemed not to. His excitement mounted, exacerbated by the effort he had to make to keep the signs of his pleasure off his face, and keep his gait steady.

He would have liked to prolong his pleasure, but he knew he couldn't risk it. And so, when he felt the first waves of his orgasm approach, he let them take him over. He had to keep walking, and he had to give no visible sign of his all-consuming climax, but those constraints didn't tamp down the feeling at all. If anything, they heightened it. Despite his best efforts at control, he couldn't stop his grip on Alexandra from tightening and the smallest gasp from escaping his mouth.

That broke into her reverie, and she looked up at him for the first time. "Are you all right?" she asked. "Am I too heavy?"

"You?" he said, striving mightily to make his tone sound normal. "I told you. You're just a slip of a thing." He forced his breathing to return to normal. "Besides, we're almost at the house."

As he said this, they rounded the last bend in the path. The house came into view and, with it, several other guests and their hostess.

"My goodness!" exclaimed Paulette, as she saw her son carrying Miss Niven toward the house. "What has happened? Are you hurt?"

Alexandra managed a smile. "We were playing tennis, and I'm afraid I've twisted my ankle rather badly. Luckily, Freddy was there to see that I had transportation back to safety."

Paulette looked from Freddy to Alexandra and back. With a mother's perspicacity, she saw immediately that there was something beyond a tennis game going on between the two. Could Alexandra be a match for Freddy? The possibilities began whirling through her mind, but she forced them into the background while she attended to the girl's immediate needs.

"We must get you inside and get ice on that ankle," she said. She could see that Freddy was exhausted, although she could not know that the cause wasn't simply the effort of carrying his charge. "We'll get you in a chair and carry you into the house in high style."

She needed two men to recruit for the task, and turned to ask Gerry, who had been standing behind her. But when she turned around, she saw that he was gone. She just caught his back as he retreated into the house. A lover's perspicacity is almost the equal of a mother's, and, like Lady Loughlin, he'd seen that there was some kind of undercurrent between Alexandra and Freddy. He didn't like it, not at all, but he decided that the prudent thing to do was not to intrude on this scene. He wanted to mull over the situation privately and decide how he should proceed now that he had a rival. Of one thing he had not a shadow of a doubt: He certainly wasn't going to cede this girl to a young whippersnapper sent down from Oxford!

Meanwhile, though, Lady Loughlin had to turn to Mr. Sheffield. "Henry," she said, "can you please get one of those chairs?" She pointed to a seating area just off the lawn, and turned back to Alexandra, still in Freddy's arms.

Mr. Sheffield dutifully brought the chair, and then he and Mr. O'Mara, who was also among the group of guests, together carried her in, sedan-chair style.

"We will put you in the front drawing room window seat, where you will be comfortable and can watch the activity out the front window," Lady Loughlin said, steering the men toward the room.

"Oh, please," said Alexandra, "I would much rather be in my own room. I'd only be in the way." She was thinking about how she was dressed, and her disheveled state, and wanted nothing more than the privacy of her own bedchamber.

"Nonsense!" said Lady Loughlin. "We all intend to wait on you hand and foot, and we can't very well do that if you're hiding away in your room."

Miss Niven was just about to protest again when her companion, Miss Mumford, came rushing in.

"Alexandra, my dear, what has happened?" she asked in agitation as she pushed her way through what was now a substantial entourage gathered around the girl.

"Don't be upset," she said to the older woman. "I've only twisted my ankle playing tennis. I'm in very good hands."

As she made her way to Alexandra's side, Miss Mumford got her first good look at her young friend and gasped openly. "What are you . . ." she began, but then stopped before she could say, "wearing?" A split second's reflection told her not to call attention to Miss Niven's attire. After a pause, she said, ". . . going to do about that ankle? It needs ice, I suppose."

"Her ankle needs ice, but I daresay her spirits need good company." Lady Loughlin addressed Miss Mumford. "Can you help us convince her to let us enthrone her in the drawing room, where all her little needs and wants will be ours to fulfill?"

Had Lady Loughlin not been so wrapped up in her own argument, she might have known that she was making her appeal in the wrong quarter.

Miss Mumford was the soul of tact. "As she would like to go to her room, I think you must give me the privilege of attending to her needs and wants, just for a while," she said with an air of finality. "I promise to share those duties just as soon as she recovers herself enough to come downstairs."

It was the first time in a long time that Alexandra had been grateful for Miss Mumford's ministrations, and she felt real relief as Mr. Sheffield and Mr. O'Mara carried her up to her room.

Freddy had watched all of this from the sidelines, and took the first decent opportunity to head to his own room to bathe and change his clothes. As he sat in the bath, he thought about Alexandra. He knew, more by instinct than by reason, that she was not a girl to be toyed with. With Lady Georgiana, he thought, he could certainly flirt. He even thought he had done himself no great harm by venturing a bolder proposition, though he had been rejected. Still, the rejection rankled. She had rejected him, and not the blasted gardener!

From Lady Georgiana, his thoughts wandered back to Miss Niven. She was a horse of another color! And, to Freddy's mind, she was a ripping fine horse of a beautiful color, and he thought perhaps she would be worth the having. He thought himself too young to seriously consider marriage, but he also wondered when another girl like her would come his way.

Dressing, he thought of the walk back from the tennis court, and how much it aroused him to have the girl in his arms. Because he was a young man of eighteen, this had predictable results, and once he was dressed he headed straight for the stable, saddled Prancer, and rode off in the direction of the Glück dairy.

When he got there, he dismounted and tied the horse to a tree, and went off in search of Gretchen. He wasn't absolutely avoiding Gretchen's parents, but he knew from experience that things went more smoothly if he didn't encounter them. Approaching on foot was, if not stealthy, at least inconspicuous.

He looked first in the barn where the cows were kept, and found it empty. The cows were out grazing, and Gretchen had evidently already finished cleaning it out and making it ready for the evening milking. There was another barn for the horses and other animals, and he found Gretchen mucking out stalls. He watched her for a moment or two. She was fresh and beautiful, spirited and strong, and any man who had her could be considered fortunate indeed.

The sound of the shovel against the wooden floor masked his approach, and when he grabbed her around the waist she started and dropped a shovelful of horse manure and straw on the clean barn floor.

It took her only a moment to know who it was, and although she was happy to see him she feigned severity. "Freddy! Look what you've made me do." She gestured to the pile on the floor.

It was the work of an instant to shovel the manure into the cart, and Freddy had it done almost before Gretchen had finished her sentence.

"You know what else I can make you do?" he said, raising his eyebrows and grinning.

"You can make me lose an afternoon's work, that's what."

"Now, how could that be when the afternoon is almost over?"

"An evening's work, then."

"Oh, I think we can get you back in time to finish all that needs doing." He again took her by the waist and pulled her toward him. She allowed herself to be pulled, but leaned away a bit and crossed her arms in front of her. "What needs doing now is that the horses need to be fed," she said, still stern.

"And would that necessitate a trip to the hayloft?" Freddy asked.

"Yes. That most certainly would necessitate a trip to the hayloft. What's that to you?"

"Well, perhaps you need some help fetching the hay."

"Since I was ten years old I've fetched the hay by myself, without help from you or anyone, almost every day of my life."

"Well, then, the novelty of assistance should brighten your day." Freddy released her, gestured toward the hayloft with one hand in the air, and bowed gallantly.

Gretchen giggled and ran for the ladder, Freddy close on her heels.

Once up, they both flopped in the hay and rolled into the back corner, which was fragrant, dusky, and familiar. Gretchen reached for the buttons of Freddy's trousers, but he checked her. "Will you take off your dress?" he said simply.

Gretchen's dress was an uncomplicated affair, a white muslin skirt topped by a blue cambric bodice with buttons up the front. She started to unbutton them, and Freddy sat back on his haunches, watching.

Their lovemaking was usually a hurried affair, without the time or the privacy to remove all the fabric that came between skin and skin. But their interludes in the hayloft were different. They weren't afraid of being discovered, and could indulge in the luxury of nakedness.

He loved to watch her undress, to watch the parts of her body be revealed one by one, knowing that they were his to touch, to caress. Gretchen wriggled out of her dress, and Freddy reached a hand out to touch her creamy shoulder, and to run his hand down the inside of her arm. When he reached her hand, he took it in his and raised it to his lips. He kissed the middle of her palm, and then released it.

She unlaced the ribbons that closed the top of her shift, and then started on its buttons. Slowly she went down the row, watching Freddy watching her. When the shift was open, she paused a moment. Freddy ran the back of his hand from her chest down to the top of her drawers, feeling her warmth and the swell of her breasts as his hand passed between them.

He opened her shift, exposing her full, heavy breasts. He loved the swell underneath and the upturned nipples, and he leaned over to kiss first one and then the other. As he took one breast in each hand he marveled that they were cool while the rest of her body was warm. He loved the way their weight filled his palm, and he caressed them gently.

Gretchen reached for his shirt and soon had it off. She touched him in much the way he had touched her, softly and gently. They were often together in a way that was urgent and almost rough, but their mood today was slow and sweet.

He eased her shift off her shoulders, and traced her waist just above the top of her drawers. She untied them, and eased them down over her knees and off. Freddy spread a soft wool blanket they kept there for the purpose over the prickly hay and Gretchen lay down on it. She reached back over her head to make a pillow with the hay, and Freddy admired the way her muscles moved under her skin.

She lay before him perfectly naked, and Freddy thought nothing could be better than this. Her hair, almost the same color as the hay, spread out under where she rested her head, and her milk-white skin stood out against the dark green of the blanket.

He stepped out of his trousers and knelt between her knees. She started to sit up, reaching for him, but he again checked her. "Let me do the touching," he said, and brushed the backs of his fingers against the insides of her thighs. She closed her eyes and let herself be immersed in the sensation.

He traced her whole body with his fingertips, starting by reaching behind him to her feet. He felt every dip, every rise, every bone, and every crevice. Her body was intimately familiar to him, but it was as though he were discovering it anew. His touch was light but certain, and Gretchen gave herself up to it. She felt it particularly in places that surprised her—behind her knee, under her arm. Slowly, slowly, her feelings mounted. Her skin tingled where his fingers touched it, and the wetness built inside her. Initially, she had found it easy to lie still, but as she became more aroused she began to want to move to him, against him, around him.

And then, as though he knew her need, he was inside her. She felt the tip of his penis penetrate the lips of her vulva, releasing the warm dew that had built up inside. And then the whole of him was deep within her.

He had one hand on either side of her, propping himself up, but she wanted to feel the full length of his body against her. She pulled him down, and he sighed as he thrust deeper.

He held her head in his hands, burying his fingers in her thick blond hair, and he kissed her. His tongue filled her mouth as his cock filled her cunt and she felt completed.

They were in perfect synchrony as he pulsed slowly and deeply inside her. With each pulse, she got a little closer to what was to come, and she could feel his increasing heat and knew he was too. Still he went slowly. Even as they both reached the edge together, he kept up the regular rhythm.

And then they were at the edge—together, but each absorbed in separate sensations. They were each attuned, momentarily, only to themselves, succumbing to the encompassing power of the pleasure inside them.

When the last pulses died down, Freddy rolled over and lay down beside her. They looked at the ceiling of the barn in silence, enjoying the calm after the storm.

Gretchen was the first to get up, and she smiled at him as she reached for her underclothes. As she dressed, she said, "Didn't you say something about helping me with the hay?"

Freddy took his cue and also got dressed. "That is why we came up here, is it not?" He picked up a pitchfork and began pitching the hay down to the floor of the barn. "But I daresay this isn't so difficult that you couldn't have done it yourself."

Gretchen punched him in the arm and laughed. They climbed down the ladder, and he kissed her and left to recover Prancer. He knew that, someday, he would have to give up this girl, but he was very glad it was not today.

TWELVE

Had Alexandra known where Freddy had gone, it might have been easier for her to sort through her thoughts. Her sheltered life had been such that Freddy's had been the first male hands to touch her in any but an ordinary way. That touch had awakened feelings and sensations that were new to her, and she needed time and privacy to sort them through.

Miss Mumford, though, was inclined to give her neither.

"My dear Alexandra," she had said, as soon as the two were alone in Miss Niven's room, "you know I am not quick to criticize."

Alexandra nodded, knowing no such thing, but knowing also that nothing was to be gained by contradiction.

"I am paid by your guardian to be caretaker of your moral development, and I take those responsibilities very seriously."

Alexandra nodded again, wishing with all her heart that her guardian, when his losses had forced him to economize, had seen fit to begin with Miss Mumford's employment. She had a vestigial fondness for Miss Mumford, left over from the years when that good lady had been her governess. But as she made the transition from girl to woman, Miss

Mumford hadn't been able to adjust, and still sometimes talked to her as though she weren't out of pinafores.

"I cannot allow your decision to go out in public wearing those clothes"—here she gestured with something like disgust at the trousers Alexandra had borrowed from Georgiana—"to go unremarked upon."

Perhaps it was her exhaustion, perhaps it was her ankle, perhaps it was momentum from having already broken some of the boundaries she had remained within all her life, but Alexandra Niven decided she'd had enough. She looked at her companion with something approaching steely resolve in her eyes and said with quiet dignity, "Oh, but you can. You can certainly allow it."

Miss Mumford wouldn't have been more surprised if Alexandra had kicked her. The girl had never stood up to her in that way! She was so taken aback that she forgot just what it was that she wouldn't allow.

But Alexandra wasn't finished. "I am nineteen years old, and I believe I have proven myself to be a young lady of good judgment and modest demeanor." Had she been able to stand, she would have drawn herself up to her full height. As it was, she sat up straighter in her chair and looked Miss Mumford dead in the eye. "I made the decision to wear these clothes, and I believe that decision to be consistent with modest demeanor. I am sorry to find that you disagree, but I am old enough to rely on my own judgment, and I will no longer disregard it in favor of yours."

Miss Mumford opened her mouth to object, but no words came out. The girl's assertion of independence struck her dumb.

"What I ask from you right now," Alexandra continued, "is simply to be left alone. I need a bath, I need to ice my ankle, and I need to think." She watched as her companion's expression changed from outrage to bewilderment, and her manner softened.

"I will see you at dinner, and I know we will be friends again."

Miss Mumford said not a word, but turned and left the girl alone to her bath, her ice, and her thoughts.

Her thoughts ran in Freddy's direction, but not to the exclusion of all else. She was an innocent girl—naive, even—but it hadn't escaped her that Alphonse Gerard's attentions had also been very particular. She knew herself to be an attractive woman, and what she felt at being, as she supposed, the object of two men's affections wasn't surprise, exactly, but more a satisfaction at the novelty and a fresh curiosity about how it all would play out.

As the possibilities ran through her mind, there was a gentle knock at the door. "It's just me, Alexandra," said Lady Georgiana's voice through the door.

Alexandra bade her come in, and she sailed through the door with a monstrously large bouquet of the finest flowers Penfield had to offer.

"I heard you were hurt," she said from behind the flowers, "and I of course had to come see you and bring you these." She put the vase on the dressing table.

"My injury is minor," said Alexandra. "It certainly doesn't merit such a beautiful arrangement of flowers." She looked at the magnificent bouquet admiringly.

"Ah!" Georgiana said. "You must know that, when it comes to flowers and young ladies, merit is not part of the equation. We simply accept them as our due. Now," she went on, taking a seat next to the bed where Alexandra was lying with her injured ankle raised, "tell me what happened."

She did, from beginning to end. She told her friend about how Freddy held her, and what she felt. She told her about Miss Mumford, and her disapproval. She even told her about Gerry and his attentions. She emptied her heart to Lady Georgiana, who heard it all with attention, sympathy, and consideration.

"My goodness," she finally said. "You have certainly had an eventful few days. And I am very sorry for the part my trousers played in your drama."

"Your trousers played the part I assigned them, and you—and they—are blameless," Miss Niven said. "And I am not sorry at all, for it was time for me to break the schoolroom bond that Miss Mumford thought gave her license to bully me."

This was a Miss Niven quite a bit different from the Miss Niven who had arrived at Penfield just a few days earlier. Georgiana marveled at the change, but also worried that her friend's newfound assertiveness might drive her to do something ill considered.

"Mightn't you want Miss Mumford's advice on those other questions, the ones involving Freddy and Gerry?" Georgiana ventured cautiously. "She and I certainly differ in our opinions, but you might benefit from hearing all sides, and I think she has your best interests at heart."

"I think she does, and I don't intend to cut her out altogether. I simply want us to be friends, and not child and nursemaid."

Given Miss Niven's spirits, which seemed almost rebellious, Georgiana thought she should refrain from offering any advice that might inflame them further. Instead, she excused herself, saying she must dress for dinner.

"As must I," said Alexandra, "and I find that, on the one day I need her assistance in dressing, I have rendered it impossible for Miss Mumford to help me." She laughed. "I suppose I must do my best."

"Nonsense. I will send Hortense to you. I have not injured my ankle, and can dress without her."

"That is very good of you." Alexandra reached her hand out to press Georgiana's. "Thank you."

Georgiana was as good as her word, and in a few minutes Hortense knocked at the door. In the maid's capable hands, Alexandra was dressed and ready for dinner with ten minutes to spare. A servant had dropped off a cane, thoughtfully sent by Lady Loughlin, and Alexandra limped downstairs.

Most of the guests were assembled, and she was fussed over no end. Lady Loughlin ensconced her in the most comfortable chair in the drawing room, and brought her the choicest tidbits from the table. Freddy, who had returned from the Glück dairy just in time for dinner, never left her side, and entertained her with stories of the trouble that he and his older brother had gotten into when they were boys. Lady Georgiana, who had known Freddy in his callow youth, sat by and laughingly interjected whenever he strayed too far from what she knew to be the truth.

But Alexandra kept looking about her for the people who weren't there. She wanted to make things right with Miss Mumford, and that lady's absence boded ill for a swift reconciliation. She also wanted to see Gerry, whose boisterous good spirits were always welcome.

When the meal was almost over, Alexandra was gratified to see Miss Mumford, as unobtrusively as possible, take a seat on the outskirts of the little group that had surrounded her. Immediately, she extended her hand. "Dear Miss Mumford," she said, "please come join us. Freddy has been telling us the most extraordinary stories, and you really must hear."

Miss Mumford was glad to be welcomed by her charge, but she had decidedly mixed feelings about what had passed between them earlier that day. She did recognize that Miss Niven was a grown woman, and knew that her own manner toward her hadn't adjusted as it should. But she also had personal pride, and faith in her own good judgment, and she couldn't have that judgment scorned without feeling it as an affront.

What resolved the issue in her mind was the prudence, if not the absolute necessity, of making sure her employment continued. The work was light, the pay was good, and she was willing to swallow the indignity and make it up with Alexandra. And so she smiled and moved in to join the group.

Gerry, however, never appeared.

Almost every one of the Loughlins' assembled guests had been busy that day, and their collective fatigue broke up the party earlier than usual. Georgiana helped Alexandra up to her room, and left her with a promise that Hortense would come and help the injured lady get to bed. As she walked back to her own room, she saw Bruce Barnes coming from the other direction.

She found that his mere appearance quickened her pulse. "Good evening, Mr. Barnes," she said with a smile.

He returned her smile. "I thought we had settled the little matter of Christian names."

"And so we have. Let me start again. Good evening, Bruce."

"Good evening, Georgiana. As it is a fine evening, and still early, I thought you might like to come out for a walk. We've electrified some of the paths, and the grounds are quite a sight at night."

Georgiana was flushed with the pleasure of the evening, with the expectation of an interlude with Barnes, and not a little with wine. "Let me get my bonnet," she said, and went into her room.

Barnes waited in the hall as Georgiana prepared herself to go out and gave instructions to her maid. "I won't be out long," she told Hortense, "and if it's possible to get some warm milk when I return, that would be lovely." Hortense said she thought such a thing could be managed, and out her lady went.

When they got out-of-doors, Barnes led them in the direction of the lake where Gerry had taken her and her friend punting just that morning. "That's the longest path with lighting, and there's more lighting around the lake. It's quite beautiful," he explained.

They walked in silence. At first, Georgiana felt the need to fill it with conversation, but it didn't seem appropriate to talk about the usual things one talked about when filling silence. The weather, the party, the house— all seemed quite beside the point. So she contented herself with the quiet, and soon began to feel Barnes's physical being as a more substantial filler of the void than any conversation could have been.

They reached the little lake, and it was as beautiful as Barnes had promised. Small electric lights had been strung around the entire circumference. They shed an eerie light on the trees lining the bank, and their reflection dotted the surface of the water.

Georgiana stopped to look, and Barnes stood behind her, his hands resting lightly on her shoulders. "It's quite breathtaking," she said, turning to address him. "I'm not at all used to electric light. We've only just begun to install it at Eastley."

"The Loughlins enjoy being first, I think," Barnes said. "And, seeing this, I can't say I blame them." He moved his hands down her back, and clasped her around the waist. "But I have something else in store for you," he whispered in her ear.

"Do you indeed?" she murmured, her eyes closing as she breathed in his nearness.

He took her by the hand and led her around to a grove of trees on one side of the lake. In the middle of the grove, almost completely obscured by the foliage, was a little shed. "You know what's in there?" he asked her.

She shook her head, not having the foggiest notion.

"The pump."

"The pump?" She was bewildered. Why was this man showing her the pump?

"We use it to circulate the water and aerate the lake," he explained. "Otherwise, it would have algae, and no one would want to swim in it."

"I am exceedingly glad to know it. And so you are a hydrologist as well as being a landscape designer?" She still had no idea what the point of all this was.

He laughed, and she saw that he was doing this deliberately. She donned her best little pout and put her hands on her hips. "Could you please tell me why I'm here, looking at a shed that contains a pump that aerates a lake and prevents algae so people can swim?"

"It's the swimming part," he said, and began to unbutton his shirt. "But not just the swimming part. Come in and you'll see."

With that, he stripped and dived into the water.

She hesitated, but only for a moment. She wore more clothes than Barnes, and it took her longer to get out of them, but within a very few minutes she dived in beside him.

The water was cool, but it refreshed rather than chilled. It had been a long time since she'd swum in a lake, and she relished the feeling of the water moving along her skin as she paddled out to where Barnes was standing in chest-high water.

What was chest-high for him was shoulder-high for her, and the buoyancy of her body under the water meant that her feet just skimmed the pebbly bottom. Until, that is, Barnes picked her up by the waist and brought her face level with his. She wrapped her legs around his middle and her arms around his neck, and they stood there together, saying nothing, enjoying the sensation of water and skin and cool evening air.

Georgiana leaned back so everything but her face was in the water, her legs still wrapped around Barnes. She swished her head back and forth, feeling the resistance of the water in her hair, and feeling also her connection to—and desire for—this man.

Barnes watched her and smiled. He reached out and caressed her breasts, which were floating almost independently of her body, their erect nipples poking up through the surface of the water. He ran his fingers down her ribs like strings of a harp, pausing at each one as though he were checking to see that they were all there.

Georgiana closed her eyes. She felt a slow, easy building of excitement, counterbalanced by the relaxing influence of the water, which now felt quite warm to her.

Barnes leaned over, put his hands behind her back, and gently lifted her up to him. "There's something I want to show you," he said.

"I hope it isn't a pump," she answered playfully.

He only smiled enigmatically and started walking toward the shore, a little off to the left of where they had dived into the water. Although they were walking toward the land, the water wasn't getting any shallower, and soon they were just a few feet from shore, but still in water that reached Barnes's abdomen.

He reached around his back and unhooked her feet, took her by the waist, and turned her around so her back was up against him, and they were both standing on the bottom, facing shore. He took her right hand in his. "Feel this," he said, and stretched her arm out under the water.

At first, she didn't feel anything, and wondered what he could possibly be talking about. But he moved her hand a little farther down under the water and then she felt it—a powerful, directed stream of water cutting through the still lake. She curled her fingers into it and felt the water rushing between them and swirling into her cupped palm.

"It's the pump," Barnes whispered. "And I think you're going to enjoy it."

She turned her head and looked at him curiously. What *was* it with him and his bloody pump? And then she saw his meaningful look, illuminated by the electric lights, and it began to dawn on her. She was glad the lights weren't any brighter, though, because she felt her face coloring as she realized how slow she'd been to take his meaning.

Barnes leaned over and reached his hands down to her thighs. He separated her legs, just a little, and stroked her inner thighs. The slippery sensation of it sent a chill up through Georgiana's body, and she gave a pleasurable shudder. Then she felt his fingers work their way up and up, until they reached the seat of pleasure where her legs met.

He traced her pubis and moved to the lips of her vulva, which he gently stroked and then opened. She gasped aloud as she felt his fingers—first one, and then two—move into her while the palm of his hand put pressure on her mound and the clitoris beneath. He held almost still, with just a hairbreadth of a motion back and forth, and she leaned back on him because she felt as though she could no longer hold herself upright. She felt his erect cock hard against the small of her back, and she mirrored his motion, just slightly back and forth, as she rubbed up against him.

And then he lifted her, one hand still in her cunt and the other supporting her ass, and moved directly into the stream of the water from the pump. She opened her eyes wide as she felt the water move over her, and her gasp was almost a scream. It was an astonishing sensation, the complete immersion of her private parts in this gushing jet.

The water flowed around, and it flowed in. It pushed and streamed and eddied, and within seconds she felt as though it would drive her to a premature climax if she let it. She maneuvered her body out of the jet and turned around to Barnes, who had a look of almost smug satisfaction on his face. "Do you like it?" he asked, knowing full well what her reply must be.

She knew he knew, and thought it unnecessary to answer him aloud. "Perhaps we could move just a little farther out," she suggested. If she could soften the pressure, she thought, she might find it easier to control her arousal.

"We can," he said, and then put her down so she was standing on the lake bottom. "Just one moment." He strode out of the water, back to where their clothes were piled on the bank, and took a small tin out of one of his pockets. Then he returned to Georgiana, who looked at him curiously. "All in good time," he said, and picked her up as he had before.

They were only a foot farther from shore, but the pressure from the pump's jet was significantly lessened. This time, as Barnes held her in the stream, she felt the water as an all-encompassing caress. The combination of pressure and motion was incomparable, and she felt the sweet, focused excitement intensify in her core.

She found she could move, ever so slightly, to change the pressure, divert the motion, and so amplify her own waves of arousal. As she felt it mounting, she moved her hips so the jet was directed to her thigh or her belly until the feeling subsided. Then she'd move back into the stream and start a new, bigger wave.

She hadn't forgotten Barnes, exactly, but she was very focused on what was happening to her when she felt a gentle pressure in the crevice between her buttocks. Barnes had his hand on her ass, and his middle finger was pressing in between her cheeks, searching for her asshole.

And then he found it and slipped his finger gently in. Because he had touched her there before, she had some idea what to expect, but the combination of the flowing water on her cunt and the pressure of his finger up her ass was all-consuming. The pleasure reached from her toes, up through the backs of her legs, concentrated in her middle, and then radiated out to her arms and even her fingertips. This was ecstasy, and her climax must be close.

Barnes sensed it, and moved her out of the stream and reclaimed his hand. He revealed the small tin, in his other hand, to be filled with white petrolatum, and he took out a big dollop of it. He put his hand under the water, found Georgiana's anus once more, and deftly maneuvered the petroleum jelly around the rim and inside. And then he put her squarely back in the jet from the pump.

This interlude had set her excitement back to simmer, but the feel of the water on her once more had it building back up, more intense than before, if that were possible.

She felt again the pressure on the rim of her asshole, and she knew it wasn't his finger. It was the tip of his cock, soft and hard at the same time, slowly working its way in. The pressure built and built as he worked himself in, and at first Georgiana wasn't quite sure what she felt. It wasn't pain, exactly, but it was a very unfamiliar feeling that wasn't quite pleasure, either. Whatever it was, it served to keep the sensations from the water in check, in a kind of sexual equilibrium.

Only for a while. As she got used to the feeling of fullness, the unfamiliarity turned to a deep, satisfying pleasure, complement to the soft gushing of the water on her labia, her clitoris. She felt every nerve, every cell, engage—and she moaned long and low.

Barnes, his hands on her hips, moved in and out in short, slow strokes. The tightness of her ass, clenching his cock, was almost more than he could bear. Had he let himself go, he would have come within seconds of easing himself into her. As it was, it took all his concentration to wait for her.

Her moan told him it was time. Together, perfectly together, they reached a climax like none either of them had ever known. As she came, she contracted harder around him, intensifying his release. As he came, he filled her wider and deeper, intensifying hers. And the water! Water everywhere, caressing, flowing, completing.

It took a long time for the last small waves to work themselves through their two bodies, and it was only after they had both fully recovered that Barnes eased himself out of her and she put her feet back on the lake bottom.

Georgiana looked Barnes full in the face. "That was truly extraordinary," she said.

"There are many extraordinary things in the world." He gave her a look full of meaning.

"And you could give me a guided tour, I've no doubt," she said, and laughed as she turned and headed for dry land.

"And what a tour it would be," he said, and followed her out of the water.

Onshore, Barnes handed her his shirt. "You can use this to dry off," he said.

"But then what will you wear?"

"Don't worry. I'll walk you back until you're in sight of the house, and then I'll just duck off to my cottage. I don't think we'll meet anyone, and I trust *you* won't mind if I'm shirtless."

"No," she said, and ran her hands down his bare chest affectionately. "No, indeed."

She put her clothes on slowly, in no hurry to return to the house and other people. The evening had had an air of unreality, and she was hanging on to the last moments, savoring them. When at last she was dressed, they strolled back toward the house arm in arm, Georgiana thinking how natural it felt to be with him.

When the house came into view, Barnes kissed her forehead and they parted company. She made her way up to her room, saying just a few polite words to dinner's last stragglers, still arranged in one or two small groups in the drawing rooms. When she reached her room, Hortense was turning down her bed and laying out her nightclothes. The hot milk she'd asked for was on the dressing table.

"Oh, what a welcome draft," she said. "I'd completely forgotten that I'd requested it."

"As soon as you left, I asked Rose to fetch it later, and she's just now brought it," said Hortense.

"Thank you," said Georgiana. "And you may go. I won't be needing you this evening." She wanted to be alone.

"Yes, my lady." Hortense gave a perfunctory curtsy and left the room.

Georgiana donned her nightdress, got under the covers, and settled in to enjoy her milk and her thoughts. The discomfort she'd felt when she first learned that everyone in the house knew about her affair with Barnes had completely dissipated. How could anything that felt so right be wrong? And if it wasn't wrong, what did she care for the world's censure?

Her determination to defy that censure felt almost virtuous. Respectable men had been enjoying such pleasures since . . . well, since the very dawn of respectability, she supposed. And why should respectable women be denied?

What never crossed her mind was the idea that something other than pleasure was at stake. That they might have a life together was a possibility she never entertained.

When—if, really—she married, she knew she would marry a man who could walk in her world, who could talk of her world, who could live in its midst. Barnes was not such a man. But such a man as he was could touch her deeply! She lay in bed reliving the moments until she began to feel drowsy.

Just down the hall was another young woman snug in her bed, drinking hot milk, reliving moments. Alexandra Niven was thinking that she had never had such an enjoyable day, and that perhaps she should make it a habit to twist her ankle. She thought of Freddy and how he'd carried her up to the house, and the attention he'd paid to her over dinner. She thought of the feeling she'd had wearing Georgiana's trousers. She thought of Gerry, and wondered why he hadn't appeared at dinner.

The soft bed and the warm covers eventually took their toll, and Alexandra felt her eyes struggling to stay open. She reached over to the nightstand to put her empty cup back in its saucer, and only then did she see the folded piece of paper that had been hidden under the cup. She picked it up with puzzlement, but with some pleasurable anticipation. A billet-doux?

She unfolded it and read the one word printed there: *Harlot.*

The pleasant thoughts of her day and her suitors turned to ashes. How could anyone call her such a thing? *Who* could want to call her such a thing? What had she done that merited such a charge?

Her mind raced. Had she opened herself to such hostility simply by wearing trousers? By letting Freddy carry her? Could Miss Mumford's reconciliation have been a sham, and this the manifestation of her disapproval? Could Gerry be jealous of the attentions Freddy was paying her?

She was now wide awake, but uncertain of what she should do. She was sitting stiffly upright in her bed, the note crumpled in her hand. It occurred to her to ring for Miss Mumford, but if that lady had sent the note she clearly couldn't be confided in. And if she *hadn't* sent the note, Alexandra thought it might be better if the secret could be kept from her.

Could she go find Georgiana? She knew she could confide in her friend, but it was too late to visit her in her room. She wanted desperately to tell *someone*, but there was no one to whom she could go.

And then she felt an unpleasant—and unfamiliar—rumbling in her bowels. At first she put it down to her distress, but then its insistence indicated that it was something more. She leaped out of bed and positively ran for the toilet, her injured ankle forgotten in the mad dash.

The toilet was where she remained for some good part of the night, her insides in an uproar. At first, she couldn't understand what had happened. She thought it must be something she ate, but the turmoil was like nothing she'd ever experienced from food gone off. Besides, her constitution was excellent, and food seldom disagreed with her.

It was somewhere near three a.m. when it dawned on her that there had been something in the milk. When she first sipped it, she thought it had a funny taste, but it didn't seem sour or rancid, and the taste wasn't unpleasant, so she drank it. And this was the price.

THIRTEEN

She woke to the sound of a timid knock.

"Alexandra, dear," said the voice of Miss Mumford through the door, "are you quite all right?"

"I am," she called. "Come in."

Miss Mumford opened the door just far enough to slip through, and then closed it behind her. She was going to make a feeble little joke about Miss Niven's lying so late in bed, but the haggard expression on the girl's face checked her. "Is something wrong?" she asked, with real concern.

Having just woken, Alexandra wasn't thinking clearly, and wasn't sure whether or not she wanted to tell Miss Mumford about last night's events. "I honestly don't know," she finally said. Then, thinking better of the ambiguity, she added, "but I think everything is fine."

"I'm glad," said her companion, but with some skepticism. "Mr. Gerard is outside. He noticed that you didn't come down to breakfast, and was concerned that your injury was keeping you in bed. He didn't think it proper to come up here alone, so he asked me to accompany him to check on you."

Alexandra was touched by this show of concern, and immediately got out of bed, donned her dressing gown, and limped to the door. "Hello, Gerry," she said, smiling at him as she opened it.

"Hullo, Miss Niven! I'm awfully glad to see you up and about. I worried when you didn't come down to breakfast."

"I overslept, I'm afraid," she said. "Please come in and sit down." Alexandra stepped aside, motioned him in, and gestured to a chair next to the bed. He wouldn't sit down, though, until he had given her his arm and helped her back up onto her bed.

This gave Alexandra a few moments to gather her wits. Under no circumstances did she want to tell Gerry about the note and the tainted milk, and she needed to put the incident in the back of her mind while he was there.

She forced a smile. "I missed you at dinner last night."

"I'm ashamed to say I was all in. I'm not used to punting, and although I didn't feel the exertion at the time—I had such diverting company—I did feel it later. I had a chop in my room and turned in early."

"You missed my coronation." Gerry looked at her quizzically. "By virtue of a twisted ankle, I was queen of dinner," she said with mock majesty. "I was placed on a throne in the drawing room and waited on hand and foot."

"By Jove, if I had been there I would have waited on you with both hands and both feet," her visitor said with feeling. "But here I am gabbing on when you haven't had any breakfast. Should you like to come down for some tea and toast?"

The very thought of food made Alexandra queasy, but she thought she could stomach a cup of tea. "Perhaps a cup of tea," she said, "but I think I'd like to ring for it. I'm not quite ready to go downstairs."

"Let me get it," said Miss Mumford, so eager to reestablish herself in Alexandra's good graces that she was willing to set aside her scruples about leaving her charge alone in the room with an unmarried man.

As soon as she was gone, Gerry turned his chair toward the bed and looked at Miss Niven with uncharacteristic earnestness.

"Miss Niven," he said, "I'm glad to have an opportunity to see you alone, because there's something very particular I want to say."

Miss Niven's experience of the world, limited as it was, had taught her what to expect when a gentleman says he has something particular to say, and she felt a warm glow at the thought of it.

"These last few days have been some of the best I've had in a very long time. And, although I know a lot of the people here, and have always enjoyed my stays at Penfield, this visit has been so particularly . . . topping." He settled for the word as he couldn't think of a better one. "And it's all been because you are here."

Alexandra looked down modestly, but didn't interrupt. "There are so many blasted clichés about men and women and love and sunshine and all that," he went on, "but this is the very first time I've ever felt a woman's presence brightening everything around me. You simply make everything better.

"I know my shortcomings," continued Gerry. "I'm old, I'm set in my ways, and I'm certainly no beauty." He swallowed and looked at the floor. "But the thing is, I love you. And I'm hoping that, perhaps, you could learn to love me." He took her hand and got down on one knee by the side of the bed. "Miss Niven. Alexandra. Will you do me the honor of becoming my wife?"

He swallowed audibly. This hadn't been easy for him. The day before, he'd spent all afternoon and evening contemplating this step, and was absolutely sure he wanted to take it. Nevertheless, the actual taking of it felt difficult and momentous.

Alexandra's head was in a whirl. What was she to say to him? She was sure she wasn't ready to say yes, but neither was she inclined to say no. And she would not, could not, must not toy with his affections.

Before she said a word, though, she had to get him off his knee.

Because the bed was high, when he knelt next to it she could see only the top half of his face, which gave his proposal a comical air. Because the matter was so very serious, Alexandra wanted him to reclaim his dignity before she spoke with him about it.

"Please, please get up." She pulled the hand that still held hers, and gestured for him to take his chair again.

Then it was her turn to swallow. Finding the right words would have been difficult even had her head been clear and her stomach calm.

"Gerry, you do me an honor that I did not look for and have not expected," she began. But the words sounded stilted and false even to her own ears, and she did not like it.

"That is," she corrected, "in the sense that good girls are never to expect such a thing." She smiled slyly and he laughed out loud. Her small joke brought back to him all the reasons he admired her, and he sat more at his ease.

"I am deeply, gratefully sensible of what an honor it is," she said, seriously this time, looking him in the eye.

"Isn't that what girls generally say when they're about to say no?" Gerry asked.

"I have very little information about what girls generally say on these occasions. I can tell you only that what I say is what I mean. I believe you to be a good, kind, well-meaning man. I have enjoyed your company." She felt the weight of her earnestness, and sought to lighten her little speech. "And I don't believe you're as old or as ugly as you seem to think."

His laugh was more of a grunt, braced as he was for what he thought was to come.

"I cannot accept you," she said gently. "But nor can I reject you. If you ask me whether I love you, I can say only that I do not. But if you ask me whether I *can* love you, I have to say that I might, with time, learn to do so. I know that is an unsatisfactory answer," she started to say, but saw that Gerry was beaming. Absolutely beaming, with a smile that took over his entire face.

"By Jove, that's no sort of rejection at all! Which makes it an absolutely satisfactory answer."

"Does it?" Alexandra wasn't expecting this.

"My dear girl," he said, "when a doddering, uncouth specimen such as myself addresses himself to a beautiful, accomplished young goddess such as yourself, he doesn't necessarily expect to win the day." After he said this, he thought that perhaps he had said too much. But to hell with it, he thought. Dissembling had never been in his nature and he wouldn't start now.

"I thought you'd turn me down flat," he said, still beaming.

Alexandra thought this admission endearing, and smiled at him tenderly. She liked it that there was no pretense, no airs with this man. He knew who and what he was, and that was all he ever set himself up to be.

"Will you give me some time to get used to the idea, and then perhaps speak to me again?" she asked.

"You can have till the cows come home! I will not press you. If I may spend time in your company while the cows are still out, that's all I can ask."

"I should like that," she said. "I should like it very much."

"And so should I," he said, and made his exit.

Just as he was leaving, Miss Mumford returned with the tea. Alexandra thought she'd never in her life been as happy to have a cup of it. Her thoughts were in a muddle, her feelings impossible to sort out. Her stomach was still unsettled, and she thought a cup of tea the very thing.

Miss Mumford, though, was not the very thing. Alexandra was bursting with the news of Gerry's proposal, but she did not want to confide in her companion.

"Thank you so much for the tea," she said with real gratitude. "And may I impose on you to ask one more favor?"

"Of course you may."

"Could you find Lady Georgiana and send her to me? It's the kind of thing I would ordinarily do for myself, but . . ."

She didn't need to finish the sentence, or even justify her desire to see the lady of whom Miss Mumford disapproved. "Of course," she said with surprisingly good grace. "I'm sure I shall be able to find her."

It couldn't have been ten minutes later when Lady Georgiana knocked at the door. Alexandra bade her friend enter.

"I hope there is nothing amiss," Georgiana said, concern furrowing her brow.

"There is. That is, I don't quite know. But there are also things that are not amiss at all. Oh! I can make neither heads nor tails of it!"

Georgiana sat down. "It's been only a few hours since I saw you at dinner last night. Perhaps the easiest way to explain this would be to tell me what's happened since then."

"Well, I believe I've been deliberately served tainted milk, and I've had an offer of marriage."

Georgiana's eyes widened. "*What?* Then it has been a very eventful few hours! And is it Gerry? I mean, who's asked you to marry him, not who's given you the milk." Because Georgiana could see that her friend had clearly survived the milk, and her health was in no danger, her curiosity about the proposal overrode her concern about that piece of malice.

"It is."

"And do you mean to accept him?"

"I don't know. It's very sudden."

"It is indeed. We can talk all about it." Her expression turned serious. "But first you have to tell me about the milk."

Alexandra told her the story of the milk. When she reached the part about the note, Georgiana interrupted her. "Don't tell me. The note said, 'Harlot.'"

"How ever did you know?" Alexandra asked, astonished at her friend's clairvoyance.

"I have gotten notes along the same line. Although I don't know who is sending them, I can at least understand why. In your case, though, it does not make any sense. Your character and conduct are beyond reproach."

Alexandra blushed deeply. "Perhaps not so far beyond as you think."

Georgiana was a little taken aback. "What is it that you have done?"

"I wore your trousers. I let Freddy carry me. But I think the gist of it is that I have been entertaining thoughts of two men, men who may be suitors. Well, one who certainly is and one who may be, but I'm not quite sure. . . ." She trailed off as Georgiana laughed.

"Entertaining thoughts of two men? Well, that *is* an offense against propriety!" But Georgiana repented her archness when she saw that her friend was genuinely distressed.

"The mere fact that you believe that your thoughts could merit censure is evidence of the purity of your spirit. You must not allow this note to upset you."

"If it were just the note, I think I could manage that. But whatever was in the milk was awfully unpleasant, and the whole incident makes me feel vulnerable and rather frightened."

"I don't blame you, but I would much rather have you angry than frightened," Georgiana said. "When I got the first note, I felt threatened and vulnerable as well, but I have since been convinced that this . . . this"—she reached for the right word—"stunt is just that. Tainted milk is certainly considerably worse than a dead peacock, but consider what it might have been. There might have been strychnine in your milk. I do believe this is a message, and not a real threat."

Alexandra thought there might be something in this, but her memories of how she had spent the night made her think that, for a message, it was awfully emphatic.

"Nevertheless," Georgiana continued, "this has gone beyond mere mischief, and we must get to the bottom of it. Who brought you the milk?"

"I suppose it was Rose—she generally does—but she left it on the table outside the door, and I don't know how long it was there. It was still warm when Miss Mumford brought it in to me."

"I saw Rose in the corridor the last time I got one of those lovely little missives, but I think she's a nice girl and I suspect there is another explanation. Lord Loughlin said he would have a word with her. Is there anyone else you can think of?"

The two women talked at length about their suspicions, and considered almost every person under Penfield's roof as a suspect, but without making much headway. "As amateur detectives," Georgiana said to her friend, "I'm afraid we fall below the mark. Perhaps it was Rose after all, and we're just too soft to believe a woman with a kind face and ingratiating manner could do this."

Alexandra still couldn't believe it, but didn't have a better explanation. Finally, their detecting efforts exhausted, the two women returned to the much more pleasant subject of suitors and offers of marriage.

Lord Loughlin had indeed had a word with Rose, upsetting her inordinately. As Alexandra and Georgiana talked over the note, and the milk, and the proposal, Rose went to find the man who'd been the source of that proposal, the man who could establish her innocence.

She found him downstairs, ostensibly reading the newspaper over one last cup of tea, but really staring out the window, marveling that Alexandra Niven had given him hope. As Rose picked up some of the used cups and saucers on the table next to him, she whispered that she needed to see him. He saw the urgency in her expression and gave a slight nod.

"You may take this, too," he said in a voice any passerby would hear, handing his cup to her. "I'm going up to my room."

She took the dishes to the scullery, went immediately to his room, and entered without knocking.

"I don't know what to do!" she said, clearly on the verge of tears.

"My dear girl, what is the matter?"

"It's Lord Loughlin and Lady Georgiana. She got this terrible note, and a dead peacock, and they suspect me because she saw me in the corridor!" This, of course, Gerry knew, but didn't let on.

"And what did you tell him?" Gerry asked, with some trepidation. Given his proposal to Miss Niven, this would be an inopportune time for his dalliance with the maid to become public knowledge. Alexandra, he thought, might not be willing to overlook such a thing.

"I told him I was making up the rooms, of course! If I told him I was with you, he would have given me the sack on the spot. But because it was so late, I don't think he believes me, and he's going to give me the sack anyway." Here she burst into tears.

Gerry tried to take her in his arms, but she pushed him away. "This is what I get for getting myself involved in this kind of nonsense. The world would be a better place without men!"

Gerry had to laugh. "That wouldn't bode well for the human species."

"Oh, I'm sure we can find a way to have babies without the likes of you."

"But only girl babies."

"Of course only girl babies. If we have boy babies they only grow up to be men, and then we'd be back where we started." Her distress was losing steam.

Gerry took her hand, and she didn't pull it away. "You can be absolutely sure," he said, looking at her seriously, "that your job is not in jeopardy. I will speak with Lord Loughlin, and I will manage it so that he knows you are innocent. You have my word."

"But how can you convince him without telling him the truth?"

"You leave that to me. I will tell him the truth, but not all the truth." Gerry was confident that, even if his host knew all, he wouldn't fire Rose, and had no doubt that he could deliver on his promise to the girl.

He saw her visibly relax, almost deflate. She believed him, and in him.

"Thank you," she said, a little embarrassed to have been so upset about a situation that had such a simple solution.

"Do not thank me for doing what is unquestionably my duty," he said, and then grinned because it sounded a bit pompous. "Will you let men back in your world?" he asked.

"Some men, I think. Some others, definitely not."

"And which am I?"

"Oh, you're all right, I suppose."

The night before, when he had resolved to ask Miss Niven to marry him, he had resolved also to put an end to the affair with Rose. But here she was, her hand in his, the door closed behind them. He felt the first stirrings, and he pulled her toward him. Just this one last time . . .

But she wasn't having it. "It's this that got me in trouble in the first place, it is," she said as she pushed him away. "From here on in, I'm keeping myself to myself."

"A policy that certainly has its advantages," he said, still keeping his hold on her hand, if not the rest of her. "But sharing yourself with someone else every now and again has advantages as well." Here he raised his eyebrows suggestively, and his look was so comical that she giggled.

"It does," she said hesitatingly, and then summoned her resolve. "I mean, it did. For I'm not to do it anymore."

"Not forevermore?"

She nodded briskly.

"Forevermore is a long, long time," he said. "Perhaps you should fortify yourself for a life of self-denial with one last act of indulgence." The eyebrows went up again.

He pressed his advantage by taking her other hand. He could see the indecision in her face. "Come, Rose," he said in a tone of gentleness. "Let's say good-bye to each other properly."

A sly look came over her. She reclaimed both her hands, and then held out the right one as though to shake hands with him. "By all means, let's do this properly. It's been very nice getting acquainted with you, Mr. Gerard." But she couldn't hold back her laughter, and the last syllable of his name was garbled by her guffaw.

"Oh, you are a naughty girl," Gerry said as he took her hand and marched her over to the bed. "Do you know what happens to naughty girls?"

She tried to look serious, without much success. "They have to wash the dishes all on their lonesome?" she ventured.

"Well, perhaps, but that wasn't what I had in mind." He sat down on the bed and pulled her down over his knee. "Naughty girls get spanked."

"Oh, no, master, please, don't spank me!" said Rose in a squeaky schoolgirl voice.

"I must spank you, for you have been very, very naughty," said Gerry, lowering his voice commensurately.

And then he matched the deed to the word.

After a few strokes, Rose turned her head to look up at him, a puzzled look on her face. "But that doesn't hurt at all." She lifted herself up and sat beside him on the bed. "I haven't been spanked since I was a wee girl, and I seem to remember that it hurt then. I guess now I have more padding."

"I think I could make it hurt," said Gerry, distinctly suggestively.

"Thanks just the same," she replied, not taking him at all seriously.

"You might find that a little pain never felt so good," he said in a tone that made her stop her bantering. She'd lived in the world long enough to have heard of such things, but she'd never imagined that it would be suggested to her.

She wasn't quite sure she wanted to take him up on the suggestion, but she had an adventurous streak, and she trusted him. "Will it really hurt?"

"It will hurt just enough," he said. "And if you say 'stop,' I will stop immediately."

A slow smile spreading over her face told him she was game. He got up, walked over to his dressing table, and opened the top drawer. He took out a razor strop, a long strip of leather with a metal fastener at one end and a kind of buttonhole in the other. He took the metal end in his hand and snapped the strap in the air a couple of times.

Rose's eyes widened in surprise not untinted with alarm. "I thought you would use your hand."

"Don't worry, my dear; you'll find that, in the right hands, this works quite well."

After a fleeting moment of indecision, Rose decided that she would try this, and let him do as he would.

"Take off your dress," Gerry said, still standing and slapping the strap against his palm.

Rose took off her dress and stood before him in her shift.

"That too," he said.

When she was standing before him naked, he walked purposely over to her and circled her once, looking at her from head to toe. Then he dropped his hands to his sides and gently started swinging the strap at her legs in a motion that resulted almost in a caress of the leather on her skin. He walked around her again, swinging the strap against the backs, fronts, and sides of her thighs.

"Open your legs," he said when he'd finished his circuit. She did, and he walked around her again, this time working the strap so it stroked the insides of her thighs.

Rose had never experienced a feeling like this. The leather was cool and smooth, and Gerry was swinging it against her gently enough so that it didn't sting at all. That, combined with the odd feeling of standing naked in the middle of a room with a fully dressed man, set her senses at sixes and sevens. There was pleasure, but there was also a little discomfort, and her mind struggled to reconcile the two.

Gerry started using the strap on other parts of her body, and she felt it brush her buttocks and the small of her back. He came around to her front and used it on her belly and her arms. He ran it up her chest, between her breasts. He went around to her back again and swung it over her shoulders, each in turn, so the end brushed the top of her breasts.

The pleasure was in the ascendant over the discomfort, certainly.

Then Gerry started using a little more force, and there was a tiny sting in each lash of the strap. It focused Rose's thoughts on the feeling of the strap, and she was completely distracted from the unease she'd felt at standing naked before him.

Gerry stopped long enough to take off his shirt and boots, and then picked up the strap again, wearing only his trousers. Rose could see the bulge of his erection through the fabric.

He swung yet harder, and what she felt, she realized, would certainly qualify as pain. Somehow, though, it was a good pain. It dovetailed with her growing arousal, and pain and arousal together occupied her mind completely, pushing out thoughts of anything else.

Gerry continued walking circles around her, lashing her with increasing force over her entire body, from her ankles to her shoulders. Soon she could see red marks where he'd strapped her hardest, and the tingling heightened all her sensations.

Just as he got to the point where she thought she wouldn't want him to hit any harder, he stopped. "Kneel down," he said, gesturing at the rug.

She did. "Down on your elbows," he almost commanded. She did as she was told, which had the result that her bottom stuck up, unprotected, in the air. He positioned himself behind her, and she braced herself for the sting of the strop.

But Gerry started gently again, running the leather over one side of her ass and then the other, and then between her knees and up through her slightly parted legs.

By this time her excitement had reached the point that any pressure on her clitoris or vulva sent shivers up her backbone, and she focused on each stroke on her backside, waiting for the gentle lashing between her legs. He once again started hitting her harder, and pain again mingled with the pleasure that was starting to cascade inside her.

And then it seemed like he was lashing her in earnest, the strap hitting the bottom of her buttocks over and over, and her mind was a jumble, unable to process the disparate sensations.

As though he had an uncanny sixth sense of it, he again stopped just before she thought she must ask him to stop. Before she even had time to savor the cessation of the pain, he was out of his trousers, kneeling behind her.

She was ready for him, wet and hot, and the sense of fullness as he slid into her was glorious. The sting of the leather was replaced by the feel of his fully engorged cock sliding in and out of her, and the feel of his skin against hers. He had one hand on each of her ass cheeks, and he worked them apart and together, apart and together, in time to the rhythm they'd established.

She lowered her head so her bottom stuck up even more, and pushed back against him as he thrust into her. He groaned, and she could feel him get harder and wider inside her. The change in the angle meant more contact with her pussy, and together they rode to climax. Rose felt her orgasm deeper and longer-lasting than she'd ever had. It spread from deep inside all the way to the surface of her skin, which was still sensitive from its ordeal.

When it finally dissipated, she collapsed on the floor, leaving him kneeling between her legs, his gleaming cock beginning to lose its stiffness.

He stood up and walked over to the basin of water on the dressing table. He dampened a cloth and wiped himself off, and then went over to her and turned her over so she was facing up.

"My dear Rose," he said as he ran the cloth between her legs and down her thighs. "I have never heard of a good-bye conducted in quite this manner, but I must say I approve of it wholeheartedly."

Rose smiled and closed her eyes, enjoying the coolness of the damp cloth against the warmth of her skin.

Gerry continued more seriously. "I know I shall never forget you, and will always think of you with fondness. It is my hope that you will do the same. But it is also my hope that you reconsider your dissociation with my gender, and find someone who can make you happy."

Rose smiled again, and propped herself up on her elbows. "I appreciate what you're saying, and that it's kindly meant, but I hope I don't need anyone but myself to make me happy. I *am* happy. I've always been happy. It's in my nature to be happy."

"I know many a nobleman who would envy you that."

Rose looked at him incredulously. "Not if happy goes with making up rooms and sweeping out fireplaces and fetching hot tea at all hours."

Gerry laughed. "You're probably right about that." He gave her his hand, pulled her up, and kissed her forehead. "You're a peach, Rose, a regular peach."

She took both his hands in hers. "And you're a . . ." She struggled to find a fruit she could compare him to, but to no avail. "You're a gentleman. You're a regular gentleman."

She kissed him one last time, with feeling, and left to return to her duties.

FOURTEEN

A lexandra and Lady Georgiana had whiled away the entire morning talking of suspects, harlots, suitors, and trousers, and it was well after noon by the time they came down together for lunch. By this time the effects of what had been in Alexandra's hot milk had worn off, and she was finally, and acutely, hungry.

The house was a hubbub of activity. The drive was lined with carts delivering items as variable as glassware, sherry, and onions. One covered cart concealed a whole load of crinkled red and white streamers. The party was the next evening but one, and preparations were beginning in earnest.

Lady Loughlin stood in the main hall keeping an eye on the provisioning, but the real work of checking deliveries against the list of what was expected and stowing the goods where they belonged was being done by Dodson, the butler. She knew the work of the day was in good hands, and when she saw Georgiana helping her friend, still limping a little, down the main staircase, she left Dodson to his job and went to the two young women.

"I was just thinking about you," she said to Alexandra. "And how is your ankle today?"

"It's much better, thank you, Lady Loughlin. I can almost walk un-assisted, but stairs are still difficult." She winced as she came down at a bad angle, as if to make her point.

"As though an injury weren't enough," Georgiana said, "Miss Niven has had another little incident."

Paulette looked at them, her head cocked to one side and her eyes questioning. "What has happened?" she asked, looking from one of the girls to the other.

The two friends had decided that, as much as they'd like to spare their hostess from knowledge of the tainted milk, they were obligated to tell her what had happened. As Georgiana had said, "If it happened in my home, I would most certainly want to know."

"Let us get some lunch for this poor, famished, injured girl," Georgiana said in mock pathos, "and then we shall tell you all about it." They did get lunch, and the three women sat down in a sunny corner of the drawing room.

The story was soon told, complete with the addendum of Alphonse Gerard's proposal of marriage.

"I declare, I don't know whether to pity you or congratulate you," Paulette said to Miss Niven. "But I do know that I am exceedingly un-happy about having my guests poisoned under my roof."

"It wasn't poison, Lady Loughlin," Alexandra was quick to point out. "It was probably a very strong laxative, and one that would do me no real harm."

Georgiana picked up that thread. "In a way, its being a laxative is proof against any truly malignant intentions. Surely, if the perpetrator had wanted to do Miss Niven harm, he could easily have put something dangerous, or even something deadly, in her milk."

"I'm not at all sure I believe that," said Lady Loughlin. "But even if it is merely a prank, I want to sort it out and get whoever is doing it out of my house." She paused for a moment. "Does Lord Loughlin know?"

"He knows of the peacock and the poison ivy, but he doesn't know about the milk," said Georgiana.

Miss Niven looked uncomfortable. "Must we tell him?"

Paulette had real sympathy for the girl, but she was firm. "We must. It's his home too. But first you must tell me whether there is anyone you suspect."

"There is an obvious suspect, but I don't suspect her." Georgiana gave a little laugh and continued. "I saw Rose in the corridor just before I found the peacock, and it was Rose who delivered the milk to Miss Niven, but I have spoken with her and she seems like a kind, sensible, hardworking girl."

"Rose has been with us only a little less than a year, but I have been very pleased with her, both as a parlor maid and as a member of our household. She works conscientiously, seems good-natured, and is not without a sense of humor." Paulette mused for a moment. "I don't know why I should value a sense of humor in a parlor maid, but there you are."

"I think a sense of humor is something to be valued universally," said Georgiana, "so I am entirely of your opinion."

"I am glad of that, but it gets us no closer to answering our question," Lady Loughlin said. "Is there anyone else whom you suspect?"

Miss Niven said, "'Suspect' wouldn't be quite the word I would use. 'Wonder about' might be more accurate, but it did cross my mind that, somehow, Miss Mumford heard about what had happened to Lady Georgiana and thought that, if she were to do something like that to me, the crime would be attributed to someone else."

"Or," added Georgiana, "it's possible that it has been Miss Mumford all along. She has certainly made her disapproval manifest."

Paulette looked doubtful. "She is such a respectable lady. It's a little hard to imagine."

Miss Niven nodded. "It's quite hard to imagine. But it's hard to imagine anyone doing this."

"We even thought about Mrs. Sheffield, for no other reason than that she is so very respectable, and her condemnation of me has been commensurate," Georgiana said. "But I think it's even harder to imagine Mrs. Sheffield doing such a thing than it is to imagine Miss Mumford doing it."

The other two women nodded, and there was a pause as they seemed to run out of suspects. When Miss Niven and Lady Georgiana had been alone, they had also talked about whether this might be Freddy's idea of a fine joke, but neither of them wanted to suggest this to his mother. His mother, though, knew her son better than either of her guests did.

"This just possibly could be the work of my younger son," Lady Loughlin said ruefully. "He's been known to pull what he's thought of as a prank, but what others consider a serious misdemeanor. And, with two distractingly beautiful young ladies under the same roof, what little judgment he has may go for naught."

Miss Niven wouldn't have dreamed of seconding her hostess's opinion, but Georgiana took the privilege of long acquaintance. "It did cross my mind," she said. "It is the kind of thing Freddy might find amusing."

"If it is Freddy," Paulette went on, "it's rather a relief than otherwise. He would never go beyond the confines of what he considers a good joke, and there is no danger. I'm much more worried that it *isn't* Freddy, and someone may get hurt."

The three women were quiet for a moment, each contemplating the possibilities. Then Lady Loughlin broke the silence. "I shall certainly speak with Robert, but I can't think that there's anything else any of us can do, except keep eyes and ears open. In the meantime, you must excuse me. The Earl of Grantsbury is due this afternoon, and I want to make sure all is right with his accommodations."

With that, she headed upstairs to look in on the suite of rooms reserved for the earl. As she expected, all was in order. Her instructions had been explicit, and her staff had followed them to the letter. She gave a quick nod of satisfaction and went off to find her husband.

The Loughlins, husband and wife, each had a dressing room and bedchamber adjoining a sitting room they shared. She had little hope of finding him in their rooms at this time of the afternoon, but she checked there before she sent her maid, Jean, to find him.

"Please tell him I must speak with him, and that he will find me in my dressing room."

"Yes, my lady." Jean curtsied and went off in search of her master.

Lady Loughlin did not have long to wait. Not ten minutes passed before her husband knocked at the door, which she had left ajar.

"Come in, my dear," she said, and Robert entered and sat in the soft chair that Paulette kept in the room for the tête-à-têtes she liked to have there.

Lord Loughlin reflected that it had been a long time since anything resembling an intimate conversation had passed between them, and wondered why he had been summoned.

"It's about the 'harlot' notes," she said, launching directly into the problem at hand.

"But we've already discussed that," he said, disappointed that a more pleasant subject hadn't been the subject of his summoning.

They had discussed the notes after the incident of the peacock, but not to much advantage. They were both angry that someone in their home—servant, family, or guest—was doing this, but neither of them knew what steps to take. It wasn't trivial enough to laugh off, but it also wasn't serious enough to call in the constabulary—at least, it hadn't been when they last spoke.

"There's a new development," Paulette said grimly, and told him about Alexandra and the milk.

Lord Loughlin sat back in the chair and took a deep breath. "That's bad."

"Yes, that's bad. But what are we to do about it?"

"I spoke with Rose, but she seemed to know nothing whatsoever about it, and was in tears at the suggestion that she could have had anything to do with it. She was quite convincing. And I must say, I can't see her being behind something like tainted milk."

"Whom *can* you see being behind it?" she asked her husband almost plaintively.

"I don't know." He thought for a moment. "But there's one thing I do know, and that is that I don't want you to have to think about it."

"But how can I avoid thinking about it?" She raised her hands, open palmed, in a gesture of frustration.

"You can assure yourself that I am thinking about it and pursuing it. We have a houseful of guests, and our biggest event of the year is the day after tomorrow. Even when all is well, we need the lady of the house to set the tone for the festivities, and I think it's even more important now. The story of Georgiana's notes has gotten out, but everyone is inclined to think of it more as a joke than a menace. We must do everything we can to ensure that they continue to think of it that way. Our friends are here for the company, and for the masquerade, and it is our obligation as hosts to make certain that they have a good time while they stay with us. Let that be what you think about."

Lady Loughlin was accustomed to taking the lead in managing the household, and slotting her husband into her plans where she thought he belonged. Now here he was slotting her—in a way that made perfect sense. She tried to keep the incredulity out of her voice. "That is, I think, an excellent approach. I shall do my level best to keep my end of the bargain."

"And I to keep mine." Robert stood, leaned over his wife, and kissed her forehead. She took his hand as he did so, and looked up at him. "Thank you," she said, with some feeling.

He stroked her cheek with his free hand, and leaned over to kiss her again, this time on the very corner of her mouth. Lady Loughlin knew this as an overture, and was touched that he was making it. Had she not had a full house, the impending visit of an earl, and party preparations to think about, she might have responded to it differently. But she did have those things, and although she was sorry to do it, she put him off.

She stood up and kissed him tenderly. "I'm afraid I must tend to the house and the guests."

"I think both the house and the guests would survive your temporary absence," her husband said.

She knew this to be true. "It is me, not them, who would struggle. You know I never can do anything but be a hostess when, well, when I'm a hostess."

"But you are a hostess so much of the time. Can you not be both a hostess and a wife?"

He hadn't intended this as a rebuke, but it sounded like one to Paulette's ears. "I believe I am always a wife," she said indignantly. "And I hope I have always been a good one."

Robert sighed. "You have, my dear, you have." And it was so. He looked at his wife rather sadly and left.

Robert knew that very little went on in his house without the servants' knowing, and he spent the next several hours making inquiries. He spoke with the kitchen staff to find out about the milk, the garden staff to ask about the poison ivy, and everyone he could think of to see who might have made off with poor Eustace. Invariably, he came up against ignorance and confusion. The house was so full of people, and the servants so caught up in the hubbub, that there was simply too much activity to make sense of.

Eventually, and reluctantly, he set off to find Jean. He generally made an effort to avoid her, both because the fact of their interludes in the dungeon made him uncomfortable around her above stairs, and because he was always afraid she would do or say something to betray him. She had never let slip any inappropriate word or expression when other people were present, but when it was just him and her, Jean put on a knowing and familiar air that Lord Loughlin disliked.

He knew, though, that she paid close attention to everything that happened in the house, and diligence required him to seek her out.

He found her in the sitting room he shared with his wife, straightening things up.

"Jean," he said, "may I have a word?"

"Of course, sir." She looked at him with just a hint of a smile at the corners of her mouth.

Lord Loughlin gestured for her to sit down, took a chair facing her, and proceeded to explain what was happening and ask her the litany of questions he'd been asking all the servants in the house. Had she seen anyone loitering on the grounds or in the kitchen? Had anyone been acting strangely? Had she heard any general disgruntlement, or any specific criticisms of Lady Georgiana or Miss Niven?

The answers were no, no, and again no. Jean had been busy attending to her mistress, and her realm was far removed from the kitchen and the grounds. What with all the activity in the house, Jean had had very little time to talk to the other servants. Her feel for the goings-on at Penfield was rather worse than it generally was, what with her many responsibilities.

When Jean came to the part about her many responsibilities, she leaned over and placed a hand on each of Lord Loughlin's legs, just above the knee. "But there's one responsibility I must never neglect," she said softly as she ran her hands up his thighs.

"Jean!" he hissed, bodily taking her hands away. "Lady Loughlin could walk in at any moment."

"I don't think so," Jean said. "She's gone out to the stables to make sure there's space and water and food for Lord Grantsbury's horses." She put her hands back on her master's thighs. "But if you're more comfortable somewhere else, we can go downstairs."

Jean stood up so her weight was concentrated on the palms of her hands, and she rubbed them up and down on his legs, inching closer and closer to where she could see the first signs of stirrings in his groin.

Lord Loughlin fought his desire. He made it a point never to use the dungeon during the day. Old Dodson, the butler, had a key to the wine cellar, and if he came there he might hear something and feel compelled to investigate. They had had one scare when Dodson did come downstairs while they were there, but they heard the heavy cellar door and were quiet until he left again.

Besides, there were so many things that needed his attention. He couldn't just disappear in the middle of the afternoon.

Jean had worked her way up to his cock, which was now fully erect, and he involuntarily closed his eyes and leaned his head back as he felt her stroking it through his trousers. She worked her thumbs into the crease between his thighs and his balls, and pressed. The combination of dull pain and acute pleasure made his mind up for him.

"Come down in ten minutes," he said, then stood up and left the room abruptly.

Jean smiled to herself, finished neatening the room, and went downstairs.

She had her own key to the wine cellar, but the other servants would wonder if they saw her use it. She made sure no one was about, and then quickly opened the door, slipped through, and locked it behind her. She made her way to the back of the cellar, where Lord Loughlin was waiting for her in the dungeon. He closed the door behind her and looked at her with a curious combination of desire and something Jean could only call hostility.

Robert clearly wanted her—he wouldn't be there otherwise—but he didn't want to be a victim to his desires. He wanted to indulge them on his own terms, and not feel so overwhelmed by them that he couldn't resist.

But she knew he couldn't resist. When Jean bent over the cask of

Armagnac in the middle of the room and flipped up her skirts, she knew exactly what to expect. She braced herself for the feeling of his hands, kneading and slapping her buttocks, and knew, without turning around, that the sight of her ass, reddened from his blows, was arousing him almost uncontrollably.

Usually, at this point in their game, Lord Loughlin would sit on a stool set up in the corner for the purpose, and watch as Jean deliberately undressed. This time, though, he told her, almost gruffly, to take her clothes off, and he went straight to the cabinet where he kept his toys. He took out the leather harness, the anal plug with the horsehair, and a large, soft sheepskin.

He removed his shirt and trousers, and Jean waited for the moment when the power shifted to her and he became submissive and yielding, but as he handed her the harness so she could put it on him, she did not sense submission. He gave her the reins, literally, but she didn't think he gave her the authority to use them quite as she would.

Robert threw the sheepskin over the cask and straddled it as though he were a stallion mounting a mare. Jean rubbed the plug in the tub of Carston's Complexion Cream, and worked it into his asshole.

They'd played this game before, with Robert in the role of stallion trying to get at the mare, and Jean in the role of handler, keeping him just out of reach of the sheepskin on the cask. Jean stood behind him and pulled on the reins to get him off the cask, but either she pulled only tentatively, or he hung on with particular tenacity, or some combination of the two. She couldn't get him off.

"Pull, girl, pull!" he said. He wanted the familiar strain against his chest. He wanted to reach for the cask but not quite get there. He wanted to be tantalized; he wanted to be controlled. But, somehow, today was different. As he yelled at her to pull, he struggled against her all the harder.

Jean couldn't quite understand why he had asked her to come down there, and then changed the rules. She didn't see that she was at fault, and she resented the displeasure in his tone.

If he wanted her to pull, pull she would. Jean was a slim girl, but she did physical work all day long, and she called on all her steely strength as she pulled the reins. She turned her back to Lord Loughlin and put the reins over her shoulder so she could brace herself against the rug and pull him away.

Away he came, and she felt strangely exhilarated. Every time she'd been in that dungeon, her power over him had been illusory, granted to her temporarily by his decree. But now this power was real. He was really fighting her, and she felt a heady mixture of arousal and adrenaline.

He was genuinely surprised that Jean had the strength to pull him off, and as he reached for the cask but came up with only air he, too, felt the reality of what had heretofore been playacting. He wasn't acting. He was feeling, and what he was feeling was anger. Angry at her, yes, but angry mostly at himself.

He reached a foot behind him to get a better purchase and strained against the harness once more. He was certainly the stronger of the two, and once he had leverage against the floor, he managed to reach the cask. He grabbed it with both hands and mounted it. The blood was coursing all through his veins, and he felt an insistence in his erection that he had seldom felt.

Jean, for her part, seemed to realize there was no point in trying to pull him off again. Lord Loughlin felt the reins go slack, and made an effort to master himself and turn around. Her look of bewilderment reached through his anger and his excitement, and he knew he hadn't been fair to the girl. He stood up and reached for her hand. She took a step toward him, and he bent her over the casket and stood behind her.

Robert spread the cheeks of her ass with his hands and laid his cock in between them. He reached underneath and gently massaged her clitoris with his index finger, and the arousal that had drained away came roaring back. She held the cask with both arms, her body braced against the soft sheepskin.

He took his hand away and slipped his cock inside her. It went in easily because she was so wet and ready for him. For the first time, they were two people making love instead of two people playing games, and the freshness of that feeling fueled both of them, enveloping them in an all-consuming warmth.

His already hard cock stiffened that last little bit, and he slowed down to prolong what he knew would be his last few strokes in and out of her.

And that is when Lady Loughlin found them.

FIFTEEN

❧

Lady Loughlin had come down to the cellar to get a bottle of port to leave in the room intended for the Earl of Grantsbury. She'd borrowed Dodson's key to do it. As she perused the racks, looking to see if there was a stray bottle of the '72 left, she heard noises of what sounded like a struggle.

She ventured back and back until she came to the cage where she knew her husband kept his prize wines, and when she looked through the bars she got what she could safely say was the surprise of her life. There was her husband, wearing a leather harness and sporting what looked like a horse's tail, fucking her maid from behind over a barrel covered with sheepskin.

She was too dumbfounded to say a word and, for a moment, Robert and Jean didn't even realize she was there. Then she must have made a sound, because they both looked up at the same time. Lord Loughlin's expression showed astonishment and horror, but apparently he had been so close to climax when he looked up that he found himself coming, ejaculating into his wife's maid as his wife watched from the other side of the iron-barred door.

Lady Loughlin didn't know how to respond to the tableau she was witnessing. It was too far removed from anything in her experience. But she knew she didn't want to stand there watching her husband and her maid extricate themselves, so she turned on her heel without saying a word and almost ran out of the cellar.

Her husband and her maid did extricate themselves and, as they did so, considered the repercussions of Lady Loughlin's discovering them.

"I'm going to get sacked, aren't I?" said Jean.

This had not been at the forefront of Lord Loughlin's mind, but he supposed it was a question that deserved an answer.

"I imagine so, yes," he said. "But I will make sure you aren't turned out without a reference." He knew full well that a maid without a reference from a long-term engagement would be all but unemployable.

Jean's immediate future was certainly a bit grim, but it was uncomplicated. She would simply have to find a new place. Lord Loughlin's future was a more difficult question. He had no idea how his wife would react, or even how he'd want her to.

Jean got dressed as quickly as she could. The idea that she was going to lose her place at Penfield, this household that had been her home these ten years and more, was taking root in her mind, and she felt herself near tears. Her personal pride was such that she would shed them alone, and she took leave of her master with no more than a nod.

Lord Loughlin was left half-dressed, sitting on the stool with his head in his hands. He had always known there was a chance it would come to this, and he knew that it was his wife, and not himself, who would decide the course their marriage would take from here. It was some comfort to know that all he could do was tell her the truth and take whatever came.

He remained in the dungeon for the best part of an hour, incapable of moving or even thinking. Finally, he roused himself. He put on his shirt, laced his boots, and went upstairs to find his wife.

He didn't have to look far. As soon as he came into the hall, he saw her, smiling brightly, arms outstretched, welcoming the Earl of Grantsbury.

The earl was a middle-aged widower with five grown children, all married. When the last of them, his daughter Serena, had wed, he'd breathed a sigh of relief in the knowledge that no other scheming parents would be pursuing him in the hopes of marrying their offspring to his.

His wife had died only the previous year, and he missed her sorely. But he was possessed of a cheerful, optimistic temperament, and her absence didn't prevent him from traveling all over England to wherever good shooting, fast horses, or interesting people could tempt him. He loved company, but also had a scholarly bent. A decade ago he'd written a monograph on ferns that was still thought to be definitive.

He was a tall, stately-looking man. His straight hair, although shot with gray, was so thick that it stood almost straight out from his head. He was kindhearted and good-natured, and the British aristocracy would have been none the worse had more of their number resembled him.

"Lord Grantsbury," Paulette said, with welcoming warmth. "I'm so glad to see you."

"My dear Lady Loughlin," said the earl, taking both her hands in both of his, "I'm delighted to be here."

"I'm sure you must be exhausted," Paulette said to her guest. "Let me show you to your room."

"Not a bit of it! If you can have someone take my man up, he'll take care of the bags. I expect you to take me around and show me all you've done." Here he offered his arm to his hostess. "I've heard stories, you know," he added with a grin.

In a way, this suited Lady Loughlin very well indeed. She knew that the events of the last several days were too public for him to not get wind of them, and she thought it best if she told him herself. This was her opportunity to color the story in such a way as to prevent its being taken too seriously by her most important guest.

If only she didn't have to do it right this moment! She was still reeling from what she'd seen in the wine cellar, and hadn't had enough time to herself to think about it properly. And now she had to direct all her energies toward the earl, whose arm she now took.

"By all means, let us go outside and take a turn around the park." Out of the corner of her eye, she saw her husband, but she would not look at him. She had to put that problem in a little box in the back of her mind while she focused on the task at hand, which was earl management.

The pair went out, and Lady Loughlin led him first to the tennis court, then to the pond, and then through the labyrinth. On the way, she told him of the events of the last several days, beginning with Lady Georgiana's affair with Bruce Barnes.

Grantsbury shook his head and tut-tutted. "I've known that girl since she was a babe in arms. She always would have her own way, and she never would understand that her own way could, if she weren't careful, be her undoing."

Lady Loughlin defended her friend. "I think she has always tempered her own way with just enough judgment to keep her on the right side of public opinion." Grantsbury looked at her and raised his eyebrows, prompting Lady Loughlin to add, "It's been a near thing, though."

"This time it's too near, I daresay. She simply doesn't understand what's at stake. She is so accustomed to the privilege she was born to that she simply can't believe that society would turn its back on her." For Grantsbury, though, this was about more than Georgiana's shortsightedness. He felt strongly that nobility brought with it responsibility, and he profoundly disapproved of her flouting of propriety.

Lady Loughlin went on to tell him of the notes, the poison ivy, the peacock, and the milk, and his surprise mounted with every new chapter of the tale. She made every effort to keep her tone breezy, but Grantsbury didn't see it as one big lark. It wasn't just the possibility of danger; it was that he thought the whole thing an offense against how things ought to be.

"I agree with you that it's unlikely any real harm is intended," Lord

Grantsbury said to his hostess, "but this kind of thing can't be countenanced. If we can't get to the bottom of it ourselves, we simply must call in the constables."

This felt enough like a rebuke to silence Lady Loughlin. But Grantsbury hadn't meant it as one, and when he saw that she had taken it that way, he stopped in his tracks and took both her hands. "Now, now," he said gently. "You mustn't see this as some kind of failure on your part. You are most certainly not to blame. All you have done is surround yourself with interesting, strong-minded people, and that is something I heartily approve of, even if it sometimes has unsavory consequences."

In her entire adult life, Lady Loughlin had not cried in front of another human being. At that moment, she thought she might. There was chaos under her roof. She had earned the displeasure of Lord Grantsbury, the guest she most wanted to impress. Her husband was fucking her maid, for crying out loud, and wearing a tail to boot! What more could a woman be expected to endure in one week?

Strangely, it was the idea of the tail that helped her keep back her tears. Even through her confusion, her anger, and her sense of helplessness, she couldn't help but see something funny in the tail. Why had he had a tail?

There was a bench near the path, under a small grove of trees, and Lady Loughlin walked to it and sat down, all pretense at good cheer abandoned. She shook her head ruefully. "I do this every year, and every year it goes perfectly smoothly. Why it had to go to smash this year, I'm sure I don't know."

"It hasn't gone to smash." The earl sat down beside her. "And we shall see that it doesn't." He patted her hands.

They talked for a bit about the servants, the guests, and how best to keep things in hand, at least until the party. Lady Loughlin would talk to Freddy, the earl would talk to Georgiana, and they would ask Lord Loughlin to get all the servants together and offer a reward for any information leading to the apprehension of the culprit. Lady Loughlin thought this was the best they could do short of notifying the police, and she didn't want to have to do that until after the party.

"We may as well begin at once," she said, sighing and standing up. The earl stood also, and they started to make their way back to the house.

As they walked, he wondered that his hostess could let her spirits be brought so low by this mischief. He couldn't know what was really on her mind, which was the image of her husband and her maid in their little dungeon. Neither said much.

They parted in the front hall, each with a job to do. For Lady Loughlin, it meant talking to her husband, and she went up to her room to pull herself together for the task. She never had the chance, for he was in their joint sitting room, waiting for her.

"Paulette." He stood as she entered.

She sat down heavily, not saying a word. He started to speak, but she put up her hand.

"Before you say anything else, there are two things I must ask of you, and I want to get them out of the way."

He nodded and sat.

"First, I just explained to Lord Grantsbury about the notes that Lady Georgiana and Miss Niven have received, and we have agreed that the best step to take is to offer the servants a reward for any relevant information leading to our finding out who is behind this. Can I ask you to take care of that?"

"Of course. Consider it done."

"Second, I want Jean out of this house as soon as is humanly possible. I don't ever want to see her face again. We can tell the guests and servants that her mother has suddenly taken ill."

"She is packing right now, under the assumption that she must be gone immediately."

The two looked at each other, and then Lord Loughlin said, "I can't imagine what you must think, but I suspect this must be causing you much pain, and I am very sorry."

"Did it have to be *my* maid?" she asked him in a low voice. "Couldn't it have been the parlor maid, or the scullery maid, or the cook, or even the sheep, for all that?" Her voice rose in tone and volume. "But my maid! *My maid!*" For the first time since she'd found them, she felt anger. There had been sadness and a sense of betrayal. There had been bewilderment and plain old surprise. But now there was anger. *"Why?"*

Her husband looked at the floor. "Do you want me to tell you how it began?" He spoke softly.

"Yes!" she almost screamed, and then, not so loudly, "No." Then a pause as she considered. "Yes, yes, I do."

The emotions she'd run through over the last hour had depleted her, and she felt her anger ebbing as quickly as it had come on. She leaned back in the chair, closed her eyes for a moment, and then opened them to look at her husband. "Tell me."

He looked at her, took a deep breath, and began. He had felt Jean's eyes on him from almost the moment she arrived. It was when Freddy was eight and Robbie was twelve, and Lady Loughlin had been so absorbed by the needs of her children that there had been very little intimacy between man and wife. But there was something about Jean—her look, her movements, the way she stood just a little too close to him—that made him think she was available to him.

Even so, he told her, nothing would have come of it had he not had certain . . . urges. At this, Lady Loughlin sat up a bit straighter. She knew nothing about these urges, and wanted to have them explained.

Explain he did: about his desire to be commanded, to submit, to play roles, to be hit. Paulette's eyes widened as he spoke. She had, once or twice, heard or read that such people existed, but she never dreamed she was married to one.

She took it all in. When he'd told the whole story, about how Jean first approached him, about how he introduced her to his urges, about their games, she really had only one question.

"Why on earth didn't you tell me?" The hurt she'd felt at being betrayed was replaced by a different hurt. There was something important about him that he felt he couldn't share with her. She had been excluded from this most intimate part of his makeup.

"How could I expose you to such a thing?" he asked, clearly distressed. "How could I ask you to participate in something like that? You're my wife; you're a lady; you have a position in society. I love you. How could I possibly expect that . . ." He trailed off.

"But how could you *not* have asked me? I'm your wife." She said it simply.

He looked at her, surprised, and said, almost in a whisper, "I thought you would laugh."

His eyes welled, and her heart melted. She went to him and knelt beside his chair. She took his hands in hers and looked straight into his brimming eyes. "I have been married to you for almost a quarter century, and in that time I have laughed many and many a time. But not one of those laughs, not one, has ever been at your expense. I never would have married a man I could laugh at."

He closed his eyes, and he wept.

Dinner that night was a blur for Lady Loughlin. She made her way among her guests, laughing and smiling, but having little idea of either what she was saying or what was being said to her. She caught glimpses of her husband, engaged also in trying to make their guests comfortable, and she could see that he wasn't quite as good at it as she knew herself to be. His smile was wooden and his laugh was forced. Still, she was happy to note, the atmosphere seemed merry and unconstrained.

Had the atmosphere seemed dampened by recent events, she might have exerted herself to remain with her guests until the last went up to bed. Since things were going well, she felt she could excuse herself with those who retired earliest. It wasn't much past nine when she went up to her room. Without a maid to help her out of her frock or into her night-clothes, she simply stepped out of her dress and left it on the floor where it lay. She didn't bother with a nightdress, and climbed into her bed wearing only her shift. Within moments, she was asleep.

She had been drained thoroughly by recent events, and her body was desperate to be rejuvenated. She slept deeply.

When she woke, she looked at the clock on the mantelpiece. It was seven, and she'd been asleep almost ten hours. It had felt like but a moment, but a moment so restorative that she felt like a new woman in a new world. Yesterday, it seemed that everything was collapsing around her ears. This morning she felt like herself again. The Lady Loughlin she knew herself to be could handle all that and more. She rang for tea and, when Rose brought it, she drank deeply and gratefully.

Her thoughts were of her husband, and when she'd finished her cup she got out of bed and pulled her dressing gown around her. She went out into their shared sitting room, and then to his bedchamber beyond. She knocked softly—she didn't want to wake him if he was still asleep—and when she got no response she carefully opened the door and slipped in. She closed it noiselessly behind her and stood for a moment, watching him.

Robert Loughlin had ever been a dignified, considerate sleeper. He never drooled or snored, and when they shared a bed he stayed on his side and used no more than his share of the bedclothes. And there he was, lying on his side with his hands under his head, mouth closed, breathing silently.

She watched him for a few moments, and then took off her dressing gown and stepped out of her shift. She walked around to the other side of the bed, lifted the covers, and slipped in beside him.

Robert woke to the warmth of his wife's breath on the back of his neck. As he came fully into consciousness, and the events of the day before came back to him, he felt flooded with gratitude and relief. He hadn't known whether she would ever forgive him, whether she would ever come back to his bed, and here she was, her body cupped to his, her arm over his waist.

He didn't know when she'd come in or whether she was asleep, and he lay still so as not to disturb her. As their bodies rose and fell with their breathing, he felt her skin moving against his, and it aroused him more than he would have thought such a small thing ever could. It had been months since they had made love, and the time apart combined with yesterday's emotions made her feel new to him again. New and very much worth having.

She stirred, and he sensed that she was awake. She had never been asleep, but had only kept still for him.

He turned over and faced his wife. His beautiful, intelligent paragon of a wife.

He took her face in his hands. "My love," he said, and kissed her.

She put her arms around him and cleaved to him. He was bare chested, and she relished the prickly sensation of his rough chest hair on her breasts. Husband and wife held each other tightly, gently rocking back and forth, each finding joy in the embrace of the other.

He was wearing simple muslin pants with a drawstring, and she reached down to untie them and push them down until he could work his legs out of them. They were both completely naked, and they ran their hands down and around each other's bodies as though they had never done it before.

Robert marveled at her skin, still supple after a twenty-five-year marriage and two children. Paulette traced the muscles of his shoulders and arms, still firm from the active role he took in managing the grounds and the horses. She put her hands on his chest, a palm over each nipple, and felt its definition with her fingertips.

She took one hand away and put his small dark nipple into her mouth. She ran her tongue over and around, and around and over, until he groaned with the pleasure of it.

She turned him onto his back and sat astride him, his cock flattened under her, against his body. She ran her hands over the contours of his chest as though she were studying them for an exam, committing each curve, every freckle to memory. She touched every part of him, and every time she moved to reach him, he felt her vulva move against his penis, each time wetter and more frictionless than the time before.

He put his hands on her thighs and started to sit up, but she put her hand in the middle of his chest to keep him from rising.

"Let me do this," she whispered.

She shifted her weight forward, came up on her knees, and put her hands on either side of his head. He felt the air, suddenly cool on his moistened cock. She bent her arms so her breasts came close to his face, and swayed, just a little, back and forth, to keep them in motion. He reached up and took one breast in each hand and buried his face between them, relishing their firm, supple, ripe feeling on his cheeks. He breathed in the scent of her. She never wore perfume of any kind, and her scent was all her. It was musty and musky, with a little sweetness and a barely detectable sharp note. He would have known it blindfolded.

She slid down his body so her breasts were on his chest and her mouth on his. She ran her tongue over the seam where his lips met, and his mouth opened to meet hers. They kissed like newlyweds, finding their connection in their intertwining.

Paulette sat back up so she could reach beneath her and find his cock. She held it in her hand, feeling its weight, its girth, and the hardness that still, after all these years, surprised her. She slipped it inside her.

Feeling him fill her, she wondered how they possibly could have lost sight of how right, and how important, this was. This was what completed them as man and wife. This was the privilege of intimacy. This was the joy of the freedom to do as you would with another's body, and to grant the same freedom to someone else. They would reclaim that as theirs and theirs alone.

Her arousal had begun when she'd slid into bed beside him and felt his naked back against her chest. It had worked itself into a pressing need as she'd touched him and felt his penis harden beneath her. Now, with him inside her, that need was being answered. She braced herself against his chest and moved up and down, feeling her wetness and their sweat ease the motion. To be emptied and filled, emptied and filled, built up her pleasure to be all-consuming.

He took both her hands in one of his so he could pull her down to him, and now her clitoris was in contact with him. The combined sensation of having him inside her and feeling the friction of his skin on her clit drove her to the edge. She felt that last buildup as the warmth concentrated down the back of her legs, and then she was over, taking him with her.

It was a deep, long onrush of pleasure, and it took her over completely. She succumbed to it, letting it carry both of them to a place they hadn't been in a very long time.

They lay together, her head on his shoulder, his softening penis inside her, for a long time. Gradually, the demands the day would place on both of them infiltrated the haze of their postcoital reverie, and Paulette extracted herself from the tangled bedding.

She pulled her dressing gown back around her and sat on the edge of the bed, smiling at her husband.

"We have a lot to do today if the masquerade is going to come off tomorrow," she said.

"We do indeed, particularly if we want to avoid any further incidents," her husband agreed.

"Will you get the servants together and tell them about the reward?" she asked.

"I did it last night after dinner, and then I made it a point to be available in the library to anyone who wanted to come forward in private, but no one did."

"Do you suppose that's because no one knows, or because no one's telling?" she asked.

"I would imagine no one knows. There aren't many on our staff who would want something like that happening in the house, and I suspect most would come forward even if there weren't a reward."

"I suppose all we can do is be vigilant and hope for the best." Lady Loughlin smiled her characteristic sunny smile. "In the meantime, I will track down Freddy and see if he knows anything about this." She leaned over, kissed him on the cheek, and headed back to her room to bathe and dress.

As she was leaving, she turned back to him and said, "Once the party is over and the house is empty again, will you take me down to the cellar and show me what you have there?"

He gave a half smile. "I will," he said.

SIXTEEN

⌒

Freddy, meanwhile, was enjoying the company of Miss Niven and Lady Georgiana. He was doing his level best to pry out of them the secret of their costumes for the party the next evening. Had he gotten Miss Niven alone, he might have succeeded, but Georgiana was too much for him.

"What is the point of going to a masked ball if you tell everyone ahead of time what your costume is? It absolutely defeats the purpose," she told him with spirit.

"I couldn't agree with you more," said Freddy. "I would never suggest that you should tell everyone. I only suggest that you tell me."

"Bah! It would come to the same thing, as your discretion is not to be relied on!"

"Not to be relied on! I say! I can be as silent as the grave when circumstances warrant." Freddy made a locking gesture over his lips.

"It is that 'when circumstances warrant' that makes me uneasy," Georgiana said.

At this, Freddy turned to Alexandra. "Miss Niven, surely you have more faith in my judgment and discretion than Lady Georgiana."

"I certainly have some faith in your judgment," she said with a smile, "but I have more faith in hers, so I am going to follow my friend's example and keep my secret."

"Well," said Freddy, stymied, "I'd like to see a little less sober judgment and a little more freewheeling devil-may-care around here, I must say."

"Then why don't you start by telling us what your costume is," Georgiana said, fluttering her lashes in a parody of innocence.

"Oh, I'll be one of the many satyrs in attendance," Freddy said.

At this point they were interrupted by Lady Loughlin. "Freddy, my son. Just the man I'd like to see."

"I suppose that you, too, are going to pry out of me my costume for tomorrow evening."

"I don't care a straw for your costume. I shall know who you are by the way you attach yourself to all the lovely young girls of my acquaintance." She nodded at Georgiana and Alexandra. "But I regret that I must pull you away from them just for a short while."

"Ah, we shall miss him," said Alexandra, who had caught Georgiana's tone. "But I daresay we shall survive his absence and live to not tell him our costumes again this afternoon."

"Then I take him away with a clear conscience," said their hostess, and led her son upstairs.

Freddy knew that his mother would take him away from company only if something serious were afoot. As soon as they were alone in Lady Loughlin's sitting room he asked, with some trepidation, what was amiss.

"You already know *what's* amiss, Freddy. But I'd like to find out whether you know *why* it's amiss."

Freddy looked puzzled.

"The notes, Freddy, the notes. Surely you know about the notes."

"Oh, the harlot thing! Yes, of course, I'd heard that Lady G had gotten a couple of censorious missives. But surely it's not serious."

"Then you don't know about Miss Niven's 'censorious missive,' as you call it."

"What? Miss Niven? What's happened?" Freddy looked genuinely alarmed, and Lady Loughlin felt sure he couldn't have been behind the milk, even if he had been the culprit in Lady Georgiana's case.

She explained to him what had happened, and he was both outraged and incredulous. "That someone would do that! That someone would do that to *her*! What's she done to deserve it?"

"And did Lady Georgiana deserve it, then?" his mother asked with some acerbity.

Freddy reddened. "Well, of course she didn't *deserve* it. But having a thing with Barnes in full view and all that. She *is* courting trouble. But Miss Niven! As pure as the driven snow."

"I certainly don't know of anything Miss Niven's done that could have earned her that kind of disapproval," Lady Loughlin said, "and I am at a loss to explain why she has been treated this way."

"Well, she's been awfully plucky about it," said Freddy, with real admiration. "She didn't breathe a word of it to me."

"At any rate, you can see that this series of incidents has taken a turn for the serious, and I'm afraid I must know whether you had anything to do with setting it in motion. A bouquet of poison ivy sounds like it might be your idea of a prank."

Freddy spluttered with outrage. "Surely you don't think . . . ! You can't suspect that I . . . ! Really, Mother." He looked at her with such bewilderment that she almost felt sorry for having asked him.

"Upon my honor as a gentleman," he said, collecting himself, "I had nothing whatever to do with any of this. And if I find out who the culprit is, I will personally take him out to the stables and horsewhip him."

"And if 'him' is a 'her'?"

"Well, I suppose it would be bad form to horsewhip a woman," said Freddy, contemplating it with a seriousness that almost made his mother laugh. "But I'd think of something."

"I daresay you would, Freddy, I daresay you would." Lady Loughlin smiled at her son with affection. "Perhaps, in the meantime, you can think about all you've seen and heard since you've been home, and tell me whether you have any ideas about the 'him' or the 'her.' Your father and I are at something of a loss."

"Oh, it's 'him' and it's Barnes," Freddy said with absolute confidence.

"What?" Lady Loughlin looked startled.

"You have only to look at the brute to know he's capable of anything." Freddy waved a hand, as though dismissing every other possibility.

"But surely you don't know anything against him." She didn't know whether he was being serious, but suspected that he wasn't.

"Do I absolutely *know* anything against him?" Freddy asked rhetorically. "No, I don't. But the man radiates animal malice. I'm sure he eats raw meat and sleeps in trees."

Paulette laughed. "Freddy, be serious. We need to get to the bottom of this."

"If it isn't Barnes, I'm as much at a loss as you and Father. I haven't been mingling much, you know," Freddy said. "It's bad, being sent down, and it's cast a bit of a pall over my socializing."

"I see you've found an exception in Miss Niven." His mother raised her eyebrows.

Freddy grinned. "That I have. And a fine exception she's been. But as to the matter at hand"—here he shrugged—"I don't think I'm going to be much help."

With that, Freddy bade his mother adieu and went off to try to find Miss Niven and Lady Georgiana—Miss Niven in particular. He went downstairs to where the three of them had earlier been breakfasting, but found that the two ladies had moved on.

Although the weather threatened, they had gone outside to take a stroll. Once outside, companionably arm in arm, they confessed to each other what they wouldn't confess to Freddy.

"I'm going to be Alice," Georgiana confided to her friend.

"Alice?"

"*Alice in Wonderland* Alice. I loved that book when I was a child. I have the dress and the apron and the stockings and the little shoes with straps. I'll wear my hair down, just like she does in the book."

"That's a wonderful idea! And, with a mask, no one will recognize you."

"It was actually my second choice," Georgiana said. "I was going to be a midshipman."

Alexandra laughed. "I don't think I know exactly what a midshipman looks like."

"A midshipman looks exactly like me, only with cotton duck trousers. I wanted to see if I could pass myself off as a man," Georgiana said. "Only I thought that, if it worked, I wouldn't be able to dance."

"I think Alice is much the better choice." Miss Niven nodded sagely.

"And now you know my secret. Will you tell me yours?" Georgiana squeezed her friend's arm.

"I am going to be Cleopatra. I have a dress with a square neck that looks a little Egyptian and a little Roman, and if I let my hair down it comes just past my shoulders. I'll brush it out when it's wet so it straightens a bit. And I'll color my eyes, which will show through the mask."

"That's a wonderful costume, and I'm sure it will set you off to great advantage."

Alexandra blushed a little, unwilling to admit that she had thought the same. "I was afraid I wouldn't be able to use it because my injured ankle made me limp, and you can't be Cleopatra and limp, but it's almost gone today and I should be completely two-footed tomorrow."

As they talked, the skies had darkened, and they now heard a loud rumble of thunder. "I think we should turn back, or we are going to get very, very wet," said Georgiana.

They turned and headed back to the house, and it looked as though they might reach it ahead of the storm. When they were just a few hundred feet from the door, though, the skies let loose and the rain fell as though from a faucet. In those few hundred feet they got soaked through, and came into the hall a sodden mass of dripping dresses, soaked boots, and ruined hats. But they were laughing as though the world were their own private joke.

They ran for the stairs to go up and change, and almost collided with the Earl of Grantsbury.

"My lord!" Georgiana said. "I'd heard you were here, but I didn't see you at dinner last night."

"I was, I regret to say, busy with my correspondence."

"It's not like you to miss dinner!"

"Not like me at all. And I can assure you it won't happen again as long as I am in this house."

Georgiana put a gentle hand on the shoulder of Alexandra, who was embarrassed to meet an earl while she was soaked to the skin, and had taken a half step back when they ran into the nobleman. "Lord Grantsbury, allow me to introduce my great friend Miss Niven. Miss Niven, Lord Grantsbury." The two nodded, and Grantsbury, seeing Alexandra's discomfort, endeavored to put her at her ease. "I expect that you will give me great credit for the acuity of my perception if I note that I think you two young ladies have been caught in the rain."

"We have indeed, my lord," said Alexandra with a shy grin, "and I hope you will excuse me if I run off to get out of these wet things."

"I will indeed, but only if you promise to return when you are warm and dry."

"I look forward to it," said Alexandra, and trotted off up the stairs.

When he was alone with Georgiana, Grantsbury took both her hands in his and kissed her forehead affectionately. "My dear girl, I am glad to see you."

"And I you," she replied. "It has been several years, has it not?"

"It has," said the earl. "Too many, I think."

"I want to find out all that's happened in the interim, but first I must follow my friend's example and change my dress. Shall I come find you when I come back down?"

"Do, my dear, please do. I will take a newspaper into the library and await your return."

She headed up the stairs, but paused before she had taken a half dozen steps and turned around to come back down. "My lord," she said, "I have been remiss. The very first thing I should have said to you is that I am so very sorry for the loss of your wife. Although I wrote to you at the time, I never feel as though a letter can do justice to heartfelt feelings—at least, my letters can't. I know you were devoted to her and it must have been a heavy blow."

"I was, and it was," he replied, and his expression softened as he thought of it. "But time works wonders, and her death has not prevented me from enjoying my life."

"I am glad to know it," Georgiana said, and went up to her room.

She came down an hour later, dry and refreshed, and went straight to the library to find the earl. He was ensconced in a corner, sitting in an oxblood leather club chair, reading his paper as promised. Georgiana stood behind him and scanned the paper over his shoulder. "Is anything of significance happening in the rest of the world?" she asked.

"Nothing I can see," said Grantsbury. "I think the masquerade at Penfield is the most notable event on the immediate horizon."

"In that case, I am glad we are here to see history made."

He folded up his paper with some deliberateness and turned to face her. "I think we have much to talk about. Do you suppose we can find some quiet corner?"

The house was full to bursting with the Loughlins' guests, and quiet corners in public rooms were hard to come by. There were several people in the library, so the two wandered through the various parlors and drawing rooms to see if they couldn't find a spot.

As the weather was still inhospitable—the rain had eased, but it was still damp and windy—almost all the guests were indoors, and their quiet corner was not to be found. "There's no help for it," said Grantsbury. "Would you consider it too improper to come up to my sitting room?"

Georgiana wasn't one to be deterred by that breed of impropriety. "I wouldn't, my lord." She took his arm and they went upstairs.

The earl's valet was in his sitting room, setting things aright. "Bertram," said Grantsbury, "Lady Georgiana and I have come up here to escape the crowds, and nothing would suit us better than a cup of tea. Could you have someone send one up?"

"Of course, my lord. I shall fetch it myself." Bertram nodded and left on his errand, closing the door behind him.

The earl's insistence on privacy and his serious manner made Georgiana think that this wasn't going to be a friendly chat about what they'd done since last they'd met. She remembered him as jovial and warm, not formal and serious, and she wondered what he might have on his mind.

He gestured for her to sit on the sofa, which she did. Instead of taking the chair across from her, he sat down beside her. "My dear," he said, "there is something particular I would like to discuss with you." The tenderness in his eyes was at odds with his serious manner.

Georgiana was taken aback. Was he going to make love to her? Her mind whirled at the possibility. He'd been recently widowed; he was connected to her family; he had always liked her. Could it be?

She had only a second or two to think about it, but in that brief time she asked herself how she would answer him. Could she think of him as a lover? She concluded, in a mere moment, that she could not. Was she, then, going to be in the terribly awkward position of refusing a man—an earl!—whom she liked and respected?

"It is a delicate matter," the earl continued, "and I am not sure how to broach it, so I will just jump in."

She wasn't looking at him. She was staring blankly into the room, her mind racing to come to terms with what she thought she was about to hear.

The earl waited, and, in the silence, she turned to him. When he could look her in the eye, he said, "It's about Mr. Barnes."

She was thunderstruck. "Mr. Barnes?" she echoed helplessly.

"Yes, my dear. Mr. Barnes."

Her mind was reeling all over again. Why on earth would this man speak to her of Mr. Barnes? It was a short hop from wonder to annoyance. What right had he to speak to her of Mr. Barnes?

The earl forged ahead. "Lady Loughlin told me some of what has gone on under her roof over the course of the last week. She was concerned for you, for your friend Miss Niven, and for the erosion of order in her household. She could not tell me of the threats without telling me also of your relationship with Mr. Barnes."

Georgiana stared mutely, not having the foggiest notion how to reply.

This seemed to suit Lord Grantsbury. He had something to say, and it was perhaps best if he got it out without too much interruption.

"I have known your family since before you were born, and you since you were a baby. From your very first steps, which, if I may say so, were willful and determined"—here he smiled—"I have liked and admired you. And, although you have a perfectly serviceable father in my great friend Lord Eastley, that has not prevented me from feeling a very paternal concern for your well-being and your future."

He sighed as he began on the substance of what he had to say.

"It gives me no pleasure to say this, and I would not say it unless I was certain that you understand that I have your best interest very much at heart, but you are behaving like an ass."

Lady Georgiana bridled. She had, by this time, expected to be rebuked, but not in such harsh terms as this.

"An . . . ass, my lord?" she said stiffly.

"I've always called a spade a spade, and I shall always call an ass an ass," he replied with a matter-of-fact tone. "Your stubbornness and pride are leading you into a situation that could very well be your undoing."

Here her color started to rise, and her anger with it.

"My lord," she said, controlling her tone with an effort, "your long acquaintance with my family and with me gives you license to talk to me in a way I would not stand for in others, but to call me an ass, and stubborn, and prideful, goes beyond what that license entitles you to." She stood, and then vacillated as she tried to decide whether or not she should stalk out in a huff.

Grantsbury stood also, and motioned her back to the sofa. "Please, my dear, sit down. Try to see beyond your anger at the liberty I have taken, and think for a moment about the substance of what I have to say."

She hesitated, and then sat.

Grantsbury was silent for a moment, giving her time to let her anger cool and her reason reassert itself. Then he began again.

"You are an earl's daughter, and the world, which thinks much of nobility, will give you as wide a latitude as it can. There are limits, though, beyond which the world will not go. I believe that your liaison with Mr. Barnes will try the world's patience."

Georgiana could not hear this without protesting. "And why is it, my lord, that Mr. Barnes's liaison—as you call it—with me does *not* try the world's patience? Is he not as much a participant as I am? Yet the world says nothing to *him*."

"He is a man, my dear. You are a girl."

"And it is because I am a girl that I am to be censured, while he, or any other man, is to get off not just scot-free, but with a wink and a nod and a nudge that all say, 'See what a fine, virile fellow he is!'"

"Yes," Grantsbury said.

The simplicity of his answer took Georgiana aback. "And you think that is fair and just?"

"I do not."

It took her a few moments to grasp this. "You do not think those constraints are fair or just, yet you condemn me and call me an ass for flouting them?"

"I do."

She was at a loss. "But why?" she asked plaintively. "How can you be so inconsistent?"

"I am not being in the least inconsistent," the earl said. "The issue isn't fairness or justice; it is your best interest."

"And is it not in my best interest to live in a fair and just world?"

"It would be, if it were possible. But the world is not fair and just, and there are times when we must do what the world expects of us, however unfair or unjust, for the simple reason that we will be made miserable if we do not. The rightness of your conduct will be cold comfort when the world turns its back on you. I am not saying you are wrong, only that you are profoundly imprudent."

She sat perfectly still as she absorbed this. She could just make out the edge of a glimmer of truth in what he said, but she was reluctant to make the effort to bring the whole truth into clear view.

"But how ever are we to make the world more fair and just if we simply do as it bids us, out of fear of the consequences?"

"I think there are ways. You can speak against unfairness wherever you find it. You can befriend and defend people who defy the world's constraints, and do your utmost to ensure that they are not made miserable. A voluble defender of the equality of women who is herself above the censure of the world will do more to forward the cause than one wayward earl's daughter."

"Can I not be both voluble *and* wayward?"

"If you are wayward, no one will listen, and your volubility will be for naught."

Georgiana knew, as she listened to this, that there had been a small voice in her own head telling her the same thing, but that she had silenced it before giving it proper consideration. Forced to consider it now, she felt chagrin.

The earl saw that she was wrestling with what he had said, and wanted to make sure she understood what the consequences of her behavior might be.

"Penfield is a very liberal place," he said. "And that is to its credit. The people here are much more inclined to think as you do, and to see your behavior in its best light, than people you will meet again back home, and in London, and most other places you choose to go. What may be regarded here as a daring dalliance will be regarded elsewhere as an inexcusable transgression."

There was a discreet knock at the door, and Bertram entered with tea and a rack of toast. Not a word was said as he put the tray down on a low table, looked at the earl, who nodded at him, and left the room.

As he poured Georgiana a cup, the earl said, "I know you have a lot to think about already, but I must give you just one more thing."

She took the cup and looked up at him. "Now that I've come this far, I suppose I want to hear it all," she said, bracing herself for this one more thing.

"It is Mr. Barnes himself," said Grantsbury. "He may be very taken with you, or very taken with the idea of allying himself with an earl's daughter, or both. If you have no intention of marrying the man, you may have toyed with his affections."

Georgiana put her cup down and leaned back on the sofa. She looked at the ceiling as she said, "I don't think Mr. Barnes attached any more significance to our relationship than I did."

"You are in a better position than I to know that, and I won't question you. I raise the issue only because I think any man, even a man with the intention of keeping his distance, might find your charms to be too much for him."

The earl leaned over to put his empty teacup back on the tray. "And that, I'm sure you'll be glad to know, is all I have to say. You may take it for what you think it to be worth." He didn't want to stand up because he knew that gesture would be taken as one of dismissal, but he also wanted Georgiana to know he wasn't waiting for an answer from her. "I'm sure this isn't the most pleasant subject for you, and we need not say another word about it, if you choose."

Georgiana looked at him thoughtfully. "I must give what you've said some consideration before I make any answer at all." She stood. "Will you excuse me?"

"Of course." He also stood, and opened the door for her. She went through it without looking at him again.

SEVENTEEN

❧

Georgiana walked back to her room with a bevy of emotions competing for her attention. The fact that the earl had rebuked her left her abashed, but she wasn't sure if she was abashed because she knew herself to be in the wrong, or abashed simply because he had been hard with her. She was also indignant because he had spoken to her in a way that no person who wasn't a blood relative ever had before.

Then there were her feelings for Barnes. What, exactly, *were* her feelings for Barnes? And his for her? She had to sort through all these thoughts, and everything the earl had said, before she could answer that all-important question: What was she to do?

The door to her room was open, and she went in and closed it behind her. She sat on the bed to unlace her boots, and it was only when she had done that, and stood the boots under the bed, that she looked up and saw the large red letter A on her mirror.

She gasped with surprise. She felt primarily the sense of violation that comes of knowing that someone had been in her room unsanctioned and didn't, at first, grasp the significance of the A. She looked at it for a moment, cocking her head. Suddenly she understood, and burst out laughing.

It was *The Scarlet Letter*! Someone knew enough to know that a red A branded a loose woman, but didn't know enough to understand that the A was for *adulteress*, which Georgiana, being unmarried, couldn't possibly be.

It was such a pathetic attempt at a threat. Not only could Georgiana not take it seriously; it colored her view of the previous incidents so she was more inclined to see them as the work of a bungling ignoramus rather than a malicious villain.

There was a soft knock on the door. She was about to ask her visitor to come in, but thought better of it. She didn't want the whole house knowing of the defaced mirror. She padded to the door and opened it. There was Barnes.

Georgiana, thinking what a spectacular piece of bad timing this was, put her hand on the doorjamb and leaned her forehead on her hand for a moment. Then she looked up at Barnes. He was the last person she needed to see right now. It was hard enough to figure out what she ought to do without the man who was the source of the problem standing in front of her, exerting his draw over her.

She felt a faint flutter in her breast, the beginning of the feeling that told her she wasn't wholly in control of herself, but it was a poor echo of what it had been. Every time she'd stood face-to-face with this man, she'd felt the same weakness, the same animal connection—until now. Somehow, her conversation with Grantsbury, if it hadn't quite yet changed the way she thought, had effectively changed the way she felt.

"I'm sorry, Bruce, but I cannot see you now."

He was surprised at this reception. "Do you have another visitor?"

"No, I am alone with my thoughts, but they are very preoccupying and I simply cannot see you now."

"Then I shall come back when you *can* see me." He did his best to take the rebuff in stride. "Perhaps after dinner."

"No," she said. "I must ask that you do not."

"Why must you ask that I do not?" Here he asserted his physical presence by leaning toward her just a bit, and looking hard into her eyes.

It surprised her that his presence, which had been so powerful to her, had lost so much of its sway. She felt his heat, but the draw did not compel her. She found that he was not, after all, irresistible.

"Is it not enough that I ask that you do not?"

"After what has passed between us? No, it is not enough. I believe I am entitled to a reason."

As little inclined as she was to talk to him just then, she did see the fairness in his request.

"Then I shall give you one, but I shall not give it to you now." She sounded imperious even to her own ears, and changed her tone. "You have come at a bad moment, but I will find a better moment and give you a better explanation. I promise." She looked at him with a pleading expression tinged with regret, but it did not touch him. He gave her one more hard look, turned without a word, and walked away.

Lady Georgiana sighed heavily and closed the door.

Barnes stalked down the hall, his temples burning with anger. He would not be condescended to! That she could lie naked in his arms one day, and talk to him like that the next!

When he'd entertained the possibility of making an alliance with an earl's daughter, the idea of an earl's daughter became much to him. Now the idea of an earl's daughter turned to ashes in his mouth. She could never forget her rank, or his. She could behave as though they were equals as long as everything was going well but, as soon as there was any fly in the ointment, her sense of what was due her rank reasserted itself.

He played her words back through his mind over and over. Her words had insulted him and her tone had infuriated him, but there was more. He knew, as a man does know, that he had lost his hold on her.

Every time he'd met her, he'd been able to close the physical, social, and emotional distance between them simply by standing close, looking her in the eye, and speaking softly. This time, though, he could not.

He had lost her, and he felt regret, but the regret was overridden by anger. In rejecting him, in breaking his hold on her, Lady Georgiana had humiliated him, and Barnes felt the fury of a man unmanned.

Almost automatically, his steps took him down to the kitchen and through to the scullery. Had his better judgment been in command of him, he would have avoided all company and gone to his cottage, alone, to recover his equanimity. But he was being piloted by the need to re-assert himself as a man.

There he found Maureen putting things in order for the dinner ser-vice. She was surprised to see him; he would know she was busy at this time of day.

"Ah, Maureen, just who I've come to see." He tried to disguise the blackness of his mood, but Maureen knew him too well to be fooled.

"What ever is the matter?" she asked.

"Nothing is the matter." He grabbed her around the waist and pulled her to him. "Nothing, at least, that can't be set right very easily." He buried his head in her neck, and she felt him pulling her flesh in between his teeth.

She tried to push him away. "It's busy here. I've work to do, and there will be people coming in and out in herds!"

He was not to be pushed. "Then let's use the jam cupboard." He pulled her in the direction of a small closet lined with shelves that the house-hold used for the jams and preserves that were put up every fall. They'd used it before, when they were afraid of company in the scullery.

Maureen didn't like the way this was going. He was often rough, and his roughness was part of what attracted her to him, but this time he was rough with an abandon that was a little frightening. Still, she let herself be led into the jam cupboard. They went in and Barnes closed the door.

There was a high stool in the cupboard, used to reach the uppermost shelves, and Barnes had her skirts lifted and her ass on the stool almost before the door was closed. He maneuvered her drawers down and pulled one of her feet, still booted, through one of the legs. The other he left on, so the garment dangled from her right calf.

Without preamble, he unbuttoned his trousers and pulled out his throbbing cock. He stepped between her legs and took her breasts in his hands. He closed his eyes as he squeezed them, and rubbed his cock between her legs.

This aroused her intensely. When they had gone into the closet, she had thought this was perhaps going to lead to an unpleasant scene, but she had been wrong. He was exercising his power over her, but she did not feel like a victim. Powerlessness, her affair with him had taught her, was heady and intoxicating.

There had been other men in her life before Barnes, and none of them would ever have dared something like this. Rough it might be, but it was proof of his strength, of his confidence—and she thought strength and confidence were the very essence of manhood.

And so, when she felt the calluses of his hands against the soft skin of her breasts as he held them so tight it almost hurt, it felt firm and forceful to her. He was pushing against her so hard she had to hold on to the sides of the seat of the stool to keep from tipping backward, and all her muscles were engaged in keeping her body next to his. She was answering his force with her own.

She had never in her life felt so aroused so quickly. His need, his immediacy, had become her own, and she wanted nothing but to have him enter her and complete her.

This he had been ready to do from the moment they stepped into the closet. When she spread her legs to accommodate him, he was inside with one thrust. The wetness that was welling up inside her hadn't worked all the way down to her labia, and there was a moment when the friction of his penis entering her caused pain. But the pain seemed to work like the powerlessness, fueling the crescendo that was building inside her.

She gave herself over to him. She watched him and she felt him taking her as though she were a possession. Taking her as though it were his God-given right. Taking her as though the laws of nature dictated that it should be so. But she knew he wasn't really taking. She was giving. She was giving and it was so erotic, so arousing, that it took her breath away. As his cock thrust in and pulled out, thrust and withdrew, she gloried in it.

Her body knew his urgency and fed on it. She caught his rhythm and matched her pace to his. She came to the verge of climax faster than she ever thought possible, and was there, coming with him, when his explosion came. It was acute and all-consuming, and it reverberated from her toes all the way up to the back of her neck.

Barnes withdrew from her as unceremoniously as he had approached her. He buttoned his trousers and carefully opened the closet door. He looked around and, seeing nobody, slipped out. On his way, he gave her a smile that looked to her to be just a little diabolical.

She put herself back together as quickly as she could, and was back in the scullery before she was missed.

Upstairs, Georgiana sat on her bed, looking at the scarlet letter and trying to align her feelings with her thoughts, and her thoughts with one another.

Her talk with Lord Grantsbury had made an impression, she realized. Had she thought him to be completely wrong, she knew her feelings about Barnes wouldn't have changed. It was because she was afraid he was right that she could no longer feel the attraction to Barnes that she had.

She needed to talk this through, and she needed a friend. She reached for her boots, put them on, and was about to leave the room when she turned, picked up a handkerchief, and wiped the lipstick off the mirror as best she could. Then she strode purposely to Miss Niven's room.

"Come in," Alexandra said in answer to her knock.

"Oh, Alexandra, I'm so glad to have found you in your room. So much has happened that I must tell you about."

Alexandra's face took on a rather confused look, and she made a downward gesture with her hand that Georgiana read as an invitation to sit, so she took a seat on an upholstered chair near the door. "You won't credit it, but I've found a scarlet letter on my mirror!" she blurted. "A great big capital A written in lipstick! Someone doesn't know any better than to label me an adulteress."

Here she sat back in the chair with a bemused look. Miss Niven didn't respond, but only coughed, and Georgiana looked at her curiously.

At that point, Miss Mumford stepped out from behind the open door of the wardrobe, where she had been setting Miss Niven's costume to rights.

Georgiana colored. She had not intended to share her news with any but her friend, and she would have preferred that Miss Niven's rather disagreeable companion not know. But it was done, and she would make the best of it.

"Miss Mumford, I apologize for bursting in on you like this," she said a little stiffly. "Had I known you had a prior claim on my friend's attention, I would have come back another time."

"Not at all, Lady Georgiana," Miss Mumford said with an oily grace. "I was simply making sure all was in order with Miss Niven's masquerade costume, and that can certainly wait. I will leave you two alone." She left the room and closed the door behind her.

"I was trying to let you know she was there," Miss Niven said almost disconsolately. She knew that Lady Georgiana would not want Miss Mumford to know about the incident. "Had I had my wits about me I would have called to her to come out and meet you. I'm so sorry."

"Never fret," Georgiana said, looking kindly at her. "I daresay no harm is done. She knows about everything else, so it means nothing that she knows about this, too."

Alexandra relaxed a little, and her thoughts turned to Georgiana's news. "When did you find the letter?"

"Just this afternoon. I returned to my room from an interview with the Earl of Grantsbury, about which I would very much like your opinion."

Miss Niven was exceedingly flattered by her friend's soliciting her opinion, and on a matter she discussed with Lord Grantsbury! But her natural modesty made her doubt that her thoughts could be of much use to one such as Georgiana.

"I am, of course, happy to give you my opinion, but I don't know that it will be helpful to you," she said.

"I disagree," her friend said firmly, "and my thoughts are in such a state of confusion that I can't make heads or tails of them. I need a clear-thinking, sympathetic friend to help me sort it out, and you are just such a one."

Miss Niven flushed with pleasure. "I shall do all I can, but first you must tell me about the A."

"I have told it already. I came to my room, and there it was."

"And you didn't see anyone in the corridor?"

"Not a soul, and the letter could have been there for an hour or more, as that is how long I was gone. But," she added thoughtfully, "I do think this tells us something about our culprit."

"Does it?"

"Yes. Because *The Scarlet Letter* is so well-known, anyone might know that an A brands a woman in that particular way. But only someone essentially ignorant would apply that to me, an unmarried woman. "

"You may very well be right that it was someone ignorant," said Miss Niven, "although it might simply be someone educated taking a semantic liberty with the word. But, even if that's not the case, might not someone ignorant be as dangerous as someone knowledgeable?"

"You are right," said Georgiana, giving this some consideration. "But it is hard for me to take it seriously when it is so comical."

The two women agreed, though, that this new piece of information made it look as though servants were more likely suspects than guests. Which servants, though, they could not say.

"One other thought did occur to me," Georgiana said, a bit tentatively.

"Yes . . . ?" Miss Niven encouraged her to go on.

"Well, at first I thought it could be Mr. Barnes."

Miss Niven looked at her wonderingly. "Mr. Barnes? But why on earth . . . ?" she said.

"In order to be the hero. It was he who identified the bouquet as poison ivy. He would have been one of the first to know when the peacock died, and he came to remove it himself."

"That seems like an awful lot of work just to make a good impression," Miss Niven said, puzzled that her friend would suggest it.

"It's not just that," Georgiana said. "I think he's a shrewd judge of character, and he might have believed that leaving those notes would have the effect of driving me closer to him, not farther away. It's not difficult to see that I'm rather a defiant sort of girl, and censure I feel to be unjust would simply make me dig in my heels."

Miss Niven thought about this. She wouldn't have described Georgiana this way, but now that the description had come from Georgiana herself, she saw its aptness.

"You may be right," Alexandra said. "And, since he certainly wouldn't have the same motive where I'm concerned, that would leave open the possibility that it was Miss Mumford in my case."

"Or anyone else who knew about the notes," Georgiana added. The girls tried to think of everyone who fell into that category, but the list was much too long.

"Anyone could have told anyone else," Alexandra said, throwing up her hands.

"You're right," said Lady Georgiana. "We can talk about it all day and all night, but it's getting us no closer to an answer." She sighed.

Their speculative efforts exhausted, Georgiana then broached the topic of her talk with Lord Grantsbury. She told Alexandra of all he had said, and again asked her opinion.

Alexandra sat silent for a time, thinking carefully about it. She didn't want to oppose her friend, or appear to criticize, but neither could she say anything other than what she believed to be true. Finally she said, "I cannot but think that he is right." Georgiana sighed and nodded but didn't respond, and she went on. "Perhaps it is because I am more accustomed than you to thinking myself at the world's mercy, and always keep in mind the importance of safeguarding my reputation."

"But why must women do that, while men need not?"

"I don't know. I know only that they must, and so I do."

They talked at some length about men and women, and reputation and restrictions, and Lady Georgiana found Miss Niven's thoughts on the subject clearer and more compelling than she had expected. At the end of a half hour, she was determined, if not to walk the straight and narrow from that day forward, at least to check some of her more outré impulses.

She didn't like it, though, and she couldn't help but resent Lord Grantsbury's harsh words.

"But he called me an ass!" she said plaintively, holding on to the last objection she had.

"Perhaps that was what the A was for, and it was someone knowledgeable after all," said Miss Niven, smiling and blushing slightly at her own daring for making fun of her friend.

Georgiana looked at her in wonder, surprised that such a joke had come out of such a girl. And then she laughed as long and loud as she had in many days.

It was only when she stopped that they heard the knock on the door. "Come in," Alexandra called, and Freddy did as he was bidden.

"What's the joke?" he asked. "It sounded like an awfully good one."

"Oh, it's much too long a story to tell," said Georgiana.

"That's what people say when they simply don't want to tell you," he said petulantly.

"All right, then, we simply don't want to tell you."

"Well, at least now you're being straight about it."

"I'm always straight, Freddy; haven't you figured that out by now?" Georgiana asked as she stood up. Her mind was still on her conversations of the afternoon, and she was in no mood for Freddy's nonsense. "And now I will go straight out of the room and leave you to our good Miss Niven."

When she was gone, Freddy sat down in her chair without waiting to be asked. He had hoped to find Alexandra alone but, now that he was with her, he wasn't sure how to begin.

"I say," he started haltingly, "my mother told me about the milk. You're a trump for not letting on."

Alexandra's color rose. The milk and the note were not something she wanted to discuss with Freddy. "It wasn't so very bad," she said, and then did her best to change the subject. "Have you played more tennis?" she asked with artificial brightness.

"Tennis?" he said. "You gave me such a thrashing that I believe I shall give up the game. Unless, of course, you would like to give me lessons." He looked at her with wide eyes and a meaningful expression.

She colored again, and began to have a sense of the direction this conversation was taking. But she would take him at his word. "Oh, I'm certainly unqualified to give lessons, but I should hate to bear the responsibility for your giving up the sport."

"I would never hold you to account," he said awkwardly, not knowing how to dig himself out of this hole. He didn't come here to talk about tennis lessons. He'd never approached a girl in this way before, and he was finding that it wasn't nearly as easy as he thought it would be.

"Devil take it!" he said, and plunged in. "Miss Niven, I think you're the finest girl I've ever laid eyes on."

Alexandra was startled at this declaration. Her mouth opened a bit in surprise.

"I mean, it's not how you look," he went on confusedly. "I mean, it *is* how you look, but it's not *just* how you look." He knew he was making a hash of it. "It's just that you're such . . . such . . ." He struggled to articulate what she was. "Such a good sport," was what he settled on.

She had to smile. She had a sense that, in Freddy's lexicon, "good sport" was a high compliment indeed, and she was ready to take it in the spirit in which it was intended. She wasn't sure, though, whether he was making love to her or not. If he was, it was a curious sort of lovemaking. But if he wasn't, as conversation it was more curious yet.

"I am glad you think me so," she said with a kind expression intended to put him more at his ease.

The two were seated in twin upholstered chairs with a small table in between them. Freddy got up from his and sat on the table, close enough to her that her skirt rustled against his legs.

He took her hand. "I know I'm making a grand muddle of it," he said, looking her straight in the eye. "But I can't help myself."

Now she was sure he was making love to her. She was less sure about how to respond. Was this to be her second marriage proposal in as many days?

Freddy put her hand to his lips, and she had only a moment to decide whether this was a liberty she ought to allow. On the whole, she thought she oughtn't, but a girlish curiosity to let the scene play out stopped her from stopping him.

Freddy tested the limits of that girlish curiosity as he took her hand from his lips and put it in both his own. He turned it over, so her palm faced upward, and ran his hand gently from her wrist to her elbow.

This was the first time in her young life that Alexandra had been touched in a deliberately provocative way, and it turned her insides liquid. Just a moment before she had been smiling at Freddy in a calm, composed manner, completely master of herself. And now, after such a simple touch, she suddenly felt a yearning the likes of which she had never known. It was as though there were a direct connection between his fingertip on her skin and the warmth and dew that were building inside her. Her body seemed to be asserting itself, separate from her, driving her, compelling her to answer Freddy in kind.

She felt the yearning, but she knew the danger. She had spent her life being prudent, understanding that a young woman in her position must be so. Although she had the benefit of noble and wealthy connections, she herself did not have the protection of high birth. A whiff of scandal could jeopardize her future in a way that she didn't want to contemplate.

She withdrew her arm.

Freddy caught her hand, though, and held tight. "It's possible that I imagine it with imaginings fueled by my feelings for you, but I believe you are not indifferent to me," he said in a low voice, keeping his eyes squarely on hers. He was now in territory where he was more comfortable.

She turned her eyes away, but her hand remained in his. "Of course I am not indifferent to you," she said, not wanting to commit herself further.

"Then you must not deny either me or yourself," he said, and moved closer to her. He put a hand on her thigh, lightly at first, and then closed his fingers more firmly around her leg just above her knee.

She closed her eyes. She felt his touch. She heard his breath. She smelled his musky, male smell.

He moved his hand up her thigh and then up to her waist. He pulled her forward, away from the back of the chair, and with the movement she opened her eyes.

She saw his face, inches from her own. His wide blue eyes and his fine blond hair. The expression that combined passion and tenderness.

She had never yet been kissed, and Freddy was determined that he should be the first to do it. He put his hand on her cheek and leaned in.

He did kiss her, but on the hand that had interposed itself between their two sets of lips.

"You must not, Freddy," she said in a whisper. "Indeed, you must not."

"And why must I not?" he asked, but he recognized something in her tone that told him the battle was lost.

"Nay, you know why you must not," she said hoarsely. And then, with more severity, "And I have been schooled to understand that a gentleman does not ask such questions."

This stung, for although Freddy understood that he was more inclined to gentlemanly behavior when it was convenient and consistent with his interest than when it was not, he did not like to be called out on his lapses.

And this was certainly a lapse. He had approached a young lady of unimpeachable moral character with a proposition—unspoken, but a proposition nevertheless—that was most disreputable. Had he cataloged all he knew of her, and considered carefully whether this was wise, he probably would have thought better of his attempt, but careful consideration had never been Freddy's long suit.

Resilience, though, he had in spades, and even a rejection and a rebuke couldn't completely daunt him.

"You were schooled correctly, and I hope you will forgive me," he said. "You must understand that I am acting under the influence of your very considerable charms, and my good manners are not strong enough to hold up under such powerful"—he searched for the word—"allure."

She stood up. "Perhaps I shall see you at dinner," she said by way of dismissal.

He stood also. "I hope you shall," he said as he left, and his parting words still had a faint echo of the tone of intimacy he had assumed with her. "I hope you shall."

She didn't see him at dinner. She didn't see anyone at dinner. She had tea and toast in her room because she felt she was too preoccupied to be good company.

She wasn't angry with Freddy. She was flattered, and fascinated by the sensations he had awoken. Still, the way he had approached her cast him in a new light, and she couldn't help but mark the contrast between his behavior and Gerry's. Freddy had been a cad, trying blatantly to seduce her. Gerry had been a gentleman, professing his love and proposing marriage.

Could she ever feel the thrill at Gerry's touch that she felt at Freddy's? She wasn't sure. What she did know was that she felt a warm glow suffusing her whole self, and she was sure it was attributable more to the older man than the younger. He had honored her in a way that touched her profoundly. She felt cherished. That, too, was a new sensation for her, and she thought it to be a more substantial and important sensation than the yearning she had felt with Freddy.

She thought about her two suitors as she sipped her tea and prepared for bed, and she knew without a doubt which of them was the better man.

EIGHTEEN

The much-anticipated day of the masquerade finally arrived. The rain of the day before had exhausted itself, and the sun was out in full force, warming the crisp fall morning. It was perfect.

Miss Niven came down late to breakfast, and was glad to spot Gerry at the buffet, taking seconds on kippers. The house was so busy and so full that the odds of finding any particular person were long.

"Hello, Gerry," she said, taking a plate and joining him.

He smiled broadly and warmly. "Hullo, Miss Niven," he said. "Have you not breakfasted yet?"

"I have not, but I certainly intend to," she said, surveying the table.

"The kippers are outstanding, and there's nothing to start the day like a kipper, I think," he said, reaching for serving tongs and picking one up. He held it out to her. "May I serve you one?"

Miss Niven had never been particularly fond of kippers, but she thought maybe it was time to give them another chance. "By all means," she said, and put her plate up to receive the fish.

Gerry started moving down the table, stopping at every dish he thought Miss Niven might enjoy. "That's a fine rasher of bacon," he said, and added that to the kipper. Then there was toast, and beautiful scrambled eggs, and a slice of melon fresh from the Penfield kitchen garden.

By the time they got to the Cumberland sausage, Alexandra's plate was already piled high, but Gerry wouldn't hear of her refusing it.

"I've had Cumberland sausage all over the kingdom," he said, "but never a finer specimen than the Loughlins serve." He put a fat link on top of her eggs.

When her plate could take no more, he took a kipper for himself, and they headed for the parlor. As it was late, the guests had begun to disperse, either to enjoy the day or to prepare themselves for the evening's festivities, and they found an empty window seat that could accommodate both of them.

Alexandra looked at her plate with raised eyebrows and a half smile. "I don't know that I eat this much in three breakfasts," she said. "I don't know how I will ever get through it."

"Oh, it's not so difficult," said Gerry. "First you take a bite of bacon, and then a forkful of eggs, and then some toast and some sausage. Then you do it over again, and before you know it you're down to crusts and bones." He took a hearty bite of kipper to demonstrate.

Alexandra laughed. This man was so very easy to be with. His manner was open, and his way was honest. She had the sense that there was nothing concealed, that she could learn everything important about him by talking to him over breakfast. His character was as straightforward as his proposal had been.

They spoke of nothing personal over their meal. The masquerade, the other guests, and the weather were their primary topics. The conversation flowed easily, and Alexandra found herself not just comfortable, but happy in his company. His good nature and enthusiasm made everything seem a source of pleasure and amusement.

After a half hour, Alexandra saw, to her surprise, that her plate was nearly empty. Gerry saw her look and chuckled. "What did I tell you? First one bite, and then another, and Bob's your uncle!"

Perhaps it was merely the thought of all the food she had eaten that made Alexandra feel suddenly full. "I must get outside and take some air to help me digest this breakfast," she said, standing up.

"May I join you?" he asked.

"I would like that very much. I must first run upstairs and get my bonnet."

As she turned to head to her room, Georgiana came down the stairs.

"Good morning!" she said. "I was just looking for you, and Miss Mumford told me you had gone down to breakfast."

"I have just eaten a breakfast that would do a blacksmith proud, and I am going with Mr. Gerard to take a walk in hopes of digesting it." She wanted to invite Georgiana to join them, but she wasn't sure whether it was appropriate to invite a second young lady on a walk with one's suitor.

"Won't you join us?" Gerry asked heartily. "It is a beautiful morning."

At that moment, Alexandra thought Gerry was a fine man indeed. That he would wish to include her friend, rather than monopolize her for himself!

"Please do!" she said, adding her invitation to his.

"Of course I shall. I can't think of anything I'd like better."

"I was just going to fetch my bonnet," Alexandra said, and trotted up the stairs.

Her room door was ajar, and she slipped through it and stopped in her tracks. It took her a moment to realize what she was witnessing, and another moment to convince herself to believe it was really happening.

It was Miss Mumford, using lipstick to put a large scarlet A on the mirror.

She was shocked. So it was her very own companion who had done all these things, had given Georgiana the poison ivy, had tainted her milk!

She recoiled in fear and disgust. She wasn't sure what she should do, but Miss Mumford hadn't heard her, so she slipped back out and ran downstairs to her friends.

Gerry and Lady Georgiana were surprised to see her return hatless and clearly distressed.

"My dear," said Gerry, "what can be the matter? You look as though you've seen a ghost."

"It's Miss Mumford," she said. "It was her all along!"

"You mean . . ." Georgiana said, looking at Gerry. "She's responsible for all the . . ."

"Yes! It's her!"

"But how do you know?" Gerry asked.

"I saw her. She was putting an A on my mirror with lipstick!"

"She was *what*?" Gerry asked. He didn't know about Lady Georgiana's A, and so Miss Niven's explanation made no sense to him.

Lady Georgiana told him about the A she'd gotten, and explained that it was the latest in the series of threats that Gerry was already familiar with.

"But this is the first threat to Miss Niven, is it not?" he asked, a little confused.

"Well, no," said Alexandra. "I had one other."

"You did? What happened?"

"Someone tainted my milk."

"Tainted your milk?" he asked incredulously. "Were you ill, then?"

Miss Niven hesitated, not wanting to make much of the incident. "I was," she finally said, "but it wasn't very bad and it didn't last long."

"This is preposterous! If this woman has done these things we must go for the police and have her arrested. This is far beyond the limits of a practical joke or an expression of disapproval." Gerry was clearly furious. "I'm going to find her right now, and keep her under lock and key until the authorities have been called," he went on.

"Wait a moment," said Lady Georgiana, a little alarmed that he might get carried away in defense of the girl he loved. "Perhaps we should find Lord Loughlin. I think he is entitled to know what is going on under his roof, and I don't think we should take any drastic steps without consulting him."

"You're right, you're right," said Gerry, looking around the room as though Lord Loughlin would simply materialize there.

He didn't, though, and Gerry said to the two girls, "You stay right here. I'll go find him, and then we'll deal with this."

Gerry went first to the library, and then to Lord Loughlin's private study. He checked all the rooms where the party preparations were going on, and even went down to the kitchen, with no luck.

He didn't think to check the wine cellar.

Lord Loughlin had been with his wife all morning, overseeing the preparations. In previous years, their efforts had been divided; he had seen to the music and the wine, she to the food and decoration. This year, though, they found themselves acting in tandem, side by side. They had recovered, in the events of the last two days, a connection both thought they had lost.

They had gone down to the cellar together, to make sure both that the wine intended for guests was accessible and that the wine not intended for guests was not. This would have taken only a few minutes, but once they'd checked everything and were heading back, Lady Loughlin had another idea.

She took her husband's hand, turned him around, and walked him toward the back of the cellar. "Show me what you have there," she said.

He smiled at her. "Do you think we have the time? There's still much to be done."

"And it will be done. In just a little while. Show me."

He nodded in acquiescence, and they made their way back to the dungeon. The door was locked but, as Lady Loughlin looked through the bars, she saw that all was changed.

The cask of Armagnac was still on the floor, but it had been moved into a corner. There was still a plush rug on the hard stone, but it was a different rug. She could not see it from the door, but the wooden cabinet that held the toys was gone.

"You changed it," she said, wonderingly.

"I changed it." He looked at her with tenderness that went straight to her heart. "That was a chapter that is now closed. You and I will embark on a new chapter, but we will build it ourselves, for us." He kissed her. And then he kissed her again.

"And is the"—what was the word?—"paraphernalia all gone?"

"Not gone, but not here." His lips had never moved more than an inch from hers.

"And will you not show me where?"

"I will, but not today."

She looked at him, and then she looked through the bars again. "Where did that rug come from?" she asked. She didn't remember ever having seen it.

"It was rolled up in the rafters in the stables," he said. "I took it down and had it given a good beating, and here it is."

"Is it lovely and plush and soft?" she asked, putting her hands on his hips and pulling him toward her.

"It is lovely and plush and soft," he said, "although a tad musty."

"Musty isn't so bad," she murmured, taking the skin on his neck softly between her lips and tasting his saltiness.

"Musty isn't bad at all," he murmured back, closing his eyes and feeling for the keys in his pocket.

He opened the door and they almost fell into the room. In a moment, she was pinned against the back wall, her hands on his ass to bring him close to her. She felt the contours of his entire body as though they were new. He was no longer young, but his active life had kept him strong and well muscled, and she relished the feel of those muscles against her softer flesh.

He was exploring every inch of that softer flesh, running his hands first down the sides of her breasts, and then her waist, and then her hips, and down to her thighs. He kissed her with a warmth that fired her, and when he stopped, he looked into her eyes.

"I love you," he said.

She nodded.

"No," he said. "I love you in a way that words can't convey. I love you in a way that means that losing you would have meant losing everything."

She nodded again, and felt a surge that was love, and desire, and renewal all together. She felt the kind of draw she hadn't felt since they first started discovering each other as newlyweds. She put a hand on each side of his face and looked at him. She smiled, and she kissed his bottom lip, just barely brushing it.

She traced his face with his fingertips, running them along his brow and around to his cheekbones. She brushed his cheeks with the backs of her hands, and then ran her fingers through his hair.

"I want to satisfy you," she whispered.

He was about to tell her that she did, but although that was true in its way, he knew that the kind of satisfaction she had brought him in the past was not what she was speaking of.

"You don't have to," he said instead. "What I sought here in this room is something I can learn to live without." He kissed her again, and she marveled that someone who could treat her with such confidence and mastery could want to be mastered in return.

But she had made up her mind. If he wanted to be mastered, she would master him.

She pushed him away from her and stood away from the wall.

"Take off your shirt," she said quietly, but very firmly. She wasn't quite sure how to proceed with the mastering, but it was clear to her that, if it were to be done, it must be done with firmness.

He looked at her for a moment.

"Take . . . off . . . your . . . shirt," she repeated, spacing the words out and almost barking them. It was undoubtedly a command.

He took off his shirt.

"Give it to me." She held out her hand, and he complied.

"And your trousers." This time she didn't have to ask twice. He took off his boots and then the trousers.

She had an idea in mind, but she wasn't sure whether the logistics would quite work out.

"Lie down on your back." She was finding it easy to assume the role of master, and the tone of her voice was severe. She gestured to where she wanted him to lie down, and told him to put his arms over his head. His hands almost reached the wine racks on one side of the room, and his feet were just a few inches from the racks on the other side. Perfect.

She tied his hands to the rack with his shirt, and his feet to the opposite rack with his trousers. She didn't have complete confidence in her knots, but she assumed that his object wouldn't be to work himself free.

When she was finished, she stood over him and just looked. He was completely naked, completely exposed, completely vulnerable. But his cock was pointing straight up from his body, so she assumed she hadn't gone too far wrong.

She took off her own boots and slipped out of her drawers, but kept the rest of her clothes on. She stood over him, with one foot just outside each of his shoulders. She knelt down, her pussy just inches from his face.

"You are going to lick me," she said, but she waited, not putting herself in his reach.

They had indulged in this act before, but not often. She always loved the feel of his tongue on her, and now she found the anticipation of it tremendously arousing.

His head was completely covered by her skirts, but she could feel him lifting it, straining to reach her. She raised herself up another inch to remain just out of reach, paused a moment, and then lowered herself down on him.

She felt his lips, she felt his tongue, she felt his warmth and his wetness and she groaned at the very first contact. How was it that something could feel that good? As his tongue explored the crevices and found the sweetest spot of her most intimate anatomy, she felt her whole body warm and yearn.

And then she pulled away.

He again strained toward her and groaned. She lifted the front of her skirt so she could see him.

"Lie down." It was harder to muster the requisite firmness when she herself was hot with desire.

He did as he was bidden. She waited a few beats, and then lowered herself again, this time holding her skirts up so she could see him. His eyes were closed, and he maneuvered his tongue and lips over her with evident pleasure.

But she didn't think his pleasure could possibly match hers. The idea that he could do this, and that she could simply demand that he do it!

The tip of his tongue met the head of her clitoris, and she almost lost control. The pressure, the warmth, and the wet muscularity of what he was doing to her were driving her mad.

She pulled away again.

This time he didn't strain. He had learned.

She kept her skirts up, hoping the cool air in the room would help tamp down the hot fire within.

She waited as long as she could stand it, and then lowered herself back to his mouth. She dropped her skirts and put her hands on the floor to steady herself as she felt the point of no return arrive. She pressed down just a little harder, and that increased the pressure of his light touch. She felt his tongue dart inside of her, and then again.

And then he went back to the head of her clitoris, nudging it with the tip of his tongue, back and forth, back and forth. She started gasping in the rhythm of his motion, feeling each wave of ecstasy build higher than the previous one.

Then arose the wave that overcame her. Every nerve in her body engaged, combining to bring her to a crest the likes of which she had never known. It took in her fingers and toes, and every part of her in between.

Her mouth opened, but she made no sound. The feeling traveled through her, and she was lost in the sensation.

When she came back to herself, she lifted her skirts and saw the need in her husband's eyes. She slid down his body and, and in a swift, powerful motion, impaled herself on his erect penis. She was so wet from both his tongue and her desire that his cock, big as it was, slid in effortlessly.

She sat up and bounced gently, knowing how close he was to his own crest. She saw his muscles tighten and strain against the knots. And she saw—and heard and felt—his release. He let out a long, soft groan, and his back arched up off the rug. His mouth was open, his eyes were closed, and she saw that he was as satisfied as she had been.

When he opened his eyes, he saw his wife smiling at him.

She stood up, and then untied his restraints.

"I hope you'll remember that I'm new at this," she said with a little laugh. "I'm not quite sure how to go about it."

"You did marvelously," he said, wiping his glistening mouth with the back of his hand. "Simply marvelously."

He stood up and dressed, and they left the little room, which no longer seemed like a dungeon. After he locked the door behind them, he took his wife's hand and kissed it.

"Thank you," he whispered.

They came out of the cellar into the kitchen, where an energetic staff was producing food of every imaginable kind. Pies were coming out of the oven as others were going in. Hams were being sliced, turkeys being carved, and salads being dressed. All the servants, whether their domain was upstairs or down, were in their best uniforms. Lady Loughlin nodded her approval to her staff. As she was saying a few words to the cook, Dodson, the butler, approached her husband.

"Mr. Gerard was here not long ago, looking for you, sir," he said. "He seemed a bit agitated."

Lord Loughlin frowned in concern. It took a lot to agitate Alphonse Gerard. "Did he say where I might find him?"

"He did not, my lord."

Lord Loughlin turned to his wife. "I must go find Gerry and see what's going on, and then I'll rejoin you." He went off in search of his friend.

His search for Gerry was as fruitless as Gerry's search for him had been. After he had told the butler he was looking for his host, Gerry had rejoined the two girls in the drawing room.

"I can't find Lord Loughlin, but I can't bear the thought of that woman on the loose. Who knows what she'll do next? We must find her and, if necessary, confine her until we can turn her over to the authorities."

Lady Georgiana thought this a little overzealous, but she, too, wanted to get to the bottom of this and put it behind her. She stood up. "Then let us go find her."

Miss Mumford was easier to find than either Gerry or Lord Lough-lin. She was in her own room, a small chamber on the top floor, sewing a white ribbon onto the bodice of her costume, that of a shepherdess.

The door was opened, and when the three visitors appeared, all looking grim, Miss Mumford was clearly flustered.

"Good afternoon," she said, looking from one face to another. "To what do I owe the honor . . . ?"

Miss Niven hadn't wanted to confront her companion when the two had been alone, but now that she had her friends with her she was up to the task.

"Miss Mumford," she said calmly, "I believe you are the person responsible for the threats to Lady Georgiana and to me."

Miss Mumford hesitated for only a moment, and then stood up, ramrod straight. "Miss Niven," she said, "I don't know how you can accuse me of such a thing."

"I saw you," said the girl. "I saw you put the A on my mirror with lipstick."

She again hesitated only a moment, and her air of injured honor evaporated as quickly as it had come on. But it wasn't replaced by the guilty resignation of someone who'd clearly been caught in the act. There was confusion, there was regret, and there were the first stirrings of panic, but there was no guilt, and no resignation.

"No, no, I can explain." She raised her hands, palms toward Miss Niven, in a gesture of innocence.

"Explain!" Gerry expostulated. "You can explain threatening an innocent young lady?" He paused, and then remembered himself. "*Two* innocent young ladies?"

"It wasn't me," said Miss Mumford, with desperation in her voice. "It wasn't me, as God is my witness."

"It wasn't you?!" Gerry scoffed. "Yet there you stand, quite literally red-handed." He pointed to Miss Mumford's right hand, which did, indeed, have red lipstick on it. At this, Georgiana had to look at the floor so no one would see her smile.

"Let me explain!" Miss Mumford said again. "I did write the A on the mirror, but that's all I did. I swear it! That's all I did!"

Here Miss Niven stepped in again. "Sit down, Miss Mumford," she said severely. "And do explain."

Miss Mumford took a deep breath and sat on the edge of the small bed.

"You see," she said, "I was in the room and accidentally heard Lady Georgiana tell Miss Niven about the A on her mirror." She took a deep breath. "At the time, I thought only that it was terrible that these young ladies keep getting these threats." She gestured at both the girls. "But then I had an idea," she added quietly.

"You see, Miss Niven and I have had words over the past few days," she said, knotting her hands together in her lap, clearly wretched. "And I thought that if I could manage it that there should be another threat— a harmless one, to be sure—and I could be with her to help her and comfort her, perhaps she might be grateful and things could go back to the way they were."

She was clearly having a difficult time getting the words out, but she went on. "I put the letter on the mirror when I knew she was going to be at breakfast, and I was going to find her and ask her to try on her costume one last time, and we'd find the letter together. . . ." With this, she burst into tears.

Lady Georgiana looked at her friend, expecting her to melt at this display of what was clearly honest misery. Miss Niven, though, did no such thing. She wasn't sympathetic; she was angry. Angry that this woman, whom she'd known long and, she thought, well, could do such a thing to her.

"It is not in my power to dismiss you outright, as you serve at the pleasure of Lord Bellingford, my guardian," she said coldly. "But it is difficult to see how, after this incident, we could ever be suitable companions again."

Miss Mumford put her head in her hands and sobbed. "I am so very sorry. I just wanted us to be friends again."

She looked at Miss Niven through her tears. "I have always loved you and wanted what was best for you. I couldn't bear the idea that you no longer needed me."

At this, Miss Niven did begin to thaw. She sat down on the bed next to her companion and laid a gentle hand on her shoulder.

"What has happened, I think, is that I have gone beyond the age where I require the services of someone in your position, and that is what I will tell my guardian. For the many years that I did require those services, you performed them ably and assiduously, and I will always be grateful. That is what I will be thinking of when I ask Lord Bellingford to write you a wonderful reference, and I'm sure we will both do all that is possible to secure another position for you. You will not be left out on the street."

Miss Mumford's sobs subsided a bit, and she tried to smile at Miss Niven through her tears. "I am sorry, you know. So sorry."

"I do know. It was a silly thing to attempt, but there has been no harm done and I shall not hold it against you. But I do think we have reached the end of our road."

Miss Mumford stood up and made an effort to muster her dignity. "Perhaps we have. Perhaps we have." She looked at her erstwhile charge once more. "I am so sorry."

The three left Miss Mumford to her regrets, and went back downstairs. They did take their walk, but it was a very subdued one. They walked here and there, talking of Miss Mumford and of the events of the last several days, and wondering—again—who might be behind the threats, as it was clear to all of them that Miss Mumford had told the truth.

Both girls, though, were getting tired of the subject. They were young, and they were vibrant, and the prospect of the evening's masquerade held much more fascination for them than dead peacocks and tainted milk. In time, their talk turned to the festivities, and their mood rebounded.

They were almost cheerful as they turned back toward the house.

They reached the drive just in time to see a carriage leave for the station. Miss Mumford would never return to Penfield.

NINETEEN

B y the time the threesome walked up the front steps, there were only a few hours remaining before the party was to start, and the house was ready for its biggest night of the year.

The orchestra was setting up on one end of the largest room, which was to be set aside for dancing. The supper was beginning to be laid in the adjoining room. One of the smaller drawing rooms had been converted to a giant coat closet, and the powder rooms were stocked with soaps and powders and creams. Supplies of cigars and port were stowed in the library for the gentlemen, and the breakfast room, farthest from the orchestra, was made comfortable for any lady who wanted to escape the bustle and noise.

The outbuildings were also ready. It was a tradition to invite the local villagers to come celebrate with roasted pig and beer, and long tables were set up in the peacock pavilion to accommodate them, the peacocks being banned for the evening.

In the stables, there were mounds of hay, buckets of oats, and troughs of fresh water for the horses. There were brushes and blankets for the visiting grooms to use, and food set out for all the servants.

Although all the guests were closeted in their rooms, preparing their persons and donning their costumes, there were people everywhere. They were the people responsible for making sure everything ran smoothly—the servants of the house, the additional help hired for the purpose, and the staff of the houseguests. They were running from place to place, cleaning up this, straightening that, laying out the other, and Penfield was a hive of activity.

And then, suddenly, it wasn't. Half an hour before the guests were due to arrive, everything was ready, and all was still. Not calm, though. There was an air of electric anticipation even where there was no movement.

The stillness was broken by the master and mistress of the house, coming down the stairs together. They were dressed as Czar Nicholas II of Russia, who had taken the throne the year before, and his wife, Alexandra. Lord Loughlin was resplendent in a genuine hussar's uniform, with a broad sash and gold epaulets, and his wife wore a purple gown with a jeweled bodice. Following a tradition that began with the very first Penfield masquerade, the host and hostess did not wear masks.

They took one last look around the rooms, but it was a mere formality. Everything was as it should be.

Just as they finished their tour they heard the sound of the first carriage pulling up to the door. And then the second. And then it was as though a signal had been sent, and the floodgates opened. The guests who were staying in the house started coming down the stairs as carriage after carriage disgorged costumed revelers at the front door.

The Loughlins' masquerade wasn't quite like other masked balls, where men wore traditional evening dress and women wore ball gowns and masks. At Penfield, all the guests were dressed as something other than themselves, and both men and women wore masks. While some people could be identified by distinctive shape, or gait, or hair, many were truly anonymous. It was that anonymity that added to the excitement of the evening, and made an invitation to the ball the coveted item it had come to be.

The array of costumes was staggering. Among the men, there were Julius Caesars and Henry the Eighths. There were, as Freddy had predicted, satyrs aplenty. There were monks and musketeers, cricketers and court jesters. There was one towering Zeus, wearing a false beard and carrying a thunderbolt.

Among the ladies, there were goddesses, goddesses, and more goddesses. There was Diana (of the hunt), several Daphnes (of virtue), a Luna with an iridescent moon as a halo, and a magnificent Pandora who came with her own gilded box. There were many faeries, and at least two Florence Nightingales. There was a threesome—sisters, perhaps—dressed as the three little maids from *The Mikado*. (There was also a man dressed as Ko-Ko, but he didn't seem to be of the same party.) There was a highly stylized cat with a sleek black dress and a headband with pointed ears.

While there were guests who clearly knew one another—husbands and wives, particular friends—everyone saw far more people whom they didn't recognize than whom they did. The costumes eased the sometimes awkward business of striking up a conversation with a stranger, and the rooms filled with the buzz of excitement and novelty.

Lady Georgiana and Miss Niven had no trouble finding each other behind the masks, as each had seen the costume of the other. Miss Niven was a thing to behold, tall and stately in a beautiful white dress with Roman-style folds of fabric, her eyes made up and her hair straightened in imitation of Cleopatra, or at least of pictures of Cleopatra.

Georgiana had used her slim, boyish figure to great advantage as Alice. Her costume precisely replicated the illustrations in the book that both she and her friend had read as children. She wore a knee-length blue dress with starched skirt and white pinafore, white stockings, and little black shoes with straps. She'd brushed her hair back simply, and anchored it with a headband. Her mask, which she'd had made specially, was the familiar face.

After they had admired each other's costumes, they surveyed the room and admired some of the others they saw. Miss Niven was particularly taken with the cat, and the way the tail integrated with the skirt of the dress to create a lithe, feline look. "She even moves like a cat," she said in wonderment. "How very clever."

Georgiana was taken with one of the many Queen Victorias. It was a favorite costume among the older women, but there was one who stood out as the very picture of the queen herself. Georgiana pointed her out to Miss Niven. "Does she not look precisely like our queen?"

Miss Niven looked and nodded. "Perhaps it *is* the queen." She raised her eyebrows in mock surprise.

Georgiana laughed, but then thought about it. "If I were the queen, and I wanted to go to a masked ball that was just a little too risqué for me to attend openly, I would certainly disguise myself as myself. It's a brilliant idea, and you've uncovered it!"

"Shall we go discuss women's suffrage with her?" Miss Niven said.

"Oh, I think not." Georgiana frowned. "That's not the right sort of talk for this sort of affair. We must ask her whether she likes champagne, or if she is enjoying the music, or whether she comes from this part of the country."

"How very dull," said Alexandra. "Perhaps we should talk to someone else."

At that point, someone else presented himself. It was a man, slight of build, dressed in animal-skin trousers with boots gotten up to look like hooves. The horns on his head completed the outfit.

"It's a satyr, I daresay," said Georgiana. "How nice to see you this evening, sir." She bowed her head slightly.

The satyr didn't reply, but quickly moved his mask so the girls could see his eyes and recognize him.

"Freddy!" Georgiana whispered, looking around to see if anyone else had seen him do it. "You know that violates all the rules!" But she couldn't help smiling. "I thought you were joking about being a satyr. And how ever did you know it was us?"

"Miss Mumford, I'm glad to say, is more susceptible to my charms than either of you two young ladies."

"She told you?" Miss Niven would have been irritated had Miss Mumford still been in the house, but now that she was gone her former charge could not but think of her with benevolence.

"She said you would be the finest Cleopatra in the room," Freddy said. "As far as I can see, you are the only Cleopatra, but I am sure you would still be the finest had there been a score more."

Alexandra curtsied in response.

Freddy held out his hand to her with all the gallantry a satyr could muster. "May I have this dance?"

Alexandra marveled at his cheerful manner. It was as though the events of the previous day had never occurred. "You may," she said with a smile, laying her hand on top of his. "Will you excuse me?" she said to Georgiana.

The two went off to the next room to dance, leaving Georgiana to continue her survey of her fellow partygoers. Most she could not identify, but she knew Zeus to be Barnes. It wasn't just his size; it was the way he moved. She was too familiar with his body, his air, his gait, to be fooled by any costume.

And he, apparently, could say the same of her. She didn't think she had thus far been recognized by anyone, but Zeus was approaching with a purpose, two glasses of champagne in his hands and his thunderbolt tucked under his arm.

Her heart sank. She knew she must talk with him, at least one more time, but she so wanted to enjoy the party. She thought that, with the mask, it would not have been clear that she had seen him and, even if it had been, perhaps he would assume she wouldn't recognize him and know that he was coming toward her.

She turned around and walked out of the room. She chastised herself for doing the cowardly thing even as she did it, but she felt a burden lift as she entered the room where the dancing had begun, the floor already crowded.

She had barely taken two steps when a stout fisherman in an oilcloth sou'wester stepped up to her, bowed, and extended his hand. She smiled and took it, grateful for the rescue, although she had no idea who the gentleman was or, come to think of it, whether he was even a gentleman.

Part of what made the Penfield masquerade exciting was that the strict conventions of dances were ignored. Although the requirement that a man be properly introduced to a lady before asking her to dance was already falling by the wayside, it was necessarily disregarded entirely at a function where anonymity was all. For all she knew, Georgiana was dancing a tarantella with an actual fisherman, who just happened to be passing by.

She danced two dances with the fisherman, and then two more with a Roman senator who seemed familiar to Georgiana, although she could not place him. Then came a quadrille with a satyr who wasn't Freddy, which finally tired her. As she headed off the floor, in need of food and drink, the satyr who was Freddy appeared at her side.

"Lady G," he said. "You must dance with me."

She smiled. "Well, you certainly have a charming way of asking, but I must have some wine and a bite to eat. I've been dancing this hour and more."

He put his hand on her elbow and gently steered her back in the direction of the dance floor. "Just one, just one, and then I'll personally escort you to sustenance."

She rolled her eyes, but gave Freddy his gavotte. As they danced, she caught sight of Alexandra, who was standing up with an admiral. Was that allowed? she wondered. If there were any real admirals here, as there undoubtedly were, they might be put out by having to dance next to a false one. She shrugged, if one could be said to think a shrug. All the ordinary rules of society seemed to be suspended for the evening.

Freddy was as good as his word, and led her out of the room and off to the buffet when the dance was over. The room with the food was almost as crowded as the room with the orchestra, and they had to thread their way through the revelers to get to the sliced ham.

They both managed to fill their plates, and then looked around for a place to sit. There were none to be had, so they settled for a spot against the wall with a little table where they could put their wineglasses.

Alexandra, carrying a plate of her own, found them there. She was still flushed from the dancing, and her pleasure and excitement were palpable.

"Did you dance with a fisherman?" she asked Lady Georgiana.

"I did. Twice."

"And did you know who it was?"

"I did not. But you do?" Georgiana was curious.

"I do. It was Gerry!"

"Did you figure it out, or did he reveal himself to you?" asked Freddy. Had he known that Gerry was his rival for the affections of Miss Niven, he might have been more interested, but it never crossed his mind that the older man would be interested in any girl, let alone the girl he was interested in.

"Oh, I figured it out," she said. "But he wanted me to figure it out, although I'm sure I don't know how he knew it was me. At first he didn't say a word, but then he started in with pleasantries about the dance because he wanted me to hear his voice. And of course, when I heard him I knew."

The three talked, ate, and drank for the better part of an hour, and speculated endlessly about who was what and what was who. There was a Florence Nightingale that Freddy swore up and down must be Mrs. Sheffield, and Alexandra thought the admiral must be Lord Grantsbury. Georgiana was quite sure that the earl would never lampoon the admiralty in that way, but she kept her thoughts to herself.

To Georgiana's relief, Zeus did not reappear.

As they were drinking the last of their wine, their hostess joined them. As was the custom of the party, they all identified themselves to her.

"May I waylay someone to get more wine for you?" she asked, looking at their empty glasses.

"Thank you, Lady Loughlin, but not for me. I'm already feeling the effects of what I've had," said Alexandra. "If I'm going to dance at all, I must try to keep my head. If I topple over during a mazurka, the floor is so crowded that I'm likely to bring everyone else down with me, like dominoes."

Paulette laughed. "I can't imagine a girl as graceful as you doing any such thing," she said.

"But we can put it to the test," said Freddy, again holding his hand out to Miss Niven, who took it and excused herself.

Lady Georgiana and her friend were left alone, and together they surveyed the room. The buzz was getting louder as the effects of the food and the drink and the company were being felt.

"It seems to me that you have more people this year than last," said Georgiana.

"We do. Every year, the list of people we absolutely must invite—or face the consequences—grows longer. If it continues, we'll have to hold it at Buckingham Palace before long."

"The outlandishness of the costumes seems to increase with the length of the guest list." Georgiana pointed to a sultan with an elaborately wound headdress, ballooning trousers, and a sword that looked like it could take down a tree. "I'm surprised he didn't come with his own elephant."

Paulette laughed. She enjoyed seeing her guests' enjoyment, and she took it as a compliment that so many of them had spent time, money, and ingenuity on their dress.

The two were so busy looking at the costumes that they didn't notice Zeus come into the room. Georgiana didn't spot him until it was too late to make an escape, and she steeled herself for the encounter.

The god joined them and bowed to Paulette. "Lady Loughlin," he said.

"Zeus," she said, bowing in return. She knew it was Barnes, but she thought he made an excellent god.

Then he turned to Georgiana. "Lady Georgiana, I presume," he said a little more stiffly, and bowed again.

"Mr. Barnes, I presume in turn," she replied, and gave a shallow curtsy.

Lady Loughlin sensed the tension between them, and thought it would be a good time to take her leave. She excused herself and left the two alone.

Georgiana took a deep breath as the details of their last conversation came back to her. Since they had last spoken, she had come to the conclusion, which she had only suspected at the time, that she had indeed behaved imprudently by becoming entangled with him.

She remembered that he had asked for an explanation, and she knew she owed him one. But she did not think this the time or the place, and she hoped they could exchange pleasantries about the party and leave it at that. Those hopes, however, he dashed immediately.

"I believe we ended our last conversation on a somewhat unsatisfactory note," he said. He was keeping his voice low so none but she would see his displeasure.

"We did," she replied. "But perhaps this is not the time for us to discuss that. It is, you know, a party." She gestured at the room and gave him a wan smile, knowing it was unlikely that she could distract him from his purpose.

"And is that why you ran for the door when you saw me approach earlier in the evening?"

She flushed. "It was," she said. "I believe that what we have to say to each other may be difficult, and I could not quite muster the courage to face it."

"And can you muster it now?" His tone was even.

"I think I need to." She sighed and dived in. "I told you that I owed you an explanation for turning you from my door, and so I do." She had been thinking about what she would tell him, and so had her explanation ready to hand.

"When I met you, I felt an attraction that was immediate and strong, and it seemed to me that you felt an attraction as well." She looked him in the eye as she said this. He nodded his agreement, but did not reply.

"We acted on that attraction in a way that was, I think, to our mutual satisfaction." He nodded again. None of this was news to him.

"Had our liaison remained private, I daresay we could have simply enjoyed it, but once it became public, I had to choose whether to continue, with the eyes of the world upon me, or desist."

Here he interrupted her. "And I did not also have a choice to make?" he asked brusquely.

She considered. "Yes, you did," she finally said. "But your choice was different."

"And why was my choice different? Because I am a gardener and you are an heiress?" he asked, his tone growing almost belligerent.

"No," she said softly, "because you are a man and I am a woman."

She owed him the truth, and she told it. "As much as I wish we lived in a time and a place where people had more freedom to do as they please . . . as much as I believe conventions about relationships between men and women are both archaic and unjust, I have been made to see that it could be harmful to flout them."

As an explanation for ending an affair, it was stilted and impersonal, and Barnes wasn't having it.

"Harmful?" he said with a sneer. "And who is harmed? You are harmed, and you would prefer not to be. That is what you are telling me. Being with me cost you more than you wanted to bear, and so you simply cut me loose, as though I were ballast weighing you down."

"That is unkind," she said, looking at the floor.

"But is it untrue?" he asked angrily.

She could not say that it was untrue. In a sense, it was certainly true. But it missed what was, to her, the heart of the matter.

"What we had," she said, choosing her words carefully now, "was a dalliance. It was a light, delicious coming together of two people who felt a pull toward each other. I don't think either of us ever gave a thought to anything serious or long-term. And a dalliance is not worth either of us making a sacrifice for."

"And how do you know that neither of us ever gave a thought to anything serious or long-term?" He looked her steadily in the eye with a penetrating gaze.

She faltered. When Lord Grantsbury had suggested that Barnes's heart might be broken, she had pooh-poohed the idea, but she did not have direct access to his emotions, and she acknowledged to herself that she might be mistaken.

"Only you know what you feel," she said. "I can only guess. But you certainly gave no indication that you thought of me as anything other than a diversion."

"And if I had not thought of you as a diversion? What then?" He was almost snarling at her. "Am I to believe that, if you thought I cared more, you would have behaved differently?"

She had been determined to be as patient and gentle as she could, but she felt her anger begin to rise at this. She did not deserve this attack.

"Mr. Barnes," she said, "I can forgive you for forgetting that a young unmarried girl has a lot at stake when she chooses to take up with a man in the way I took up with you, as I forgot it myself. But when I look the ramifications in the face and decide that what is at stake is too much, I do not expect to be rebuked in this way." She looked him in the eye, and showed him that he did not have the corner on anger.

"As for your feelings," she went on. "It is difficult for me to deal in the theoretical," she said, making an effort to control the tone of her voice. "So let me simply ask you: Have you cared for me in a serious way?"

He was nothing if not blunt, and she fully expected him to say yes or no. Instead, he glared at her and said, "It doesn't matter now, does it?"

Suddenly Georgiana understood the game he was playing. Had he loved her, she felt sure he would have said so unambiguously. Instead, he was simply playing on her guilt by making her think she'd wounded him mortally.

"*If* you have loved me, I am truly sorry for the pain this causes you," she said, with a knowing emphasis on the *if* and a look that was intended to tell Barnes she was onto him. "But if you did not, then I hope we can agree to remember this week fondly, and part friends."

She extended her hand to him, but he did not take it. He looked from her hand to her face, turned, and strode off.

TWENTY

❧

Lady Georgiana found herself angry, but at herself rather than at Barnes. Grantsbury had made her see that she had erred in taking up with him, but she hadn't fully realized what the repercussions of that error would be. As unjust as she thought Barnes had been to her in trying to make her believe in his love, he had made a point that struck home: She *had* discarded him, and she had done it because she was protecting her own interest.

She felt deflated, and she wandered from room to room in an attempt to revive her festive mood. At first, the conviviality all around her felt false because it was at odds with her state of mind. After a while, though, she found it was infectious, and the dark clouds that swept in after her talk with Barnes began to dissipate. When the Roman senator she had danced with earlier in the evening approached her again, she was happy to join him on the dance floor.

Again, she felt as though he was familiar, and the idea that she knew him was reinforced by his total silence. Had he been a stranger, surely he would have spoken. But then, how did he know who she was? It was a puzzle, but a pleasant one.

As they danced, she saw Freddy and Alexandra dancing a few couples away, and she was alarmed to see that Alexandra looked unhappy. When Georgiana saw her friend abruptly break off dancing and leave the room, she excused herself from her senator and followed.

Once she caught up to her, she took Alexandra's elbow. "My dear Miss Niven, you seem upset," she said. "Has something happened?"

"Yes, it has," she said. "But I don't mean to give the impression that it's serious. It's just that . . . It's . . ." She sighed. "It's Freddy."

"Oh! Freddy, is it?" Georgiana said. She tried not to laugh, as Alexandra seemed a bit disquieted, but she couldn't suppress a smile. "What has he done?"

Alexandra saw the smile, and felt a little silly for letting Freddy unsettle her. "He has . . ." She sought the right words. "He has been making inappropriate advances to me."

"To *you*!" Georgiana fully expected that he might make inappropriate advances to a girl, but thought the girl might be a milkmaid or a villager, not a member of his own set.

Miss Niven didn't want Georgiana to think he had done her any real injury, and she hurried to explain. "Please don't think it's all his fault. It's my fault, too. In fact, it may be mostly my fault. You see, when he came to my room yesterday, and you left us alone, that's when it started."

The story of Freddy's clumsy assault on her virtue was soon told, and Alexandra laid the blame at her own feet. "I should have dismissed him the moment he crossed the line," she said, with much more firmness than she had felt at the time. "And because I essentially gave him permission, he tried again just now."

Lady Georgiana did not need the details to understand what had happened. The party atmosphere, the free-flowing spirits, the protection of masks all combined to fuel Freddy's fire until it was sufficiently stoked for a renewed attempt.

She took Alexandra's arm and steered her away from the crowds, toward a little veranda off one of the drawing rooms. "I am glad to see that he has not truly upset you," she said. "I'm sure you understand that there is no harm in Freddy. If you consider that you are up to the task of protecting yourself from such advances—and I certainly consider that you are—then you have nothing to fear, and you can see this as the misplaced ardor of a callow youth. A callow youth with excellent taste, I may add."

Alexandra by this time was a little embarrassed about the fuss she had made. "I have made a mountain out of a molehill and, in so doing, kept you from the party for too long," she told Lady Georgiana. "Let us go rejoin the other guests."

They did rejoin the other guests, and found that the party seemed to be losing its self-control. It was well past midnight, and the orchestra was playing a cakewalk, a new dance that very few of them knew, reportedly imported from America. Debris from food and drink was accumulating on every surface, despite the best efforts of a host of servants. The volume of talk had increased to the point where it nearly drowned out the music.

The crowd, though, had actually thinned somewhat. From the veranda, Georgiana and Alexandra had seen a few carriages taking their leave, and had assumed they were some of the older, more staid guests, who had limited tolerance for late-night revelry.

And someone had turned down the lights.

As the two young ladies wandered from room to room, they saw things that, a week ago, would have made Miss Niven blush uncontrollably. Since she had arrived at Penfield, though, she had matured considerably, and the sight of a bobby and a barmaid kissing—actually kissing—behind a very large potted plant did not discompose her.

They didn't venture as far as the tables set up outside for the villagers but, had they, they would have seen a great deal more. Although the local people were not in costume and didn't have the lack of inhibition anonymity invariably begets, they did have a freewheeling spirit. Drink was undoubtedly partly responsible, but so was the simple—but temporary—

release from the grind of daily routine that their social betters knew little of.

Women sat on tables, their skirts hiked up over their knees. Men leered, and fondled, and caressed, and the women's efforts to rebuff them were clearly only for show. Dark corners and large bushes provided shelter for all manner of intimate activity.

A way down a well-trodden path was one such shelter, a well-enclosed glade with a small clearing and a bench. It was there that Freddy, no longer a satyr but a mere mortal, had led Gretchen.

When Miss Niven had rebuffed him for the second time, he had taken it philosophically. Since he was coming up empty at the big house, he ducked upstairs to his room, put on real clothes, and shimmied down the drainpipe (something he'd gotten good at in childhood) so as to avoid causing comment by walking through the party unmasked.

He knew he'd find Gretchen and her parents at the party outside, but as he wanted to see Gretchen alone, he skirted the edges, shrouded by the darkness, until he got her attention. She was surprised to see him, having assumed he'd be at the masquerade, but he was always a welcome sight to her, and she slipped away from the party to join him as soon as she had the opportunity.

He took her by the hand and led her down the path—familiar to him, new to her—to the glade. There, he took her by the waist rather unceremoniously and kissed her, hard.

They were young, enthusiastic, and more than a little drunk, and each fumbled at the clothes of the other until skin met skin. The night was cool, and the two of them almost glowed with warmth and pleasure.

Freddy, with his cock sticking straight out of his trousers, took Gretchen's hand and climbed up on the bench. He then put her hand on his erection and stroked her hair.

His cock was just at mouth level, and she knew what he wanted. She was happy to oblige him—but not right away. She ran her hands up and down the insides of his thighs. She laid her warm cheek against his hard cock. She caressed the base of his penis, running circles around it with her fingertips, and then her tongue.

Freddy groaned in pleasure and anticipation as the circles got tighter and tighter. And then she was licking—using the tip of her tongue at first, and then, gradually, more of it—the shaft of his cock. She could feel it throbbing and bouncing as though it had a life its own.

Up the shaft she went, toward the sensitive tip. Freddy resisted the urge to draw her head toward him and force himself into her mouth. He *wanted* this to go on this way, but he kept having to remind himself of that.

And then she was there, running her tongue around the ridge of the glans, barely making contact, but doing it in a way that drove him mad. And then she was doing it a little harder, and a little harder still.

Then, suddenly, she took all of him in her mouth. Her lips were on the base of the shaft and the tip of his cock was at the back of her throat. She held him there for a moment and then slowly, slowly withdrew.

When he was all the way out, she flitted her tongue around the ridge again, and again took in all of him. She did this over and over, each time a little faster and a little harder, until Freddy could barely stand it. Then she started going in the other direction: moving more slowly, easing up on the pressure, deliberately calming him down.

After one last, long, slow stroke, she backed away from him, and again stroked his thighs and laid her cheek on his cock. She had taken him full circle.

She leaned back and smiled up at him, and he jumped down from the bench. He kissed her again, and moved his arms around to take her ass firmly in his hands. He held her to him, moving her ever so slightly back and forth against him, and then he lifted her off the ground.

She automatically wrapped her legs around his waist, and he carried her around the bench and put her down next to the large elm that stood behind it. He was inside her almost before she got her balance.

She was more than ready for him. The feel of him getting ever harder in her mouth gave her a kind of pleasure almost commensurate with his. She had felt her insides turning warm and liquid, and now he was answering her need.

The hum of the party would have been barely audible, had they been listening. But they were not listening, raptly absorbed as they were in the matter at hand. Gretchen was thrilled that Freddy had left the party at the house to steal away with her, and the feel of him now, all his muscles taut, his skin warm to the touch, compelled her.

She moved her hips against him, meeting him thrust after thrust. She was hotter and wetter and needier with every stroke. She needed him deeper, and harder, and she put her foot on the bench behind Freddy and put her hands on his ass to draw him to her, into her.

He responded by moving even closer; he grabbed a branch above her head to hold himself cleaved to her, every inch of his body against hers, the two of them moving as one.

And then they came as one, in an explosion of energy that enveloped them so completely that they almost lost their balance. Together they felt the storm of sensation, and together they enjoyed the feeling of its ebbing and then dying away, leaving them profoundly satisfied.

"And is this why you left the party at the house?" Gretchen asked him in a soft, teasing tone as they extricated themselves.

"It was an easy decision," Freddy said. "You have much more to offer than the party does."

He was thinking, of course, of his aborted attempt at Miss Niven, but had Freddy known what was going on in some of the more secluded corners of the party, he might not have been so quick to condemn what it had to offer.

As the hour had grown later and the liquor had flowed and the lights had dimmed, what was left of the inhibitions dropped away. The bobby and barmaid Alexandra had seen kissing behind the plant had found a commodious closet and were engaged in exactly the same activity—in the same position, even—that had just occupied Freddy and Gretchen.

Two floors above the heads of the bobby and barmaid, in one of the smaller guest rooms, a cricketer's costume lay scattered on the floor as the erstwhile cricketer made love to the Queen of Sheba on a bed that belonged to they knew not whom.

All over the house, in tucked-away nooks and shaded corners, small groups were forming. Some were engaging only in conversation, others in genteel versions of what the villagers were doing outside: teasing, flirting, tantalizing.

The dimmer the lights, the less genteel the version, and nowhere were the lights dimmer than on the path around the pond. The electric lights that Barnes had been so proud to show Georgiana were not lit. Earlier, they had been, but somewhere along the way one of the partygoers had decided that an unlit lake was more in keeping with the spirit of the proceedings than a lit lake was.

Strolling along that path, with a silk-sheathed Isis on his arm, was Napoleon. Isis was unsure of her footing, and cleaved as closely as possible to the general as they made their way slowly around the pond, talking of the loveliness of the evening and the pleasures of the party. And then Napoleon took Isis in his arms, and the talk ceased.

The sheer silk dress of the young lady had left little to Napoleon's imagination, but he wanted very much to have his hands confirm her shape and her feel. Where the fabric had hung, just so, over the gentle rise of her ass, there was a fine, firm hillock that fit his palm perfectly. Where it had brushed against her leg as she walked there was a smooth, muscular thigh. Where it had dipped provocatively at the neckline, there was a valley between two lovely, upward-facing breasts.

Napoleon felt all of this, and Isis reveled in it. A powerful hand on her flesh, warm lips on hers, and she gave herself over to the pleasure of the moment. She let her hands explore his body as his hands explored hers, and she felt the solidity and strength of a well-made older man. His shoulders were broad, and still tapered to his waist, although he had none of the slimness of youth.

She unbuttoned his uniform and the shirt beneath, and ran her hand through the abundant hair on his chest. He groaned as she took his nipples between her fingers and pinched softly.

When she put one of the nipples in her mouth, his grip on her tightened and he held her clenched against his erect cock, rocking her back and forth across it.

She put her arms around his neck and jumped up to wrap her legs around his waist. He staggered back a step, and then balanced against a tree.

He put one hand under her ass to hold her up—she was delightfully light—and used his other to free the folds of her dress from between him and her. And then he found skin. He ran his calloused hands over it, first lightly and then harder, up from her knees to the tops of her thighs, as she threw her head back and leaned away, staying anchored by her hands around the back of his neck.

And then she looked at him with a mischievous smile. "Do you swim?"

"Do I swim?" Napoleon was surprised at the question, but only for a moment. "Of course I swim. I learned to swim when I learned to walk."

She released her legs' hold on him, hopped down, and reached for his hat. "Let's go for a swim."

He had never, in a lifetime of fairly adventurous living, had an offer like that.

"By all means, let's," he said, and took off his coat.

She had her dress off in one small motion, revealing the briefest of drawers and a tightly laced corset. As she reached behind her to unlace it, her breasts jutted provocatively in his direction.

There was just enough moonlight for each of the lovers to make out the shape of the other. She was slim and sylphlike, old enough to be no longer a girl but young enough to have lost none of her shape. He was compact and substantial, older than she but not so old as to have lost his appeal.

He reached out to take her by the waist, but she slipped from his grasp and was in the water before he could turn around. He followed and reached her in two strong strokes. He reached for her waist again, and this time she did not slip away. She clung to him, and again wrapped her legs around him as he stood on the sandy bottom.

He had marveled at her lightness when they were on land; in the lake, buoyed by the water, she was weightless. He held her to him and felt again her thighs, her ass, her breasts. His hands slipped over her wet body and his heart beat faster as she squirmed against him.

She reached between her legs, where his cock was lodged, and took it in her hand. She pressed it up against his own abdomen, pointing straight up, and rolled her palm back and forth against its underside. Almost involuntarily, his hands stilled as all his attention was focused on what she was doing to him.

She shifted so there was a little space between them, and had started to maneuver his cock inside her when he stopped her.

"Shhhh," he said. "Listen."

She listened. Voices were coming down the path. It was a man and a woman. Although their words were hard to make out, their tone indicated that they were at least a little tipsy, and their accents indicated that they were villagers, rather than Penfield guests.

Had the moonlight been brighter, Isis would have seen that Napoleon was grinning. "I think they have the same idea we have," he whispered to her.

"Should we make a noise, so they know we're here?" she whispered back.

"I think perhaps we should just let them get on with it," he said.

Getting on with it was just what they were doing. Napoleon and Isis heard no more voices, but they heard sighs, and little moans, and the unmistakable sounds of clothing being removed.

"Here goes," Napoleon whispered. And then, aloud, "Come on in, the water's fine!"

The woman gave a gasp that was almost a shriek. "What? Is someone out there?"

"Someone is," he replied. "In fact, two people are."

"You could make it four," Isis added.

The woman giggled. "Oh, I think we'll just leave you two in private," she said. "Come on, let's go," she said to her companion.

But her companion had other ideas. "It does look lovely out there." He could just barely make out the shape of two heads above the water. "And perhaps you'd enjoy a swim," he added.

They heard a female murmur that had the tone of reluctance, and then a male murmur that had the tone of encouragement. And then a little more reluctance, and then a little more encouragement.

And then a splash, and another splash.

It started off awkwardly. None of the four knew any of the others; both the pairings had been impromptu affairs, as was the pairing of the pairings. When the villagers joined Napoleon and his lady, they first treated it as though they all just happened to be taking a late-night swim in the same body of water. They stayed at some little distance away, and talked quietly to one another.

But they became accustomed to the charged atmosphere just as they became accustomed to the bracing water. Both couples picked up where they had left off.

Isis, as she reached again between his legs, found that Napoleon's erection had softened. She took the base of it between her thumb and forefinger and, pressing gently, ran them slowly up the length of him. He felt it first as almost a tingling, and then as a tantalizing omen of what was to come.

He groaned softly, aware of the other couple just a few feet away. But as his pleasure grew, so his scruples faded, and he found that the presence of other people was beginning to heighten, rather than dampen, his ardor.

Isis was fascinated, and very aroused. She took her hand away and started rubbing her pussy against his cock, which was now fully erect and stiff as a board. She made the tip of it rub against her in just the right spot, over and over, and her groans joined his own.

As she was doing this, Napoleon started to drift over in the direction of the other pair. Slowly, without making a ripple, he was inching closer and closer. It was too dark to make out features, but Isis could see which was the man and which was the woman, and it seemed that the man was holding his lover just as Napoleon was holding her—against him, with her legs wrapped around him.

When they got close enough, Isis patted Napoleon's shoulder in a way that told him she wanted him to stop. He did. The other pair clearly knew they were there—there was only about a foot between them—but they didn't move away.

Isis reached her foot out under the water and ran her big toe up the other man's thigh. He gasped in surprise, and she did it again. And then he moved closer.

Isis put her leg behind Napoleon's back once more, released her hands, and leaned backward to float on the water. She reached her hand over and, as if by chance, grazed the arm of the man.

The woman with him was fascinated by this, but felt a coy sense of propriety that prevented her enthusiastic participation. She wasn't quite ready to jump in, but neither did she want to put a stop to the proceedings. Instead, she climbed around and hung on her partner's back, leaving his front exposed, but hers comfortably covered. From there, she felt almost like an observer.

The man's cock, erect and monstrously large, was floating on the surface of the water, and Isis reached for it. She held it in her hand, feeling its heft and its hardness.

The villager put his large, rough hands around Isis's small, soft ones and tightened her grip. "Harder," he said, as he moved both their hands up and down the shaft.

Napoleon watched this and felt his own cock harden in response. He had lived long, and had had many sexual encounters, but he had never held a naked girl as she touched another man. He was riveted.

He watched as the man turned Isis's head and brought her mouth up to his penis. She flicked her tongue out and licked the very tip, which she was holding above the water.

The man moaned softly, and the woman on his back felt her body begin to respond to what was going on around her. The stirrings she'd felt before Napoleon had made his presence known were returning in full force, and she maneuvered her legs so she could better rub up against the back of the man.

He felt her movements, and understood. As Isis licked his cock, he reached one of his hands behind his back and found the woman's asshole. Gently, he played around its outside edges and then began to work his finger inside. She responded by gasping and pushing harder against his back.

And then she froze.

"Stop!" she whispered, but it was a whisper with urgency. "Listen!"

And then they all heard what she had heard. It was a man's voice, still distant. "Esme!" he called. "Esme, are you out here?"

"Oh, lordy!" said the girl, still whispering, as she slid off the man's back. "It's me young man, come to find me. We're supposed to be married Sunday next and if he spots me here it'll all go for nothing!"

"That's news to me," said the villager whose back she had just climbed down from, but he said it in a low voice, not wanting to give her away. He had just met her this hour, and saw the situation as more amusing than offensive.

"Sorry," she whispered to him. "I just wanted to have a spot of fun before I got all settled down, like." None of them could see her grin and her shrug, but they felt it in her voice. Then, loudly, she said, "I'm right here, Henry. I went for a little swim is all." She splashed toward shore, making what she hoped was enough noise to cover any sounds that might escape the other three. Once on dry land, she quickly found her clothes and moved down the path toward her accepted lover, hoping that darkness would shroud the activity in the water and the other heaps of clothes on the bank.

The three listened to their erstwhile companion go down the path and reunite with Henry. Then, when the two voices had faded into the distance, they turned their attention back to one another.

Isis, still with her legs around Napoleon, still with her back floating on the water, reached both hands out for the stranger. She coaxed what remained of his erection back to its previous hardness. She fondled his balls; she felt the contours of his ass. And then he began to touch her in return. He stroked her face and he ran his hands under her shoulders, under the water. He held her arms in his huge hands, almost encircling them. He ran his fingers over her breasts, fingering her hard little nipples until she moaned.

Napoleon watched the man's hands on her breasts, and he put his hands on her waist. The man looked up, for the first time, into Napoleon's face. Napoleon couldn't see his features, but could get only a sense of what he looked like and what he wanted.

The man ran his hand down from her breasts, down between Napoleon's hands on her waist, and down to her pussy. With one finger, he found her clitoris and rubbed it gently. Isis let out a long, vibrant moan.

Then the man moved his hand so that, as his finger rubbed Isis, the back of his hand brushed Napoleon's cock. Napoleon closed his eyes and abandoned himself to the feeling of another man's hand on him. The combination of the naked girl being coaxed to climax while her legs were around him and he himself being led in that same direction by that same hand was electrifying.

Then the man turned his hand around so the back of it was against Isis's cunt and he circled his fingers around Napoleon. His rhythm was slow, and his touch was sure, and the rest of the world faded into the distance.

The man stopped just as Napoleon couldn't have taken much more, and moved around behind him. He unwrapped Isis's legs from around Napoleon's waist so he could step in and nestle his own cock up against Napoleon's buttocks. Then he put her feet behind him so she had both men encircled in her legs.

The stranger reached around and put his hands on her thighs, holding her so that she was pressed up against Napoleon's rock-hard penis, and he rocked the three of them back and forth. He felt his cock nestle in the space between Napoleon's ass cheeks. Napoleon and Isis were rubbing up against each other, and the threesome felt the ecstasy mount.

Isis, still lying in the water, felt far away, and she pulled herself up and put her arms around Napoleon's neck. The stranger's head was right there, and she explored the contours of his face. When she traced his lips with her index finger, he took that finger in his mouth and sucked it, hard. He didn't let it go, and the wet warmth of his mouth echoed the wet warmth that was emanating from inside her.

Still the man kept control of all of them. He held Isis to Napoleon's front, and himself to his back. He would speed up, just a bit, and then slow. He would hold them all together more firmly, and then give them some breathing space. He would take them right to the edge, and then he would make them all step back. It was all but unendurable.

Finally, he let it happen. Napoleon felt Isis tense in every muscle and push herself against him at the same moment that the man behind him did the same. And then the three of them were enveloped by an orgasm that ran through them like a tidal wave.

After it died away, Isis let go her hold and floated away on her back, and the two men separated and drifted in different directions. After a minute or two, the stranger walked out of the lake, put on his clothes, and simply walked away. Napoleon and Isis got out a few minutes later, dressed as best they could, and headed back toward the house. No word was spoken.

The three had shared an experience, but they shared nothing else.

None had ever met the others until this night, and chances were good that the three would never meet again. They hadn't even exchanged names, and Isis and the stranger would no doubt have been very surprised to find that they had shared such an experience with the Earl of Grantsbury.

TWENTY-ONE

The changed atmosphere of the party and the charge in the air made Alphonse Gerard, still wearing his oilcloth sou'wester but not his mask or his hat, think about Rose. If only he could find her . . .

But no. He had said his good-byes to her already, and he had sworn to walk the straight and narrow, at least until his courtship of Miss Niven was resolved one way or the other. But he had a lascivious side, and his abstemiousness cost him a pang.

Instead, he went to find Miss Niven. There were still a few couples dancing, and perhaps he could lure her out on the floor once more.

He found her on a sofa, unmasked, sitting in a large group of guests, most of whom were somewhat older than she, and all of whom seemed to be at the point of exhausting their party endurance. Gerry stood behind her and put his hand on her shoulder.

"Hullo, Miss Niven," he said.

She turned around, and he was delighted to see that a smile lit up her face. "Gerry! I was just thinking about you." She stood up and walked around the sofa to where he was standing, but not without stumbling and almost falling into the lap of a man Gerry did not recognize.

"I'm so glad to shee you," she said. Her eyes were unnaturally bright, and even a man without Gerard's experience with drunken companions could see that she had had far too much wine.

"And I you," he said gallantly, taking her elbow firmly. "Let us find a quiet spot and see if there isn't a cup of coffee to be had."

"Oh, I don't want coffee," Miss Niven said. She waved her hand in dismissal, and the gesture almost cost her her footing. "I know I've had too much to drink, but I daresay I shall be fine tomorrow without coffee tonight. But let us by all means find a quiet spot."

They did. And as soon as they had sat down, Alexandra said, "I have something important to tell you."

Gerry raised his eyebrows. "Do you indeed?"

"I do." She hiccuped, in what Gerry thought was almost a parody of inebriation. He half expected that little bubbles would come out of her mouth.

"Do you remember when you asked me to marry you?" she said. She flopped back in her chair and looked at him as though he might really have forgotten.

He was surprised. This was the last topic he expected her to embark upon at such at time, in such a state.

"You may not credit it, but I actually do have a hazy memory of just that," he said with a smile. "But perhaps such a serious topic isn't appropriate conversation for such a festive occasion." He was terribly afraid that her liquor had emboldened her to tell him no, and he knew that, once the word was said, it would probably not be unsaid.

Since he had made his proposal, he had steeled himself for her eventual refusal. He understood that he was not without his charms and attractions, but he understood also that those charms and attractions might very well not be enough for a beautiful, intelligent girl twenty years his junior.

"I think it is the perfect occasion. I think you should know that I mean to do it. To marry you." She said this with the tone of a mother telling her young child that she meant to let him have cherry pie for breakfast.

Gerry sat back in his chair and looked at Miss Niven openmouthed. How was he to respond to this? If she really did mean to marry him, she would make him the happiest man in the empire. But was this simply the wine talking, and was this a decision she would repent in the cold light of morning?

He would not let her take such a step under the influence of strong drink. And, in his characteristically straightforward way, that was what he told her.

"My dear girl. If you decide to accept the hand I have offered you, it will be a source of joy unbounded to me. But I will not allow you to make the decision in your current state."

She waved her hand. "Oh, don't worry. I didn't make it in my current state. I made it before. I'm perfectly certain." But then she looked uncertain as to just what it was she was certain about, and Gerry laughed aloud.

Drunk as she was, she knew her own mind, and her acceptance of his proposal was in earnest. Before the evening began, she had been leaning toward accepting him, and the incident of Freddy and the dance pushed her over the top. The contrast between the two men was so great, and showed Gerry to be such a superior, considerate, gentlemanly man, that she could not help but decide in his favor.

And she liked him. She liked him greatly, and she thought she could love him. She was at her ease in his presence, she enjoyed his conversation, and, most important, she thought she could entrust her future to him. She felt safe with him. Safe and loved. Hours before the wine caught up with her, she knew she wanted to marry him.

Gerry knew none of this, of course. He knew only that he had to get her upstairs.

"This is a conversation we will certainly continue in the morning," he said as he helped her to her feet. "Or perhaps the afternoon," he added, skeptical that she would be in a talking frame of mind any time before midday.

A young servant girl was clearing glasses nearby, and Gerry motioned to her.

"This lady could very much use our assistance, I think," he said. "Perhaps you would be so good as to come with us upstairs and help get her to bed."

The girl looked doubtful; this wasn't part of the job she'd been hired to do for the evening. When Gerry slipped her a half crown, though, she thought she could see her way clear to making it part of her duties.

Gerry got Miss Niven up to her room and left her with the girl, trusting that, with the servant's assistance, she would get to bed.

On his way back down the stairs, he encountered Lady Georgiana going up them. Like most of the remaining guests, she had taken off her mask.

"Off to bed so soon?" he asked.

"No, I'm afraid," she answered, and waved a small note she held in her hand. "I have been summoned upstairs for a late-night chat." She said it breezily enough, but Gerry sensed she wasn't happy about the prospect of the interview.

"Nothing alarming or disagreeable, I hope," he said.

"I hope the same." Her mouth stretched into something halfway between a smile and a grimace, and then she continued up the steps.

It was clear she was not happy about her summons, and, as Gerry watched her go, he wondered if he should offer to accompany her, or intervene in some way. Had she turned around, he probably would have made such an offer, but she did not turn around, and he continued on downstairs.

———

Georgiana was indeed unhappy about the note that asked her to come upstairs to what was laughingly referred to at Penfield as the grand laboratory. It was a small room, tucked away in a far corner of the house, where Lord Loughlin kept a telescope. When he was younger, he had been interested in astronomy, and used to go up there of an evening and make notes about stars and planets. In recent years, though, his interest had waned and the room was little used.

Lady Georgiana had been in it only once in all her years of visiting Penfield, and it struck her as very odd, and even a little suspicious, that she was to meet there for a tête-à-tête.

It was Barnes, naturally, whom she was to meet. She had been in the drawing room talking with the same group Gerry had extracted Alexandra from, when Rose, the parlor maid, came to her with a little folded note on a tray.

She had unfolded and read it. *Meet me in the grand lab. I must speak with you. B.*

She folded it up again and held it in her lap as she considered her options. She could understand that Barnes might want to speak with her again, and she could even understand why he might like to speak with her privately. It was possible, she knew, that she had hurt him rather badly, in which case she should now be as kind to him as she could.

But why the grand lab?

She wasn't sure whether she ought to go. Was it conceivable that he meant to do her harm? Had he wanted to harm her, she felt sure he simply would have done it, and not asked for an appointment, but her last two interviews with the man had made her see that there might be menace in him. She considered that he might be the person behind the threats to her and Alexandra, although she could think of only the flimsiest of motives for his missives to her, and none whatsoever for those to her friend.

She thought also of the times they had spent together. She thought of the pull she had felt for him, and the way he had made her feel. She thought particularly of their evening in the lake, and thoughts of menace receded. Surely she knew this man better than to think he would harm her.

She resolved that she would go, and made her excuses to the company.

As she made her way to the staircase, it was the good memories she had of him that she replayed in her mind. The more she thought of them, the less trepidation she felt about the upcoming interview. When she encountered Gerry on the stairwell, though, the meeting derailed her thoughts, and as she continued up the stairs the trepidation returned, and she even thought about asking him to accompany her.

When she had gone some ten steps beyond him, she decided she would do just that, but when she turned around he was already on his way down the stairs, and she changed her mind.

Up she went. She had to pass through the wing of the house where many of the guests' bedchambers were, and she occasionally heard the murmur of conversation, or the sounds of more intimate activities. Fortunately, Penfield had electric lights throughout, and the corridors were bright. She felt sure she would have had trouble facing an eerie dimness at this time of night, in these circumstances.

She passed through the guest corridor and mounted a staircase at the far end. Lord Loughlin had placed his observatory in the top corner of the house, as far as possible away from the electric lights and as close as possible to the stars he was intent on observing.

Why the grand lab? The question revolved around and around in her head.

Once at the head of the staircase, she was on the top floor of the house. All that remained between her and the grand lab was a long gallery with the relics of Lord Loughlin's family. There were portraits of his Irish ancestors dating back hundreds of years, and objets d'art that Lady Loughlin had deemed too fusty for the main house. There was even a suit of armor that dated back two centuries, the memento of an ancestor who fought King William at the Battle of the Boyne.

Of Paulette's family, there was of course nothing. When Lady Loughlin had first shown the gallery to Lady Georgiana, she had made a joke about it. "What would we put here, the formula for the complexion cream?" she had asked. "A coat of arms with a microscope and a factory?"

Georgiana thought of that as she made her way through the gallery, looking at the pictures, but she was not in the mood to see the humor. She found that she was profoundly uncomfortable, almost frightened. This part of the house was completely empty and absolutely silent, but she did not feel alone. The hairs were up on the back of her neck, and she slowed her steps as she strained to hear any sound.

She was almost through the gallery when the lights went out.

Georgiana's first thought was that it was an unfortunate coincidence, that a servant had been sent to turn out lights simply because it was so late. A split second told her she was wrong.

She heard footsteps running toward her, but she couldn't see a thing. There was some light filtering into the hall from a skylight, but her eyes had been accustomed to the brightness of the electric lights, and the semidarkness seemed total to her.

That is why she didn't see the suit of armor topple over. She heard a metallic creaking, and automatically turned her head in the direction of the noise. She still didn't see it as it barely missed her head, grazed her shoulder, and almost knocked her down. She jumped back instinctively as the armor clattered to the floor in front of her.

She was desperate to see what was happening, and her eyes finally started to make out some of the shapes in the darkness.

The shape she saw bearing down on her horrified her. It was a person, arms overhead, carrying some kind of weapon, presumably intent on bringing it down on her head. She turned to flee, but tripped on the helmet from the armor, which had come loose from its body and rolled behind her. She fell, sprawling on the floor, and steeled herself for the blow that was to come.

She heard the whoosh of whatever weapon it was, and then the clang of metal on metal and then a grunt of pain. Her assailant had hit the helmet instead of her. Georgiana turned over as quickly as she could. Her eyes were now accustomed to the dimness, and she could see that her attacker wore some kind of robe, and was holding his wrist in his hand.

The blow had made him drop the weapon, which she could now see was a battle-ax of some kind.

She reached for the ax, thinking first to take it to defend herself. Feeling its weight, though, which was too substantial for her to handle deftly, she decided against that and instead slid it along the floor, far enough down the gallery to be out of reach, in order to give herself time to escape.

Before she could recover her footing, her assailant was upon her, trying to get a grip on her throat. Although she knew she ought to be terrified—and, on some level, she was—she found herself thinking remarkably clearly. She didn't know who this was, and she didn't know why she was being attacked, but she did know that she would not let this be her fate if she could help it.

She fought. She fought with all her strength and all her guile. She kicked and she bit as she tried to shield herself from the blows of her attacker and protect her throat. But her attacker was bigger and stronger, and Georgiana was just beginning to feel that she must lose when the lights went on again.

Her attacker immediately stood up and pulled the hood of his robe over his face so he could not be identified. He knew someone was there, someone who would help, and that his only chance was to run.

He did run, straight into the arms of the Roman senator Georgiana had danced with earlier in the evening.

The senator was no longer wearing his mask, and Georgiana was astonished to find herself face-to-face with Jeremy Staunton.

"Are you badly hurt?" Jeremy asked her as he wrestled to hold what Georgiana could now see was a man dressed as a monk.

She took inventory of her limbs even as her mind reeled to make sense of Jeremy's presence there. "I believe I am barely hurt at all, just quite shaken," she answered as she stood up.

Both Jeremy's hands had been occupied in restraining the monk, whose hood still covered his face. Georgiana lifted the hood, and saw that it wasn't a man at all. It was a young red-haired girl whom Georgiana thought she recognized as a servant of the house.

It was Maureen.

TWENTY-TWO

There was much that Georgiana wanted to know, but she was so
addled by her experience, and by Jeremy's sudden appearance,
that she could think only of the one question that was to her
most relevant.

"Why did you do this?" She asked it plaintively. She really had no
idea, and it was important for her to know.

Maureen said nothing, and looked at the floor.

"Will you not tell me?" Georgiana said.

Maureen again said nothing.

"We need to find Lord Loughlin, and call the local constables," Jeremy said, as he started walking Maureen down the hall. "There is no
point in trying to get information from her."

"Wait," said Georgiana, and ran down the hall in the other direction
to take a look into the grand lab. As she suspected, Barnes was not there.
The note had been a ruse to get her to the gallery.

She returned to Jeremy, and they went off to search for Lord Loughlin.
They found him in the library with his Armagnac and a few friends. He

was startled to see a man he didn't know holding one of his servants, dressed as a monk, firmly by the wrist. He looked at Georgiana inquisitively.

"I think we have a great deal to tell you," she said to him. "But I don't know that you know Jeremy Staunton." She nodded toward Jeremy, and some of the confusion on Lord Loughlin's brow cleared.

He extended his hand. "Mr. Staunton, I am glad to see you. We were, of course, expecting you, but I did not have the chance to make your acquaintance earlier." He looked at Maureen. "But you must tell me what is going on here. Perhaps we can find a more private spot." He made his excuses to his friends and bade them enjoy his Armagnac, and the four went to one of the parlors, which was completely deserted at this hour.

The story of the assault, which horrified Lord Loughlin, was soon told.

"And are you hurt?" he asked Georgiana with real concern.

"I am not," she said. "Shaken, but not hurt."

"I am glad of that." He turned to Maureen. "This is a very serious matter."

She still said nothing, but looked down at the carpet.

Lord Loughlin looked at his guests. Lady Georgiana, now that the incident was over, had been overtaken by a tiredness that penetrated to her bones, and her weariness showed on her face. Jeremy, who had risen at dawn to make the trip to Penfield, was manfully trying to stifle a yawn.

"Nothing can happen at this hour," Robert Loughlin told them. "I will make sure Maureen is confined, and I will send a messenger to the police first thing in the morning." He looked at the clock on the mantelpiece and added, "Which is only an hour or two from now. In the meantime, though, we must all get some sleep."

This was the first thing to make sense to Georgiana since she had received that note, and she was perfectly ready to excuse herself.

She turned to Jeremy as she was leaving. "In the morning, you will have to tell me what on earth you're doing here."

"In the morning, I will do just that," he said, smiling.

The morning came and, with it, the constable. Cowed, perhaps, by his presence, Maureen told all.

Lord and Lady Loughlin, Lady Georgiana, and Jeremy Staunton had assembled to hear it.

She did it because she was desperately in love with Bruce Barnes. When she learned of his affair with Lady Georgiana, she was afraid she would lose him. She thought it would be easy to scare off her rival, and her first attempts at threats were harmless enough.

But her rival would not be scared off. And that was why she tried the tainted milk.

"But why did you give that to Miss Niven?" Lady Loughlin asked, bewildered.

"I didn't," said Maureen. "Rose did. It was supposed to go to Lady Georgiana, but the stupid girl mixed up the trays." That explained a great deal, and Georgiana was sure Miss Niven would be relieved to hear that she hadn't been the target, after all.

At the moment, though, Georgiana was busy assimilating the fact that she had been someone's rival. She had no idea whether Maureen's obsession with Barnes had been born of an affair the two of them had been having, or whether she had formed it without any assistance from him, but her bet was on the former. She knew, firsthand, how he could exert his pull with women, and Maureen was an attractive girl.

She sighed and stood.

"I think I know everything I need to know," she said to the company generally. "Do you need me for anything else?" she asked the constable.

He answered in the negative, and she turned to go. Seeing that she was leaving, Jeremy stood also. "May I join you?"

"Of course."

They left together, and at first said nothing to each other. After a while, Jeremy said, "Perhaps we can find a quiet place to sit so I can tell you how I came to be here."

She nodded, and they found a window seat in the room that, the night before, had housed the buffet. Georgiana marveled at how quickly, and how thoroughly, it had been restored to its regular condition.

As soon as they had taken their seats, Jeremy said, "Lord Grantsbury wrote to me."

Lady Georgiana took this in. "He did, did he? And what did he say?"

"He said your high spirits might have gotten you into a bit of a fix."

Georgiana raised her eyebrows at this. "A bit of a fix?"

"That's what he told me."

"And is that all he told you?"

"That is all he told me. But he pressed that I should come to the masquerade—he had gotten Lord Loughlin's leave, of course—and the pressure lent his concern some urgency. So of course I came."

"When did you get here?"

"Just an hour or two before the party began. Grantsbury let me use his rooms, and had arranged the costume."

"And what did Grantsbury tell you when you arrived?" Georgiana needed to know how much Jeremy knew.

"He told me only that I should perhaps look out for you. He had learned what your costume was, but I would have recognized you regardless."

"Yet you did not identify yourself to me when we danced."

"I did not. I wasn't sure what my reception would be." He stopped, evidently thinking he was treading on dangerous ground. "Had nothing happened, I might not have revealed myself to you at all, and gone home this morning. I thought you might be offended had you known I was watching you."

Georgiana considered this. "I might have been," she said. "I'm not at all sure."

They looked at each other for a moment, and then Georgiana decided she ought to tell him everything. It wouldn't be fair, she thought, when everyone at Penfield knew what had gone on and he, her particular friend, did not. She also thought he was bound to learn the truth sooner or later, and better he should hear it from her.

And she did, giving the story no gloss and making no excuses for her own conduct, of which by now she had come to be somewhat ashamed.

Jeremy listened silently, and when she was finished he sat back in his chair and let out a long, slow breath. When Lord Grantsbury had written to him about Georgiana's "high spirits," he had expected something along this line, but nothing so bad as this.

Grantsbury had written to Jeremy because he was concerned about Georgiana, both because he thought she was behaving badly and because she was under some sort of vague threat. Jeremy had come because Lady Georgiana was his most particular friend, and if he thought that she could do herself harm, or that someone else would do her harm, he wanted to do everything in his power to prevent it.

But it was more than that. The knowledge that he loved her had come on him gradually, and the absolute conviction that it was so, which was quite recent, surprised and discomposed him. He had been happy, he thought, with the casual nature of their intimacy and the pleasure of their stolen moments. When he understood that he wanted more from her, that he wanted to be with her always, he found he could not tell her. He was afraid she would bolt, of course, but he also had a sense that, if she could be happy with their relationship as it was, so should he be able to.

He was not able to.

He had inadvertently disclosed his love to Lord Grantsbury when the earl, a family friend of the Stauntons as well as of Georgiana's family, had visited the Stauntons that spring. Grantsbury, who made a habit of using old friendships as an excuse to say anything he liked, had asked penetrating questions about Jeremy's prospects and intentions. Jeremy had tried to avoid answering the substance of the questions, but also tried not to tell blatant untruths, and had thus given himself away to the canny old nobleman.

The earl, seeing the kind of trouble Lady Georgiana was bringing on herself at Penfield, had summoned him in the hopes that everything could be set right if only Jeremy's love could be returned.

Sitting in the drawing room, listening to Georgiana's story, Jeremy was not at all sure he wanted his love to be returned. As a matter of fact, if he could have wished his love away at that very moment, he might have done it. He was dismayed, and he was angry. He was also jealous.

Georgiana, when she had told her tale, looked at him and saw the coldness in his eyes. His distance and his disapproval pierced her very being. Her regret at what she had done—which, up until this moment, had been somewhat grudging and resentful—suddenly became real and heartfelt and almost overwhelming. Her eyes welled, and she fought manfully to keep from weeping.

She almost succeeded, but two rogue teardrops betrayed her.

She put her head in her hands and shook it back and forth. It was as though a veil had been lifted. How could she have been such a bloody fool? How could she have failed to understand that you couldn't gallivant through the world acting on your own impulses without regard either to what was expected of you or, more important, the feelings of the people with whom you gallivanted? How could she not have seen what was so clear to Lord Grantsbury?

"Oh, Jeremy," she said, almost choking on the words. "I have been such an ass."

Her distress tempered both his anger and his jealousy. When he handed her his handkerchief, it was not without some tenderness.

As she saw his coldness begin to melt she lost her grip on her emotions and wept like a child. He laid a hand on her arm and waited. Like a heavy thunderstorm that blows out as quickly as it blows in, her tears subsided in just a few minutes.

"I am so sorry," she said, looking at the sodden handkerchief in her hands.

"You have done me no injury."

"Have I not?" She looked up.

"We have explicitly said, all along, that we owe each other nothing. You are not bound to me any more than I am to you."

She looked down again. When they had made that agreement, she had thought it both liberal and liberating. Now it sounded stupid.

"Perhaps our saying it doesn't make it so," she said in a small voice. She knew that she had taken his closeness for granted while she had it, and now that she was in danger of losing it she understood its value.

"Perhaps it doesn't," he replied.

They sat in silence for a few moments, each absorbing the meaning in the other's words.

Then Jeremy stood up and extended his hand to Georgiana. "I have not seen the grounds here, and I should very much like to. Won't you come on a walk with me?"

She took his hand and smiled. "Of all things, I think I should like that the best."

As they were heading toward the front door, they encountered Lord Grantsbury, who had just come down in search of breakfast.

"Good morning, my lord," Jeremy said, and Georgiana seconded the greeting.

Grantsbury looked at them with some satisfaction. "And good morning to you. Are you off to enjoy the grounds?"

"We are," said Georgiana.

"Well, I am off to enjoy some coffee and cold ham," said Grantsbury. "Have a lovely walk."

The couple turned toward the door, but after they'd gone a few steps, Georgiana turned around and called to the earl.

He turned around. She walked over to him and kissed him on the cheek. "Thank you," she said.

TWENTY-THREE

⁓

After Jeremy and Georgiana had been gone for an hour or so, the house slowly began to come to life. Guests trickled down from upstairs, some looking refreshed and others looking rather haggard. Coffee and tea were in great demand.

Miss Niven, who made her way down sometime after noon, was not looking her best. She had been up for an hour or two already, and had tried to banish her headache and nausea with tea and toast, but had met with little success. Her memory of the previous night's interview with Gerry was indistinct. She knew she'd told him she'd marry him, but she had no recollection of what had happened after that. She woke that morning in her own bed, wearing nothing but her shift, and she'd no idea how she'd come to be in that state.

She had no doubt that Gerry would not have made an assault on her honor, but she was worried that she might have embarrassed herself, or perhaps him. She was determined to find him and clear the air as soon as she could.

She found him breakfasting alone, looking a bit the worse for wear himself.

"May I join you?" she asked.

He looked up, and his delight at seeing her was evident.

"You need not ever ask," he said, and gestured to the chair next to him. "How are you feeling?"

"I have certainly had better mornings," she said a little ruefully, "but I daresay I can muddle through."

"Would you like some breakfast or some tea?"

Her stomach churned at the thought. "I have tried that already, and it didn't answer."

Neither was sure how to broach the subject of last night's conversation. They were quiet for a time, and then each started at the same moment.

"I must—" Alexandra said, and then broke off as she realized that Gerry was speaking also.

"I should—" he had begun, but also broke off.

Gerry gestured to her. "Ladies first."

She took a deep breath. "I must tell you that, drunk as I was, I was most certainly in earnest last night."

He smiled broadly, and she went on. "I am ashamed to have accepted your proposal, which was made in such a generous way, without the dignity and seriousness that it deserved."

She took a breath to go on—she had a whole speech planned—but he interrupted her. "My dear, you could have accepted it while swinging from the chandelier in a monkey suit, and I wouldn't have cared a fig! My only care is that you have accepted it." There was wonder in his eyes. "You have accepted it!"

His joy was palpable, and her heart leaped. To be loved, to be sincerely loved, and by a sincere man who was worthy of the best she had to give.

Her speech and her headache were alike forgotten when he took her hand and kissed her gently, softly, on the cheek. "I will do everything in my power to make your life as happy as mine is this day."

She knew that it was so, and she rejoiced.

As Alexandra's future was being settled, Georgiana was feeling very unsettled. Walking the grounds with Jeremy, she felt very much as she always had. He was so familiar to her, and she was comfortable in his presence. Their walk had been subdued at the start, but they had soon fallen into the bantering style they were accustomed to.

For Georgiana, though, there was a difference. When she had told him her story and seen his anger, she had known that the casual nature of their intimacy was a sham. Her distress at the thought of losing him through her own bad behavior put her feelings for him in stark relief, and as they walked around the Penfield grounds she felt as nervous as a schoolgirl with a crush.

When he took her hand, she felt butterflies. When he kissed her, she felt her knees weaken.

They were by this time quite far from the house, walking along a stream that was almost a river in spring, but was now just a trickle. The path they took ran across the slope that went down to the water. It faced south, and the leaves on the maples and oaks were just beginning to turn. It was a lovely spot, and the solitude made Georgiana feel as if she were far, far away from everything that had caused her trouble at Penfield.

They were evidently not the first people to enjoy the hillside spot, though, as there was a gazebo built under a stand of trees just ahead of them. They made their way to it and admired the view of the stream and the nearby countryside.

Jeremy sat down on the bench, and Georgiana sat down beside him. He moved a little away from her, which startled her for a moment, but then he pulled her shoulders down to his lap and gestured that she should put her feet on the cushioned bench.

She lay on the bench, using his thigh as a pillow, and reveled in the sensation of having her hair stroked by his hand. She closed her eyes, and he brushed his hands against her forehead and rubbed her temples. It was an odd combination, she thought, the profound relaxation coupled with the nervous excitement.

He ran his hands over her cheekbones and massaged her earlobes. He curled the loose tendrils of her hair around his fingers, and then let them go. He fit the tip of his index finger in the little indentation over the middle of her upper lip, and then used that finger to trace the outline of her mouth.

She felt his touch running along her lip as though it were electric. While all the muscles in her body were at rest, her energy was focused on that one spot.

He moved down and traced her jawline. He stroked the soft skin of her neck and ran his hands across the ridges her collarbones made. Her dress was cut low enough that he could make out her top few ribs, and he traced each of those in turn.

Georgiana felt her breathing grow shallower and her muscles begin to tense. Jeremy ran his fingertips under the neckline of her dress, all the way from her shoulder to the hollow between her breasts and back up to the other shoulder. Then he did it again the other way.

By now she was on fire, with a heat centered deep inside her and radiating out. When he slid his hand under her dress and caressed her breast, it was as though his hand had a direct line to her very soul.

She couldn't help comparing what she felt now with what she had felt with Barnes. Certainly he had excited her, piqued her, aroused her. But there was a connectedness with Jeremy that added depth and richness to her bodily sensations.

It was that thought that made her open her eyes. It was that connectedness that made her sure that this wasn't right. What she felt was meaningful and important; it wasn't the stuff of casual encounters in gazebos. She sat up.

"I don't think we should do this," she said quietly.

He gave her a questioning look.

"I have learned many things over the course of the last week. One of them is that I shouldn't trifle with affections, either mine or someone else's."

"And whose do you believe you trifle with now?" Jeremy had just a hint of a smile as he asked this, but she answered him seriously. "My own," she said. "I do not know about yours."

"Do you not?" he asked, the smile gone.

She had an inkling, of course, and was searching for a way to say it, but Jeremy was too much of a gentleman to let her answer such a question.

"I love you. You must know that I love you."

She flushed deeply, a blush not of embarrassment but of deep, fulfilled pleasure.

"I did not know. I could not know. I could only hope," she said. "It was the fear that my missteps could have cost me you that made me realize how fervently I did hope." She looked him in the face, her eyes shining. "And you must know that I love you."

The pleasure, this time, was his. "I know it now," he said.

He put one hand on each of her cheeks and brought her face to his. He kissed her deeply, warmly, lovingly, and then pulled back, keeping his hands on her cheeks.

"Marry me," he whispered, but it was a compelling whisper, a whisper almost urgent.

She said nothing. She simply nodded, as though it were a conclusion foregone.

For a moment, they only looked at each other, absorbing their happiness. And then he let go of her cheeks and took her hands. He put them to his lips and kissed first one and then the other. "You will be my wife," he said, as though he couldn't quite believe it, and then he pulled her to him.

Lips had never felt so soft to Lady Georgiana. A tongue had never felt so warm, so right. She felt as though she wanted to be consumed, subsumed, to become a part of him.

She climbed onto his lap, facing him, and laid her head on his shoulder, her face buried in his neck. She sat there, still, for a few moments, feeling her own breath and his, absorbing his warmth.

Then she kissed his neck, tasting his salty-sweet taste. He put his hands on her buttocks and pulled her closer to him. She felt the contours of his body against hers, familiar but freshly exciting. She ran her hands down his arms and felt as his muscles tightened to pull her closer still.

She groaned and threw her head back with the joy of it, and he ran the tip of his tongue from the base of her collarbone, up her neck, to the point of her chin. And then her mouth met his once more, and they kissed with a passion that amounted almost to greed.

She felt his cock, hard beneath her, and she shifted her body to one side so she could reach the fastening of his trousers. In a heartbeat, it was undone and he was released. She stroked him, slowly and gently, noticing every detail. Her fingertips ran over every bump, every ridge, every vein, as though this intimate braille would tell her all she needed to know.

Again she felt their connectedness. This was his cock, but it was also hers.

Then it was his turn to release her. He ran his hands under her skirts, over her taut legs. Her body was warm, and got ever warmer as he moved up her thighs. If he was going to take her drawers off, she would have to stand up, and he couldn't have that. He simply ripped a hole in the seam.

Georgiana was surprised at the sound, and then laughed softly as she realized what he had done.

Then she shifted over him and he was inside.

She felt him slide into her and had an overwhelming sense of completion, of rightness. They began to move as one and she felt as though they *were* one, that they would be one until death did them part.

She wanted him very badly, but not with the sharp-edged urgency that she had sometimes known. It was instead a deep, soft compulsion, and the knowledge that he wanted to satisfy it filled her with happiness.

She rocked back and forth, back and forth on his lap, and the small motion gradually built up the tension in their muscles and the firmness of the hold they had on each other. Georgiana felt Jeremy's hands on her ass, holding her tightly, moving her back and forth. She felt that he was restraining both himself and her, and the restraint piqued her ever-growing pleasure.

She felt her arousal mount. What had started as dewy moisture building inside her became a torrent as he got harder and they both gave themselves over to the motion and the pleasure.

As the waves built higher, her impulse was to speed up. She wanted to move faster, she wanted to feel more of him pulling out and thrusting in, but he had his grip on her and kept rocking her back and forth, back and forth, slowly.

It was tantalizing, it was agonizing, that little pulse she felt every time she moved never getting bigger!

And then, with one of those little pulses, she knew nothing could stop her. Just as she knew it, she felt that last hardening in his cock that told her he could not be stopped either.

Still he kept the motion small, the rhythm slow, and at last an orgasm washed over them as though they were one, feeling it together. It started small, and she felt it first as a tightening in her chest. And then it spread and it grew, pulsing into strength. And then, finally, it crested as an all-consuming sensation, binding them together in intoxicating joy.

For several minutes they sat as they were, letting their heartbeats slow and the heat from their bodies dissipate. Then she put her hands on his cheeks, kissed him, and climbed off his lap.

"I shall have to get new drawers," she said as she tried to reassemble her dress.

"Oh, I don't know about that," Jeremy said. "This kind certainly has convenience in its favor. Perhaps you should convert your entire under-garment wardrobe."

"Well, it's good to know that, if I decide to do so, I have someone with experience to do the conversion," she said as she straightened his shirt collar and brushed off an inchworm that had lit on his shoulder.

He in turn straightened her neckline and tucked a lock of her hair back into her loose chignon.

"How do we look?" she asked.

"As though we've been cavorting in a gazebo, I'm afraid," Jeremy said, looking at his wrinkled trousers.

"Well, there's no help for it," she said, and took his hand. If her dress had been grass-stained and torn, it wouldn't have detracted one whit from her happiness.

They headed back to the house to seek out Lord Grantsbury in order to tell him what his interference had wrought.

They found him, and they told him, and his congratulations were hearty and heartfelt. They also told Lord and Lady Loughlin, whose mild surprise did not stop their congratulations from being just as sincere as the earl's. It was only a couple of days ago that she was conducting an affair with their landscaper, and here she was engaged to another man.

Georgiana saw their surprise, and did not wonder at it.

She touched Jeremy's arm. "This is not new," she said to her hosts. "It is only newly discovered." She paused for a moment. "I have discovered much at your house this week."

Paulette understood her friend, and nodded. "I am very happy for you," she began, "and anyone who has ever loved understands that these things sometimes come about in odd ways, ways that are opaque to any but those who are in love."

Georgiana was grateful to her hostess for understanding, but was skeptical that others would. "Under the circumstances, perhaps it is best if we do not announce this to the company at large," she said. "I daresay it would be talked of in ways that would not be flattering to any of us."

"I think that's probably prudent," Lady Loughlin said. "When it is time to tell the world, though, I hope you will come back and let us give a dinner in your honor."

"We would be delighted," said Jeremy, and his affianced bride nodded her agreement.

Georgiana was relieved that she would not have to tell Barnes that, only days after she had been in his arms, she agreed to be the wife of another man. She told herself that he would possibly be hurt, or even unmanned by this piece of news, and that she would spare him that, but the real source of her relief was that she would spare herself the discomfort of that interview.

Still, she thought, there must be an interview. After what had passed between them, and the events of the previous night, she could not leave Penfield without trying to say a few healing words.

She and Jeremy were planning to leave for home in the morning, and so Georgiana thought she may as well try to say those words as soon as possible. She excused herself to the Loughlins, gave Jeremy a quick explanation, and went to find her erstwhile lover.

She found him, with some help from the gardening staff, in the peacock pavilion, supervising the mending of a wall that had been damaged in the revelry of the masquerade.

His back was to her, and she knocked on the doorframe, hesitant to go in.

He turned, and was apparently surprised to see her. "Lady Georgiana," he said, and nodded his head stiffly in greeting.

"Mr. Barnes." She nodded in return. "If your duties allow for it, would you care to take a turn with me?"

He took a backward glance at the work underway, and then followed her out the door.

She was prepared to launch into her healing words, but he beat her to it. "I heard what happened to you last night," he said. "It must have been dreadful, and I'm terribly sorry."

"It was dreadful, but it is not for you to be sorry, as you had no part in it."

Barnes, when he had heard what Maureen had done, knew that he had been cavalier with her, and that Georgiana had paid the price for it. He was in the habit of being cavalier with women and, although he acknowledged to himself that he was unlikely to change, he also acknowledged that the events of the night before were, to some degree, his responsibility. And, although he might be cavalier, he was also fair.

"I believe I had at least a small part," he said.

"No part," she said firmly, although she understood from what he said that he had been having an affair with the girl. "But what I want to say to you is not about that, or about her. It is about you, and about me."

She took a breath. "I don't know how you feel now or how you felt when you met me. What I do know is that I am not happy with my own behavior and, if I caused you any pain, I am terribly, dreadfully sorry."

He was silent, and she feared for a moment that his anger might flare up again. But it did not. Last night Barnes had been angry indeed, but news of the assault on Georgiana had squelched his fury. Beyond his genuine concern that she might have been hurt was the realization that he had toyed with Maureen in just the same way he had accused Georgiana of toying with him.

And he admitted to himself as well that he did not love her. She was beautiful, and she was interesting, but she was more a conquest to him than a woman. It was the idea of a noblewoman in his bed, and the idea that he might keep her there forever after, that appealed to him.

Instead, he sighed, and said, "We had our moments, though, did we not?"

She laughed with relief, and from that moment they were able to talk with humor and even affection of the week that had passed.

When Georgiana realized she had to return to the house to dress for dinner, she took her leave of him. "I'm glad we part friends, Mr. Barnes," she said, and held out her hand to him. He shook it, but then put it to his lips and kissed it. And then he was gone.

Penfield had been gradually emptying throughout the day, and the evening meal that night was a much smaller affair than it had been the last couple of nights. When Georgiana came down, she had barely a chance to survey the room before Miss Niven, positively beaming, rushed to her side and took her arm.

"Oh, Lady Georgiana, I have been looking for you all afternoon! I heard what happened to you last night!" Her expression of regret was at odds with the look of joy on her face.

They talked of it for a minute or two, but Georgiana could see that something else, something good, was distracting her friend. "But has something else happened?" she asked tentatively.

"Oh, yes! I have such news," Alexandra positively gushed.

Georgiana smiled broadly. She could guess at the news, but she wanted to give her friend the pleasure of saying it aloud.

"I am going to marry Mr. Gerard," she said.

Georgiana embraced her with warmth and affection. "I am so very happy for you! I am sure he will be an excellent husband and that the two of you will be happy together."

"I believe we will," said Alexandra. "I believe we will."

After the two had extolled Gerry's virtues, Georgiana decided she must tell of her own engagement.

"I have some news of my own," she said, "but you must promise me to tell no one but Gerry. I don't want it known here quite yet."

Her friend looked at her quizzically, but pledged her silence.

"I am also to be married."

Alexandra's eyes widened in surprise. "To Mr. Barnes?" she blurted out, unable to contain her astonishment.

"No, not to Mr. Barnes."

Alexandra blushed to the roots of her hair. "I'm terribly sorry. That was very rude of me. Please tell me your news."

The news took some time to tell, as Miss Niven hadn't known until that afternoon that Jeremy Staunton existed, let alone that he was in this very house. And now he was engaged to her friend Lady Georgiana Vernon!

By the time the story was told, most of the other guests had helped themselves at the buffet and were choosing seats in one of the two rooms being used that night. The two young ladies did the same, and then each found her fiancé. Introductions were made, and the foursome took a quiet corner in the farther of the rooms.

Once Gerry was sworn to secrecy, the news was told once more. He was more successful than Alexandra at concealing his surprise, and offered robust congratulations.

Four happier people had never sat down at table together.

After dinner, Lord Loughlin, who, with his wife, had been told of Alexandra's engagement to Gerry directly after he'd been told of Georgiana's engagement to Jeremy, stood in the doorway between the two rooms and asked for attention. He raised a glass, requested that all his guests join him, and announced his pleasure that the engagement of Miss Niven and Mr. Gerard had been sealed under his roof.

There was general surprise at the idea of a union between a middle-aged man like Gerry and a beautiful young girl like Alexandra, but both were liked by everyone who met them, and there were good wishes and congratulations all around.

The only person in the room who couldn't quite adjust to the idea was young Freddy. It was unfathomable to him that a lovely young girl could reject his advances and then go marry this veritable troll of a man! But he shrugged, and consoled himself that any girl who would go in for the likes of Alphonse Gerard wasn't for him anyway. And, although Freddy was wrong about many things, he was certainly right about that.

———

The next morning saw all the remaining guests take their leave, and there were many plans for autumn visits made among them. Gerry was to go visit Miss Niven and settle things with her guardian, Lord Bellingham. And then Alexandra was to go visit Lady Georgiana at Eastley. Gerry insisted that the entire company come join him in Sussex for Christmas.

There were handshakes and embraces all around as they parted company and, at long last, Lord and Lady Loughlin turned back to an empty house.

"Shall we take a stroll around the grounds?" Paulette said to her husband, taking his hand. "We have at least an afternoon before we must start planning for next year."